Child of the Ghosts

Jonathan Moeller

ISBN: 1481918109
ISBN-13: 978-1481918107

EPIGRAPH

"God, whose law is that he who learns must suffer. And even in our sleep pain that cannot forget, falls drop by drop upon the heart, and in our own despite, against our will, comes wisdom to us by the awful graces of God."

-Aeschylus

OTHER BOOKS BY THE AUTHOR

CHAPTER 1
THE ANCIENT SCROLL

Caina loved her father's library.

It had high windows, with a fine view of the town and rippling Bay of Empire beyond. Her father's desk stood by those windows, covered with papers and books and curiosities he had picked up over the years. Count Sebastian Amalas worked there in the evenings, writing and sealing letters with his heavy gold signet ring. Caina liked to sit on the nearby couch, reading as he wrote.

He had taught her to read when she was three or four years old. First in the High Nighmarian tongue, as befit the daughter of an Imperial Count. Then in Caerish, the commoners' language, and then in the tongues of the eastern Empire; Saddaic, Disali, Kagarish, Cyrican and Anshani. His library held books in all those languages and more, and Caina devoured them, working her way through his oak shelves over and over again, reading new books as her father bought them from printers in the Imperial capital. Sometimes she spent all day in the library, and old Azaia the cook brought her meals, and Caina read as she ate.

"You read too much, daughter," her father said, with a slight smile.

"No, I don't," she answered. "If you're meeting with the town's decimvirs, you should just tell me to use another room."

Count Sebastian lifted an eyebrow. "And just how do you know that I'm meeting with the decimvirs?"

"Because," said Caina. "You always meet with petitioners at your desk. You don't care if I overhear those. But if you're meeting with the decimvirs, that means you're discussing criminal cases, which don't want to discuss in front of me." She stood from the couch. "I'll go read in the solar."

Sebastian laughed, leaned down, kissed her forehead. "Why do I even

1

try to keep secrets from you, my clever child?"

Caina smiled, picked up her book, and left the library, her skirts whispering against the polished marble floors of the villa's corridors. Busts of long-dead Emperors stood in niches, gazing down with stern marble eyes. Sebastian was a Loyalist, and so he had busts of Emperors like Soterius, who had ended slavery in the Empire, or Helioran, who had forced the magi to abide by Imperial law. Caina had read about them in her father's books of history.

She opened the solar door and stopped.

Her mother stood at the windows, gazing down at the sea with a scowl.

Caina slipped away before her mother could notice her.

She loved her father's library. It gave her a place to hide from her mother.

Caina was eleven years old, and she could not remember ever hearing a kind word from her mother.

Countess Laeria Amalas was the opposite of her husband, short where he was tall, slender where he was thick. She had long black hair and icy blue eyes that seemed to burn when she was angry.

And she got angry a lot.

Caina's earliest memory was her mother's fury. She had been no more than two or three, so young that she had not yet learned to read. Her mother had been alone in the dining hall, practicing simple sorcery - making a goblet float, summoning light from her fingers, conjuring gusts of wind.

Caina blundered into her, disrupting her concentration. The goblet fell from midair and shattered against the floor.

"You stupid girl!" screamed Laeria. Her backhand sent Caina to the floor atop the shattered goblet. "Useless brat!" She started to kick. "I wish I had never borne you! I wish had I never met your father! Get out of my sight! Get out of my sight! If you interrupt my concentration again, I'll beat you so bloody that..."

Caina fled, wailing, and hid herself beneath the table.

Her father came, and Sebastian and Laeria shouted at each other. After Laeria stalked from the room, Sebastian carried Caina, still weeping, to her bed.

"Why does she hate me so much?" whispered Caina.

Sebastian hesitated before he answered.

"I don't know."

She spent much more time with her father after that.

###

But her mother still did things to her.

Laeria knew a spell that let her reach into another's mind. And she used it upon Caina whenever she had the chance, digging through Caina's thoughts and turning her into a puppet. Caina hated it, hated the feeling of her mother's thoughts digging through her mind like wet, groping fingers. She loathed how the spell forced her to do without question whatever Laeria commanded.

And she grew to hate her mother, the rage becoming hard and sharp.

One day when Caina was seven, Laeria held her immobile in the grip of her sorcery.

"Do you know," murmured Laeria, taking Caina's chin in her hand, "why I had you?"

Caina said nothing. She couldn't, not with Laeria's spell wrapped about her mind.

"I wanted to go back," sighed Laeria, black hair sliding over her pale face. "They put me out, only four years into my novitiate. They said I wasn't strong enough, that I could never wield the power of a full magus. But if I had a talented child...then the Magisterium would have to take me back."

She growled and slapped Caina across the face.

"But you're useless," she said. "Not a spark of arcane talent. Utterly useless. How I wish I had never had you. I should have purged my womb of you, spared myself the bother."

Caina's fury writhed inside her like something alive.

"And your father," said Laeria. "I cannot believe I let myself be chained to that sniveling weakling. It is not fair! I was meant for so much more. For greater things than to waste my life with a useless child and a pathetic weakling of a husband..."

Caina's rage flared.

And she felt her mother's spell shiver.

"Don't talk about him like that!" Caina shouted. "He's better than you!"

Laeria flinched as if she had been slapped.

"Don't talk!" she said, making a clenching gesture, the chains of her will tightening against Caina's mind. "I command you not to talk!"

But Caina's anger could not be denied, and she thrust it against her mother's will.

The spell shivered again, and then shattered. Laeria stumbled back, eyes wide with shock, and perhaps a touch of alarm.

"I hate you!" said Caina, clawing at her mother's skirts. "I hate you, I hate you, I hate you..."

"Get off me!" said Laeria, shoving, and Caina fell to the floor.

"What is this?"

Sebastian hurried towards them, expression thunderous.

"Husband," said Laeria, voice heavy with contempt. "You've returned early from town. I suppose the rigorous duties of the Count of the Harbor cannot fill your entire day."

"You were casting spells on her again, weren't you?" said Sebastian, placing himself between his daughter and his wife.

Laeria lifted her chin. "What if I was? The little whelp is useless for anything else."

"Enough," said Sebastian, voice quiet. "That is the last time you will cast spells upon her."

Laeria laughed. "Or what?"

"Or I'll report you to the Magisterium for practicing unlicensed sorcery," said Sebastian.

"You wouldn't," said Laeria. "You're a Loyalist, not a Restorationist or a Militarist. You hate the Magisterium, and won't have anything to do with it."

Sebastian took a step towards Laeria. "Cast a spell my daughter again, and you'll find out just what I'll do."

Laeria met his gaze for a moment, and then stalked away.

Sebastian sighed and scooped up Caina. "Did she hurt you?"

"She didn't hit me," said Caina.

He carried her to the library, sat upon the couch. Caina leaned against his shoulder, crying softly.

"Why does she hate me so much?" said Caina at last.

"I suppose you're old enough to understand now," said Sebastian. "Do you know what the Imperial Magisterium is?"

Caina had read about it. "It's...the brotherhood of the magi, the sorcerers. The only ones allowed to use sorcery inside the Empire."

Sebastian nodded. "Before I met your mother, she was a novice of the Magisterium. The novices take a seven-year course of study before they become full magi. The Magisterium expelled your mother in her fourth year. She was simply not strong enough with sorcery to become a full magus. When she married me, I thought she had gotten past that, but I was...I was wrong."

"Why did she marry you," said Caina, "if she hates you as much as she hates me?"

"She thought I was a different kind of man than the one I really am," said Sebastian. "I am the Lord of House Amalas, and a Count, besides. Do you know the difference between a Lord and a Count?"

Caina thought back to her reading. "A Lord is a noble of the Empire," she said, remembering. "But a Count...a Count is a noble appointed to an office by the Emperor himself."

"I was already appointed Harbormaster of Aretia when I met your mother," said Sebastian. "I think she hoped that I would rise higher, become the commander of a Legion, or maybe the Lord Governor of an important province."

"Someone powerful enough to force the Magisterium to take her back?" said Caina.

"Yes," said Sebastian. "Very good. But I am not that sort of man, Caina. I have no stomach for Imperial politics. Aretia is my home, and I am content to stay here."

"And Mother hates it here," said Caina.

"Yes," said Sebastian. "She would rather return to Artifel and the Motherhouse of the magi, but they will not take her. So she takes her frustrations out upon me...and upon you."

"Do you wish you had never married her?" said Caina.

Sebastian smiled. "How could I," he said, touching her hair, "for without her, I never would have gotten you."

Caina smiled.

"But this has gone on for too long," said Sebastian. "I am ashamed that I let it go on for so long. If she strikes you again, tell me and I will put a stop to it. And if she uses her sorcery against you, tell me...and I will go to the Magisterium."

"I don't think she will," said Caina. "I made her stop. I got angry and pushed her out of my head."

"You did?" said Sebastian, surprised. "That takes great mental strength."

"She said bad things about you," said Caina. "I got angry."

"You defend me more than I deserve," said Sebastian. "But if Laeria lifts hand or spell against you, tell me. I will not let it pass."

###

But her mother left them alone after that.

Perhaps Sebastian's threat daunted her, or Caina's unexpected resistance alarmed her. After that day, Laeria ignored them, spending almost all her time shut away in her rooms, practicing her spells, or corresponding with the few magi who did not ignore her. She emerged only to appear with Sebastian and Caina at public functions, and left as soon as possible.

As Caina grew older, more than once she wondered why her father simply did not divorce Laeria. The gods knew he had endured enough. Perhaps he thought Laeria could change. Perhaps part of him still loved her.

Caina did not love her mother, not even a little.

Eventually, she realized that her father preferred reading and thinking and writing to any sort of action, and would put off confronting Laeria as long as possible.

She loved him nonetheless.

But Laeria left them alone, and Sebastian continued with his duties and his scholarship, and Caina worked her way through his library. Sebastian hired new tutors for her, and she began learning new languages.

It was a pleasant enough life.

Night had fallen by the time her father finished meeting with the decimvirs, the ten magistrates who governed the town of Aretia.

Caina let herself into the library after they left. A bright fire crackled in the fireplace, covered by a bronze screen to protect the books and the carpet from any sparks. Sebastian sat at his desk below the windows, fiddling with a pen, his expression distant.

He smiled as she approached.

"How was your meeting with the decimvirs?" she said.

"Simple enough," said Sebastian. "Not a major criminal matter, thankfully. A smugglers' ship ran ashore a few miles south of here, and the smugglers fled before the militia could take them in hand."

"What were they smuggling?" said Caina. "Not slaves?" Slavery had been banned in the Empire for a century and a half, since the War of the Fourth Empire, but Istarish slavers still sometimes raided the coasts.

"No, nothing so grim," said Sebastian. "Spices, mostly, from the Cyrican plantations. Some Anshani silks. And scrolls."

"Scrolls?" said Caina.

He beckoned her closer. "Come look at this."

A tattered scroll lay across his desk, the thick papyrus yellow with age. An intricate diagram filled most of the scroll, an elaborate sigil of swirling lines and crossing circles. Lines of strange characters filled the rest of the scroll, the symbols resembling birds and animals and men.

"I think it is a Maatish scroll," said Sebastian. "What can you tell me about the land of Maat?"

Caina smiled. Her father was a scholar at heart. Had he not wed, she supposed, he would have been quite happy as a priest in the Temple of Minaerys, tending to the collections of books and scrolls the priests kept in Minaerys' honor.

"Maat was called the Kingdom of the Rising Sun," said Caina, thinking. "Its pharaohs ruled a great empire long before our Empire arose. The Maatish priests were all powerful sorcerers and necromancers, but grew too proud, and destroyed the Kingdom of the Rising Sun in their folly."

Sebastian nodded. "Much as our Empire's own magi almost did, during the War of the Fourth Empire. Caina, I think this is a genuine Maatish scroll."

Caina blinked. "But...I read that the Kingdom of the Rising Sun fell thousands of years ago. All that remains are stone ruins in the desert. For a scroll to have survived..."

"It is rare," said Sebastian. "And incredibly valuable. The smugglers must have looted it from a Maatish ruin and hoped to find a buyer for it within the Empire."

"What will you do with it?" said Caina.

"I will study it, make certain it is authentic," said Sebastian. "If it is...I think I shall make a trip to the capital, to the priests of Minaerys at the Imperial Library."

Caina's eyes widened. The Imperial Library was the Emperor's own library, the largest collection of books in the Nighmarian Empire.

The thought of all those books made her hands tremble.

Sebastian laughed. "Would you like to accompany me?"

"Yes," whispered Caina. "Yes, I would."

"Then it is settled," said Sebastian. "If the scroll proves authentic, we shall go to the capital and the Imperial Library. Now get some sleep, daughter. You're still too young to stay up half the night reading."

"You do, father."

"Yes, but I'm old enough that it doesn't matter. Now, off to bed."

Caina smiled, kissed his cheek, and left for her bedroom. Though she doubted she would be able to sleep. The Imperial Library!

She entered the hallway, and stopped.

Laeria stood at the end of the hallway, staring at her.

Caina stopped and stared back, readying herself to fight, if her mother tried to invade her mind.

But Laeria only smirked, and walked away without another word.

CHAPTER 2
A PRICE OF BLOOD

Sebastian spent over a week closeted with the scroll, pouring over his books and scribbling into a notebook. Caina realized that he was attempting to translate it, converting the Maatish hieroglyphs into legible Caerish. She read in the library, but otherwise let him work in peace. When the scholarly fit came upon her father, nothing could distract him.

So when she got hungry, she visited the servants.

Caina got on well with her father's servants. They had always been kind to her, even during her mother's rages. As Caina got older, she realized that they felt sorry for her, and feared and detested Laeria. She knew that some nobles treated their servants badly, but her father always said that the true measure of a man was how he treated his servants, or those who could not hurt him or repay him.

So Caina tried to repay the servants' kindness in turn. The gods knew they took enough abuse from Laeria, after all.

Caina wandered into the villa's kitchen, looking for Azaia, the old Saddaic cook who prepared the family's meals. The kitchen had four large ovens and a dozen tables, but Count Sebastian rarely entertained guests, and Azaia and her few helpers never lit more than one oven.

"Azaia?" Caina called to the empty kitchen. "Are you there?"

Her voice echoed off the stone walls.

Caina blinked in surprise. Where was Azaia? She usually had breakfast ready by now.

But the ovens were dark, and the kitchen quiet and empty.

"Azaia?" called Caina again, looking around. Had the old woman overslept? That seemed inconceivable. Or maybe she had gotten sick, and hadn't told anyone? Caina made up her mind and headed to the kitchen's back door. Azaia lived in a small room behind the kitchens, and Caina would see if she had fallen ill...

She stopped.

There was a strange smell in the air, something metallic.

She turned, frowning.

Something dark and wet trickled down the wall, leaking from the leftmost oven. Had Azaia left something in there? That, too, seemed out of character. Caina walked to the brick wall, gripped the iron handles, and pulled the metal door open.

Azaia stared at her from within the oven, dead eyes glassy, torn throat covered in blood.

The scream ripped out of Caina like something alive.

Her father's seneschal Morus found her, drawn by the screams, and almost started screaming himself. He shouted for the rest of the servants. Eventually her father arrived and pulled her from the gruesome scene.

"What happened?" said Sebastian.

"I...I don't know," said Caina, trying to talk through the tears. She had read about violence, of course, but to see it with her own eyes was something else. "I came down for some food, to see if Azaia was cooking breakfast. No one was around, so I looked for her, and I saw the...I saw the blood leaking from the oven..."

Sebastian looked stricken. He had known Azaia for longer, after all, before Caina had even been born.

"Who could have done this?" said Caina.

"I don't know," said Sebastian, voice quiet. He fiddled with his heavy signet ring. "But we're going to find out, Caina. I promise you that. Whoever did this will be brought to account."

He stared at the bloodstain, his expression grim.

"Why would anyone kill Azaia?" said Caina. "She is...she was...so kind. Who would have hated her enough to do this?"

"I don't know," said Sebastian. "Azaia had no money, no influence. There was no reason for anyone to kill her. No reason at all. No reason to spill her blood." He sighed and rubbed his forehead. "Except for the blood itself."

He said the last so quietly she almost didn't hear it.

"You...know, don't you?" said Caina, puzzled. "You know who did this?"

"Maybe," said Sebastian. "I hope I'm wrong." He closed his eyes. "But if I'm wrong...then I've been blind. A blind fool." He opened his eyes. "I'm going to need help with this. Morus!"

The seneschal hurried over, face pale.

"Lord Count?" he said.

"Stay here," said Sebastian. "Don't let anyone inside."

"Where will you go, my lord?" said Morus.

"To town," said Sebastian. "I will inform the decimvirs of the murder, and...arrange for additional assistance." He took Caina's hand. "Come with me. Quickly."

They hurried through the villa's hallways and entered the library. The Maatish scroll still lay upon the desk, held open by two heavy books. Sebastian knelt behind the desk, opened the bottom drawer, and reached inside. He drew out a small wooden box and unlocked it.

Inside rested a single tarnished silver coin, its inscription and portrait worn with age.

"That's...the Emperor Cormarus, isn't it?" said Caina, curiosity overriding her fear.

"It is," said Sebastian, picking up the ancient coin.

"I've never seen him on a coin," said Caina. The Emperor Cormarus had ruled millennia ago, during the age of the Second Empire. Most of his coins would have been lost or melted down long ago. "Why would you need such an ancient coin?"

"I don't," said Sebastian, sliding the coin into a coat pocket. "The coin itself has no value. But it will send a message to the right people." He took Caina by the shoulders. "Stay in the library until I return. It shouldn't be long."

"I don't want to be left alone," said Caina. She remembered Azaia's dead eyes. "What if...what if the man who killed Azaia comes for me?"

Sebastian looked away. "I don't think he will. But I will have Morus send one of the maids to keep you company." He kissed her forehead. "I will be back."

Then he left. Caina walked to the windows, and in a few minutes saw her father on horseback, riding towards Aretia. Galloping, actually.

He rode through the town's gates and vanished from sight.

Caina turned towards the shelves, running a finger along the leather spines of the books, but her mind was in too much turmoil to read. Why would anyone want to kill Azaia? Had thieves done it, perhaps? But why hadn't they tried to break into her father's strong room, or the library? Maybe the smugglers had returned to reclaim their Maatish scroll?

But the scroll sat untouched on Sebastian's desk. Caina doubted that Azaia had even known about it. And it was just a dusty old scroll, written by people long dead. It couldn't be worth spilling blood over.

All that blood, dripping down the wall...

No reason to kill her except for her blood itself. That was what her father had said. But that made no sense. Why kill Azaia for her blood?

What use would her blood be to anyone?

Caina turned and flinched.

Her mother stood in the library doorway. Laeria Amalas wore an elaborate gold gown, the drooping sleeves and the skirts slashed with black. As usual, her hair was coiffed and arranged, jewels glittering on her fingers and ears.

Laeria never let anyone see her the slightest bit disheveled, even when angry.

They stared at each other for a while.

"So," said Laeria, walking towards the desk. "I suppose you came here to weep over that lazy cook?"

"This is Father's place," said Caina, voice low. "You shouldn't be here."

Laeria sneered at her. "I am the Countess of House Amalas. I may go wherever I please in this house, girl." She stopped and looked at the desk, staring at the ancient scroll.

"That belongs to Father," said Caina, worried that Laeria would tear it up out of spite. She had done such things before.

"Is it?" said Laeria. "Everything that is his is mine. Including this. I would put it to far better use than the fool ever could."

"Doing what?" said Caina. "You'll sell it and spend the money on jewels? Or wine, perhaps? Or maybe you'll bribe the Magisterium to take you back?"

No sooner had the words come out of her mouth than she realized they had been a mistake. She would send Laeria flying into a rage.

But her mother only smiled.

"You'll find out soon enough," Laeria said. "Because you are mine, child. Mine to do with as I please."

"No," said Caina. "I hate you and I don't want anything to do with you." She glared at her mother. "Someday I'll have my own children, and I'll be a better mother to them than you ever were to me."

"You won't," said Laeria, voice quiet. She laughed. "Have you been crying over that cook? Why? She was old and fat. Utterly useless."

Tears rose in Caina's eyes. "She was better than you."

Laeria laughed again. "Then you are as stupid as I always thought. I was a student of the Imperial Magisterium, a wielder of arcane science..."

"You were a novice for four years," said Caina, "until they threw you out because you were too weak. And useless."

Laeria's blue eyes blazed, and Caina knew that she had pushed her mother too far.

"Am I?" said Laeria. "Tell me again if I am weak."

She lifted her hand, palm out, fingers spread, whispering an incantation under her breath. Caina braced herself, expecting her mother to reach into her mind.

But instead, invisible force slammed into Caina, throwing her across the room and into a shelf. Books fell around her, bouncing off her head and arms. She struggled to regain her balance, to get away from the shelf, but the invisible force held her in place like a giant unseen hand.

Laeria had never been able to do anything like that before.

"Still think I am weak?" said Laeria, her face flushed, her eyes wide with something like ecstasy.

Caina struggled against the invisible force. Strain came over Laeria's face, beads of sweat rising on her forehead. Then the force sputtered and vanished, and Caina fell hard to the floor, rolling over the carpet. She staggered back to her feet, breathing hard, back and shoulders aching from the impact.

Laeria sneered again, and took a step forward, but had to grab the edge of the desk for support. Whatever she had done, whatever spell she had cast, had exhausted her.

"You belong to me," said Laeria. "Never forget that, you worthless, useless brat. You belong to me...and I will do with you what I please!"

"My lady?"

Caina and Laeria looked to the door. One of the maids, a young Caerish woman named Gwen, stood in the hallway, looking back and forth.

"What?" said Laeria.

"Morus sent me," said Gwen in Caerish, "said that I was to..."

"Be silent! Or speak High Nighmarian in my presence, rather than the babble of commoners" said Laeria, turning away with one last glower at Caina. "Never forget, girl. You are mine to do with as I please."

Laeria stalked from the library without sparing Caina another glance.

Caina let out a long breath. She was shaking, her hands clenched into fists, tears trickling down her cheeks.

"My lady?" said Gwen. "What...what should I do?"

Caina closed her eyes. "Help me clean up these books."

It did not take long to clean up the books, and afterwards Caina sent Gwen away. She was not afraid that Azaia's murderer would come after her.

She was afraid that her mother was the murderer. Or that Laeria knew who had done it.

Caina spent the day leafing through books, her eyes moving over the pages without seeing anything. Again and again she looked towards the window, hoping to see her father riding back from Aretia.

He did not come.

Eventually Caina fell asleep on the couch by her father's desk. She dreamed of the kitchen, of Azaia's dead eyes gazing at her. She fled, screaming, but the dead woman lurked in every door, reaching for her with pallid, lifeless hands.

Caina awoke with a start, her heart racing.

She heard shouting. A man's voice, and a woman's, both raised in anger.

Her mother and father.

The voices came from the hallway. Caina rose and crept towards the door.

"Don't take that tone with me," said Laeria, her voice full of contempt.

"Tone?" said Sebastian. "One of my servants lies butchered in her own oven, and you're worried about my tone?"

"Simply hire another one," said Laeria. "The woman's cooking was deplorable. Aretia is thronged with idle commoners. You should have no difficulty replacing her."

"She was murdered!" said Sebastian.

"What of that?" said Laeria. "Commoners murder each other for the stupidest reasons."

"I think the reasons had nothing to do with Azaia, or any other commoner," said Sebastian.

There was silence for a moment.

"So you are blaming me?" said Laeria, laughing. "You think I snuck down to the kitchens in the dead of night and cut the fat old cow's throat? Yes, indeed, that is how I like to spend my evenings."

"Not you," said Sebastian. "Your friends."

"My friends?" said Laeria. "Yes, dear husband, I have so many friends worthy of my attention, living in this miserable backwater."

Her voice had grown shriller.

"You know what friends I mean," said Sebastian. "Your correspondents. The sorcerers."

Laeria sniffed. "If I choose to correspond with the magi of the Imperial Magisterium, then that is my own affair..."

"The Imperial Magisterium is a collection of fools, tyrants, and murderers," said Sebastian, "but even they know better than to have anything to do with you. They cast you out after four years, after all."

Caina could just imagine Laeria's expression at that.

"Do not think to insult me," said Laeria, voice cold. "If I..."

"You've been writing to...other sorcerers, haven't you?" said Sebastian. "Not the magi?"

Laeria said nothing.

"The outcasts and the criminals," said Sebastian. "The sorcerers outside the Magisterium, the ones who practice forbidden sciences."

Laeria still said nothing.

"Tell me that I'm wrong," said Sebastian.

"You've been reading my letters?" said Laeria. "Such a worthy pursuit of a nobleman..."

"It wasn't necessary," said Sebastian. "I know you, Laeria. I know what sort of woman you are, even if I didn't when we first met. You only want power. That's all you've ever wanted. You thought the Magisterium would give you power, but they rejected you. So you've turned to outlaw sorcerers instead."

Laeria said nothing.

"Tell me that I'm wrong," said Sebastian.

"You are a narrow-minded fool," said Laeria.

"Damn it, woman," said Sebastian. "Necromancers? Are you insane?"

"You are as blind as the Magisterium," said Laeria. "They could not appreciate my talent, my potential. But the outlaws can. They understand me. Why should I not associate with them?" Her voice dropped, so quiet that Caina could barely hear it. "And not all the Magisterium thinks as you do. There are magi who appreciate the potential of necromancy and the other banned arcane sciences. They would see the magi rule the Empire again, and the glory of the Fourth Empire restored."

"The Fourth Empire was built upon the blood of the innocent and the sweat of slaves," said Sebastian. "I will not have anyone in my house associate with necromancers! Not even you, Laeria. If need be, I will stop this."

Laeria laughed. "You are a weak and craven man. How will you stop me?"

"I will contact the Ghosts."

Laeria's laughter redoubled. "The Ghosts are a myth. A story fools use to excuse their failures."

"I will not tolerate this, Laeria."

Again she laughed at him. "And how will you stop me, dear Sebastian? You are a coward. You always have been a coward. Even now you are afraid of me. Stay out of my way, little boy, and perhaps you will not be hurt."

Her heels clicked against the floor. Silence hung over the library for a moment. Then the door opened, and Sebastian walked into the room. He looked tired and disheveled, his clothes rumpled and his thinning hair sticking up at odd angles. He crossed to the desk, reached into a drawer, drew out a dusty bottle of brandy, and poured himself a glass.

Only then did he look up and see Caina.

"Daughter," he said. "What are you doing here?"

"I fell asleep on the couch," said Caina.

Sebastian gave a distracted nod. "I'm sorry. My business in town took...longer than I anticipated. I should have been back sooner."

"What were you and Mother fighting about?" said Caina.

Sebastian closed his eyes. "You heard?"

Caina nodded.

"The same thing we always fight about," said Sebastian.

"It didn't sound like it," said Caina.

Sebastian sighed. "This...was not something I wanted to discuss with you, Caina. But..." He sighed again, and took a sip of his brandy. "I suppose it cannot be kept from you." One more sip of brandy, and he looked at her. "Tell me about the Imperial Magisterium."

Caina shrugged. "The magi of the Magisterium oversee the use of sorcery in the Empire."

Sebastian nodded. "Go on."

"They all learn to use the sorcery of the mind," said Caina, remembering how her mother had dug into her thoughts. "They can also learn to control the elements of earth, wind, and water."

"But not fire," said Sebastian. "Why not?"

"Because using fire sorcery drives the wielder insane," said Caina. "They're also forbidden to use necromancy."

"Why?"

"Because," said Caina, thinking back to the books she head read, "because...other kinds of sorcery draw their power from the mind, or the elements. Necromancy draws its power from death, from blood, and...and..."

She remembered Azaia's corpse, all that blood dripping down the wall...

"Azaia?" whispered Caina.

Sebastian sighed and nodded.

"Some...some necromancer killed her?" said Caina.

"The Magisterium," said Sebastian, his voice heavy, "would have us believe that they have total control over sorcery in the Empire, that the forbidden arcane sciences have been stamped out. But that's not true. Bands of rogue sorcerers have operated within the Empire for years. And many brothers and sisters of the Magisterium are...sympathetic, to say the least. And some of the nobility, for that matter. They would see the magi rule the Empire once more, would see the forbidden sciences restored, and slavery reestablished in all the provinces."

"What has that to do with Mother?" said Caina.

"Your mother," said Sebastian, tugging at his signet ring, "has been corresponding with one of these outlaw sorcerers."

"Why?" said Caina.

"The Magisterium rejected her," said Sebastian. "Perhaps the outlaws will not. Never mind that necromancers fuel their powers with the blood of the innocent. Your mother, Caina...your mother would not scruple at any crime, if she thought it would give her power." He shook his head. "I had thought better of her. I had...I had hoped to think better of her."

"What will we do?" said Caina.

Sebastian looked out the windows, at the moonlight rippling on the sea. "The Ghosts."

"Ghosts?" said Caina. "Will the necromancers call up spirits?"

Sebastian smiled, briefly. "Not quite. Most people think the Ghosts are only a legend. But they're very real. They are the Emperor's spies, his eyes and ears. And occasionally his assassins. And they are bitter enemies of the magi, and all who practice forbidden arcane sciences. If any one can deal with your mother's 'friends', the Ghosts can."

"Or with Mother herself," said Caina.

Sebastian shook his head. "Your mother is...brittle, Caina. She's..." His voice trailed off. "There are bruises on your face. Did she hit you?"

"No," said Caina, touching her cheek. It still hurt, come to think of it. "No...she did something. Some kind of spell. She pushed out with her hand, and this...invisible thing hit me. It threw me into the bookshelf."

Sebastian frowned. "She's...never been able to do anything like that before." He looked at her, at the shelves, and then back to her. "She didn't have the power. That is why the Magisterium put her out...she simply wasn't strong enough to become a magus."

"Then how did she get so much stronger?" said Caina.

Blood. Her father had said that necromancers used blood to fuel their powers. To make themselves stronger. And Laeria had become stronger. Caina had watched her practice sorcery for years, and Laeria had barely been able to lift a goblet into the air with her powers.

And now she had the strength to throw Caina across the room with a single gesture.

"Oh, gods," whispered Caina. "She killed Azaia, didn't she?"

Sebastian said nothing, but his sickened expression told Caina everything.

"What are you going to do?" said Caina, her voice shaking with panic. "She's going to kill us. She's going to kill me, she's going to kill me, she's..."

"Caina!" Sebastian stood, took her by the shoulders. "I will not let her hurt you."

"How?" said Caina.

"I will confront her with the truth," said Sebastian. "She was right about one thing. I have been a coward, and I have put this off for too long. I will give her one chance to leave with her life. If she is still here when the Ghosts arrive, they will kill her."

Caina grabbed his hand. "No. Don't. Don't! She'll kill you."

"She won't," said Sebastian. "Bad enough that she killed a servant. But if she kills an Imperial Count, she knows that the Ghosts will never stop hunting her."

"Don't," said Caina, her fingers squeezing his hand. "Please, don't do this."

"I have to," said Sebastian. "It is the right thing to do."

"She murdered Azaia!" said Caina. It was the first time she had ever shouted at her father. "How is giving her a chance to run the right thing to do?"

"Because," said Sebastian. "She is still my wife, and I swore before gods and men to be faithful to her until death. And even if I hate her, even if we haven't spoken a civil word to each other in ten years…she still gave me you, Caina."

Caina had no answer for that. Yet every nerve in her body screamed that warning Laeria was a mistake, that Sebastian should contact the Ghosts at once, that he should avoid Laeria until the Ghosts arrived to deal with her.

But she could find no words to articulate her desperate fear.

"Don't," she whispered.

"I must," said Sebastian, squeezing her hand. "Go to bed, Caina. This will all be settled in a few days, I promise you."

Caina didn't believe him. But he was her father, and she trusted him. So she nodded and let him lead her to her bedroom. He lifted her, kissed her on the forehead, and placed her upon the bed.

"Good night," he said. "I love you."

"I love you, too," said Caina.

Sebastian smiled and left.

Caina lay alone in the darkness.

The shadows seemed to swallow her, and at last she fell into a feverish, dream-haunted sleep.

CHAPTER 3
MAGLARION

Caina awoke from a nightmare, her heart pounding. In the dream, she had seen her mother standing over Azaia, a shining knife in her hands. Azaia screamed and pleaded for her life, to no avail, while Laeria laughed and laughed.

Caina rolled out of bed, shivering.

It was still dark out. Only a glimmer of moonlight came through her bedroom windows. Silence hung over the villa, complete and unbroken.

Something was wrong.

Caina could not say what it was. Yet she was afraid, more afraid than she had ever felt in her life. Even the worst of Laeria's rages had never frightened her so badly.

She wanted her father.

Caina pushed open the bedroom door.

It struck something. Caina blinked in surprise and looked into the darkened hallway.

A body lay upon the floor.

It was Morus, the seneschal, flat upon his back, arms flung to either side. A scream rose in Caina's throat, but then she saw his chest rising and falling, and all at once she felt foolish. Had he gotten drunk? Or had he fallen sick, and collapsed outside her door?

Caina stepped over his outstretched legs and stopped.

His eyes were open, staring at her. He did not move, did not blink. Caina hesitated, then stooped over him and waved a hand in front his face.

He blinked, once, but otherwise did not move. A foul smell struck her nostrils, and she realized that Morus had soiled himself.

What had happened to him?

Her father, she needed her father.

Caina broke into a run, and almost tripped over another body. It was Gwen, the maid who had helped her clean up the books. Like Morus, she was still alive. And like Morus, she stared unseeing at the ceiling.

What had happened to them?

Caina ran through the hallways. More of the servants, men and women she had seen every day of her life, lay open-eyed and immobile upon the floor. Caina pushed at some. She shouted at others, tugged at their ears, tried to get them to wake up.

They did not respond.

At last Caina came to her father's bedroom. He and Laeria did not share a bedroom, had not shared a bedroom for years, and kept their rooms on opposite sides of the villa. Sebastian's room had more bookshelves, of course, and numerous curios and relics from the Empire's history.

His bed lay empty.

Caina stared at it panic, breathing hard. He had gone to confront Laeria. Had Laeria hurt him, or killed...

No. No. He would be upset after fighting with her, he would have gone to the library to settle his nerves.

Caina raced out of the bedroom, hurrying past the servants lying motionless in their own waste. The library doors stood open, a glimmer of moonlight spilling through the windows, and a dying fire crackled in the fireplace. Sebastian sat at his desk, and relief surged through Caina. He would know what to do, he would know how to help the servants...

"Father?" said Caina.

She skidded to a stop before his desk.

He stared at her.

Unblinking.

"Father?" said Caina.

He wasn't sitting in his chair, she saw. He was slumped against it, his limp arms hanging over the sides, his heavy signet ring gleaming on his finger.

"Father!" shouted Caina.

He did not respond.

She rushed around the desk, shook him. He blinked a few times, but did not otherwise react.

"Wake up," she said, starting to cry, "wake up, wake up, wake up..."

He did not. He gave no sign that he heard her. Her father started to slide out of the chair, and she pushed him back into place, hoping to keep him from falling to the floor.

Someone laughed.

Caina whirled.

Laeria Amalas walked into the library, smiling. She looked...energized.

Stronger, somehow, stronger than Caina had ever seen her. Radiant, even.

Caina walked around the desk, hands curled into fists.

"You did this," she whispered, "didn't you?"

Again Laeria laughed at her.

"Your father," said Laeria, looking at Sebastian. "He said he knew what I had been doing. Who had been teaching me. He would give me one chance to flee before the Ghosts came." She stepped behind the desk and slapped him. His head turned with the blow, but his blank expression did not change. "The fool. He did not understand what I have become. What the Master has taught me."

"What did you do to him?" said Caina.

"The Master desires secrecy," said Laeria. "So I thought to reach into their minds, to erase their memories of the old woman's death." Her smiled widened. "Except...I'm afraid I didn't quite master the spell. I wanted to erase a few days' worth of memories. I wound up destroying their minds."

"You...you killed them," said Caina.

"Not quite," said Laeria. "Living blood is the fuel of necromancy, and the Master might yet have a use for their lives. I merely erased their minds. They are little more than vegetables, now. They will lie there and drool in their own waste until they finally die of thirst."

She crossed to the desk and ran a finger over the ancient Maatish scroll, smiling.

"Why?" whispered Caina, tears trickling down her face.

"Why?" echoed Laeria, mocking her tone. "Because the Master will not take me as a disciple unless I show my worthiness. First by ridding myself of the attachments of family. And then by offering a gift."

Her hand strayed to the ancient scroll again.

"The scroll?" said Caina.

Laeria looked at her, eyes narrowed. "How did...yes, child. The scroll. Dear Sebastian didn't know what he had found. This scroll is a spell of Maatish necromancy, ancient and powerful. The Master desires it. I offered it to him, in exchange for his teachings, and he agreed to take me as a disciple."

"That's it?" said Caina. "You did...did this to my father for some stupid old scroll?"

"The Master desired one other thing, as the price of my discipleship," said Laeria, her smile widening. "You, my dear child."

"You hurt Father," whispered Caina, "for that?"

"I told you that you would be of use to me yet," said Laeria. "The blood of a virgin has power...power that can fuel the most potent spells of necromantic science. The Master will make good use of you, child, better use than you could have ever achieved with your worthless waste of a life."

"You hurt Father!" said Caina, her voice rising to a scream.

Laeria scowled and strode around the desk, and Caina backed away until she bumped into the fireplace. "And I wish I had done it years ago. I loathed you both, you and your worthless craven of a father. At least I shall find some use for you in the end. Though I wish I had never met your father!" She smirked. "No, that's not quite true. I wish I had killed him ten years ago..."

Caina screamed. Rage drowned both her fear and pain alike. She wanted nothing more than to make Laeria pay, to smash the gloating smirk from her face.

Her hand closed about the fireplace poker.

Laeria laughed at her. "Weep for him all you want. You are weak and useless, and I shall..."

Caina screamed again and swung the poker with all her strength. It raked across Laeria's face, sent her stumbling. Laeria's feet tangled in the heavy skirts of her golden gown, and she lost her balance and fell backwards.

The back of her head bounced off the corner of Sebastian's desk with a sickening crack. Laeria hit the floor and did not move.

Caina cringed against the fireplace, clutching the poke. She had yelled at her mother, fought with her...but Caina had never dared strike Laeria Amalas before. Surely Caina had gone too far. Surely Laeria would rise in wrath and beat her senseless, or unleash her sorcery and twist Caina's mind into nothingness, as she had done with Sebastian and Morus and Gwen...

But Laeria did not move.

In fact, she wasn't even breathing.

Caina stared at Laeria, frozen. After a long time she mustered the courage to move closer. Still Laeria did not move. At last Caina stood over her mother, gazing down at her.

At the puddle of blood spreading beneath her head.

Her blue eyes stared unblinking at Caina. Even in death, they still seemed to burn with hatred and contempt.

The poker fell from Caina's hand and struck the floor with a clang. She backed away, breath keening through her lips.

"Oh gods," whispered Caina, "oh gods, oh gods, oh gods..."

She had just murdered her mother.

Caina stared at the corpse, panic threatening to overtake her. She had hated Laeria, hated her for years, but to have actually killed her...no. Matricides were accursed, everyone knew that.

Caina didn't know what to do.

Her father would know.

She hurried to his chair, shook him.

"Wake up," she said. "Wake up, wake up, please, please wake up."

Sebastian did not answer. He blinked, once or twice, but did not move, his breath steady and shallow.

"Please!" shouted Caina, shaking his collar.

Sebastian slid forward, falling upon the desk, his cheek resting against the ancient Maatish scroll. His outstretched hand overturned a pewter inkwell, the ink dripping down the front of the desk to mingle with Laeria's blood. Sebastian was fastidious with his inkwells. He never spilled ink, not ever.

Whatever Laeria had done to him, he really was gone.

Caina wept, grabbing the heavy chair for support. In the past, she had always gone to her father for help. But he sat empty-eyed and limp in his chair. She could have gone to Morus, or old Azaia, but Morus lay motionless in the hallway, and Azaia in her own oven. Caina was alone, and she didn't know what to do.

Time passed. Caina could not have said how long. She stood over her father's chair and cried.

A single footstep cracked against the floor.

Caina looked up, blinking.

A gaunt old man stood in the library doors, looking at her. Pale white hair seemed to float around his head, one gray eye glinting in the glow of the fireplace, the other hidden beneath a strip of black cloth. He wore a fine black coat that hung to his knees, black trousers, and a white linen shirt. The leather of his boots gleamed, and a jeweled dagger rested in a sheath at his belt. He leaned upon a polished black cane in his left hand.

He looked...kindly. Almost grandfatherly.

"Child, child," said the old man, smiling at her. He spoke High Nighmarian with a calm stateliness. "Why do you weep?"

"My father," said Caina. "He's...he's..."

"His mind has been wiped, yes," said the old man, taking a step into the library. His one eye flicked over the scene.

"Can you help him?" said Caina. The old man had seen what had happened at once. And if he knew what it was, then perhaps he would know how to reverse it.

The old man chuckled. "No, I am afraid not. The mind is rather like a mirror. Or a vase, perhaps. Once shattered, it cannot be remade."

Caina bowed her head.

"Tell me," said the old man. "Who did this to your father?"

He took another step closer. He had a limp, and leaned upon the black cane for support. Something about him, something about his unwavering gaze, frightened Caina.

She felt as if something watched her from behind the black cloth covering his left eye, something cold and terrible and alien.

"My mother," said Caina. "I...I...."

The old man glanced over Laeria's body, prodded it with the cane.

22

"Ah, Laeria. Clumsy to the end. A capable practitioner could have removed the necessary memories and left the victims none the wiser. Instead, she used a hammer when a needle would have served. Incidentally, how did she die?"

"I killed her," whispered Caina.

For the first time, the old man looked surprised. "Did you, now? Did you indeed?" He looked at her, at the poker lying discarded on the floor, and back at her. "How amusing. Laeria thought of herself as a master magus, a brilliant flower crushed by the tedium of her surroundings. And so she was killed by a scrawny eleven-year-old girl with a poker. Appropriate, really." He laughed aloud, and beckoned.

More men came through the doorway behind him, hard-faced men in leather armor. Swords rested in their belts, and they carried ropes and chains.

"What?" said Caina, backing away in fear. "Who...who are they?"

"No one of importance," said the old man. "Tell me. You are...Caina, I believe that was the name, yes? Laeria's daughter?"

Caina nodded. "Who are you?"

The old man smiled, the skin around his good eye crinkling. "You can call me Maglarion, if you wish." He peered at the desk for a moment, his smile widening as he saw the ancient papyrus scroll. "Ah. Yes. You know, I have been seeking this for a very long time." He rolled up the scroll and tucked it into his coat. "A very long time, indeed. I was even willing to teach your mother, blockheaded fool that she was, in order to obtain it. She is dead now, true, but I have made the long journey to Aretia, and I am entitled to my payment, am I not?"

"You were the one who taught her necromancy," whispered Caina, backing away from him.

A woman entered the room, and the men made way for her. She was tall and slim, with white hair, despite her youthful face. Like the men, she wore leather armor, but only bore one weapon, a single black dagger at her belt.

Her expression was blank. Utterly blank. Like there was nothing behind her eyes at all.

Maglarion blinked. "Yes. A most perceptive child, you are. A pity you have no arcane talent. I suspect you would have made a far better student than Laeria ever would. Still, I shall take the second half of my payment."

"What's that?" said Caina.

Maglarion grinned, and for the first time Caina realized how cold that gray eye was, like a disk of ice glinting in his face.

"Why, you are, my dear. Laeria assured me that you were virgin, and I have much need for a virgin's blood in my work."

Caina ran for the door.

23

Maglarion laughed and crooked a finger.

And his will fell upon her mind like a thunderbolt. Her mother's will had been a slender hand, groping and clawing its way through her thoughts like a shuffling rodent. But Maglarion's will was a mailed first, an iron hammer, and he beat through her resistance with ease. Caina went rigid, every muscle locked in place by the power of Maglarion's sorcery. She struggled against his grip, but it was like trying to fight a stone wall.

Even with the aid of stolen blood, Laeria had never been able to do anything like that.

"Still fighting?" said Maglarion. "You are strong. A pity, indeed, that you do not have any arcane talent." He looked away from her. "Ikhana?"

"Master?" said the tall woman, stepping to Maglarion's side.

"Gather up Laeria's victims and take them to the sanctuary," said Maglarion. "The foolish woman broke their minds, so they will be useless as slaves...but I still have a use for their lives. And so might you, come to think of it."

For a brief moment something almost like a smile flickered across Ikhana's face, her eyes kindling.

"Also, secure the child," said Maglarion. "Have her bound and hooded, and taken to the sanctuary as well."

Ikhana turned to the men. "Do as the Master bids."

"Why?" said an unshaven man with ragged hair.

A hushed silence fell over the others.

Maglarion looked at him, a bland smile on his face.

"Why?" said the unshaven man, glaring at Ikhana. "I signed up for profit. And there's no profit in selling drooling idiots as slaves."

Slavers, Caina realized. The men were slave traders. Sebastian had told her how sometimes Istarish and Alqaarin slavers raided the Bay of Empire, capturing women and children to sell in the markets of Istarinmul and Nhabatan.

"We won't get much profit with one little girl," said the unshaven man. "So let the old man use his witchery to keep her bound. I'm not lifting another finger until I get paid."

Maglarion crooked his finger, his smile never wavering.

For the briefest moment, something like green fire flickered beneath the cloth covering his left eye.

And the unshaven man's throat exploded in a crimson spray. He fell to his knees, choking and coughing, blood pouring down his chest, and then toppled onto his face.

"Does anyone else," said Maglarion, "have any objections? Anyone? No. I thought not."

"Do as the Master bids," repeated Ikhana.

The slavers hastened to obey. Some hurried into the hallway, while two stepped around the desk and picked up Sebastian. Maglarion released his mental grip on Caina, and she turned to run. But the slavers were faster. Two of them seized her arms, while a third pressed a rag over her face.

A strange, chemical stink filled Caina's nostrils, and everything went dark.

CHAPTER 4
THE NECROMANTIC SCIENCES

Caina awoke in darkness, her cheek against a rough stone floor.

For a moment she thought she had rolled out of bed in the night. Then she remembered Maglarion and his sorcery, Ikhana and her empty eyes, and the slavers.

She remembered her father slumped motionless in his chair.

Caina scrambled to her knees in sudden terror.

She was in a cell, the stone walls rough and glistening with dampness. A massive iron-banded oak door sealed the cell, a strange blue glow leaking through the barred window. The walls and floor were icy, and Caina started to shiver.

What were they going to do with her?

Boots clicked in the hallway, and a key rattled in the door's lock. The door started to open, but got stuck against the frame. Someone cursed and kicked it, and the door swung open with a shriek of rusted hinges.

Ikhana stood in the corridor outside, two of the Istarish slavers besides her.

"Good. She is awake," said Ikhana, fingering the black dagger at her belt. "The Master requires her now. Take her."

Caina pressed herself against the far wall, heart hammering with dread. The men reached in the cell, seized her arms, and dragged her out. Caina fought, or tried to, but the men held her fast.

"Also, gag her," said Ikhana, her face expressionless. "If she disrupts the lesson, the Master shall be wroth."

One of the men nodded, produced a length of rag, stuffed it into Caina's mouth, and tied it behind her head. Then they carried her out the corridor and up a flight of stairs. Ikhana opened another door, and they stepped into an vast stone room, dozens of square pillars supporting a vaulted ceiling. More strange blue light filled the room, coming from glowing glass spheres upon iron stands. The Magisterium manufactured and enspelled those spheres, Caina remembered, selling them by the thousands.

A dozen men and women stood near the far wall, speaking in low voices. Unlike the slavers, they wore ornate black robes, tied about the waist with crimson sashes. Magi, Caina realized, brothers and sisters of the Imperial Magisterium.

A metal table stood before the assembled magi, its corroded surface marked with dark stains. The slavers wrestled Caina onto the table and shackled her wrists and ankles to the corners. The metal felt very cold through her clothes, and even colder against the bare skin of her wrists and ankles.

A cane tapped against the flagstones, and the assembled magi felt silent.

Maglarion limped between the table and the magi, leaning upon his cane, his white hair ghostly in the pale light, his good eye hidden in shadow.

"Welcome," he said, speaking in High Nighmarian. "Welcome." He smiled and spread his hands. "Do you know why you are here?"

"This had better be worth the risk," said one of the magi, a sullen man with a square jaw. "The practice of necromancy carries the death sentence. If the high magi or the Ghosts get word of this..."

"Nothing is accomplished without risk, Kylan," said Maglarion. "If you are too timid to face that, then you may leave. But if you are strong enough to stay, then you will indeed see the power that lies within reach of the strong."

Kylan scowled, but said no more.

"You are here," said Maglarion, "because you are wiser than your peers. You realize that the Emperor's ban against the necromantic sciences is foolish and short-sighted. In the days of the Fourth Empire, when the magi ruled, the Empire was strong. The commoners knew their place, and the magi used the blood of slaves to fuel mighty spells."

The magi nodded in agreement.

"And I am here," said Maglarion, "because of my mastery of the necromantic sciences, and I mean that in the most literal sense. For I was born four hundred years ago, during the War of the Fourth Empire, and I studied at the feet of the great masters of those days, whose like cannot be found in the Magisterium today. And it is through necromancy that I have done what every god has promised, but cannot do - I have transcended death through my skill, attained immortality through my power. And you, too, may attain immortality - if you are strong enough."

"And how did you attain this?" said Kylan, still dubious.

"Power is the essential principle of sorcery," said Maglarion. "Or, more precisely, the source of a spell's power. A magus can draw upon his mind to empower a spell," he gestured, and his cane floated into the air, "or upon the elements of earth, wind, and water. And the necromantic sciences draw their power from death, from the consumption of life. Just as burning coal produces light and heat, so also does the destruction of life produce necromantic power. Observe."

He turned towards Caina, a glittering dagger in his hand.

Caina shrieked and fought the restraints, her wrist and ankles scraping against the steel. Maglarion cut open the bottom of her shirt, revealing her stomach.

"And blood," said Maglarion, "is the foundation of necromancy."

He drew the tip of the dagger across Caina's stomach, slicing the skin and opening a long cut below her navel.

Caina screamed into her gag, but the shackles held her fast.

"Come now," said Maglarion, digging the dagger deeper, hot blood welling over her chilled skin. "I wouldn't thrash about. You will only do further damage to yourself."

A chuckle went through the magi.

It hurt worse than anything she had ever known. Caina lay trembling and helpless, sobbing into the gag, as Maglarion sawed the dagger back and forth. Finally he grunted in satisfaction and produced a small silver cup, its sides black with age and tarnish. As her blood drained into grooves on the metal table, he held the cup below it, catching the crimson droplets.

"Observe," he said, lifting up the cup. "A virgin's blood. It can be used for a variety of useful necromantic applications, but the most potent is that of a bloodcrystal."

He whispered an incantation, green flames snarling and crackling around his fingertips. Again emerald light flickered beneath his eye patch. Caina felt a sudden sharp tingle, in addition to the pain, and for a moment her stomach clenched with nausea.

That only made the gash on her stomach hurt worse.

Then the green fire faded, and Maglarion reached into the cup.

"Behold," he said, holding out his hand. "A bloodcrystal."

A black gem perhaps the size of Caina's thumb rested in his hand. It was the exact color of dried blood, yet looked as hard and as sharp as obsidian.

"It stores the force, the raw life energy, that was latent in her blood," said Maglarion, gazing into the crystal's black depths.

"Fascinating," said another of the magi. "So the power can be stored for later use?"

"Yes," said Maglarion. He paused for a moment, as if just remembering something, and tucked the bloodcrystal away in a pocket of his coat. "Any blood can be used, of course, but the best results are obtained from the blood of a virgin."

"Then you'd best make as many as you can now," said Kylan. "The way the child is bleeding, you won't have the opportunity."

Caina sagged against the cold metal table, the room spinning around her. Her emotions numbed, and so did her pain. She was going to bleed to death, she realized. That thought did not trouble her.

At least she would be free of this place, and these men.

Maglarion chuckled. "Not yet. I still have a use for her, you see."

He made a slashing motion, and again green flame erupted around his hand. He dragged his glowing fingers across Caina's wound, and fresh pain exploded through her, worse than before. She screamed again, and Maglarion's hand burned like ice against her skin.

Then the pain faded, leaving only numbness. The cut on her stomach had vanished, leaving a ugly crimson scar.

"Necromantic power can also be used to heal," said Maglarion. He ran a finger along the new-made scar. "Though the experience is often...unpleasant."

"Why not simply kill her outright, and use all her blood at once?" asked another magus.

"No need to be wasteful," said Maglarion, flexing his fingers. "With proper care, we can continue to bleed her for several months yet. Once she has her first menstrual cycle, then I'll kill her. The womb of a virgin contains tremendous potential for necromantic energy. Think of all the children that might have grown there, the lives that might have begun within her...then imagine all that potential power consumed and used to your ends. The womb of a virgin can be used in the most powerful workings of arcane science. Though, alas, the process of removing it is almost invariably fatal."

"Fascinating," said Kylan. He seemed intrigued, even excited. "The Empire is filled with useless mouths. If their blood were harnessed to empower mighty spells...think of all that we could accomplish. We could restore the glory of the Fourth Empire. We could surpass the glory of the Fourth Empire!"

Maglarion smiled. "I am pleased that you recognize the potential." He glanced at Ikhana. "Take her. Bring another. One of the mind-wiped ones. The old seneschal, I think."

Two of slavers unlocked Caina and dragged her from the metal table. She tried to fight, but the loss of blood made her light-headed, and she sagged against them, the room spinning around her.

"What we have seen," said Maglarion, "uses only a small amount of blood. But by using every drop of blood in a human body...dramatic effects can be achieved."

More slaves appeared, carrying old Morus between them. They

dumped him on the metal table without bothering to shackle his wrists and ankles.

"Observe," said Maglarion, crossing to the table, his glittering dagger in hand.

The slavers had just opened the door to the cell when Caina felt the crawling tingle of another spell.

Maglarion had just murdered Morus.

The slavers dumped Caina back into her cell and shut the door. She tried to stand, but her head kept spinning, and she collapsed against the wall, sinking into darkness.

Time passed.

Caina knew neither day nor night in this dark place, but some slavers arrived with a plate of food and ordered her to eat. Caina refused. The slavers grunted, disappeared, and returned with Ikhana.

The woman knelt before Caina, pale eyes blank and empty. Caina shied away from her, pushing into the corner.

"You will eat, child," said Ikhana, her voice soft.

"No," said Caina.

Ikhana almost smiled.

Her hand blurred, and suddenly her black dagger rested against Caina's cheek. The gleaming blade had been carved with strange, flowing symbols.

"You are fortunate, child," said Ikhana, "that the Master requires you alive, for now. Because I would enjoy killing you. I would very much enjoy killing you." She caressed Caina's face with the blade. "You are young and strong. For now. How I want to devour you." Again her eyes kindled with something like madness. "Perhaps I will, before the Master leaves you used up and empty."

Gently, she pushed the tip of the dagger into the skin of Caina's jaw.

All at once a horrible cold filled Caina. The tip of the black dagger felt like an icicle stabbing into her. The symbols on the blade flickered and danced with green light, and Caina felt a terrible emptiness radiating from the blade, something cold and hungry.

As if the dagger yearned to suck away all her life and warmth.

Ikhana sighed and straightened up. "But...not yet. The Master has a use for you. After he is finished with you...then I shall feast upon you, yes." She turned and left, the door closing behind her, leaving Caina alone with the food.

Caina tried to ignore it, but she was soon so hungry that she ate and drank anyway. Then she sat alone in the darkness, alternating between fits of weeping and shocked numbness. From time to time she heard an agonized scream as Maglarion continued his lessons, and she felt the crawling tingle of arcane spells.

Sometimes she fell asleep in brief, feverish snatches. But every time she closed her eyes, the nightmares filled her mind. Her father, slumped in his chair. Her mother, laughing at her.

The way the poker had felt when it connected with Laeria's face, the sound her skull had made, bouncing off the edge of Sebastian's desk.

She woke up screaming.

Perhaps four days passed before Ikhana returned. The cell door screamed open, rust falling in flakes from the iron hinges.

"Take her," said Ikhana.

Caina tried to scramble out of reach, but she felt tired, sluggish, and the slavers seized her with ease. The memory of Maglarion's glittering dagger filled her with terrified strength, and she tried to fight. Finally one of the slavers cursed in annoyance and cuffed her across the face, while a second man twisted her arms behind her back. A third one gagged her once more. They marched her back into the vaulted room and shackled her to the metal table once more.

Numerous fresh stains marked the table.

The assembled magi sat upon chairs, watching, while Maglarion stood nearby, drumming his fingers on the head of his cane.

"Now," said Maglarion, as the slavers finished chaining Caina to the table. "As I have demonstrated, specific amounts of blood, used properly, can fuel potent necromantic effects. But let us turn from the specific to the general. Death itself, the sundering of spirit from flesh, generates power, and that power can be tapped and controlled by the skilled practitioner. Any death releases power. The younger the victim, the more energy that is released, but even the deaths of the elderly and the sick can be used. But first," he turned towards the table, dagger in hand, "we must prepare a receptacle to store that power."

Caina screamed into the gag, muscles going rigid with horrified anticipation. Maglarion paid no heed, but brushed aside the bloodstained rags of her shirt and slashed his dagger across the scar.

It hurt worse than before.

The blood welled across Caina's skin, and Maglarion sawed deeper, ignoring Caina's trembling. Then he produced the black crystal he had made from her blood, and rubbed it through the gash, whispering a spell as he did so. Green flames danced around his hand, filling Caina with cold pain, and she howled into the gag until she thought she might bite through it.

When Maglarion lifted his hand, the bloodcrystal was twice the size it had been before, and a green glow flickered in its dark depths.

"In addition to its latent energy," said Maglarion, turning the crystal back and forth before his covered eye, "and its ability to serve as a reservoir, the bloodcrystal can now act as a...trap, of sorts, absorbing the energy released from any death in the nearby area."

"How large of an area?" said one of the magi.

"It depends upon the size of the bloodcrystal," said Maglarion. "A crystal this size can absorb the energies from any death within, oh, perhaps thirty yards or so. The distance increases exponentially with the size of the crystal." He peered to the side. "Ah. As we shall now demonstrate."

Another of pair of slavers entered the chamber, dragging a man between them.

Caina moaned into her gag.

It was her father.

He did not look well. No doubt the slavers hadn't bothered to feed him, and had only been pouring enough water down his throat to keep him alive. His face still looked vacant and slack, his mind ruined by Laeria's sorcery.

But he was still alive. Maybe his mind could get better with time, maybe he could one day recover...

Maglarion walked towards him, dagger in hand.

Caina screamed, threw herself against the restraints so hard that the shackles drew blood, that the heavy metal table rocked a bit. Maglarion turned, eyebrows raised in surprise.

"She seems upset," said Kylan.

"I believe," said Maglarion, "that is her father. So I doubt she has the objectivity to appreciate our noble purpose just now."

A chuckle of amusement went through the magi.

Caina shouted into the gag, but Maglarion paid her no mind. One of the slavers tore open Sebastian's filthy shirt, exposing his chest. Maglarion squinted at it for a moment.

Then he drove the dagger between Sebastian's ribs, directly into his heart. Sebastian shuddered once, his arms twitching. Then he slumped forward, his blood dripping upon the floor. Maglarion wrenched the dagger free and held up the bloodcrystal.

For a moment green light flared its in depths, and then it shivered. Before it had been the size of a grape. Now it was the size of a walnut. The green light faded from the bloodcrystal's depth, but the size remained.

Caina sobbed, the gag's foul taste filling her mouth.

"You can see," said Maglarion, "how the power released by his death has been trapped in the bloodcrystal, stored to use as I see fit. The application, I think, should be obvious. Simply killing a large number of people to empower a potent spell is often impracticable. However, killing them one by one, and storing the power as you go...that is far easier. Waste not, want not, after all."

Again the magi laughed.

"Speaking of which," said Maglarion, crossing to the table.

Again he slashed his hand across Caina's torn stomach, his fingers crackling with green flame. Again the horrible, nauseating pain filled her, her skin crawling beneath the force of his sorcery.

Her wound sealed itself shut, the pain vanishing into sick numbness. In its place the scar returned, wider and more livid than before.

"Take her," said Maglarion.

Ikhana nodded to the slavers, who hauled Caina from the table and carried her back to her cell. They dumped her on the floor and locked the door behind them, the rusted hinges screaming.

Screaming, as Caina wanted to scream.

Instead, she lay curled on her side on the cold stone floor, weeping.

The torture continued for weeks.

Every three or four days, without fail, the door opened with a rusty shriek, and Ikhana and the slavers dragged Caina to that horrible metal table and Maglarion's dagger. She fought and screamed, bit and punched, but it never did any good. The constant blood loss left her weak and dizzy, and she could barely stand up.

She could not stop them from dragging her to that table again and again. She could not stop Maglarion from cutting into her, siphoning off more and more off her blood to demonstrate some new aspect of necromancy to his watching students.

She hated him. She hated them. But she could do nothing to stop the pain.

Caina prayed, begging the gods for help. She prayed to Minaerys, the god of scholars, Markoin, the god of the soldiers, Joravius, god of the Empire, the Living Flame, the god to whom Azaia had prayed, and a dozen others.

None of them answered.

Her sensitivity to sorcery grew. At first she only felt the crawling, nauseating sensation whenever Maglarion cast a spell. Then when the magi practiced their lessons. Even when she lay in her cell, she felt the presence of their spells, the arcane power washing over her like tiny needles.

And Maglarion kept cutting into her stomach. Caina thought she would grow used to the constant agony, but every time was worse than the one that had come before. He cut through skin and muscle alike, the blade slicing deeper every time. Sooner or later he would cut too deep and kill her.

She hoped he would.

When the lessons ended, Caina lay shivering on the floor of her cell, alternating between sobbing and blank numbness, unable to think, unable to function. Hunger cramps kept her from sleeping. And even when she did sleep, the nightmares tormented her. She saw her father dying, saw him slumped in his chair, eyes glassy and unfocused. Or she lay again upon Maglarion's metal table, unable to tell the dream from the reality.

She would have given anything to see her father again, to hear his voice.

She would have given anything to see the sun again.

But she would not.

Caina realized that she was going to die here. Maglarion would never let her go, and would kill her once her usefulness to his spells had ended. Death was the only way out.

And she wanted to die.

But she didn't want to kill herself. Some part of her, the part that burned with hatred for Maglarion and the magi, refused to contemplate the idea. She wanted to go down fighting. She wanted to make them kill her.

But how?

Then one day the slavers tried to open the door, and it stuck. The hinges had jammed with rust. Caina heard them curse, heard them kick at the door. Finally it shuddered open, flakes of rust falling to the grimy floor.

One of the slavers stepped into the cell. He did not look at all well, his eyes sunken and his face flushed, and Caina wondered if the man was drunk. The slaver dropped her plate of food on the floor, turned, and slammed the heavy door behind him.

The hinges screamed.

And then the top hinge cracked. A shower of rust fell to the floor, followed by one of the heavy pins.

It rolled to a stop against Caina's knee.

She picked it up. The thing was as thick as her thumb, its end sharp and jagged.

She could plunge it into her throat. She had seen Maglarion cut enough throats, after all. It would hurt, true, but she had already endured so much agony. What was a little more? A little more pain, and all her torments would end. It could all end.

She remembered her father, bleeding in the slavers' grasp.

Caina growled, staggered to her feet, limped to the door.

If she was going to die, then let them kill her! She would not give them her life.

The door had three hinges. The top one had shattered when the slaver had left, and the door had begun tilting inward. The middle and bottom hinges remained intact, but rust caked them both.

Caina knelt before the middle hinge and started digging. Her hands shook and trembled, but the rust had chewed through the hinges, and she kept at it.

It was not as if she had anything better to do.

Hours passed. She kept digging and digging, the jagged pin scraping against the hinge. Chunks of rust fell across her knuckles and rolled down her sleeves. The pin made a scraping sound as she dug it into the hinge. Vaguely she wondered why the guards hadn't heard the noise yet.

More hours passed. Her arms ached and trembled with fatigue, her head spinning. She couldn't keep doing this. She was going to pass out, and...

Something cracked. The middle hinge splintered, the pin falling loose.

The massive door fell towards her, the bottom hinge ripping free from the stone.

Caina scrambled backwards, sudden fear lending her strength. She crouched back against the far wall as the heavy door slammed against the floor a few inches from her toes. The echoes lingered for a long, long time.

She braced herself, expecting to see the slavers leap through the door, weapons in hand. Then she would throw herself at them, forcing them to kill her.

No one came.

Caina waited, her heart hammering in her ears.

Still no one came.

She hesitated, stepped onto the door, the wood rough against the soles of her feet. A deep breath, and she crossed into the corridor.

It was empty, with no sign of the slavers. Or Maglarion, or Ikhana, or anyone else.

What was going on? Had Maglarion decided to kill everyone?

But she didn't feel the crawling tingle of sorcery.

Caina looked back at her cell. She could either go back, or she could keep moving.

She kept moving.

CHAPTER 5
THE GHOSTS

Caina found the first dead slaver a few moments later.

It was the man who had brought her the plate of food. He lay on his back, eyes bulging, hands clutching his throat. His lips had turned black, bloody foam encircling his mouth. A strange smell, like rotting flowers, hung over him.

Poison, Caina realized. He had been poisoned.

Two more dead slavers lay against the door to the vaulted room. Like the first man, both had bulging eyes and black lips, blood drying around their mouths. The door was locked, the hinges free of rust, but one of the dead slavers had a ring of keys on his belt. Caina took the keys and tried them in the door until she found one that fit. The lock released with a clang, and she leaned her shoulder against the door, straining with all her strength, until it swung open.

Her head spun, and she fell upon the floor. Distantly she wondered if she had been poisoned, as well. Or, more likely, she had overtaxed her weakened body.

Caina passed out.

She awoke some time later, chilled from the stone floor. With a grunt she heaved herself to her knees, and then her feet.

The vaulted chamber was silent, the glow from the glass spheres spilling over the thick pillars. The metal table sat in its usual place, stained with Caina's blood. Terror filled her at the sight, the scars on her stomach clenching, and she forced herself to look away.

She shrieked.

The magi sat at a long wooden table, staring at her.

They did not move.

Bit by bit, Caina calmed down, saw their bulging eyes and blackened lips. And some of the magi lay slumped over the table, or had fallen to the flagstones of the floor.

They, too, had been poisoned.

She stared at the dead men and women for a long time, wondering if it was a trick, some scheme of Maglarion's.

But if Maglarion and the magi were dead, if someone had indeed poisoned them...then perhaps Caina could simply walk out of this place.

Assuming she could even find her way out.

She took a step forward, and heard voices. Men's voices, raised in argument. Torchlight flared in the distance, drowning out the pale glow of the glass spheres. Caina froze for a moment, then hurried to one of the pillars. Her head spun with the effort, but she ducked behind the thick pillar, breathing hard.

Two men, she heard, and one woman. All of them speaking Caerish. That made her feel a little better; Maglarion and the magi had spoken High Nighmarian, and the slavers had spoken Anshani, when they had bothered to speak at all.

"Nothing," said the first man, who spoke with a thick, rolling Caerish accent. "This place is as silent as a tomb."

"That's because it is a tomb," said the woman, her voice sharp. "That poison I brewed for you worked too well."

"The poison did as it was intended," said the second man. His voice was cold and hard, empty of emotion. "Would you rather have dealt with twelve magi, especially ones dabbling in necromancy?"

"Of course not," said the woman. "But we've killed all the captives, as well."

The man with the rolling accent sighed. "I doubt it."

"What do you mean?" said the woman.

"Because I poisoned the wine," he said. "That was quality wine, from the vineyards of Caer Marist, and the magi wouldn't have shared it with the captives. But I doubt that matters. The magi have been hiding here for seven weeks. Odds are they killed the captives long ago. No doubt they would have sent their pet slavers to snatch more victims from the countryside, had we not slain them."

"So there is no one to rescue?" said the woman.

"I doubt it," said the man with the rolling accent.

"But these magi, at least, will not shed another drop of blood," said the second man, some satisfaction coloring his cold voice.

"Little comfort that will be to their victims," said the woman.

"Perhaps their spirits will rest easier, now that they are avenged," said the man with the rolling accent. "Best we make a thorough search, though, in case some wretch lies chained in a cell."

"Very well," said the cold-voiced man.

Caina risked a look around the pillar.

She saw the man with the rolling accent first. He was in his middle forties, with stringy iron-gray hair, a bushy gray beard, and arms thick with corded muscle. He dressed like a caravan guard, or perhaps a brigand, with battered leather armor and a short sword and dagger at his belt. Besides him walked a woman of about the same age, with blondish-gray hair and a lean, lined face. Like the man, she wore worn leather armor, though she bore no weapons.

The cold-voiced man stood behind them both.

He frightened Caina, in a way the other two did not. He was much younger, no more than twenty-five, with close-cropped blond hair and deep-set eyes. He wore a black leather jerkin, steel mail glimmering beneath it. Sheathed daggers rested at his belt, and he carried a long spear like it was an extension of his arm. He had the same sort of cold eyes she had seen in the Istarish slavers.

"Cells, over there," said the cold-voiced man, gesturing with the spear.

"Aye," said the man with the rolling accent, "if we're to find any survivors, they'll..."

Caina leaned back, intending to slink behind the pillar.

Instead her head spun once more, and she fell to the floor.

Both men whirled at once, the cold-voiced man lifting his spear, while the older man drew his sword. Caina scrambled against the pillar, breathing hard, holding the rusted pin out before her.

Compared to a spear and a sword, it made for a pathetic weapon.

"Wisdom of Minaerys," breathed the woman. "A child."

"Stay away," said Caina in Caerish, the pin trembling before her. "Stay away from me."

"We mean you no harm, child," said the older man, putting his sword away.

"No," said Caina. "You could be working for him. Stay away."

The woman's eyes fell upon Caina's tattered clothes, the scars across her stomach. "Great Minaerys," she breathed, "what did they...Halfdan, I think the magi used her blood."

The older man, the one the woman had called Halfdan, nodded. "You look half-starved. Come with us, and we'll get you some food, perhaps find your mother and father."

The younger man shook his head. "Not likely."

The woman glared at him.

"No," said Caina. "You could be one of them. The magi. One of his disciples."

Halfdan smiled. "If I was one of the magi, why would I have killed them all?"

"You killed them?" whispered Caina. "You...poisoned them, didn't you?"

Halfdan nodded. "Aye. We're not far from the town of Aretia, and the slavers visited every week to buy supplies. We noticed it. I asked Komnene here," he gestured at the woman, "to brew up something special for them. And I added it to their wine."

The cold-voiced man jerked his head at the magi, his eyes never leaving Caina. "Looks like they drank it."

"Why?" said Caina.

Halfdan glanced at Komnene and the cold-voiced man, and something seemed to pass between them.

"Because," said Halfdan, "we are Ghosts."

"Ghosts?" said Caina. "The...the spirits of his victims?"

The cold-voiced man laughed.

"Not quite," said Halfdan. "We are the spies of the Emperor, his eyes and his ears. We hunt those who break his laws, those who enslave his people, those who use sorcerous power to terrorize and destroy."

"A fine speech," muttered the cold-voiced man.

"Why did you come?" said Caina.

"We were summoned," said Halfdan, reaching into a pouch at his belt. A coin gleamed in his hand, worn and ancient. A coin inscribed with the portrait of the long-dead Emperor Cormarus.

The coin she had seen Sebastian take out of his desk.

Caina stared, transfixed.

"Count Sebastian Amalas summoned us," said Halfdan. "He wrote that his wife had been associating with outlaw sorcerers, with necromancers. We came to investigate, though too late, I fear."

"My father," whispered Caina.

Halfdan blinked. "Gods. Sebastian Amalas...you're his daughter?"

Caina started to cry, something like a scream coming from her throat. She could not keep herself together any longer. Komnene rushed over, knelt besides her, and Caina did not resist, did not try to run. Again the dizziness washed over her, and she would have fallen again to the floor, if not for Komnene's grasp.

When Caina came to her senses, she heard Halfdan and Komnene arguing. The man with the cold voice stood to the side, looking bored.

"She's in no state to do anything," said Komnene. "Look at her scars. Look at what they did to her."

"Aye," said Halfdan, "and if we don't find out what happened to her, it might happen to others. She's the only one who can tell us what happened."

"What happened?" said Caina, her voice scratchy. She closed her eyes. "My mother. She did this. She did all of this." Something halfway between a sob and a laugh escaped from her lips. "I made her pay, though. I did."

"What's your name?" said Halfdan.

"Caina."

"What happened?" said Halfdan. "Tell me."

Caina closed her eyes. It was hard to think, and the memories had blurred into one long morass of agony. "I...my mother. She sent letters, to outlaw sorcerers, to necromancers. She was in the Magisterium, but they expelled her. She wasn't strong enough. My father had a scroll, something that...that he wanted. My mother promised him the scroll, and me, if he would take her as a student."

"So he did?" said Halfdan.

Caina nodded. "My father found out. Said he would contact the Ghosts."

Halfdan lifted the coin. "He did."

"My mother wanted to stop him," said Caina. "She tried to...to erase his memory, I think, so he would forget. Except she didn't know what she was doing, and she broke his mind. She did the same to all the servants. All of them."

"What happened to your mother?" said Halfdan.

"I killed her," said Caina.

Komnene looked disturbed. Something like approval flashed over the cold-voiced man's face.

"I didn't mean to," whispered Caina. "I was so angry. I hit her with a poker. She lost her balance and hit her head against the desk. And then...he came. And he took me here. He cut me, used my blood for his spells. I'm going to die here."

"No," said Komnene, her voice sharper than Caina had yet heard it. "You are not."

Halfdan frowned. "This man," he said, "this necromancer. Do you know his name?"

"Maglarion," said Caina.

She could not have gotten more of a reaction out of the Ghosts if she had slapped them.

Komnene's eyes went wide. Halfdan reached for his sword. The cold-voiced man raised his spear, his face taut with readiness.

"What?" said Caina.

"The necromancer called himself Maglarion?" said Halfdan.

Caina nodded.

"What did he look like?" said Halfdan.

"An old man," said Caina. "His left eye was missing. He had expensive clothes. He limped when he walked, and carried a cane."

"That's him," said the cold-voiced man. "We have to go, now."

"But...you poisoned them all," said Caina.

"It would take more than poison to kill Maglarion," said Halfdan.

"He must be gone," said the cold-voiced man, looking back and forth.

"I don't understand," said Caina.

"We're only still alive because Maglarion isn't here," said the cold-voiced man. "And if we're still here when he returns, we won't be alive for long. Or we'll wish we were dead before much longer."

Caina stared at the metal table, a scream rising in her throat. The thought that Maglarion might return, that he might shackle her to that table once more...

"Go!" said Halfdan. "Now!"

Caina staggered to her feet, almost lost her balance.

"Halfdan!" said Komnene. "She can't walk on her own."

"Riogan," said Halfdan to the cold-voiced man. "Take her!"

Riogan grunted, shifted his spear to one hand, and reached for her. Caina tried to flinch away, but Riogan's arm felt like a bundle of iron cords, and he scooped her up as if she weighed nothing at all.

"Quickly, now," said Halfdan.

They hurried through the vaulted room, past the table of dead magi. More of the slavers littered the floor beyond the table, their mouths black from the poison. Halfdan's poisoned wine had indeed killed them all.

All except for Maglarion.

Something glittered in the light of Halfdan's torch.

"Wait!" said Caina.

"What is it?" said Halfdan.

She pushed out of Riogan's grasp and fell to her knees besides one of the dead slavers. She pawed at the man's shirt, pulling it open.

Her father's heavy signet ring rested against the dead man's chest, hanging from a leather thong. No doubt the slaver had looted it from Sebastian's corpse. Caina tugged at the cord, but it would not give.

Riogan snorted. "We're stopping to loot corpses, now? This is folly, Halfdan. We should be gone."

"This was my father's!" said Caina, pulling. "I can't leave it, I..."

Steel flashed, and Halfdan's sword severed the thong. Caina fell back, the heavy ring clutched in her hands.

"Now," said Halfdan, "we must go. Riogan!"

Riogan picked Caina back up, and broke into a run, the others following. An archway on the far side of the vaulted chamber opened into a spiraling staircase, and Riogan headed up the steps. Despite sprinting up the stairs while carrying Caina, his breathing remained slow and steady.

Then sunlight stabbed at Caina's eyes, and she cried out. She had spent too long in the darkened gloom below the earth, and her eyes had grown used to the shadows.

When her vision cleared, she saw that they stood in the ruins of a long-abandoned villa. The roof had fallen in, and only the walls remained, rising out of a field of jagged stones and tall weeds.

"What is this place?" said Caina.

"It was once the seat of a noble house, extinguished during the War of the Fourth Empire," said Halfdan, beckoning them around a corner. "Forgotten by almost everyone living, save a few scholars and priests of Minaerys. Maglarion likes to use forgotten places for his lairs."

"The hills," said Caina. "We're in the hills above Aretia."

Halfdan nodded, heading towards a stand of trees. Three horses stood tethered there.

"Where are you talking me?" said Caina. "Are you..."

She started to ask if Halfdan would take her home. But that didn't matter any more, did it? Home was where her father was. And her father was dead.

"We'll talk later," said Halfdan, untying the horses. "First, we need to flee. We need to be well away from here by the time Maglarion returns."

Halfdan swung into the saddle, and Riogan passed Caina up to him. She clutched as the saddle's pommel, just barely keeping her balance, and Halfdan's hand settled upon her shoulder. Riogan and Komnene climbed into their own saddles, Riogan with considerably more grace.

"Where?" said Riogan.

"South of Aretia, I think," said Halfdan. "Somewhere along the Imperial Highway. Maglarion is probably in Aretia. We'll want to be well away by nightfall."

"Agreed," said Riogan.

They rode along a narrow, weedy track winding its way back and forth down the hill, shaded by stubby trees and piles of boulders. The constant jouncing rhythm of the horse's stride made Caina's legs hurt, but she didn't care. At least she was in the sunlight again. At least she was leaving that horrible vault behind.

The horses rounded a stand of trees, and Caina saw the blue expanse of the Bay of Empire, the town of Aretia standing at its edge. She also saw her father's villa, standing on its hill overlooking the town.

Or, rather, the burned ruins of her father's villa.

The roof was gone, the remaining walls blackened with soot. Caina stared at it in horror. It was all gone. Her bedroom, Azaia's kitchen, the garden with the fountains, the courtyard and the dining hall, all gone in ashes and smoke.

Her father's library. All his books. Gone.

"They burned our home," said Caina. "Why?"

"To cover their tracks," said Halfdan. "Maglarion doesn't like attention. So he burned your father's villa to throw us off the trial. It worked, too. We only found his hiding place when we saw those slavers buying supplies in Aretia."

Caina said nothing. But the tears trickled down her face, and her fists squeezed against the pommel, so hard that the leather started to crackle.

###

They stopped well after dark, maybe twelve miles south of Aretia. Komnene tended to the horses, Riogan walked about, sweeping everything with his cold green eyes, while Halfdan started cooking supper.

Caina watched them in silence.

"What are you going to do with me?" she said at last.

Halfdan looked at her. "I don't know. We can't take you anywhere near Aretia. Maglarion may not care that you're still alive. Or he might come after you." He shook his head. "And it's certainly not safe for us to remain near Aretia. Once Maglarion realizes we killed his students, he will try to kill us, if he can find us. And if he finds you with us, well...he'll either kill you or take you captive once more."

Caina shivered. "I can't go back to Aretia, then." Not that she had any reason to, with her father dead and his house burned.

"Do you have any other family?" said Halfdan. "Elsewhere in the Empire?"

Caina shrugged. "I don't know. My father's parents died when he was a boy. My mother's parents, perhaps. Not that I want anything to do with them."

Halfdan nodded. "Once we reach safety, we'll decide what to do with you. Until then, you'll stay with us. You should eat something."

Caina shook her head. "I'm not hungry."

"You should eat anyway, child," said Komnene. "And let me find you some better clothes, and treat some of those cuts."

Caina did not care, but she let Komnene give her clean clothes, and bandage the cuts and scrapes she had acquired. Komnene sucked in her breath at the sight of the scars across Caina's hips and belly, but said nothing.

Afterwards, Caina wrapped herself in a blanket and fell asleep by the fire.

###

Halfdan volunteered to take the first watch, ordered Komnene and Riogan to get some sleep. Komnene made some effort to protest, but Riogan rolled himself in his cloak and fell asleep at once. He knew how to take his rest when he could.

Not surprising, given his background.

Halfdan sat by the fire, thinking. Nearby Caina thrashed and muttered in her sleep. Of course the girl had nightmares. Probably she would have nightmares every night for the rest of her life.

No surprise there.

What did surprise him was how the girl had responded to her pain. Halfdan had been with the Ghosts a long time, and he had seen people endure every kind of pain and loss and tragedy. Very often they went numb, stunned into catatonia.

Caina had not. He doubted that she cared if she lived or died. But she had rage. He had seen it in her face, as she gazed at the ruins of Count Sebastian's home.

And they had found her wandering through the chamber of dead men.

Which mean that, somehow, she had gotten herself out of her cell.

Halfdan thought about that for a long time.

CHAPTER 6
A KEEN EYE

The next day, the Ghosts disguised themselves.

A wagon had been hidden near their campsite, concealed beneath loose branches and piled leaves, the bed empty save for a few empty wine barrels. Halfdan cleared it off, dressed himself in an old cloak and a worn cap, and hitched the horses to the wagon. Komnene dressed herself in a plain gray dress. Riogan kept his armor and weapons, though he concealed them beneath an old cloak.

They looked, Caina thought, like a common-born farmer and his wife, accompanied by a caravan guard chance-met on the road. Which Caina supposed was the point.

No doubt people would think that she was Halfdan's daughter. That made her think of Sebastian, and she wept a little.

Still, she did not mind the wagon. Sitting in the wagon's bed was an improvement over the horse's jouncing back.

Halfdan drove the wagon south along the paved stones of the Imperial Highway, while Riogan walked besides it, hand beneath his cloak, eyes cold and suspicious. Komnene rode in the bed with Caina, attempting to talk to her from time to time.

Caina didn't care. She sat slumped, swaying with the wagon's motion, lost in her own grief.

The nightmares came again when she slept, worse than before.

###

The next morning, though, she was curious.

"Where are we going?" said Caina.

Not that she cared. But perhaps asking questions would keep her mind from dwelling on the nightmares.

On what she had endured.

Komnene looked at her in surprise, and then at Halfdan.

"Mors Anaxis," said Halfdan. "It's a town..."

"About forty miles south of Aretia, along the Imperial Highway," said Caina.

Komnene smiled. "How did you know that?"

"I read it in one of my father's books," said Caina.

"Do you know why it's called Mors Anaxis?" said Komnene.

"The Emperor Anaxis," said Caina, remembering. "His tomb is there, along with his funerary cult. He was buried there in ancient times, during the Second Empire."

"Very good," said Halfdan.

"I didn't even know that," said Komnene.

Riogan snorted. "Not that it matters. The bones of one dead Emperor are much the same as another."

"Why are we going there?" said Caina. She looked at Riogan. "Do you want to pray to the Emperor's bones?"

Riogan scoffed and looked away.

"Mors Anaxis is a port," said Halfdan. "We'll hire a ship, and sail to the eastern side of the Bay of Empire. Maglarion would expect us to flee north, towards Malarae. Hopefully this will throw him off our trail."

Caina nodded.

"How are you feeling?" said Komnene.

Riogan snorted. "A foolish question."

Komnene gave him a withering glance. "I meant physically. She took some terrible wounds."

Caina shrugged. "They hurt. But not as bad as they did." She closed her eyes. "Maglarion always healed them when he finished."

"Hardly from charity," said Riogan. "He only wanted to keep you alive so he could drain more blood from you."

"I know that," said Caina.

"It's well that he did," said Komnene. "You would have died from infection, had he not."

"Maybe that would have been better," said Caina.

They rode in silence for a moment.

"After Mors Anaxis," said Caina. "Where then?"

"Then, I think," said Halfdan, looking back at her, "we will take you to Malarae. The Ghosts have many friends in the Imperial capital. One of them will take you in."

Caina didn't care. But Halfdan had been kind to her, and her father had always said to thank those who did you kindnesses. "Thank you."

Halfdan nodded.

"And thank you," said Caina, "for taking me out of that...that place."

"I would leave no one in Maglarion's clutches," said Halfdan.

"You should eat something," said Komnene.

"I'm not hungry," said Caina.

"You should eat something anyway," said Komnene. "You were starved for all those weeks. You need to keep your strength."

Caina looked at her, looked at her for so long that Komnene started to frown.

"What is it, Caina?" said Komnene.

"You used to be a priestess of Minaerys," said Caina, "didn't you?"

Halfdan snorted in surprise and half-turned in his seat. Riogan looked at Caina with cold eyes, reappraising her.

"How did you know that?" said Komnene.

"Did you read her mind?" said Riogan. "Perhaps you learned a spell or two from Maglarion?"

"What?" said Caina. "No. I don't have any arcane talent. My mother said so. Maglarion said so."

Halfdan watched her for a moment. "Then how did you know Komnene used to be a priestess of Minaerys?"

Caina shrugged. "I just did."

"How?"

Caina thought it over. "She was the one who looked at my cuts. And I saw all the drugs and potions she has in her bags. You said she brewed up the poison that killed the magi. So that means she's a physician. And the only women who become physicians are priestesses of Minaerys."

"So?" said Riogan. "Practically every village from here to Marsis has a shriveled old crone who knows a thing or two about herbs."

"She also swore by Minaerys," said Caina. "In the vault. 'Wisdom of Minaerys', that's what she said. Only the priests and priestesses of Minaerys talk like that."

"Maybe she's still a priestess of Minaerys," said Halfdan.

"No," said Caina. "She's not. Physicians in the service of Minaerys are not allowed to brew any drug to cause harm. So if she made that poison, she's not a priestess of Minaerys any more."

Komnene looked away, as if in sudden pain, and Caina felt a brief twinge of guilt.

"You are," said Riogan, "a clever little thing, aren't you?"

"Indeed," said Halfdan. "What kind you see about me?"

Caina shrugged. "You're...harder. It's like...it's like you went out of

47

your way to disguise yourself, to hide things about yourself. Riogan, too, except he's better at it."

Riogan guffawed.

"Well, you're right," said Halfdan. "We did go out of our way to disguise ourselves."

"I think...I think you used to be a farmer," said Caina, frowning. Thinking about the puzzle kept her from thinking about the grief. "Or...a vintner? Yes, a vintner. Your arms...you look like you're used to lifting things."

"True," said Halfdan. "But why a vintner?"

"Wine barrels," said Caina, kicking one of the empty barrels. "I watched you move them around when we started. You looked like you had done it before."

"So I have," said Halfdan. "And I was indeed a vintner, long ago. What do you see about Riogan?"

Caina shrugged. "Not very much. I think he's spent a lot of time practicing with weapons."

"Why?" said Halfdan.

"Because he's been carrying that spear for days," said Caina, "and I've never once seen him trip over it. And he doesn't make any noise when he walks."

Riogan's face went blank as he looked at her.

"You're very observant," said Halfdan. "Who taught you to do that?"

"I don't know," said Caina. "I used to watch my mother. She'd get angry for anything, start hitting me, or start hitting the servants. Or casting spells on us. So I'd have to watch her, in case she got angry."

"You're very clever," said Halfdan.

"My mother always said I was stupid," said Caina.

Halfdan gave sharp shake of his head. "Then your mother was a fool, not to see a treasure when it was before her eyes."

Caina blinked, wondering what he meant by that.

They arrived at Mors Anaxis later that afternoon.

The town held perhaps five thousand people, and did not look very different from Aretia. The same houses with white-plastered walls and red-tiled roofs, the same wooden warehouses, the same stone wharves cluttered with fishing boats and the occasional merchantman. The half-ruined tomb and mortuary temple of the long-dead Emperor Anaxis stood on a hill over the town, looking desolate. Evidently very few pilgrims came to pray to Anaxis's bones.

"To the docks, I assume?" said Riogan as Halfdan steered the wagon through the town's narrow streets.

"Almost," said Halfdan, bringing the cart to a halt. He swung down from the driver's seat and passed the reins to Riogan. "You and Komnene go to the docks, find us a ship. One heading to Craton, preferably, but Mors Nicoron or Kratekon will do. Hire a fishing boat, if necessary. I'd like to put on tomorrow's tide."

Riogan frowned, but took the reins. "Where are you going?"

"Caina and I will be visiting the market square," said Halfdan.

"Why?" said Caina and Riogan in unison.

"Indulge me," said Halfdan.

Caina shrugged, climbed out of the wagon, and followed Halfdan. In truth, she did not mind. Other than Aretia, she had been to only a few other towns, and never to Mors Anaxis. She rather enjoyed looking at the people going about their business, the men with tools and wagons, the women carrying jars of water or bundles of laundry.

It made her think of her father's promise to visit Malarae and the Imperial Library.

Tears came to her eyes, but she blinked them back and followed Halfdan.

They came to town's market square, a broad space ringed with merchant shops and stalls, a fountain bubbling in the center. A magistrates' hall stood on one end of the square. No doubt ten decimvirs judged in Mors Anaxis, as in Aretia. On the other end of the square stood a high building of timbered stone, and Caina supposed it was an inn or a drinking house.

"What do you think?" said Halfdan.

"It seems busy," said Caina.

Halfdan snorted. "Not quite. The Great Market in Malarae, that is busy. Or the Plaza of the Tower in Marsis, or perhaps the Grand Bazaar in Istarinmul. This is a quiet little town in the heart of the Empire."

"If you say so," said Caina.

"Your father," said Halfdan, "he never took you to the capital? Or to any of the Empire's great cities?"

"No," said Caina, blinking back tears again. "We...were going to go to Malarae soon. But...other things happened."

"Yes," said Halfdan. "So you've had no...schooling? Your father never took you to the Temple of Minaerys, for instance, for a course of study?"

"No. Why does it matter?"

"I am just curious," said Halfdan, "how you became so observant."

"I read a lot of books in my father's library," said Caina.

"So I see," said Halfdan. He stood in silence for a moment, then gestured towards a man walking across the square. "That man. What can you tell me about him?"

Caina squinted at the man. He was tall and rangy, with skin like old leather, his hair pale. He walked with a rolling gait, and had a knife at his belt.

"He's a fisherman," said Caina.

"How do you know?"

"He's been in the sun a lot," said Caina. "You can tell, from his skin and hair." Halfdan nodded. "And he...walks funny. Like he spends a lot of time on a boat. The fishermen in Aretia always walked that way. And that's a scaling knife on his belt."

"Good," said Halfdan, gesturing again. "That man, the one leaving the inn. Tell me about him."

Caina watched the man descend the inn's stairs. He moved with a heavy stride, sweat dripping down his forehead, his gut straining against his belt and fine coat. He wore a short sword, but the weapon looked ornamental. Not like the simple, deadly blades that Riogan carried.

"He's a merchant," said Caina. "I think he sells...spices. Yes, that's it. Spices. Also, his money pouch is in the inside pocket of his coat."

Halfdan lifted his gray eyebrows. "Now, how did you know all that?"

"He's fat and sweaty," said Caina. "So, he doesn't labor for a living. His clothes are too nice. And there's black powder on the sleeves of his coat. Probably pepper, I think. And he keeps reaching into his coat and looking around, making sure his money pouch is still there."

"Very good," said Halfdan. "That fellow, there?"

"A courier. He's wearing spurs, has mud on his boots, and he's got the sigil of a noble House on his coat. House...Basilicus?"

"Yes," said Halfdan. "And that woman?"

"A shopkeeper's wife," said Caina. "She squints and has a stoop, so she must do his account books." She blinked again. "Like my mother always said reading would do to me."

"You have a gift for observation," said Halfdan. "And for deducing facts from those things you observe."

Caina shrugged. "What good is that?"

A smile flickered over Halfdan's face. "You'd be surprised, I think." He gestured again. "What about that woman, the one in the blue cloak?"

"She's the wife of a linen broker," said Caina, "and she has four children."

Halfdan frowned. "Now how did you work that out?"

"Because my father's seneschal would buy linen from her husband. He came up to Aretia sometimes," said Caina.

Halfdan burst out laughing.

Caina almost smiled. It had so long since she had smiled, or laughed, that the motion felt strange on her face.

"An eye for observation, and a knack for remembering detail," said

Halfdan. He smiled at her. "Truly, Caina, you are a remarkable child."

"I...thank you," said Caina, unsure of how to respond.

"I wonder," said Halfdan, "do you..."

Caina froze.

A man stepped down from the magistrates' hall, a man in a black robe with a red sash about the waist.

A magus, a brother of the Magisterium. Caina remembered the men and women in black robes staring at her, watching as Maglarion had cut deeper and deeper into her flesh...

"Get on the ground," said Halfdan. His voice was hard, but his face remained calm. "Act like you tripped. Do it now."

His voice cut through Caina's fear, and she let herself fall to the flagstones. Halfdan knelt besides her, took her arm. The magus glanced once in their direction and kept walking.

"Do you recognize him?" said Halfdan. "Was he with Maglarion?"

"I...I don't know," said Caina. "It was dark. I couldn't see their faces. He looks like them. But...I don't know." Hatred boiled up inside her, like a pot threatening to overflow. "But they're all villains, they're all murderers, every last one of the magi..."

"Keep your voice down," said Halfdan, helping Caina to her feet, hand around her elbow. "This way."

He led her away from the market square and through a maze of narrow streets. The air smelled of salt and dead fish, and seagulls cawed and circled overhead. Finally they came to the waterfront itself. A row of taverns faced the quays, and crews of porters worked at unloading ships. Caina spotted Komnene and Riogan driving the wagon along the street.

"That was quick," said Riogan.

"Change of plans," said Halfdan. "I saw a magus coming out of the decimvirs' hall."

Riogan swore.

Komnene glanced at Caina. "Was the magus one of Maglarion's students?"

"I don't know," said Halfdan. "She couldn't recognize him. He might be here on perfectly innocent business. Or he could be hunting for us, or for the girl. I'd rather not stay to find out. But if he is looking for us, then he'll surely be smart enough to check the outgoing ships."

"So we're to travel around the Bay of Empire on foot?" said Riogan. "That's a long walk."

"It is," said Halfdan. "So we'll travel another day south. To Koros, I think."

Riogan scowled. "Koros is barely a village."

"Correct," said Halfdan. "We'll charter a fishing boat and sail across the Bay. Safer that way. I doubt Maglarion or any of his disciples would bother searching for us there."

"Then," said Riogan, "we had better get moving, hadn't we?"

###

They drove south for the rest of the day, and after five miles left the Imperial Highway for a weedy dirt road along the shoreline. Koros lay a few miles from the Imperial Highway, Halfdan said, which meant that the magi would be less likely to search there.

"Which also means," said Komnene, "that smugglers and pirates like to stop in Koros. We'll need to be careful."

Caina frowned. Smugglers...she remembered her father's Maatish scroll, the one that Maglarion had taken. The scroll, she realized, that had started this whole thing.

"Maybe we shouldn't," said Caina.

They all looked at her.

"Why not?" said Halfdan.

"That Maatish scroll," said Caina. "The one my father got from the smugglers. Maglarion came for us because of the scroll. If...those smugglers came from Koros..."

"Then it's all the likelier that Maglarion won't come back," said Halfdan. "He already got the scroll. Why bother with smugglers?"

Caina hoped that he was right.

They drove for the rest of the day and made camp on the beach, above the tide line. Komnene had purchased supplies in Mors Anaxis, and they had a good supper of stew and biscuits. Caina found that she was hungry, and ate more than she had in a long time.

"Good," said Komnene.

"What?" said Caina.

"Your appetite is coming back," said Komnene.

"Well, I'm hungry," said Caina.

Afterwards, she rolled in a blanket and fell asleep by the fire.

The nightmares assailed her again.

CHAPTER 7
AN INVITATION

"It's time we talked," said Halfdan.

Riogan and Komnene looked at him in surprise. Riogan sat on side of the fire, cleaning and sharpening his weapons. Komnene sat on the other, mixing up some sort of herbal tea. She claimed that it let one sleep without nightmares.

Caina lay between them, wrapped in her blanket. She muttered in her sleep, from time to time lifting one arm as if to ward off a blow.

"About what?" said Riogan, returning his attention to his blades. "We're talking now, aren't we?"

"We need to decide," said Halfdan, "what we will do about Caina."

"You're circlemaster," said Riogan. "So decide."

Komnene laughed. "No, he wants to hear what we think, first. And then he'll decide to do what he wanted to do anyway."

Riogan sighed, got to his feet in a single fluid motion. "Let's get this over with, then."

They walked a short distance from the fire, far enough that their conversation would not wake Caina. Though given the nightmares the girl had, Halfdan supposed, waking her might have been merciful.

"So," said Halfdan. "What do you think of her?"

"Just a child," said Riogan. "Her mother killed her father, but what of it? Orphans are as common as sand. Live long enough, and everyone is an orphan, in the end."

"She is an unusual child," said Komnene.

Riogan laughed. "You only say that because she realized the Temple threw you out."

"Komnene's right," said Halfdan. "The girl is...observant, unusually so.

53

When we were in Mors Anaxis, I bade her observe things about the townsmen and women. Without fail, her deductions were accurate."

"So that's where you went," said Riogan. "You were testing her."

"And she passed," said Halfdan, glancing at the sleeping girl. She still thrashed and muttered in her sleep. "Not many people are that observant, let alone a girl of eleven years."

"So she's clever," said Riogan. "What of that?"

"She's also got steel in her," said Komnene, voice quiet. "Consider what she has endured in the last two months. Her mother's betrayal. Her father murdered in front of her. The things Maglarion did to her. It should have broken her. She should be huddled in a corner, weeping and clutching her knees, but she isn't."

"Because we rescued her," said Riogan, "not because she's got steel in her."

"I'm surprised you didn't notice it," said Halfdan. "When we entered that vault. She was already walking around."

"So?" said Riogan.

"There were cells in the vault," said Halfdan. "She had already gotten out of the cells on her own."

Riogan opened his mouth for another cutting remark...and fell silent.

"An unusual child," repeated Komnene.

"So she's strong and clever," said Riogan. "Why does that matter? You said you wanted to decide what to do with her. So decide. The Ghosts have many friends among the Loyalist Houses. Some of them must need another daughter. Find a friendly noble House and have the Lord adopt her."

Komnene shook her head. "That is a poor choice. Her life will be miserable."

Riogan laughed. "Life is misery. Better she learns that sooner that later."

"You don't understand," said Komnene. "Maglarion...he cut too deeply into her. He probably left her barren."

"A virgin's womb," said Halfdan, shaking his head. "Useful for all kinds of necromantic spells."

"We won't know for sure until she has her first menstrual cycle," said Komnene. "Or until she doesn't, to be more accurate. But I am almost certain she will not be able to bear children. And the life of a noble spinster is hardly a pleasant one. She will never be able to wed, and will gradually become an outcast."

"What of that?" said Riogan. "Nobles are tedious company, anyway. The girl likes to read? Make her into a priestess of Minaerys. She can spend all day reading. And it's not as if you have to give her to a noble House. The Ghosts have friends among the merchant and craft collegia, don't they? Give her to a merchant, or to a craftsman. She could actually do something useful, unlike most nobles."

"A craft collegia would be a waste," said Komnene. "I am not...welcome among the priests of Minaerys, not after what I've done. But Caina, I think, would find a welcome home among them."

Riogan scoffed. "Assuming she even wants to go. I doubt any god answered her prayers, sitting in that cell."

"No," said Halfdan. "Turning her into a priestess of Minaerys would be as much of a waste as making her into a noble spinster or some merchant's daughter. No, I have something else in mind. We shall make her into one of us. We shall make her into a Ghost."

Neither Riogan nor Komnene seemed surprised.

"That's what you wanted to talk about?" said Riogan. "Asking her to join the Ghosts? Of course she'll join the Ghosts! We saved her life, and the Ghosts want eyes and ears everywhere. Whether maiden aunt or priestess, she'll join the local Ghost circle."

"Not quite," said Halfdan. "I want to make her into a nightfighter."

And as he expected, that met with a barrage of protest.

"A nightfighter?" said Riogan, his voice dripping with scorn. "This scarred waif of a girl, and you think she can be a nightfighter? You've finally gone mad, Halfdan."

"A nightfighter?" said Komnene. "You want to inflict that upon her? Recruit her into the Ghosts, by all means. The Emperor needs eyes and ears everywhere. But to turn her into a Ghost nightfighter, to make her into an assassin and a spy..."

"Yes," said Halfdan. "That is exactly what I intend, to turn her into an assassin and spy in the service of the Ghosts."

"Why?" said Komnene.

"The girl has strength," said Halfdan. "She got out of her cell on her own. How many other children could have managed that?"

Riogan laughed. "So what? Had we not already poisoned the magi, she would have just gone right back into her cell. Or they'd have killed her on sight."

"You'll agree she's not stupid?" said Halfdan.

Riogan nodded.

"Then she found her way out of her cell, and tried to escape...even though she knew the magi would probably kill her," said Halfdan.

Riogan fell silent.

"How many children could do that?" said Halfdan. "For that matter, how many grown men and women could summon that kind of courage?"

"So she has nerve, I'll grant," said Riogan.

"And think how much more she could do with knowledge, with training, with experience," said Halfdan. "You saw how she deduced that Komnene was once a priestess of Minaerys, that I was once a vintner."

Riogan flipped one of his daggers into the air, caught it. "She deduced nothing about me."

"She almost did," said Komnene. "She could see how long you have been training with weapons. How many people would notice that you never lose your balance? Had she little more knowledge, a little more experience, I'm certain she would have realized that you were once an assassin of the Kindred."

Riogan's eyes narrowed, but he said nothing.

"There's more," said Halfdan. "I think she's developed the ability to sense sorcery."

Komnene frowned. "How?"

"It's been known to happen," said Halfdan, "in people who survive sorcerous attacks. They develop a...sensitivity, for lack of a better word, to sorcery. It usually manifests as a tingling sensation, perhaps with some nausea attached. You know the difficulty the Ghosts face in combating sorcery, especially the mind-control spells the magi enjoy so much. Someone with the ability to sense sorcery would be invaluable to us."

Riogan snorted. "The best way to deal with magi is a spear down the gullet." He grinned at Komnene. "Or poison, eh?"

Komnene looked away.

"There you have it," said Halfdan. "The girl is brave and strong, and clever. Plus, she can sense the presence of sorcery. With proper training, I think...she could be a capable nightfighter, an infiltrator and spy without equal. The Emperor has many enemies, and the Ghosts need all the talent we can find. Caina could be of great help to us."

"So you want to take this girl, this child who has lost her parents," said Komnene, "and turn her into a weapon."

Halfdan nodded.

"And you are comfortable with this?" said Komnene. "This will not trouble your conscience in the least?"

"It will not," said Halfdan. "For consider the alternatives. What will become of Caina? She has no family. Shall we make her into a noble spinster, have her spend her life attending meaningless balls? Or shall she be a merchant's daughter, and keep his books and count his inventory? Or will she be a priestess of Minaerys, spend her days in a dusty library reading forgotten books? Or can she become something more?"

Riogan laughed. "Why are you surprised, Komnene? This is what Halfdan does. He wanders the Empire, doing the Emperor's dirty work...and he finds wounded souls and turns them into weapons for his Emperor. That's what he did to you, after all."

"And to you?" said Komnene.

Riogan laughed again, his cold eyes flashing. "I was already a weapon."

"So I have your support, then?" said Halfdan.

"You'll do what you want, anyway," said Riogan.

"But I have your support?" said Halfdan.

Riogan nodded and walked back to the fire.

"And you?" said Halfdan.

"Very well," said Komnene. "But...you will give her a choice, won't you? You'll ask her?"

"Of course," said Halfdan.

Komnene gave a sad smile. "Though your choices, Halfdan...they tend not be any choice at all."

She walked back to the fire.

Caina awoke the next morning with a headache and a foul taste in her mouth. She could remember nothing of her nightmares. Or, at least, nothing specific, only a jumbled blur of blood and screams and dark images.

She wondered if she would ever stop having nightmares.

She wondered if they would last for the rest of her life.

For that matter, what would she do for the rest of her life?

Caina ate breakfast in silence, washing it down with Komnene's tea. She claimed it would help Caina sleep better. Caina doubted it, but at least the bitter tea cleaned the foul taste out of her mouth.

"We should reach Koros later today," said Halfdan around a mouthful of biscuit. "We'll hire a fishing boat, and depart with the tide."

Caina nodded. "And...then what?"

Halfdan lifted his eyebrows. "You mean, what we are going to do with you?"

Komnene looked at her, while Riogan smirked and checked his daggers.

"Well," said Halfdan, "what do you think we should do with you?"

"I...I don't know," said Caina. "My father's dead. He doesn't have any other family. My mother's dead, but I hated her, and if she has any family, I don't want anything to do with them." She closed her eyes, felt the tears well up, blinked them away. "I don't have anywhere to go."

"I'm sorry," said Komnene.

"So what are you going to do with me?" said Caina.

"You have a few choices," said Halfdan. "The Ghosts have many friends among the nobility. One the Houses could adopt you as a daughter, take you in."

"But I won't be able to have children, will I?" said Caina.

Komnene flinched. "How did you know?"

"Maglarion," whispered Caina. "He...told the magi that, as he was...he

57

was cutting into me. I always wanted children when I grew up. I told my mother...I told her I would be better than her someday." She stared at the dying fire. "I suppose that will never happen now, will it?"

"No," said Komnene.

"We could also put you with the family of a merchant friendly to the Ghosts," said Halfdan.

"But I still wouldn't be able to have children, would I?" said Caina. "I could never marry." She sighed and rubbed her stomach, feeling the hard ridges of the scars beneath the cloth.

"We won't know for sure until you're old enough to have your first menstrual cycle," said Komnene. "But you could join the Temple of Minaerys as an initiate. You enjoy books, do you not? The Temple sponsors scholars and physicians. You could become a priestess in time, a scholar, or perhaps a physician."

"That sounds nice," said Caina. And it did. She thought of the Imperial Library, and wondered what it would be like to see all those books.

"But?" said Komnene.

"It...seems like hiding," said Caina. "Like I'm hiding from what happened to me, what the magi did to me. If they did it to me, then they've probably done it to lots of other people, too. Haven't they?"

Halfdan nodded. "More than I care to recall."

"That was why I left the Temple," said Komnene, the words spilling out of her. "There was a magus in the city of Arzaxia, he would buy slave children and kill them to empower his spells. I couldn't let it continue. One day he came to use the Temple's library, and I...slipped poison into his tea. I murdered him, and I was put out of the Temple. But...I couldn't have let him continue. I couldn't."

"I don't think I could join the Temple of Minaerys," said Caina. "Not now. Now when I know that the magi are doing these things to people, and no one is trying to stop them." She sighed and shook her head. "I can't say it any better than that."

"I think you mean," said Halfdan, "that you want to fight against the magi, and the slavers, and all those who would do to others what they did to you. That you could not have peace, otherwise."

"Yes," said Caina. "Yes. That's exactly what I meant."

Komnene closed her eyes and sighed.

"There is," said Halfdan, "another way for you."

"What is it?" said Caina.

"You could join the Ghosts," said Halfdan.

Caina frowned. "You mean...spy for the Emperor?"

Halfdan nodded.

"But...wouldn't I do that anyway?" said Caina. "If I became a priestess or a merchant's daughter? If I saw something bad happening, I would send a coin of Emperor Cormarus to the Ghosts, the way my father did."

"Aye," said Halfdan, "the Emperor needs eyes and ears...but who do you think answers their calls for help?"

"You?" said Caina.

Halfdan laughed. "When I can, yes. The Emperor has special...agents, Caina. Those who spy when necessary, who kill when necessary. Those who kill men like the magus Komnene slew, or Maglarion...or women like your mother. The nightfighters."

"Are you a nightfighter?" said Caina.

"No," said Halfdan. "I am the head of a Ghost circle, a circlemaster."

"Which means he tells nightfighters what to do," said Riogan.

"Komnene is a nightkeeper," said Halfdan. "She assists the Ghosts whenever she can, using her skills and abilities to aid us. Riogan is the only nightfighter with us."

Caina looked at the cold-eyed man sharpening his blades. "So...what exactly is a nightfighter?"

"A spy," said Halfdan. "An infiltrator. The Emperor's unseen hand."

"And an assassin, if necessary," said Riogan, sheathing one of his daggers and drawing another.

"One who does what is necessary, for the good of the people of the Empire," said Halfdan, "that they may be free from the cruelty of lawless sorcery and the tyranny of corrupt nobles."

Riogan snorted. "Or we just kill people who need killing."

"That, too," said Halfdan.

"But it is a hard and lonely life," said Komnene. "And the training is long and difficult."

"Only if you are too weak for it," said Riogan.

But something within Caina had kindled at Halfdan's words.

"If I join the Ghosts," said Caina, "then I can fight against slavers? And magi? Against men like Maglarion?"

"Yes," said Halfdan. "But I warn you, Riogan and Komnene are right. The training will be hard, and it is not an easy path."

Caina hesitated. She knew, then and there, that this decision would shape the rest of her life. Did she want to spend her life wandering around the Empire, lurking in the shadows as Halfdan and Riogan and Komnene did?

Would she ever know peace?

But her father was dead, her home reduced to rubble and ashes.

Caina would never know peace, not ever.

"Yes," she said. "I will join the Ghosts."

"So be it," said Halfdan.

CHAPTER 8
THE BLOODCRYSTAL

Maglarion walked alone through the hills.

The night was pitch-black. No moon shone, and storm clouds blotted out the stars. The hills rose around him like walls of shadow, black and impenetrable.

The darkness did not hinder him in the least.

Not with the thing that had taken the place of his left eye.

But darkness put him in a contemplative mood, as it always did. How many dark nights had he seen, over the centuries? How many sunrises and sunsets, how many summers and winters? So many, and they all had passed into the bottomless depths of time.

But he was still here.

He smiled at that thought.

Three hundred and eighty years he had seen. He had been born during the Fourth Empire, when the magi ruled the Empire and the nobility knew their place. When the commoners toiled as slaves, as was proper. The Empire had stretched from sunrise to sunset, and the magi raised glittering towers in the sun, their mighty sorcery empowered by the spilled blood of slaves.

But all that was gone now. The great magi had been overthrown, necromancy banned and the slaves freed at the Emperor's command. The sorcerous wonders of the Fourth Empire had passed away, and Maglarion's teachers had long ago perished, their bones moldering to dust.

But he was still here.

His smiled widened at that.

He considered the magi waiting for him in the ruined vault, so eager to learn the few scraps of knowledge he was willing to impart. The current age considered them full brothers and sister of the Magisterium. In the glory days of the Fourth Empire, they would have been little more than novices, fit only for carrying out the menial chores of the great magi. They were insignificant children...but how they yearned to restore the glory of the Fourth Empire, to wield the power possessed by the magi of old.

Maglarion did not care about that.

He paused for a moment atop a hill, looking at the town of Aretia. His eye of flesh saw the harbor lanterns, the light scattering on the bay's rippling waves.

His other eye, the one hidden beneath the black patch, saw...other things. The pulsing life energies of the townsmen. The power flowing through their blood. Waiting to be harvested by one with the skill to wield it. So many nobles saw the commoners as nothing more than beasts of burden, fit only to be slaves. Those lords would follow anyone who promised to overthrow the Emperor and restore the commoners to slavery.

Maglarion did not care about that, either.

He saw the commoners as raw material in a rather more...literal fashion.

His left eye, the one not made of flesh, twitched, its rough edges scraping against the inside of the socket. He saw death in the air. Death, as he had taught the petty little magi, released its own power, just as flame released heat and light. A lot of people had died nearby, and recently.

He did not care about that, either.

Or, at least, not quite yet.

For he had transcended death, transcended mortality itself. His parents, his family, his teachers, his allies, and so many different enemies...all had passed into death. Yet still he lived. He breathed, walked alive under the sun. He had conquered death, by his own skill and power.

He had become immortal.

His smile thinned.

Almost immortal.

For he could still be killed. His spirit was anchored to his body of flesh and bone. His mastery of necromancy conquered aging, kept disease at bay...yet he still could be slain. A foe of sufficient power, of sufficient skill, could kill him.

Or a lesser foe could simply get lucky. There was such a thing as mischance.

And Maglarion had enemies. Rival sorcerers, for one. And the Ghosts, the Emperor's pet spies and assassins. They had hunted him for centuries, and he had littered his path with their dead. But sooner or later, some enemy would get lucky, and Maglarion would die.

Unless, of course, he found the path of true immortality. A way to transcend the flesh itself, forever.

And here, in Aretia, he had found the way at last.

Maglarion stopped, took a moment to savor the energy of death crackling around him. He didn't need it, not yet. But he would, very soon.

How ironic that the secret to everlasting life lay in such a vast quantity of death.

Chuckling to himself, he continued up the path to the ruined villa. No doubt the aspiring necromancers desired a new lesson. Well, he would give it to them. Laeria Amalas's little daughter still had some blood in her. Maglarion could wring some more use out of her, until he fed her death into his growing bloodcrystal.

Ikhana waited for him in the ruined villa, a darker shadow among the crumbled walls.

"Ikhana, my dear," said Maglarion, leaning upon his cane. "So good to see you this night."

Her expression, as usual, did not change, but her fingers strayed to the black dagger at her belt.

He had first met her...two hundred years ago, was it? She had once been an ambitious young assassin of the Kindred. She thought to seduce him, to lure him to her bed and cut his throat as he slumbered.

Instead, he had enslaved her.

The black dagger had been one of Maglarion's early creations. It allowed Ikhana to steal the life force of her victims, to heal her wounds, to make her younger and stronger. But as it happened, stolen life force was more addictive than any liquor, any drug...and the dagger only functioned at Maglarion's command.

Ikhana had not tried to rebel against him for almost a century now.

He wondered if it even occurred to her to try any more.

"The guards," said Ikhana. "They are missing from their posts."

"Perhaps they went to town, to tumble a few fishermen's wives," said Maglarion.

"No," said Ikhana, voice flat. "I commanded them to stand guard. They would not disobey me."

That was true. Ikhana had that effect on people. Maglarion found her most useful for inspiring loyalty in his various hirelings. He closed his right eye, his eye of flesh, and looked through his left eye. Again he saw the energy of death simmering around him, fresh and potent.

A great many people had died here. Recently.

"There," said Maglarion, opening his right eye once more. "And there. You'll find them both behind that wall."

Ikhana stalked to the ruined wall, black dagger in hand. Maglarion followed, his cane scraping against the rocky ground. He saw two Istarish slavers lying sprawled against the earth, their bodies concealed by the wall.

Their throats had been cut.

Expertly.

Maglarion had cut a lot of throats in his time, and he knew skill when he saw it.

He supposed his lair must have been attacked during his absence.

Had he been here, things would have gone rather...differently.

"We have been betrayed," hissed Ikhana. Her face remained expressionless, but rage burned in her voice, and the black dagger glittered like a serpent's fang in her grasp. "The slavers have sold us to the Ghosts. Or one of your useless students panicked, and went to the Ghosts in exchange for clemency."

Maglarion shrugged. "No matter. The Ghosts would have found us here sooner or later anyway. After all, my dear, how many times have we moved over the centuries? One more is no great inconvenience."

He started towards the stairs.

"The enemy may still lie in wait for you," said Ikhana.

Maglarion laughed. "Then pity them."

Something halfway between a grin and a feral snarl flickered over Ikhana's features, and she followed him.

The dark energies of recent death grew stronger as he reached the bottom of the stairs. The enspelled glass spheres still glowed on their iron pedestals, bathing the vaulted chamber in pale blue light. Motionless forms littered the floor.

The Istarish slavers Maglarion had hired.

Dead to the last man.

"Pity," murmured Maglarion.

Finding new hirelings was always such a bother.

The Ghosts, undoubtedly. Maglarion wondered how they had accomplished it. He prodded one of the corpses with the tip of his cane. The dead man's head turned, his features already starting to swell with decay.

Black foam stained his lips and mouth.

"Poison," said Maglarion. "Clever, indeed. The Ghosts must have seen the slavers buying supplies in town. Rather than risk a direct confrontation, they poisoned the wine. Very clever."

Ikhana hissed. "Drunkards always come to a bad end."

Maglarion lifted an eyebrow. For a woman addicted to stolen life energies, Ikhana took a dim view of any other vices.

It still amused him, even after all these years.

"Come," said Maglarion, "let us see if any of my students survived."

He found the magi near the table, slumped in their chairs or prone upon the ground. Like the slavers, they all had black foam on their mouths. Maglarion cast his eye over the table, saw a pewter goblet still half-filled with wine.

He took it, lifted it to his mouth, drank.

"Ah," he murmured, tossing the goblet aside. It clattered against the floor and rolled into the darkness. "Yes. Blackroot extract, distilled and refined. A most potent poison. Two drops into a cask of wine would be enough to kill anyone who drank from it."

Poison had long since ceased to trouble Maglarion. Much to the dismay of the Ghosts, no doubt.

"Then it was the Ghosts," said Ikhana. "They are the only ones in the Empire who use blackroot extract."

"Along with a few other assassin bands," said Maglarion. "But then they have no reason to wish me dead. I always pay on time, do I not?"

"The Ghosts know you are here," said Ikhana.

"Perhaps," said Maglarion. "Or perhaps not. Dear little Laeria mentioned that her husband was an idealistic fool. If he realized that Laeria played at necromancy, he might have sent a coin of Cormarus to the Ghosts. Or we may have drawn the attention of the Ghosts in other ways." He sighed. "I really shouldn't have let you burn the Amalas villa to the ground."

"It was necessary," said Ikhana, "to conceal our presence."

"Or it drew the attention of the Ghosts," said Maglarion. He sighed again, thumped his cane against the floor. "No matter."

"Then our task here was a failure," said Ikhana.

Maglarion lifted his eyebrows. "Not at all."

"It was not?" said Ikhana.

"No," said Maglarion, turning from the table of dead men.

"What of your students?" said Ikhana.

"Useless fools," said Maglarion. "And our trip to Aretia was not a failure. I found exactly what I came here to claim."

He kept walking, past the corridor leading to the cells.

"What of the prisoners?" said Ikhana.

"I don't care," said Maglarion. "The Ghosts rescued them. Or they starved to death." He thought for a moment. "If any of them are still alive, you may have them."

Ikhana vanished down the corridor, black dagger flashing in her hand.

Maglarion chuckled, stopped before the stained metal table, and whispered a spell. One of the flagstones shifted, revealing a hidden compartment below the floor. Maglarion gestured, and the ancient papyrus scroll he had taken from Sebastian Amalas's desk floated to his hand.

He unrolled it, gazing upon the ancient hieroglyphs and strange diagrams.

His smile returned.

The ancient Maatish sorcerers had been necromancers beyond peer. They had reared mighty pyramids to house their pharaohs, their god-kings, and by their necromantic sciences they had raised their pharaohs, and themselves, to everlasting life. Or almost everlasting life. The Kingdom of the Rising Sun had fallen long ago, its spells and sorceries undone, and now only its ruins remained, littering the deserts like bleached bones.

And their secrets, waiting for those bold enough to claim them.

For this scroll held the secret, the thing that Maglarion had sought for so very long.

A spell to transcend the flesh itself. To escape the body, and live as power forevermore.

The secret of true immortality.

Maglarion rolled up the scroll and tucked it into his coat.

He gestured again, and the bloodcrystal he had made from Laeria's virgin daughter - Maglarion could not recall her name - floated from the compartment to his hand.

He blinked in surprise.

When he had left, the bloodcrystal had been the size of a walnut. Now it had grown to the size of a child's fist, its edges jagged and sharp. From time to time a green light writhed in its crystalline depths.

The deaths of the magi and the slavers, Maglarion realized. The power released by their deaths had fed the bloodcrystal. He felt its increased potency crackling beneath his fingertips, the trapped power within it yearning for release.

That was just as well. If Maglarion had read the scroll correctly, he was going to need a great deal of power very soon.

And what better way than death, a great deal of death, to harvest that power?

Ikhana returned, her face empty. No doubt the Ghosts had taken any surviving prisoners. Or the prisoners had all starved to death, or died from their wounds. Or Ikhana had killed them, feasting upon the feeble remnants of their life energies.

Maglarion had greater things on his mind.

"What shall we do now?" said Ikhana.

Maglarion closed his living eye, thinking of the scroll's hieroglyphs. Of what he would need to transcend the flesh.

"First," he said, opening his eye, "I shall need some new followers."

CHAPTER 9
THE VINEYARD

They reached Koros the next day.

The village perched on a spit of land jutting into the Bay of Empire. Thirty or forty ramshackle houses stood around a dilapidated tavern and a stone shrine to Tethene, the goddess of the sea. Dozens of fishing boats floated at wooden docks, bobbing with the waves.

The place stank of rotting fish, salt, and tar. The villagers gave them furtive looks as Halfdan drove the wagon to the tavern. Many of the women wore mourning black, and the few men that Caina saw looked sullen and unfriendly.

"I think they want to rob us," whispered Caina.

"Undoubtedly," said Halfdan. "And they would, too, if Riogan were not here."

Riogan grinned, drew one of his daggers, tossed it to himself.

"All the women are wearing black," said Caina. "Like they're in mourning."

"She's right," said Komnene.

"I passed through here a year past," said Halfdan, frowning, "and there were not so many women in mourning."

"The black looks new," said Caina.

"Some plague, perhaps?" said Komnene.

"Let's find out," said Halfdan, halting the wagon before the tavern. "Riogan, Komnene, stay here. Caina, come with me."

Caina blinked, but followed Halfdan to the tavern's door.

"Two things," said Halfdan. "First, don't speak unless I tell you."

Caina started to say "yes", but nodded instead.

Halfdan grinned. "You learn quickly. Good. Second, as you might

66

expect, it behooves me to take different identities from time to time. Here, I am known as Paulus, a broker for the grain merchants in the Imperial capital."

Caina nodded again, and followed Halfdan inside.

The interior had a dirt floor, rough wooden benches, and a crumbling fieldstone fireplace. A lean man in a greasy leather apron approached, squinting beneath a shock of unkempt gray hair.

"Aye?" said the man in the apron. "Paulus, you scoundrel, is that you?"

"It is," said Halfdan, "Baccan, you old dog." Caina blinked in surprise. Halfdan's accent had changed, and he now spoke Caerish with a heavy Disali accent. "I see you haven't choked on your own filth."

Baccan snorted, and spat upon the floor. "Not yet. What brings you here? You've picked a bad time to come."

"Why?" said Halfdan. "What's happened? Your womenfolk are wearing mourning black. Did a storm take half the fishermen?"

"No," said Baccan. "No storm. Sorcery."

Caina flinched.

"Sorcery?" said Halfdan, fear entering his own voice. "Did you offend the Magisterium?"

"I don't know," said Baccan. "You remember Wyfarne and his lads? Did a bit of smuggling?"

Halfdan nodded.

"Well, they had some big cargo from the south," said Baccan. "All these old scrolls, looted from some tomb in the desert."

Old scrolls? Like the one her father had found?

"They were the sort of things a sorcerer would want," said Baccan. "Well, Wyfarne's ship ran ashore near Aretia - the fool never could navigate at night. The Count of Aretia seized the scrolls, and that was that. Then two days ago this old man comes to the village. A cane and a patch over his eye, and he's got this woman with him. Pale thing, looks like she's dead herself."

The scars on Caina's belly clenched, painfully.

So that was where Maglarion had gone.

"He says he knows about the scrolls, and asks if we have any more," said Baccan. "Wyfarne says he doesn't, told the old man to go to hell."

Caina saw where this was going.

"So the old man...he killed them," said Baccan, shaking his head. "All of them. Wyfarne's entire family. And anyone else who got in his way. Thirty-four dead."

"Wyfarne's own fault," said Halfdan. "The idiot bought something dug up from an old tomb. Anyone with a lick of sense stays away from old tombs. Nasty things in there...the sort of things sorcerers and magi like."

Baccan spat again. "We're lucky the old fool didn't bring destruction down upon the entire village. Now. Why are you here?"

"I need passage across the Bay," said Halfdan. "To Craton, as quickly as can be found."

"Well," said Baccan, "my son Racus, he's got a fishing boat, and the catch has been slim of late. Scared off by all the sorcery, I'll warrant."

"I also have a wagon and a team I need to sell," said Halfdan. "Doubt they'll fit on the fishing boat, after all. I'll sell them to you in exchange for passage and say...oh, two hundred denarii."

"Two hundred?" said Baccan, incredulous. "You're little better than a thief, Paulus..."

Halfdan and Baccan launched into a convoluted negotiation, and Caina listened with fascination, the news about Maglarion temporarily forgotten. After numerous insults, emphatic gestures, and occasional threats, Halfdan and Baccan settled on one hundred sixty-eight denarii and passage across the Bay in exchange for the wagon and team.

They shook hands, and Caina followed Halfdan back to the wagon.

"Maglarion was here," she said, her voice low.

"Aye," said Halfdan. "Your mother lured him here with the scroll. It only makes sense that he would come here to look for more."

"He might return," said Caina.

"No," said Halfdan. "I doubt he'll bother. One day the Ghosts will bring him to account for his crimes. But not today, I fear."

They spent the night at Baccan's tavern, in his guest rooms.

Caina took one look at the bedbug-infested bedding and decided to sleep on the floor, as far from the bed as she could manage.

As usual, she had nightmares. The metal table, her father in his chair, Maglarion's glittering knife, her mother's laughter.

But when she awoke, breathing hard, she wondered what it would have been like to take up a dagger, to strike back at her mother, at Maglarion. Perhaps Caina could have stopped her from destroying her father's mind.

Perhaps she could keep others from suffering what she had suffered.

Perhaps the Ghosts, the nightfighter training, could give her what she needed.

Caina thought about that, lying awake in the dark.

###

They left before dawn, sailing on Racus's fishing boat.

Racus was a younger, thinner version of his father, with the same sullen squint and slovenly appearance. Yet his fishing boat was well-maintained, and Racus and his brother handled the rudder and the sails with deft skill. Though everything did stink of dead fish.

"How long?" said Halfdan.

Racus grunted, squinted at the sky. "Four days, I think. Maybe five, if the winds turn sour." He grinned. "Course, a storm could come up, send us all to the bottom in an hour or so. Hope you thought to leave an offering at Tethene's shrine."

But they encountered no storms. The wind filled the boat's sails, and soon they left Koros and all sight of land behind. Rippling blue-green water filled the world in all directions. Caina saw at the prow, fascinated. All her life she had lived within sight of the sea, but she had never been on a boat before.

She had never been out of sight of land before.

Riogan stepped besides her, eyes narrowed.

"What's so fascinating, girl?" said Riogan. "It's seawater."

Caina shrugged. "I...have never been on a ship before, that's all."

Riogan laughed. "This? This tub is a boat, not a ship. Go to Malarae, or to Marsis, and you will see ships. Not just fishing boats." He spat over the side. "Fool child. Is that why you followed us? To ride upon a boat?"

"My father is dead," said Caina. "I have nowhere else to go."

"You could have had a life of comfort and ease," said Riogan. "Instead you chose to become a nightfighter. And for what? Hmm? To see a boat?"

Caina started to answer, fell silent.

"What, girl?" said Riogan. "What were you going to say?"

"You don't like me very much," said Caina.

"No," said Riogan. He smirked. "Are you going to cry? Complain to Halfdan? Or maybe you'll do something clever, figure out why I don't like you?"

"I think I remind you of a bad memory," said Caina. "Something you don't like to remember."

Riogan did not move, his expression did not change, but his eyes grew cold.

He stalked away without another word.

Caina wondered what she reminded him of, what dark memory rose up whenever he looked at her.

She decided she didn't want to know. She had enough dark memories of her own, after all.

###

Racus was as good as his word. Four days later, the boat put in at Croton.

The town looked much like Aretia or Mors Anaxis. The same white-walled houses with red-tiled roofs, the same paved streets, the same warehouses, the same plump merchants and lean fishermen. Halfdan paid Racus, and they went into the town.

"Will we buy another wagon?" said Caina.

"No," said Halfdan. "Mules."

"Mules?" said Caina. "Why? Are we going mining?"

Halfdan smiled. "Consider this your first lesson. Figure out why we need mules."

Halfdan bought eight mules, loading them down with supplies and equipment. Caina took one, as did Riogan and Komnene, while Halfdan led the remaining beasts. Then they left Croton, heading north along the Imperial Highway.

Caina's mule was ill-tempered, and tried to bite her whenever her hand strayed too close to its head. Yet the beast continued its steady, plodding pace, and they made good time.

Soon she saw the distant shape of mountains to the northeast.

"Disalia," said Caina the next morning.

Halfdan looked back at her.

"We're going to one of the Disali provinces," said Caina. "Disalia Superior or Disalia Inferior, I'm not sure which."

"Disalia Inferior, actually," said Halfdan. "How did you know?"

"The mules," said Caina, closing her eyes as she remembered the maps in her father's study. She jerked her hand back as she felt the mule's hot breath upon it. "Disalia is hilly. Too hilly for wagons. So merchants have to take mules."

"Most merchants don't bother traveling through Disalia at all," said Komnene.

"It's easier, and cheaper, to ship goods through the Narrow Sea, past Arzaxia," said Halfdan.

"So the Disali provinces are isolated," said Komnene.

"Perfect for the Ghosts," said Halfdan.

###

The hills rose up around them the next day, high and jagged, layers of yellowish-brown rock jutting from sandy soil. Pine trees clung to the earth here and there, along with tough grasses and thorny bushes, and streams trickled through the hills, sometimes falling in dramatic waterfalls. The Imperial Highway wound back and forth through the hills, sometimes climbing the hills, sometimes circling around them, and occasionally crossing a steep ravine with a stone bridge. Caina found herself admiring the skill of the engineers who had carved the Highway through those curves and ravines.

"Tell me," said Halfdan, as the mules picked their way along the Highway. "What do you know about the Ghosts?"

Caina thought it over, swaying in her saddle.

"Well," she said at last, "you did save my life."

Halfdan smiled. "Before that, though. Before what happened to you. What did you know about the Ghosts?"

Caina shrugged. "Not very much. Most of the books said that the Ghosts were legends, that they never existed. I never really thought about them. Not until my father showed me that coin of Emperor Cormarus."

"The Ghosts began here, in Disalia," said Halfdan, waving his hand at the jagged hills.

"How?" said Caina.

"It was long ago, during the Second Empire," said Halfdan.

Riogan snorted and rolled his eyes. "Here we go again."

Halfdan ignored him. "In those days, the Disali clans acknowledged no king or emperor, and spent their time fighting among themselves. They fought with stealth and ambush, from the shadows, and every clan had its spies among the others. And then the Ashbringers came."

"Who were they?" said Caina.

"The sorcerer-priests of the Saddai," said Halfdan. "They worshiped the flames, and practiced pyromancy, burning their victims alive to fuel their arcane powers. They conquered Disalia and enslaved the Disali clans. The Disali tried to fight back. Their honor and rituals compelled them to seek out the Ashbringers in open battle. But the clans could not stand against the power of the Ashbringers, and every time they fought, the Ashbringers slaughtered them."

"The Disali must have won," said Caina.

"Why do you say that?" said Halfdan.

"Well, there are no more Ashbringers," said Caina.

Halfdan nodded. "How did they fight back?"

Caina thought about it. She remembered her father going to warn

71

Laeria one last time, because it was the right thing to do. The fair thing to do.

She remembered how that had ended.

If only he had listened to her. If only he hadn't done the right thing.

"They...didn't fight fair," said Caina.

"Go on," said Halfdan.

"They couldn't fight the Ashbringers openly," said Caina. "They'd get slaughtered. So...they didn't fight openly. They fought in secret. With ambushes, and poison, and spies, and assassins."

Halfdan nodded. "The Disali formed organizations called circles. Each man knew two others in the circle, and only the circlemasters knew everyone. They built hidden lairs and tunnels throughout Disalia, moving undetected through the hills. And the circles fought back against the Ashbringers. They poisoned wells and supplies. They arranged the assassination of the Ashbringers' supporters and generals. And they passed information to the enemies of the Ashbringers - to the Emperor in Malarae, and to the Magisterium in Artifel. Time and time again the Ashbringers sent a general to pacify the Disali hills, and again and again the generals failed because of the circles. When the generals complained of the circles, the Ashbringers claimed that they blamed failure upon shadows and ghosts, and executed the generals."

"Ghosts," said Caina. "That's where the name came from?"

"There are no Ghosts," said Halfdan, "only whispers and rumors." He grinned. "Sensible men know that the Ghosts do not exist."

"But the Ghosts couldn't defeat the Ashbringers on their own," said Caina.

"No," said Halfdan. "So they sought help, and found an ally in the Emperor Cormarus of Malarae. They made a pact. Cormarus would lead his Legions into Disalia, and drive the Ashbringers out, ending their tyranny. He would defend the commoners, and protect them from the cruelty of sorcery. And in exchange, the Ghosts would become his servants. They would spy for him, shield him from his enemies, and kill for him when necessary."

"So the Emperor drove the Ashbringers from the hills," said Caina, "Disalia became an Imperial province, and the Ghosts have served the Emperor ever since."

"For the most part," said Halfdan. "The Ghosts defend the commoners from lawless nobles, from corrupt sorcerers, from slavers and brigands. We stand with the Emperor, we spy for him, because he is the commoners' strongest shield against the tyranny of the nobility and the tyranny of sorcery. And if the Emperor turns from the common people, if he sides with the nobility and the magi...then the Ghosts will turn on him."

Riogan laughed. "A noble speech. But an obscuring one. We kill people who need killing. Even Emperors, if need be. Anything else is nothing but flowery language."

"Fortunately," said Halfdan, "our current Emperor, Alexius Naerius, rules with a strong hand, and keeps the nobility and the magi in their place."

"The Fourth Empire," said Caina.

"Oh?" said Halfdan.

"That's when Ghosts killed Emperors," said Caina. "When the magi ruled the Empire, and slavery had not yet been abolished."

"You put your time in your father's library to good use," said Halfdan.

"Yes. The magi practiced necromancy openly then, and slaughtered slaves by the thousands to fuel their spells. That is what the Ghosts fight against, Caina. To prevent a return to those days."

And against men like Maglarion, she realized.

The thought pleased her.

The Imperial Highway climbed ever higher into the hills. Soon they left the Highway, and made their way along narrow rock-cut roads and graveled paths.

They stopped in small villages to buy supplies. The Disali houses were tall and narrow, no doubt to conserve space, since the hills had very little in the way of flat land. The villagers themselves wore brown and green, colors that matched the hills around them. At every village men stopped to greet Halfdan, and carry out long conversations in the Disali tongue. Sometimes they gave him bundles of letters, which he took and secured in his mule's saddlebags.

"Why were you talking about wine?" said Caina.

Halfdan blinked in surprise. "You understand Disali?"

"Yes," said Caina. "It was in..."

"One of your father's books, yes," said Halfdan. "I should learn not to underestimate you."

"I don't know about that," said Caina. "But why talk about wine?"

Halfdan smiled. "I used to be a vintner. Perhaps I keep my hand in the trade."

"It's...a code, isn't it?" said Caina. "He was giving you messages."

"The Disali vineyards make some of the best wine in the Empire, and perhaps the world," said Halfdan.

Caina decided that meant yes.

"My father always said he preferred Caerish wine," said Caina.

"No, too sweet," said Halfdan. "Disali wine has more vigor to it."

Komnene laughed. "Careful, child. If you get Halfdan started about wine, you'll never have another moment of silence."

"It's only appropriate," said Halfdan. "We've almost reached our destination. Where you will begin your training."

Caina looked up.

"A vineyard," said Halfdan.

The reached the Vineyard the next day.

It sat atop a high crag, overlooking a narrow valley, a fast river bubbling and rushing past it. And at first glance, Caina thought it was a fortress, not a vineyard. Terraces climbed their way up the crag's side, surrounded by a stout wall of lichen-spotted gray stone. Watchtowers stood at the corners of the walls, and Caina saw armed guards pacing with crossbows at the ready. The fortified gatehouse looked as if it could repel a Legion attack, and Caina saw a stream bubbling from within the walls, no doubt coming from a cave within the terraces.

Hidden lairs and tunnels, Halfdan had said, and she wondered how much of the Ghosts had hidden beneath the towers and walls.

Yet she saw the grape vines growing on trellises upon the terraces. The place looked beautiful, sitting among the soaring hills and the falling water.

"The Vineyard," said Halfdan, leading the mules up the narrow path to the gatehouse.

"So it's a fake?" said Caina.

His look was almost reproving. "Not at all. It's a working vineyard, and the vintages fetch good prices in the markets of Malarae and Arzaxia."

"But the Ghosts...work here?" said Caina.

"Yes," said Halfdan. "The cultivation of grapes is not the only thing that happens in the Vineyard. Here, you will learn to be a Ghost nightfighter."

The gates swung open to meet them, and Caina followed Halfdan, Riogan, and Komnene inside.

CHAPTER 10
KNIVES AND POISONS

Six weeks later, Caina awoke before dawn, as she did every day.

She slept in a small room built in the base of the Vineyard's outer wall, one that had no doubt once been used for storage. It had enough room for a narrow bed, a chest to store her possessions, and a stool.

And just enough room to do her exercises.

Caina stood, stretched, and began the exercises that Akragas had taught her, moving her arms and legs through the forms. The middle palm strike. The unarmed throw. The leg sweep. The high kick. The low kick. Blocks, high, middle, and low.

When she finished, her heart was racing, and a light sheen of sweat covered her forehead. But she was not tired. Not nearly as tired as she had been after the first lesson.

That was good.

After she finished the exercises, Caina dressed in a gray shirt and gray pants. She remained barefoot. At first, not wearing shoes had felt strange and uncomfortable, but after a month and a half at the Vineyard, it seemed natural.

Her father's signet ring went on a slender cord around her neck, the heavy gold resting against her chest. She kept it with her, most of the time.

Then Caina left her room for the Vineyard's lowest terrace. She saw no one else. The workers would not begin tending the vines until after sunrise, and the Ghosts who came here on various errands had not yet awakened.

Except for the guards on the wall. They never seemed to sleep.

Caina took a deep breath and started to run.

She sprinted along the terrace, feet slapping against the flagstones, past the vats and the winepresses. Then up the steep stone stairs to the next terrace, and she darted along its length.

And then up to the next terrace.

And the next.

Finally, she reached the top of the seventh and final terrace, her heart pounding, her breath heaving. Caina slowed to a walk, pacing back and forth at the base of the high watchtower crowning the final terrace. From here she had a splendid view of the valley, with the churning river below and the white spray of the waterfall above.

Akragas waited for her beneath the watchtower.

He was an old man, with bushy white eyebrows and scraggly white hair. He wore a white shirt and black pants, the sleeves of his shirt stark against the sun-bronzed skin of his face and hands.

"Well, child," he said in Kyracian, "your time is improving. When you first ran the terraces, I had time to eat a fine breakfast and take a pleasant nap afterwards. I still have time to eat a fine breakfast, but only three courses instead of four."

"That is...doubtful," said Caina in Kyracian. He had been teaching her the language, which was similar to Cyrican, but she still had trouble with it. "You eat...like a monk. Nothing but oats and...wine that is watery."

"Watered wine, you mean, impudent girl," said Akragas.

"Yes," said Caina.

He stared at her.

She stared back, and waited.

His right hand blurred, swinging towards her face. Caina hopped back, his fingertips blurring inches from her nose. His left hand came up, and Caina caught it in a high block, beating away his palm.

And while she was distracted, his right hand came up and slapped her across the cheek.

"Better," said Akragas, "but still not satisfactory."

"You will have to learn to fight," Halfdan had said during her first day at the Vineyard, "and Akragas will teach you to fight without weapons."

Akragas looked her with eyes full of disdain.

"You are a pampered noble child, yes?" said Akragas in accented Caerish, "soft and weak. The Ghosts should teach her to be perfumed and pretty, to lure our enemies into her bed when she is older. Until then, waste not my time with her."

"I used to be a noble child," said Caina in Caerish, "and now...now I don't know what I am."

Akragas grunted, reached down, took her chin in his hard hand. He titled her face back, looked into her eyes.

"Ah," he said. "You have known pain, yes? That is good. Life is pain. You may either let it break you...or you may let it make you stronger. Perhaps your pain will make you stronger. Or perhaps you will let it break you." He looked at Halfdan. "Very well. I shall teach her."

"Splendid," said Halfdan. "Caina, listen to him. He is a hard teacher, but a good one."

He left, leaving Caina alone with Akragas.

"Halfdan tells me you are very observant," said Akragas. "So. What do you observe about me?"

Caina shrugged. "You're Kyracian. I can tell from your accent. And...I think you used to be a soldier, one who spent a lot of time on a ship."

"Very good," said Akragas. "Perhaps you are observant enough to see this coming?"

He slapped her. Not very hard, but Caina stumbled, losing her balance. His hand had moved so fast that she hadn't even seen it.

"Why did you do that?" said Caina, rubbing her cheek.

"To see if you could block it," said Akragas.

"You could have warned me, at least," said Caina, scowling at him.

Akragas scoffed. "Little girl, I did warn you. My feet said that I would slap you. My shoulders said that I would slap you. My hands all but shouted that I would slap you. If you are to deaf to hear...well, then it is your own fault. You should listen better."

"Then teach me," said Caina.

Akragas nodded. "Very well. Let us see if you can learn to hear or not."

After the first session, she was so sore and bruised that she could barely sleep. Which wasn't all that bad, considering it meant no nightmares.

Six weeks after that first lesson, she sparred with Akragas, as she had every morning since.

"Faster!" barked Akragas, swinging an open-handed blow that Caina just managed to avoid. "You will be faster! You will never be as strong as a man. So you must end your fights quickly."

"I must never fight fair," said Caina, thinking of her father.

"Yes!" said Akragas. "That is true. You must never fight fairly! Only fools fight fairly. All men have their strengths and their weaknesses. You must pit your strengths against your enemies' weaknesses, always."

Sometimes he talked about history. The Ashbringers had forbidden the Disali to bear weapons. So the Disali had developed different forms of fighting, learning ways to transform their hands and feet into lethal weapons. The Kyracians had a similar system of fighting, one that they called the storm dance.

"These are ancient traditions I am teaching you, yes?" said Akragas. "Very old. And you will respect them! For they shall make you strong, if you follow them. And faster, child! Your enemies will not pause for you!"

He kicked at her. Caina caught his ankle between her hands and twisted. Akragas rolled with the movement, and his hand caught her on the side of the head. Caina stumbled, losing her grip on his foot. Akragas caught his balance and swung around, his leg sweeping beneath Caina's.

She lost her balance and landed upon her rump.

"We are done now, I think," said Akragas. "It is time for my breakfast."

"With only three courses?" said Caina. "Why bother?"

"When you leave me with no time for breakfast, then you may boast," said Akragas, and walked away.

###

Every morning without fail, Caina trained with Akragas, learning how to fight without weapons.

For the rest of the day, she learned other things from other men and women.

One day Halfdan introduced her to a tall man with black hair and a sweeping black mustache. He wore black pants with red stripes and a bright red vest that left his well-muscled arms bare. He looked like one of the traveling carnival performers that had passed through Aretia from time to time. She had laughed and clapped at their tricks, at feats of juggling and acrobatics and knife-throwing.

"This is Sandros," said Halfdan. "He will teach you to fight with knives, when necessary."

"And so I shall," said Sandros, speaking Caerish with a booming voice. "All of Akragas's fancy tricks are well and good. But when you need to kill a man, and kill him quickly, there's nothing better for the job than a good sharp blade. Come. We shall learn in a civilized environment!"

A massive villa occupied the Vineyard's sixth tier, and Sandros led her to the villa's courtyard garden, a leather bundle under his arm. He set the bundle on a stone bench and unwrapped it. Dozens of blades rested in the bundle, the steel gleaming.

Caina flinched. She remembered lying shackled in the darkness below the earth, Maglarion lecturing the magi with that knife glittering like ice in his hand...

"What?" said Sandros, lifting a dagger. "Do not be afraid! I will not hurt you. I am a very wicked man, as many lonely noblewomen will attest, but I certainly will not hurt a child...ah, I see. Halfdan did not tell us where he found you, but someone has hurt you with knives, yes?"

Caina nodded.

"Well, then," said Sandros. He reversed the dagger, took Caina's hand, and pressed the handle into her grasp. "You should not be afraid of knives."

"Why not?" said Caina, her throat dry.

"Because knives, they teach respect," said Sandros. "All the techniques that Akragas will teach you, all the moves with your hands and feet, they are useful, but they are limited. Most men, they will always be stronger than you will ever be."

"Akragas says I must never fight fair," said Caina.

"True," said Sandros. "Hand to hand, it will be hard for you to defeat a man of equal skill. But blades...ah, blades, are the great leveler. In a skilled hand, a knife can kill anyone. And knives, as I said, teach respect. A man may view you as a victim, as prey to be exploited...until you hold a knife to his throat. Or to his balls." He chuckled. "Then he will think of you rather differently."

Caina frowned, examining the dagger in a new light.

"There," said Sandros, pointing. "Do you see that flower, on that bush? About twenty paces away?"

Caina nodded. "What about it?"

"I will show you something," said Sandros. He lifted a slender, flat knife from the bundle, its blade as long as its handle. "Knives have many different uses. Observe."

He flung his arm back, his entire body snapping like a bowstring, and hurled the knife. It shot through the air and neatly snipped the flower from its branch.

Caina blinked. "You..."

Sandros sighed. "Ah, the trick is more impressive when I can hit an apple resting upon the head of some comely young maiden, but you see the point? Why fight hand to hand when you can kill quickly with a blade? Or from a distance with a throwing knife?"

"Show me," said Caina.

"I will," said Sandros, handing her a dagger with blunted edges. "Now, you hold it like this...no, like that. Yes. Good! First, you..."

###

Sometimes Caina spent the afternoon with Komnene, who also had things to teach her.

"This is called redshade," said Komnene, lifting a small jar of dried leaves. "An herb, it grows in the Disali hills, and on the shores of the Inner Sea, but nowhere else. Mixed with the juice of the Anshani southwood tree, it is a useful medicine for reliving the pain of arthritis. But taken in too large a dose, undiluted, it causes hallucinations, delirium, and eventually death, if the body is not purged with a strong emetic."

Komnene had an infirmary in the villa, a spacious room with three beds and wooden shelves sagging beneath countless jars and vials of dried herbs. A shrine to Minaerys rested in the corner, candles standing over a small silver bowl.

"And this is blackroot," said Komnene, indicating a glass vial half-full of dark powder. "This only grows on the borders of the Cyrican desert, far to the south. It is quite rare, and most expensive. It has absolutely no medicinal use, but can be used to brew a poison of exceptional lethality."

"That's what you used on the magi, isn't it?" said Caina, remembering the dead men lying in the vaulted cellar. The foam around their mouths had been the same color as the powder in the vial.

"Yes," said Komnene. Guilt flickered over her face for a moment, and she glanced at the shrine to Minaerys.

Then she composed herself, and kept talking.

On other days, Komnene treated injuries. Sometimes injured or wounded Ghosts came to the Vineyard, or men and women from the nearby villages, and Komnene treated them. She taught Caina how to clean wounds, how to suture and stitch, how to set broken bones, how to prepare poultices to prevent infection and draw out poison.

"Do you still pray to Minaerys?" Caina asked one afternoon, as she blended medicines under Komnene's watchful eye.

Komnene smiled. "You deduced that from the shrine, no doubt."

"Why?" said Caina. "You were expelled from the Temple."

"Because I still believe in Minaerys," said Komnene. "In his teachings."

"But...the Temple forbids its physicians to make poison," said Caina. "And you poisoned that necromancer, and all those magi and slavers."

"Yes," said Komnene. She closed her eyes, thought for a moment. "I...think the Temple is wrong. We have a responsibility to use our knowledge and our abilities as best as we can. And for me to stand by and to do nothing when men like that necromancer have their way with the innocent...no, I cannot do it. I cannot, Caina. I believe that Minaerys wants his followers to use their abilities for the greatest good...and if that means poisoning murderous magi, then so be it."

"But you're not entirely sure," said Caina.

"No," said Komnene. She stared at the shrine for a moment. "It is a dark world, Caina, and the right thing to do...it is so hard to see." She shrugged. "If I had never brewed that poison, I could have stayed in the Temple of Minaerys, and my conscience would be clear."

"But then I would be dead by now," said Caina. Or, worse, still chained in that dark cellar, screaming as Maglarion came at her with his knife again and again.

"Perhaps a heavy conscience is a small price to pay to save a life," said Komnene.

They resumed mixing medicines.

###

And sometimes Halfdan himself spent the afternoon teaching her things.

He often left on business, but when he returned, he took the time to teach her. And Halfdan was far more important to the Ghosts than she had understood. At first she thought he had only been a circlemaster, commanding a circle of nightfighters and nightkeepers like Riogan and Komnene. But many couriers and messengers arrived with letters for him, and he was the unquestioned commander of everyone at the Vineyard. Caina realized that Halfdan was one of the high circlemasters, one who commanded the lesser circlemasters.

He was one of the most knowledgeable and dangerous men in the Empire of Nighmar, a man who knew every trick that had ever been used.

And he taught those tricks to her.

"You have to understand," said Halfdan, "that people see what they expect to see. The best place to hide anything is in plain sight. That coin of Emperor Cormarus your father sent to us? Most men would look at the coin and see nothing but a coin, spend it on wine or a whore. But to eyes that know where to look, there was a message."

"Hiding in plain sight," said Caina.

"Precisely," said Halfdan.

He taught her pick locks. The Vineyard had a small workshop where the guards' armor and crossbows were repaired. Caina sat at one of the workbenches, working with picks as Halfdan showed her how to open a lock. He also taught her to disarm mechanical traps. Powerful nobles and wealthy nobles liked to build traps into their locks, preparing poisoned needles or even toxic gases for would-be intruders. The needles in the practice traps stabbed into Caina's fingers again and again until she mastered the trick of disarming them.

She did not complain.

"Pain teaches best," said Halfdan. "But...you know that already, don't you?"

Caina nodded, and kept practicing.

The trap released without stabbing her fingers.

"Motivation," Halfdan told her some days later. "That is the key."

"The key to what?" said Caina.

"To understanding your enemies," said Halfdan. "Many nobles betray the Emperor. Why do they betray him?"

Caina shrugged. "Why does anyone betray anyone? Wealth and power and ambition."

"Yes," said Halfdan, "but what kind of power? Where does the wealth come from, what does the ambition desire? The nobles want different things. Some are loyal to the Emperor. Some want to see the Magisterium returned to power, see slavery restored in the Empire. Others want to see the Legions in command of the Empire. And some want nothing more than to be left alone with their families."

"But not very many, I suppose," said Caina.

Halfdan laughed. "Not really. So. Why is important to know what your enemies want?"

Caina thought about it. "Because then you can use it against them."

"Exactly," said Halfdan. "Your enemies will have weak spots, levers that you can use against them. Weaknesses you can exploit. Akragas told you this, I suppose?"

"That I should never try to fight fair," said Caina. "He said most men are stronger than I will ever be, so when I fight, I must strike first, and strike hard."

"Very good," said Halfdan. "That is the nature of the Ghosts. We are spies, not soldiers or sorcerers. We cannot face our enemies in a contest of strength. We would quickly lose. Our minds must be our weapons, our cunning our armor. We must understand our enemies, for that is our only hope of defeating them."

Caina thought about that.

"What about," she said, "what about Maglarion? What does he want?"

"I don't know. No one in the Ghosts knows," said Halfdan. He sighed. "Which is why the Ghosts have not been able to defeat him, not in three hundred years."

Halfdan also taught her to move silently, to walk without making a sound. There was a room in the Vineyard's cellars where the slightest noise produced dozens of reverberating echoes, and he took her there to practice. At first she could not take a single step, even barefoot, without setting off the echoes.

"Your footsteps are wrong," said Halfdan, walking in a circle around her, his boots making no noise against the floor. "Look at my feet. Toe first, then heel. The weight upon the outside of my feet, not the heel. Yes. Yes, that's it. Again now. Turn your ankle a bit to the left. Yes. Now. Again."

He kept her practicing. It would have been difficult, once upon a time. But open-handed practice with Akragas and weapons practice with Sandros had made her stronger, tougher, and Halfdan's exercises came easier and easier. Soon she could move in perfect silence around the echoing cellar, even while wearing boots.

"A good start," said Halfdan. "But moving silently while alone in a room isn't very useful, is it? You'll need to practice on someone else."

So he set her to creeping up behind various people around the Vineyard. If she could walk upon behind a man and tap him on the shoulder, without being detected, she passed the test. At first she failed, over and over again. The Vineyard's residents kept close watch over their surroundings, and Caina suspected Halfdan often used them to train new Ghosts.

But bit by bit, she learned. She learned when to move, and when to remain motionless. When to take cover, and when to stay in the open. She learned to gauge shadows, to watch where they pooled in the walls and the corners, and how to conceal herself within their folds.

When at last she sidled up behind a guard and slapped him on the back, and the man jumped with a startled yell, Caina felt so proud that she could burst.

Evenings, she spent doing chores. The Vineyard was, after all, a vineyard, and Caina helped tend grapes or roll barrels along the terraces.

After dinner, her time was her own, and she spent it in the Vineyard's library.

For the Vineyard had a huge library, easily six times larger than the one once housed in Sebastian Amalas's study. Caina had seen many of the titles on her father's shelves, but she read them again anyway. But most of the books she had never seen before, and she started to devour her way through the library, making her way through book after book.

And at night, she returned to her tiny room, and had nightmares.

She would probably have nightmares for the rest of her life, Halfdan had told her.

"Nightmares," he said, "are scars of the mind. Your body can recover from a wound, but it will bear a scar for the rest of your life. The mind is much the same way. It can recover from an injury...but it will retain a scar. And you will carry that scar for the rest of your days. Whether you let it destroy you...that is up to you."

But as the months passed, as summer became winter and then spring again, Caina grew used to the nightmares. Sometimes she woke up, heart pounding, hands trembling, sweat pouring down her brow, tears streaming from her eyes. She saw again Maglarion cutting her father's throat, felt again the cold metal table against her back and legs.

But sometimes she slept the night. Her lessons and training often left her exhausted, and on those days she sank into a black and dreamless sleep.

Or, at least, if she did dream, she did not remember it.

"Work is the best medicine for grief," Halfdan told her once.

So Caina worked hard.

One night Halfdan walked to Komnene's infirmary. He had frequent headaches, and Komnene prepared a bitter tea that helped him sleep.

Komnene was awake when he arrived, mixing the herbs by candlelight.

"Ah," said Halfdan. "You received my message, I see."

Komnene laughed. "Yes. Do you know where Caina left it this time? Upon my pillow. While I was sleeping, no less! I locked the door, I am sure of it. So your student picked my lock, crept across my room without disturbing me, slipped the note under my pillow, and left - all without waking me!"

"Caina," said Halfdan, "is a fast learner."

"So I see," said Komnene. She handed Halfdan a cup of steaming tea, and poured one for herself. "Have a seat."

Halfdan sat, took a drink, smiled behind the cup.

"The things you are teaching Caina..." said Komnene.

"You think they won't be useful?" said Halfdan.

Komnene shook her head. "I think she will find them most useful."

"So you think that the things I am teaching her are useful," said Halfdan, "but you don't think I should be teaching them to her."

"No," said Komnene. She sighed, looked into her cup. "You are turning her into a weapon, Halfdan."

"I know," said Halfdan.

"She will never have a chance at...at a quiet life, at happiness," said Komnene.

"We make our own happiness," said Halfdan. "And she will never have a peaceful life, not after what happened to her. You examined her yourself, Komnene. She will probably never bear a child."

"I know," said Komnene. "She could have been a priestess, though. A scholar, a physician."

"You have peace in your profession," said Halfdan. "Do you think Caina could have peace as a physician?"

Komnene sighed again. "No."

They sat in silence for a moment, drinking the tea.

"She will have to do terrible things," said Komnene.

"She's already done terrible things," said Halfdan. "She killed her mother, after all."

"That was an accident," said Komnene.

"Nevertheless," said Halfdan. "Laeria Amalas is dead. And she deserved to die. She sold Caina to Maglarion. She destroyed the minds of every man, woman, and child in Count Sebastian's villa."

Komnene said nothing.

"And consider how much evil would have been averted," said Halfdan, "if Caina had killed Laeria before she contacted Maglarion. Her father would yet be alive. His servants would yet be alive. Those smugglers in Koros would still be alive."

Komnene closed her eyes.

"Caina will become a Ghost nightfighter," said Halfdan. "She will have to do terrible things. The Ghosts do terrible things, I know. But sometimes it is necessary. Sometimes we must do terrible things, to keep even worse things from happening. Killing her mother was a dreadful thing. But if Laeria Amalas had died a month earlier...think how much evil might have been averted."

Komnene kept her eyes closed...but nodded at last.

Caina kept training, kept working.

And one day she looked up and realized that she had spent over a year at the Vineyard.

CHAPTER 11
YOU'RE TURNING HER INTO A WEAPON

The day after her thirteenth birthday, Caina stood on the Vineyard's highest terrace, watching Akragas. The old man seemed relaxed, his stance loose, his eyes wandering.

Caina knew better.

She waited, weight balanced on the balls of her feet, breathing slow and steady. She heard the roar of the waterfall, the buzz of insects and the chirp of birds, felt the cool wind against her face.

But her whole attention was on Akragas, on his arms and legs.

On his hands.

On the hand blurring for her face...

Caina moved.

Her right hand shot up, catching Akragas by the wrist. She thrust his arm over her head and spun, intending to force his arm behind his back. But Akragas spun with the movement, his free hand coming for Caina's head. She released his arm, ducked, and swept her leg, intending to knock the old man from his feet.

Akragas jumped back, the tips of Caina's toes brushing his knees. She spun back to her feet and came at Akragas, refusing to surrender the momentum, palm swinging for his face. Akragas slapped aside her blow, and then the next one, and the next one, and then his foot drove for her leg. Caina hopped aside and kicked at Akragas's extended leg, hoping to knock him off balance. But Akragas anticipated the blow and swiveled, regaining his feet, and his hand shot towards Caina's face. Her block knocked his arm aside, and she tried to counterstrike with her free hand. But Akragas saw the strike coming and blocked it, though just barely.

Then he came at her, launching a barrage of punches and short sharp kicks. Caina ducked and dodged and blocked, her breath coming harder, her heart pounding. Every ounce of her concentration went into blocking Akragas's attacks, and she could spare no effort for a counterattack.

Then one of Akragas's kicks got through, and Caina landed on her back.

Akragas sighed, wiped the sweat from his brow.

"Better," he said. "But still not good enough." He grunted, wiped more sweat from his face. "Though I will have time for only one course at breakfast."

He walked away, still breathing hard.

Later Caina stood in the courtyard garden, a slender steel throwing knife in hand. Sandros stood behind her, arms crossed over his chest.

"Again!" he said. "With your entire arm - it must snap like a bowstring. And roll your wrist - all in one motion! The knife must spin when you throw it. Otherwise it shall flop to the ground like a dead fish, and it is very hard to kill a man with a dead fish, yes?"

Caina took a deep breath and stepped forward, her right arm and shoulder thrown back, the flat of the blade grasped in her fingers. Then her arm shot forward, her entire body going into the motion, her wrist rolling as she released the knife.

The knife spun end over end, burying itself in the shoulder of a straw dummy against the courtyard wall.

"Better!" Sandros said. "But again! The throat, put the knife in the poor fool's throat!"

Caina drew another knife from her sash and flung it.

This time the blade embedded itself in the dummy's groin.

"Well," said Sandros, "you certainly won't have to worry about that fellow fighting back."

"I was aiming for his throat," said Caina.

"Though he will probably spend a great deal of time screaming," said Sandros. "Which, if you were trying to kill him quickly, would rather defeat the point, would it not?"

Later they sparred with practice daggers.

A practice match might drag on for minutes, Sandros explained, but real fights ended in a matter of seconds, of heartbeats. A solid dagger or knife blow to the throat, the heart, or the eye, and a man would die in seconds. Or at least be too incapacitated to fight.

"You are a woman," said Sandros, "or you will be, anyway. So you will be weaker than all but a few men. Almost certainly you will be faster than most, and more skilled than many, thanks to our excellent training. But they will almost always be stronger than you. Fighting hand-to-hand is a mistake."

"Fighting fairly is always a mistake," said Caina, thinking of her father.

Sandros chuckled. "Indeed! Now you are thinking like a Ghost. Your enemies may be stronger than you, but a knife...if you know how to use it, that will negate their strength. Even the strongest man cannot fight when the veins in his throat have been cut. You must strike first..."

"And quickly," said Caina, finishing the proverb Sandros and Akragas and Halfdan had told her over and over again.

"Yes," said Sandros, "you must..."

She jabbed him in the chest, between the ribs.

Sandros flinched, hissing in pain. Then he laughed. "Yes. You are learning."

A few days later Caina awoke with twisting cramps in her stomach. She felt lightheaded, and a little nauseous. At first she thought to push aside the sensations, to go for her run and training with Akragas, but she did not feel up to it.

Instead, she went to Komnene's infirmary.

"This just began today?" said Komnene.

Caina nodded. "I didn't feel quite right before I went to bed. I thought I just pushed myself too hard."

"Before you went to bed, how did you feel?" said Komnene, frowning.

"A little feverish, I guess," said Caina. "I just felt...off."

Komnene nodded, began to mix up one of her teas.

"Did I accidentally poison myself?"

Komnene laughed. "Not at all. You're experiencing your first menstrual cycle, that's all."

Caina blinked. "Oh."

"I'm surprised that it took so long," said Komnene. She was speaking carefully, slowly, as she did when worried. "Though given your...injuries, I suppose it was to be expected." She put the tea into a cloth bag, dropped it into a clay cup. "I suppose your mother didn't warn you what to expect?"

"No," said Caina. "We never talked about anything, except how much she hated me." She shrugged. "But my father had books about medicine in his library. So I know what should happen." She thought for a moment. "Isn't there supposed to be blood?"

Komnene closed her eyes. "There's no bleeding?"

"None," said Caina.

"What Maglarion did to you," began Komnene, "the things he did..."

"He cut me open and drained out my blood for his spells," said Caina. "I know what happened. I was there." It came out harder than she intended.

"He cut too deeply," said Komnene. "You said he would...heal you, somehow, after he finished, but I don't think he was actually healing anything. He was just patching you up enough to stay alive. I think he cut deeply enough to destroy your womb, Caina. The blood...if a woman of childbearing years is not pregnant, her womb will purge itself every month, that's where the blood comes from. You probably don't have much of a womb left, not after what Maglarion did to you. So you'll never..."

"Never have a child, I know," said Caina. "You already told me that."

"But we wouldn't know for sure until you had your first cycle," said Komnene.

"And you told me that too," said Caina, getting to her feet. "I already knew that. I..."

She blinked, and was surprised to see that she was crying.

Komnene guided her back to the chair, helped her to sit.

"I just..." Caina rubbed at her eyes, furious at herself. She had known she would never have children. But it had hit her harder than she had thought. "I just...thought that my father would find a suitable husband for me, and I would have children. That I would be a better mother...a better mother than my mother ever was." She scowled at the floor. "But she took that from me too, didn't she?"

"She did," said Komnene.

"That's why...that's why I'm becoming a nightfighter, isn't it?" said Caina. "Not many women become nightfighters. It's because I can't have children."

"I'm sorry," said Komnene.

Caina scrubbed the tears from her eyes and gave a sharp nod. "Then so be it. I'll become a nightfighter. And if I find someone like my mother, or like Maglarion, I'll make sure they never hurt anyone else ever again."

"Into a weapon," said Komnene, her voice low.

"What?" said Caina, blinking the last of the tears from her eyes.

"Nothing," said Komnene. She rose, took the kettle from the fire, and poured tea into the clay cup. "Here. Drink this. It will help with the cramps."

Caina took the cup, drank. The tea, as usual, did not taste very good, but it spread a gentle warmth through her. "Did you ever have children?"

"No," said Komnene. "Nor did I ever want them, I'm afraid. My father was a bookbinder in Caer Rhyfel, with seven daughters and no sons. I was the youngest, and I saw my sisters get married off one by one to advance my father's business. They all seemed miserable, and I didn't want to end up like them. I preferred to spend my time reading the books in my father's workshop. So when the chance came, I ran away, and joined the Temple of Minaerys in Malarae. I never regretted it."

"Never?" said Caina. "Not even a little?"

"No," said Komnene. "The things I regret came later. After I left the Temple."

"I always wanted a family of my own," said Caina. "It was just my father and me, against my mother. I thought it would be different, someday, when I could have children of my own. That I would be better to them than she was to me."

"You would have been," said Komnene.

"Thank you," said Caina. She shook her head. "Not that it would have been very hard."

"Perhaps you'll find your family elsewhere," said Komnene. "In other things."

After a day or two, Caina felt much better, and went on with her training.

A week later, Akragas sent her to the gate.

Riogan was waiting for her.

Caina had not seen him for a year and a half, not since he had left the Vineyard on some task for Halfdan. He looked much as Caina remembered, the same lean build, the same close-cropped blond hair, the same cold eyes and cold voice.

And still he held her in contempt.

"Child," said Riogan. "You've changed."

"People do that," said Caina.

"You're taller and you've started growing teats," said Riogan. He laughed. "No doubt Halfdan will soon have you made up like a whore, ready to lure men into bed so you can steal their secrets."

"He's been teaching me to fight," said Caina.

"He's been teaching you to kill," said Riogan. "The purpose of fighting is to kill. The purpose of the knife is to kill." For a moment he almost sounded as if he were reciting some long-remembered lesson. "And death isn't pretty, child. All those books you've read, all those stories about wars and swordfights? Did they tell you how the blood will spray across your fingers when you cut a man's throat, how the very air will smell like hot copper? Or if you crush a man's head, his brains will look like oatmeal mixed with blood? Of if you stab a man in the belly, and pierce his entrails, you can smell his own filth, and leave him to wallow in it?"

"I've seen people die," said Caina.

She remembered the sound her mother's head had made as it bounced off the edge of Sebastian Amalas's desk, remembered the dark blood pooling on the floor.

"So you have," said Riogan. "But seeing people die is not the same as killing them yourself. Come. Let us see if you are hard enough."

Caina followed Riogan, apprehensive. For a moment she wondered if he had brought prisoners back to the Vineyard, prisoners that he wanted her to kill in cold blood. They passed through the Vineyard's fortified gate, walking below the walls.

A herd of goats waited below one of the stone watchtowers, staked and leashed in place. A wooden shed stood nearby, and Riogan led Caina inside. Within one of the goats hung from a crossbeam, still alive, its legs tied together.

"Blood," said Riogan. "That necromancer friend of yours was right. It all comes down to blood in the end."

Caina scowled. "Maglarion's not my friend."

"Regardless," said Riogan, picking up a heavy knife. "He was right. Halfdan's been teaching you to kill...and we'll see if you have the stomach for it."

He reached up, grabbed the goat's head, and cut its throat. The animal thrashed against its bonds, the blood draining into a trough running along the floor, and soon died. He cut it down, dumped its corpse in the corner, and retrieved another one from outside. The goat started to panic as soon as it smelled the blood, but the cords held fast, and Riogan hung it from the crossbeam.

"Now," he said, "let's see if you have the stomach for it."

He held the bloody knife out to her, handle first.

Caina took it, staring at the stained blade, and started to laugh.

Riogan blinked.

"Really?" said Caina. "I know that you're trying to scare me, but...seriously? A goat? You're trying to scare me with a goat?"

She reached up, grasped the goat's head, and dragged the knife across its throat. She wasn't as strong as Riogan, and she had to saw the knife back and forth to cut everything. But Sandros had taught her well, and she did not flinch as she felt the blood spatter against her fingers, as the crimson spray splashed into the trough.

Riogan stared at her, expressionless.

Caina laughed. "What, did you expect me to start crying, or to run out screaming because of a little blood? I told you, I've seen people die. What are a few goats next to that?" She gestured with the knife. "Do you want to do the rest of them, or should I?"

They had goat meat for dinner that night.

###

A few weeks later Halfdan summoned Caina to the Vineyard's villa.

He awaited her in the library.

A magus in a black robe stood besides him, a red sash around his waist.

Caina hissed in sudden alarm, reaching for the dagger she now carried everywhere.

Halfdan's hand closed about her wrist. "Calm yourself."

"An interesting reception," said the magus, speaking High Nighmarian with a precise accent. He was tall and thin, with sunken cheeks and a jaw shaded with a close-cropped black beard. "Fiery little thing, isn't she? I do believe she would have plunged that dagger into my chest, if you weren't here to stop her."

"Did he sneak in?" said Caina. "Is he here to spy on us?"

"Suspicious, too," said the magus. "I am going to enjoy this, I think."

"This is Rekan," said Halfdan, "a brother of the Imperial Magisterium. Do you remember what I told you about motivations?"

Caina nodded, keeping her eyes on Rekan. "Find out what your enemy wants, and use it against him."

"The Magisterium puts up a united front in public," said Halfdan, "but like the rest of the Empire, it has factions. Politics. And some brothers and sisters of the Magisterium find that their interests align with ours."

"So he spies for you," said Caina. "Is that why he's here?"

Rekan chuckled. "I think of it as passing along information of mutual interest."

"Yes," said Halfdan. "He's also here to train you."

"To do what?" said Caina.

"To defend against sorcery," said Halfdan.

Again Rekan chuckled. "Insofar as someone without the talent can defend against the arcane sciences, after all. Properly wielded, arcane science can defeat even the most prepared adversary."

"But sorcery has limits," said Halfdan, "and sorcerers, even more so. Fighting a sorcerer is no different than fighting a man with a sword or a bow. A sword or a bow has limitations, and so does sorcery. And if you know where those limitations are, and if you know the limitations of your enemy, you can defeat a magus."

"In theory, of course," said Rekan, glancing at Halfdan. "Shall we begin?"

"Are you ready?" said Halfdan, looking at Caina.

Caina nodded.

"You are being trained as a Ghost," said Rekan. "And that means you have secrets, secrets that the Magisterium would like to know. And a skilled magus can break into another's mind, ferret out its secrets. Or turn that mind into a puppet - control it so thoroughly that the victim doesn't even realize that anything is amiss." His smile widened, his eyes glinting with anticipation. "Do you notice, my dear, how friend Halfdan hasn't told me your name?"

"Just as well," said Caina. "I wouldn't have told you, either."

"There's no need to ask your name," said Rekan, "when I can merely reach into your mind and find it for myself."

He lifted his hand, whispering under his breath. And Caina felt the electric surge of sorcery, her skin crawling, her stomach clenching.

And then Rekan's will battered upon her mind.

Caina gasped and fell back a step. Rekan's will felt like groping fingers, digging and rummaging through her thoughts. She saw the magus smile with pleasure, saw Halfdan frown.

"Tell me your name, child," said Rekan, "I command it."

Rekan's will squeezed against her, compelling her to obey.

And the old familiar fury welled up in Caina. Her mother had done this to her, again and again. Caina had hated it then, had hated her mother...and she hated it now.

"No," she growled, hands shaking with the effort.

Rekan's eyes narrowed, and his outstretched hand curled into a fist.

"You will tell me your name!" he said.

"No!" said Caina. Maglarion had been able to overpower her, to dominate her will. But Maglarion had been powerful beyond the reckoning of most magi. Rekan was stronger than her mother had been...but not by very much.

She filled her mind with rage, her hatred of sorcery, and Rekan's will scrabbled against it.

"Tell me your name!" said Rekan, his will flexing against Caina's thoughts.

"No!" said Caina.

Rekan's mind strained against hers, and Caina's will started to buckle. She pulled up memories - the things her mother had done to her, the things Maglarion had done to her, and let them inspire fresh rage.

She saw Rekan's eyes widen a bit, saw sweat bead on his forehead. Then she pushed against his will, meeting the scrabbling hand of his sorcery with a wall of her fury, and shoved.

Rekan stumbled back a step, staring at her.

Halfdan smiled, briefly.

"She pushed me out!" said Rekan.

"So it would seem," said Halfdan.

"Is she a magus?" demanded Rekan, glaring at Halfdan. "Does she have any talent of her own? A fourteen year old girl should not be able to resist my spells!"

"Her mother had some training at the Magisterium's motherhouse in Artifel, I understand," said Halfdan. "Evidently she used to break into the girl's mind on a regular basis."

"You could have told me that she had been trained!" said Rekan. "Entering a mind is a dangerous business! I could have damaged myself."

"Or you could have damaged her," said Halfdan. "But, no harm done, true? One girl without arcane talent could not possibly harm a skilled wielder of arcane sciences."

The look Rekan shot him was just short of murderous.

"She still hasn't told you her name," said Halfdan. "Try again?"

"You could have told me what was going to happen," said Caina, as she left the library with Halfdan.

She wasn't quite angry. Or she couldn't decide if she wanted to be angry or not. She loathed the magi, hated everything about them, and confronting Rekan had brought a score of dark memories.

On the other hand, the magus had failed to break into her mind. Utterly.

"I could have," said Halfdan, "but that would have defeated the purpose. You'll be spying on the magi, one day, and you'll need to know how to resist their mental attacks."

"And you don't trust him," said Caina.

"Not in the least," said Halfdan. "How did you know?"

"You didn't leave me alone with him," said Caina. "You've left me alone with Akragas, Sandros, Riogan, all the others. But not Rekan."

Halfdan nodded. "By Imperial law, a magus can only enter the mind of another with proper writ from a magistrate. In practice, the magi tend to disregard that law. And some magi have the habit of taking mind-enslaved lovers."

"Oh." That was a revolting thought.

"And Rekan is still a magus," said Halfdan. "I don't trust him at all. He works with the Ghosts because it happens to align with his interests."

"Which are?" said Caina.

"Wealth," said Halfdan. "We bribe him."

"Ah."

"But he would turn on us in a minute, if he thought he could enhance his standing by doing so," said Halfdan.

"So that was why you brought me here to practice," said Caina. "You wanted to...take Rekan down a notch. You knew I could fight him off. You wanted him to fail against a fourteen-year-old girl."

"Very good," said Halfdan. "And you need to learn more about sorcery, anyway. You know the mission of the Ghosts. We defend the people of the Empire against brutal lords, against slavers...and against the magi, or against outlaw sorcerers. So you need to know everything you can about sorcery...and who better to teach you than a magus?"

"So I can know my enemies," said Caina, "and know what weaknesses to use against them."

"Exactly," said Halfdan.

So Rekan became one of Caina's regular teachers.

She did learn a great deal from him. In a fight, he said, magi preferred to use blasts of psychokinetic force, charging their thoughts with the force of fists and clubs, or to stun the minds of their enemies. They also had the power to ward themselves against steel weapons. And some magi, the more powerful ones, could command the earth itself to swallow their enemies, or the wind to turn to ice, or water to erupt from the ground.

But the magi were dependent on their sorcery, Caina realized. They trusted too much in their power, and neglected their bodies. If she could close to hand-to-hand with a magus, she could kill him. Or if she could kill a magus before he could even work a spell, that was better.

She continued to train, and another year passed.

CHAPTER 12
HARVESTING DEATH

Maglarion stood on the balcony and watched the crowds.

The docks of Malarae, the Imperial capital, never grew quiet, not even for a moment. Wagons laden with goods rolled up and down the streets below the inn's balcony, while a forest of masts crowded the harbor and the Megaros River. Ships came from the Empire's farthest corners, and from a score of nations beyond, from New Kyre and Catekharon, from Istarinmul and Anshan, from Alqaarin and Nhabatan. Dozens of languages filled the streets with a constant babble, and the stream of wagons never stopped, climbing the streets to the grand mansions and high towers of the city's nobles and magi, some even reaching the lofty towers of the Imperial Citadel itself, perched upon its mountain spur.

So many people.

Maglarion watched from the inn's balcony, his lip curling with contempt.

Vermin, every last of one of them. Stupid animals, rutting and eating in their own filth. They spawned like rabbits, or perhaps like rats, filling the world with their useless, worthless offspring. They cared about nothing but filling their bellies, or filling the bellies of their brats. Their concerns were petty, material.

Meaningless.

Maglarion had transcended them. He had mastered death itself, had already lived four times longer than even the strongest of them would manage, and he would live longer yet. He was above them, like a man looking down at rats.

Like a god looking down at rats.

He smiled at the thought. A god could do as he pleased with his creation.

And one day Maglarion would put the people of Malarae to very good use indeed. Not yet, not quite. He had a great deal of work to do first. But...soon, very soon.

And then their lives would have more meaning than they had ever dreamed.

His left eye, the eye that was not flesh, saw their potential.

Maglarion turned and descended from the balcony, into the inn.

Malarae's dockside inns were well-known for their danger, but the Grey Fish Inn had a particularly evil reputation. According to rumor, if a man drank too much in the Grey Fish, he might wake up naked in the gutter, his possessions gone - or he might wake up manacled to the oar of a Kyracian galley, or chained in the hold of an Istarish slaver.

Or worse things might happen to him.

Maglarion smiled.

Worse things had happened.

The common room was empty, save for the innkeeper, a sullen, doughy man named Drugen. Or he had been sullen, at least, until Maglarion shattered his will and took control of his mind. Drugen still acted the same, spoke the same - and it would take a sharp-eyed observer to notice the glassy cast in the fat innkeeper's eyes.

Drugen was not his own man any longer.

"Master," said Drugen.

"Take me to the cellar," said Maglarion. "I wish to resume my work."

"Of course, Master," said Drugen, hurrying to a door behind the bar. He slid back the massive iron bolt, undid the lock, and opened the door. Stone stairs descended into the darkness, and Maglarion hobbled down them, his cane scratching against the steps. The door boomed shut behind him, the lock slamming home. Maglarion approved. No mere lock could contain him, of course, but he did not want any of his...experiments to escape.

The Grey Fish Inn had quite an extensive cellar. Drugen had once dabbled in slave trading, snatching victims from the streets and selling them to the Istarish slavers for a considerable profit. Later, fear of the Emperor's Ghosts had forced him to stop, but the cellars had remained - deep, dark, and soundproof.

Maglarion had a better use for them.

He walked to the table in the center of the cellar, his left eye unhindered by the darkness. A row of newly made bloodcrystals stood in a row atop it, alongside the curled Maatish scroll. A stack of papers held his notes, the records of his experiments.

"Is anyone there?" came a cracked, shaking voice.

A man hung in iron shackles from the wall. Ikhana's men had

kidnapped him from one of the dockside tenements.

"Have no fear," said Maglarion. "It's only me."

He lifted the patch from his left eye, ghostly green light spilling over the cellar.

The shackled man shied away from the light.

"Please," he whispered. "Let...let me go. I have a wife, a daughter."

"I know," said Maglarion, examining the row of bloodcrystals. "Your daughter was...four years old? Five? I killed her first, in front of your wife. She screamed and begged me to spare the child, even offered to go to my bed, if I would but spare the girl. After I killed the child, I killed your wife, slowly, draining away her blood drop by drop until she grew cold and limp."

Maglarion was watching, so he saw the exact moment when the prisoner's mind snapped. The man bellowed and raved, flinging himself against his shackles until the blood ran down his wrists and ankles. Maglarion suspected that a charged emotional state lent all the more power to the stolen life energies. Savor to the stew, as it were.

Besides, to watch these petty mortals break, to see them shatter, was something of a thrill.

He took a moment to refresh his memory with one of the scroll's spells, and then picked up a dagger and a bloodcrystal, the one made from the blood of the man's wife. The prisoner thrashed and cursed as Maglarion approached, his eyes filled with grief and madness.

Maglarion gestured, summoning power. The man went rigid as the spell held him in place, his rage no match for Maglarion's arcane power.

Then Maglarion lifted the dagger and began to cut.

He severed the tendons in the man's wrist, making sure to leave the veins intact. He worked the dagger over the prisoner's arms and chest, cutting deep furrows, poking the blade into the nerves below the skin. The man could not scream, not with Maglarion's spell holding him, but sweat poured down his face, and his eyes bulged in agony.

Which reminded Maglarion to put them out.

Some time later, Maglarion stepped back, wiping blood from his forehead. The prisoner was still alive, but reduced to a crippled husk of a man. If he survived his injuries, he would be helpless for the rest of his life, his body ruined by Maglarion's blade.

A perfect test.

Maglarion pressed the bloodcrystal into the prisoner's ragged wounds and whispered another spell.

Green light flared in the crystal's black depths. The bloodcrystal shivered in Maglarion's grasp and shrank, the green glow spilling over the man's torn flesh.

And then the prisoner's wounds began to heal.

The hideous cuts vanished, the skin knitting itself shut, the wounds closing as if they had never been. Maglarion released his spell, and the man's arms and legs shook as the tendons repaired themselves. White fluid filled his eye sockets, and a moment later his eyes returned, wide and terrified. The regeneration continued as the life energy from the bloodcrystal poured into the man's flesh, restoring him.

And then the bloodcrystal vanished into nothingness, and the prisoner was healed.

In fact, he had gotten younger.

Maglarion gripped the prisoner's chin, turning his face back and forth. The man had been in his early forties. Now he looked no more than twenty, his body lean and muscled, his face bright with the energy of youth.

Interesting. He hadn't anticipated that, not at all.

"What," whispered the prisoner, "what did you do to me?"

"It healed you," said Maglarion. "The stolen life force of your wife, stored in the bloodcrystal. It even rejuvenated you." He smiled. "So in a way, I killed your wife...and forced you to eat her. Ironic, really, if you think about it."

The prisoner started to scream and rave again, thrashing at his chains. It was rather annoying.

Fortunately, Maglarion had no further use for him, and cut the prisoner's throat. The man thrashed for a few moments, drowning in his own blood, and then died.

Maglarion felt it. His left eye, the eye that was not flesh, saw the power released by the man's death, the dark energy crackling free. It also saw the power...captured, sucked down towards a small wooden table in the corner of the cellar.

He smiled, retrieved his cane, and crossed the room.

His own bloodcrystal, the one he had made from the blood of Laeria Amalas's virgin daughter, sat on the corner table. It was perhaps half again the size of a large man's fist, grown potent with the lives of his victims over the last two years. Even as he watched, the thing seemed to swell a little larger as it drank the life of the man hanging in chains from the wall.

And it would continue to grow, until at last he was ready.

Time for another test.

Maglarion slashed his left palm with the dagger, his own blood welling forth. It hurt, but physical pain had long ago ceased to mean anything to him. He put his right hand on the jagged bloodcrystal and whispered a spell. Arcane power surged through him, and he tapped a portion of the bloodcrystal's strength, the tiniest part of its stored energy.

The wound on his hand sealed, the skin smooth and unmarked.

His smiled widened.

He was close now, very close. A few more years of work, and then he would at last ascend to true immortality. He would leave the flesh behind forever, stand above the world of common mortals like a god towering over insects.

But first, he had more work to do.

Best to get on with it.

Maglarion left the cellar, leaving the dead man hanging in his chains.

###

He washed the blood away and put on better clothes, covering his left eye with the patch once more.

No sense in terrifying the poor fool before it was necessary.

Ikhana waited for him in the common room, cold as ever. Besides her stood a stout figure wrapped in a heavy cloak. No doubt the cloak was meant for anonymity, but the richness of the material rather gave it away.

A lord of the Empire.

Maglarion hid his smile and approached, making sure to lean on his came.

"He came, Master," said Ikhana.

"So I see," said Maglarion. "May I welcome you, my lord?"

The stout figure drew back his hood. The nobility of the Empire divided into petty factions, and Maglarion never bothered to keep them straight. But one of those factions, the Restorationists, desired to restore slavery and see the magi returned to power. They often worked with the magi...and with outlaw sorcerers like Maglarion.

And the stout man, Lord Haeron Icaraeus, was one of the most powerful Restorationists lords in the Empire.

Where he led, others would follow.

"So," said Haeron Icaraeus. He had a thick, corpulent face, and a receding hairline, but eyes that glittered with deep cunning. "You are the famous Maglarion. I have heard so much about you. I believe the Ghosts offer fifty thousand denarii for your head, and the Magisterium thirty-five thousand."

Maglarion bowed. "The Ghosts are fools, my lord, as you well know. And the Magisterium...let us say that many brothers and sisters of the Magisterium recognize that the ban on necromancy is foolish."

"Perhaps," said Lord Haeron. "But I shall be blunt. How can you be of use to me?"

Maglarion smiled. "How would you like to live forever?"

Lord Haeron remained impassive, but Maglarion saw the lustful glitter in his eye.

Yes, he would put this fool to very good use, indeed.

CHAPTER 13
ASSASSINS

A few days after her fifteenth birthday, Caina blinked in astonishment, her heart hammering, sweat pouring down her face.

It was a cool morning in the Vineyard, the terrace chill beneath her bare feet. A breeze blew down from the hills, and she saw the sun just beginning to peek over the eastern hills.

She also saw Akragas lying sprawled at her feet, breathing hard, eyes wide with surprise.

It had been so...easy. She had seen the hole in his defenses, assumed it had been a trap. But he had tried to compensate, tried to change his stance. So Caina attacked with all her strength and speed, throwing everything she had into the opening, expecting any moment for Akragas's trap to close around her.

But there had been no trap. He had simply been too slow to stop her.

Akragas grunted, sat up.

"Did I hurt you?" said Caina. "I didn't hurt you, did I?"

Akragas barked out a laugh. "I have been teaching you to hurt people, yes? So if you did hurt me, it would be my own fault." He got to his feet, shaking his head. "I thought I would have ample time to work around that opening. But I am getting too old, too slow. And you are getting too fast." He sighed. "And now I will have no time for breakfast. Or a nap afterward."

Caina blinked. For over three years, she had sparred with Akragas almost every day.

She had never expected to beat him.

"I'm sorry," she said at last.

Akragas snorted. "Since you are so fast, why do you not run to the

101

kitchens and fetch an old man his breakfast? Getting beaten by a fifteen-year-old girl works up quite an appetite, no?"

Caina smiled, and ran for the kitchens.

Later Halfdan summoned her to the library.

He sat at one of the tables, frowning at a stack of letters. Rekan waited nearby, his expression souring as Caina approached. She had spent a great deal of time with the magus, learning how to defend from sorcery, and their mutual dislike had only deepened.

And much to Caina's satisfaction, he still had failed to learn her name.

Riogan leaned against a shelf, sharpening a dagger.

"Ah, child," said Halfdan. He always called her "child" in front of Rekan. "It's time you left the Vineyard."

"Why?" said Caina.

"Because we need you," said Halfdan. "There's trouble. What can you tell me about the Empire's nobility?"

Rekan frowned. "This is a waste of time…"

Halfdan raised his hand, and Rekan scowled, but stopped talking.

"They have three factions," said Caina. "The Loyalists support the Emperor, oppose the return of slavery, and," she glanced at Rekan, "sensibly oppose letting the Magisterium rule the Empire once more."

Rekan's scowl deepened.

"The Militarists," said Caina, "want the Lord Commanders of the Legion to elect the Emperor, not the nobles. And the Restorationists want to restore slavery, and restore the magi to control of the Empire. The Loyalists are friendly to the Ghosts, the Militarists indifferent, and the Restorationists hostile."

"Very good," said Halfdan. "And what can you tell me about Lord Haeron Icaraeus?"

"The fat bastard," muttered Riogan. It was the first time he had spoken.

"He's a Lord from the Cyrican provinces," said Caina. "One of the most powerful and influential of the Restorationists."

"And why is that significant?" said Halfdan.

"Because," said Caina, "the Cyrican provinces are the only ones in the Empire that allow slavery. Cyrica broke away from Istarinmul, during the War of the Fourth Empire, and offered to join our Empire. But only on the condition that the Cyrican lords would get to keep their slaves."

Riogan snorted. "Quite the little scholar you've trained there, Halfdan."

Halfdan smiled. "Perhaps that explains why Rekan has yet to break into her mind."

Riogan's eyes narrowed, and Rekan's scowl deepened further, but neither man said anything.

"Anyway, you're right," said Halfdan. "The Cyrican lords kept their slaves, and they want to expand slaveholding into the rest of the Empire. The most powerful Restorationist lords are from Cyrica, and of them, Haeron Icaraeus is by far the most influential."

"So Lord Icaraeus is an enemy of the Ghosts," said Caina.

"Of the Ghosts, the Emperor, and the commoners of the Empire," said Halfdan. "He has contracts with the assassin brotherhoods of Istarinmul and Anub-Kha, the Kindred and the Red Hands, and sends them after his enemies. He frequently hires outlaw magi and foreign sorcerers, and uses their sciences against his opponents. The slavers' brotherhood of Istarinmul is allied with him, and he permits them to raid inside the Empire for captives. And he kills any Ghost informant or agent within his reach."

Caina remembered the Istarish slavers descending upon her father's villa and shuddered.

"And he's gotten worse lately, much worse," said Halfdan. "A gang of Istarish slavers have been kidnapping people from the streets of Malarae, smuggling them to the slave markets in Istarinmul and Cyrica. They've even infiltrated the Disali hills, and have been kidnapping Disali peasants and travelers."

Riogan scoffed. "That's foolish. There are too many miles of road between Disalia and the sea. Easier to snatch slaves from the coasts and escape to a ship."

"Not if the profits are worth the risk," said Rekan. "Disali slaves can fetch a high price."

"Why?" said Riogan.

"In some parts of the world, the Disali are an exotic curiosity. Disali men are tough and strong, and valued in the mines," said Rekan. "And the Disali women...well, some Anshani satraps have a taste for Disali women."

"That's contemptible," said Caina.

Rekan shrugged. "It is merely the way of the world." Caina suspected he would enjoy a an enslaved Disali woman in his bed.

"So we're going to shut them down," said Halfdan, "and you're going to help."

"How?" said Caina.

"I will disguise myself as Marcus Antali, an independent merchant," said Halfdan. "Riogan will be Raccard, a mercenary guard in my employ. And you, I think...we shall disguise you as my daughter Talia. Marcus Antali will bring you along in hopes that your beauty would ensnare a noble-born husband, or at least a wealthy one."

Caina nodded. "As you say...father."

It felt strange, saying that. Almost four years now, Sebastian Amalas had been dead, and Caina thought of him often. But Halfdan and the Ghosts had taken his place. If she had to masquerade as Halfdan's daughter to stop men like Maglarion and women like her mother, then so be it.

They left at dawn.

Caina dressed in a gown of blue wool, with boots and belt of soft black leather. Komnene helped her wash and style her hair. Caina felt odd, wearing a gown again, but she supposed she would get used to it.

"She'll stick out like a thief in a satrap's harem," said Riogan. He dressed as he always did, black leather over chain mail, daggers at his belt and spear in hand.

Halfdan shrugged, clad in the robe and cap of a prosperous merchant. "That's the point. How many fifteen-year-old girls look comfortable when their fathers try to sell them off like a side of meat? She'll learn social graces soon enough."

Caina wondered what he meant by that.

She kept a dagger in her belt and a pair of throwing knives hidden beneath each sleeve. After so many hours training with Akragas and Sandros, she would feel naked if she went anywhere without a weapon.

They left the Vineyard by pack mule, the beasts making their way along the narrow roads. Caina watched the Vineyard recede behind them and felt a pang. It had been her home for almost four years, a refuge from the terrible things that Maglarion had done to her.

But it was time to move on.

It was time to start fighting against those things.

And it was good to travel again. She had seen so little of the Empire, of the world.

"We're going east," said Caina.

"Aye," said Halfdan.

"I thought we were going west," said Caina.

"Why's that?" said Halfdan.

"If the slavers are taking their victims to the sea," said Caina, "then they would go west, towards the Megaros River and the Bay of Empire...no. They're taking their captives east, towards the Narrow Sea, aren't they?"

"They might be," said Halfdan. "All shipping coming out of the Narrow Sea has to travel through Arzaxia, and thousands of ships pass through Arzaxia every year. A clever slaver could easily smuggle his captives through the city. And the northwestern coast of the Narrow Sea is lightly populated, nothing but fens and swamps. Plenty of places for slave ships to come and go unobserved."

A few days later, they reached the Vytaagi swamps.

The Vytaagi had once been a nation of barbarians, following the other tribes during the great invasions of the Second Empire. After the Legions and the warrior-Emperors of the Second Empire had been victorious, the remnants of the Vytaagi had accepted the Emperor's authority and settled in the swamps along the northwestern coast of the Narrow Sea. Now the province of Vytaagia was a quiet backwater, with no major cities or towns, the Vytaagi themselves making a living from fishing, farming, and hunting their swamps.

The perfect place, Caina supposed, for slave traders to operate undetected.

"We may have made a mistake, father," said Caina as they reached the first village.

"Oh?" said Halfdan.

"You couldn't possibly find a wealthy husband for your daughter here," said Caina.

Riogan laughed at that.

The Vytaagi villages all looked alike. Built upon grassy islands, the houses stood on high beams, no doubt to keep flooding at bay. Or perhaps the Vytaagi built their houses upon stilts to keep out the vicious crocodiles that wallowed in the swamps. Wooden planks covered the streets, and rickety stairs led up to the houses. Men and women alike wore clothes of loose linen, though some men wore vests and belts of crocodile leather.

"Hunters," said Riogan, pointing with the butt of his spear. "Among the Vytaagi, only a man who slew a crocodile can wear leather made from its hide."

Every village had its own tavern, a roomy hall standing upon thick logs. Inside the Vytaagi men sat around peat fires, telling stories and drinking a vile beer brewed from the swamp plants. And Halfdan visited every tavern, Caina and Riogan trailing behind them.

Marcus Antali was well-known among the Vytaagi.

She watched Halfdan with amazement.

He held the Vytaagi enthralled, buying, selling, and telling stories. He had a remarkable gift for stories, and could hold an audience rapt. The Vytaagi roared with laughter and clapped at all the right places, and more than once Caina found herself laughing with them.

Even Riogan smiled, once or twice.

And in return, the Vytaagi told Halfdan things. Most of it was trivial - grumblings about taxes, complaints about the weather and the crocodiles, but some of it was not. Istarish ships had been sighted in the Narrow Sea, and had sent canoes into the swamps. The Vytaagi hated the Istarish, had nothing to do with them, but the Istarish were smart enough to avoid the Vytaagi villages. But the Vytaagi hunters spied on them, and saw the Istarish canoes carrying cargo to Kaunauth.

"Where's that?" murmured Caina to Riogan.

"Village a few miles from here," answered Riogan, his eyes roving over the tavern. "Smugglers' nest. You can buy or sell anything there, including people. Big lagoon, room for a lot of ships. Every smuggler, slaver, pirate, and corsair on the Narrow Sea weighs anchor in Kaunauth, sooner or later."

Halfdan told a few more stories, and then they left the tavern.

"We're going to Kaunauth, I take it?" said Riogan.

"Aye," said Halfdan. "Word is a man named Jakob operates out of a tavern near the lagoon, a man who takes cargoes from the Istarish canoes. And we're going to talk to him."

"Is that wise?" said Riogan, glancing at Caina. "Walking into a den like Kaunauth with a girl?"

Halfdan shrugged. "I'll tell them that Marcus Antali has suffered business reverses as of late, and is interested in entering the slave trade."

"Or you could always offer to sell me to them," said Caina.

Halfdan laughed. "Confident, isn't she?"

"Or foolish," said Riogan.

"Hopefully it won't come to that," said Halfdan. "I merely plan to look around, gather information. Then we'll send a letter to the Lord Governor of Vytaagia Province, and the militia will come, burn Kaunauth to the ground, and shut down the Istarish slavers. And if we're fortunate, we'll find proof that Haeron Icaraeus was involved."

"That would be sweet," said Riogan, lifting his spear. "Perhaps we'll have the proof we need to burn the fat old bastard ourselves.

###

They reached the town of Kaunauth the next day.

Caina had thought that Koros was disreputable, but the fishing village was tidy compared to Kaunauth. Ships from a dozen different nations crowded the lagoon, pulled up to rough stone quays. Ramshackle wooden buildings ringed the lagoon in no discernable pattern, forming a wild maze of narrow, stinking alleys. Hard-eyed men walked those alleys, hands near their weapons, and more than one cast acquisitive glances in Caina's direction.

She was very glad she had not come here alone. And even gladder of the knives hidden beneath her sleeves.

"This is the place," said Riogan, stopping before sagging wooden building that might have been a house, or a barn, or perhaps a tavern.

"You know it?" said Halfdan.

"Oh, aye," said Riogan. "Been here once or twice before, doing your little errands. Watch yourself. This is a rough place, even for Kaunauth."

But the inside of the tavern was almost deserted. The only light came from burning peat piled in a central fire pit. Six men sat on benches, nursing clay cups of beer. Five of them looked like common thugs, but the sixth...

Caina stared at him, fascinated.

The sixth looked like a killer. He rose from the bench with fluid grace, glanced at Caina once, and then his cold eyes returned to Halfdan and Riogan. His hands never strayed far from the sheathed sword and dagger at his belt.

As she watched, the man drew a dagger. Halfdan and Riogan tensed, but the man merely reversed his grip on the blade and started to clean his fingernails.

Caina stared at his hand, at the way his knuckles tightened against the dagger's handle. Something about that seemed familiar, somehow...

"So," said the man, "you must be Marcus Antali."

"And you, I assume," said Halfdan, "are Jakob?"

"Some call me that." Jakob squinted at his fingernails for a moment. "I presume you have business for me?"

"I do," said Halfdan. "I've heard rumors that Istarish slave traders have returned to the Narrow Sea."

"A man of your age should know better than to listen to the idle gossip of housewives," said Jakob, gesturing with the dagger. Something about the movement screamed a warning in Caina's brain, but she could not explain it. "So slavers have returned to the Narrow Sea, hmm? Will you run to the Lord Governor, call the militia down upon our heads?"

"Hardly," said Halfdan. "I am a man of business. If there's profit to be made, I make it...in any merchandise. And I can supply you with merchandise."

"The girl?" said Jakob, not looking at Caina. "You wish to sell her? She's pretty enough, would fetch a fair price in Istarinmul or Anshan."

"My daughter?" said Halfdan. "Perhaps if she gets mouthy. Her mother never shut up, either."

Jakob and Halfdan shared a laugh at that.

"But, no," said Halfdan, "I have other things in mind. I heard you're shipping slaves down from the Disali hills. Wouldn't it be cheaper to take them from the Vytaagi villages?"

"Too much trouble," grumbled Jakob. "These damned swamps have never been mapped, and the Vytaagi are good with those bows. Kidnapping peasants from Disalia Province and shipping them through the swamps is difficult, but less trouble than kidnapping the Vytaagi out of their villages…assuming we can even find the damned villages."

Halfdan grinned. "But the Vytaagi trust me. I've been selling them baubles for years. I know where all the villages are. And I could show you the way…for a cut of the profits, of course."

Caina felt her lip crinkle in disgust and forced her face to remain still. Halfdan…almost seemed to have become someone else. She knew him as the levelheaded Ghost circlemaster. Now he had become an obsequious, grasping merchant, one eager to sell his customers to slavers in exchange for a few coins. It was almost as if he had disappeared and become another man.

And Jakob was buying it.

"You've interested me," said Jakob. "Come out back and we'll talk. Leave your pet thug and your daughter here, and we can work out the details."

He flipped the dagger and slid it back into its sheath.

And Caina realized why that seemed so familiar.

She grabbed Halfdan's elbow.

"His dagger," she murmured.

"What about it?" said Halfdan.

Caina swallowed. It sounded so foolish, but she could not shake the feeling that it was important. "He holds it the exact same way that Riogan does."

"Antali?" said Jakob. "Is something amiss?"

For a moment they stared at each other.

Then Jakob jerked his head. Two of the thugs shot to their feet, moving to block the door. Halfdan drew his short sword from his belt, and Riogan adjusted his grip on his spear, the blade glimmering.

"What is this?" said Halfdan. "I am only a simple merchant, trying to turn a profit…"

Jakob laughed, drew his dagger in one hand and his sword in another.

"You're no merchant, old man," said Jakob. "Our employer warned us that the Ghosts would come sniffing around…and, well, here you are. Looks like the old devil was right."

"And you're no slaver, either," said Halfdan.

Jakob grinned, white teeth flashing in his face. "Oh? Then what am I?"

"An assassin of the Kindred, I should wager," said Halfdan. "Let me guess. From the Arzaxia family? Or do I merit an assassin from Malarae itself?"

"Malarae," said Jakob, his eyes shifting to Riogan. "You two. Take the girl. Keep her unharmed; we can sell her later. You three, deal with the old man. I'll take this one myself."

The men fanned out to carry out Jakob's orders. Three converged on Halfdan, two moved towards Caina, and Jakob himself moved towards Riogan, face hard, blades raised. Riogan started to circle him, spear drawn back for a stab.

They were going to die.

Caina could see it. Four against two was not a winning combination. Riogan was deadly in a fight, but Jakob looked just as skilled. Halfdan would not doubt kill one or even two of his attackers, but the third would take him.

They were going to die.

Unless Caina did something right away.

She began to cry.

The thugs approaching her laughed, and she saw disgust ripple across Riogan's face. Caina shied away from them, sobbing.

Her right hand closed around her dagger's hilt, the motion shielded behind her body.

"Come along, my pretty," said the nearest thug, grinning, "and we'll have ourselves a good time, eh?"

Strike first, Akragas had always said.

The thug's thick hand closed about Caina's left wrist, yanking her towards him.

She spun into the movement, and buried her dagger in his throat.

The thug screamed, or tried to scream, but Caina's blade had lodged in his windpipe. She ripped the dagger free, tearing the wound open, and the man fell to his knees, clutching at his neck, his blood hot against her knuckles.

Goats, she thought. It was just like killing those goats.

The second thug yelled and stabbed at her with his sword. But his form was pitiful, his stance wrong, his movements slow and sluggish. Akragas could have taken him down in the space of two heartbeats. Caina sidestepped and brought her dagger up. He jerked back, but not fast enough, and the side of her blade sliced across his throat. The thug staggered, and Caina stabbed up, the dagger angling up beneath his jaw and into his mouth.

He fell besides his companion, choking.

The entire thing had taken only a few seconds.

Riogan dueled Jakob, sword and spear and dagger forming a blurred web of steel. Halfdan backed towards the wall, the three other thugs prowling around him. He was fighting defensively, but he could not hold off three men forever.

So Caina rolled her wrist, one of the throwing knives dropping from its sheath into her hand. She flung back her arm and shoulder and then hurled the knife, her entire body snapping like a bowstring.

The knife buried itself in the nearest thug's calf. The man stumbled, and Halfdan darted to the left. His sword flickered out, and blood sprayed from the thug's throat. The two survivors hesitated, trying to choose between Caina and Halfdan. Then Halfdan bellowed and attacked, sword rising and falling, and the thugs backed away.

Which gave Caina all the opening she needed.

She leapt forward and fell upon the nearest man's back, her dagger raised. Sandros's words echoed in her mind, and she stabbed him once, twice, thrice, aiming her dagger between his ribs each time.

He should really have worn armor.

Finally the man screamed and knocked Caina off his back, but he fell to his knees, blood tricking from his lips. She scrambled backwards as Halfdan killed the remaining thug with a quick thrust. Then she rolled to her feet as Riogan and Jakob continued their dance of blades. They both moved so fast that she couldn't hit Jakob with a throwing knife, and if she tried to close, he would probably gut her...

Then Riogan sidestepped, whipping the butt of his spear in a circle. The heavy wood smashed across Jakob's face, snapping his head around. Several bloody teeth fell to the floor. Riogan reversed his spear and drove its point into Jakob's belly.

Jakob fell, gasping, and Riogan finished him off with a dagger to the throat.

Caina took a deep breath, trying to steady her breathing.

The entire fight had taken little more than a minute. Perhaps less. Sandros had been right.

A serious fight did not last very long at all.

"You made a mistake," said Riogan, pulling his spear from Jakob's gut.

That made a mess.

"Aye," said Halfdan, wiping his sword clean on a dead man's shirt. "I knew the slavers would be on their guard against the Ghosts. But to have a Kindred assassin waiting for us...no, I did not suspect that. We'd have been finished, if not for Caina." He looked at her. "Good work."

Caina nodded.

"How did you know he was a Kindred assassin?" said Riogan.

Caina shrugged. "I didn't. But he held his dagger in exactly the same way you do."

Riogan's expression tightened.

Halfdan ignored him. "Are you all right? Killing your first man is hard."

"I'm fine," said Caina. She knelt, retrieved her blades, and cleaned them. "And these two weren't my first. I killed my mother."

"You're sure?" said Halfdan.

"I am," said Caina. She looked at the men she had killed and felt...very little. Satisfaction, mostly. "They would killed us. Or they would have killed you, raped me, and then sold me to slavers. Either way, they deserved it."

"Damn it," said Riogan. "You wanted to turn the girl into a weapon, well, she's a weapon. Do you think it might be a good idea to get away from here before someone notices all the dead bodies?"

Halfdan shook himself. "You're right. Check the corpses, first. And search the tavern, quickly."

"For what?" said Riogan, but he knelt and started rummaging through Jakob's clothing.

"Anything interesting," said Halfdan. "This was a trap for us. I want to know if the slavers only suspected that the Ghosts might show up, or if they knew for certain."

Riogan pulled a crumpled piece of paper from Jakob's belt, smoothed it out. "Looks like they knew. Come read this."

Halfdan walked over, and Caina followed. It was expensive paper. Neat lines of High Nighmarian marched across the sheet.

"To my friends of the Kindred," the note read. "As you undoubtedly know, my patron and I have commissioned the Istarish slavers' brotherhood to procure slaves from Disalia and the lands around the Narrow Sea. This will attract the attention of the Ghosts, and while I do not fear their meager interference, I do not wish to deal with the annoyance. Therefore, I wish you to dispatch assassins to Vytaagi province to hunt down and kill any Ghost agents. My patron will pay a bounty of three thousand denarii for any slain Ghost."

The note had neither signature nor seal at the bottom.

But Caina felt her blood run cold nonetheless.

"Haeron Icaraeus," said Riogan. "The fat bastard. Has to be."

"No," said Caina. "Maglarion wrote this."

Halfdan frowned. "How do you know?"

Caina pointed. "I saw him write notes. I'd recognize his handwriting anywhere." She shivered. "I couldn't forget it, no matter how hard I try."

"Then he's working with Haeron Icaraeus," said Riogan. "That must be the 'patron' the note mentions."

"Why?" said Caina. "Why would he work with an Imperial noble, even a Restorationist one?"

Halfdan had said that the best way to defeat an enemy was to understand his motivation, to understand what he wanted. But she had no idea what Maglarion wanted. She had heard him talk for weeks to his students about immortality and power. But Maglarion had already lived for centuries, and he was probably stronger than nearly any other sorcerer or magus.

What more did he want?

"We can discuss it later," said Riogan, handing the note to Halfdan. "Let's go."

They searched the tavern and found nothing else of interest. Riogan did, however, find several amphorae filled with oil, no doubt for cooking. He spilled most of them on the floor, and kicked the final one into the peat fire.

The floor caught fire at once, the flames spreading over the floorboards and the clothes of the dead.

"Time to go," said Halfdan, and they left Kaunauth.

CHAPTER 14
THE KINDRED

Things happened very quickly after that.

They fled Kaunauth and headed north to Mors Insidion, a town built around the tomb and mortuary temple of Emperor Insidion of the Second Empire. The town also served as the capital of Vytaagia Province. Halfdan left a message with the Lord Governor, and the town's militia marched. Caina later found out that the militia surprised the Istarish slavers at Kaunauth, killed dozens of them, scattered the rest, and freed hundreds of captives taken from the Disali and Saddai provinces.

No one suspected that the Ghosts had been involved.

Caina smiled at the thought.

###

The day after the militia left, she decided to talk to Riogan.

They were staying Mors Insidion's chief inn, an establishment with the somewhat mordant name of The Dead Emperor, while Halfdan communicated with the local Ghosts. Fortunately, the inn was comfortable, and the sitting room even had its own fireplace.

Caina found Riogan sitting before the fireplace, sharpening his blades.

"You knew Jakob," she said.

Riogan grunted, but did not look up. "I did not. Never saw the man before in my life."

"But he fought the way you do," said Caina. "Like he'd been trained the same way. He held his dagger the same way you're holding yours right now. And when I told that to Halfdan, he realized Jakob was a Kindred assassin. Whatever that is."

Riogan looked at her and smirked. "You don't know what the Kindred are, girl? All those books you read, and you've never heard of the Kindred?"

"Then what are they?" said Caina.

"Assassins."

"Obviously. But what kind of assassins?"

"The last brotherhood of assassins left in the Empire," said Riogan. "During the Fourth Empire, when the magi ruled, there were a dozen competing assassin brotherhoods. The Ghosts helped the Emperor overthrow the magi and return to power, and the assassins' brotherhoods were hunted down and banished. But the Kindred remained. They're organized into five clans, one for each of the great cities of the Empire. They're the favored assassins of the magi and the Restorationists."

"And you used to be a Kindred assassin," said Caina, "didn't you?"

His cold eyes grew colder.

"Do you really want to know?"

Caina shrugged. "I already figured it out, didn't I? How did you go from a Kindred assassin to a Ghost nightfighter?"

"I started as a slave."

"How?"

"Twenty years ago," said Riogan. "We lived near Caer Mardon. My father was dead or gone, and my mother was a whore. And Lord Haeron Icaraeus had just started buying slaves. So my mother sold me to them."

"My mother sold me, too," said Caina.

"Do you think I care?" said Riogan, flipping his dagger into the air and catching it. "At least your mother had the wit to set a better price. My mother only got a few silver coins for me. I was...eight, at the time. Maybe nine. I can't be bothered to remember." His eyes grew distant. "They took me to Istarinmul, to the great slave market there...and the Kindred bought me. That's how they recruit their assassins, you know. Buy them young, and raise them up to know nothing but death and fighting."

"And you hated it," said Caina.

Riogan laughed. "Not at all! I loved it. I loved killing fat merchants and lords, seeing the terror in their eyes. I loved the power, I loved knowing that so long as I had this," he patted his spear, "that no man could harm me. And the Kindred paid me well. Whatever I wanted, I had. Gold and wine and the finest weapons and armor. And women and girls, too. When I saw one I wanted, I took her, whether she willed it or not. I had my first girl when I was fourteen, some slave girl I bought in Istarinmul...she was no older than you are now, I think."

Caina edged away from him, just a bit.

"It was a fine life," said Riogan. "Do you think I felt guilty about it? That I cried myself to sleep, the way you probably do, weeping about all the innocent blood on my hands? No! Every man and woman I killed, I would do it again. I regret nothing."

"Then," said Caina, "why are you a Ghost, and not a Kindred assassin?"

Riogan said nothing. He remained silent for so long that Caina thought he had decided to ignore her.

She turned to go.

"Haeron Icaraeus," said Riogan.

"What about him?" said Caina.

"He hired the Kindred to kill a rival lord," said Riogan. "I received the contract. I was to kill the lord, his wife, and their daughter. I broke into their townhouse in the middle of the night." His voice grew so quiet that she could barely hear him. "And...I found the daughter first. A girl. Eleven or twelve. No older than you were, when we found you in Maglarion's little pit. She saw me. I expected her to scream. I wanted to cut her throat before she could scream. But she didn't scream. She didn't even cry. She just kept staring at me. And...I couldn't do it. I couldn't kill her. I left."

"You had mercy," said Caina, astonished.

"A weakness," spat Riogan. "A weakness I should have excised from myself. I had broken a contract. My life was forfeit, and my brothers and sisters from the Kindred hunted me. Then I found Halfdan...and he took me in." He laughed, testing the edge of his dagger with a fingertip. "That's what he does, you know. He finds men and women that have been broken, and turns them into weapons. He turned Komnene into a poisoner. And you...you're a weapon now, too, little girl. I saw how you cut down Jakob's hirelings. I didn't think you had it in you, but you do."

Caina didn't want to think about that. "Why do you stay with the Ghosts?"

"Because," said Riogan, "someday, I'll take revenge on Haeron Icaraeus, for all he did to me. If he hadn't sent me to kill that girl, I'd still be in the Kindred. I would not have these...doubts, these weaknesses. My life would be better." He lifted his spear. "So someday I'll take this and shove it into his fat belly."

Caina said nothing.

"Don't look at me like that," said Riogan. "You're just like me. I thought you might be innocent...but you're not, not any more. You want someone dead, too. I can see it in your eyes. You want to kill Maglarion, the same way I want to kill Icaraeus." He leaned closer, eyes on her face. "Admit it. You're just like me. I want to kill Haeron Icaraeus for what he did to me. And you want to kill Maglarion for what he did to you."

Caina closed her eyes. "Yes."

"You see?" said Riogan. "I thought...perhaps you might be an innocent, like that girl. But you're not. You're a weapon, like me, and all you want is revenge."

"I want," said Caina, opening her eyes. "I want more than that."

Riogan snorted. "There is no more than that. That is life. Death and pain and endless struggle, the weak preying upon the strong."

"I wanted children," said Caina. "I wanted a family of my own. But that won't happen, not for me. So instead...so instead I want to keep it from happening again. To other people. So they don't have to suffer the way I have suffered."

"That's foolish," said Riogan. "The strong do as they like, and the weak suffer for it. That is the way of the world. You cannot stop it."

"No," said Caina, "but we can stop some of it. We just did in Kaunauth, didn't we?"

She left him by the fire, sharpening his daggers.

Halfdan returned that night with a goblet of wine, a smile on his face.

"Things are going well," he said, sitting down by the fire. Riogan had retreated to the common room to drink and to find a prostitute. "The Lord Governor of Arzaxia agreed to release his warships. In four weeks there won't be a single Istarish slaver left in the Narrow Sea."

"Good," said Caina. She hesitated, and then said, "Tell me about Maglarion."

Halfdan blinked, took a sip of wine, set down his goblet. "Why?"

"He tried to kill us," said Caina. "Set those assassins to wait for us in Kaunauth."

"He didn't try to kill us, specifically," said Halfdan. "Just any Ghosts who happened to wander along."

"He still tried to kill us," said Caina. "And...my father..."

"Ah," said Halfdan. "So that's what this is about. Revenge."

"Yes. And no," said Caina. "It...I want to kill him, for what he did to my father." Her hand twitched towards her belly, and she forced it to remain still. "For what he took from me. But...what I want doesn't matter, does it? He has to be stopped. Otherwise he'll hurt and kill other people."

"He has been killing people for a long time," said Halfdan, voice quiet. "A very long time. And no one has been able to stop him." He thought for a moment. "All right. You deserve to know, but I doubt it will bring you any peace."

He gestured, and Caina sat in the chair opposite him.

"Maglarion," said Halfdan, "is almost four hundred years old. Maybe older."

"So he really is that old?" said Caina. "He wasn't boasting when he told his students that?"

"No," said Halfdan. "There are records. He was born towards the end of the Fourth Empire. In those days, the magi commonly practiced necromancy, and used the blood of slaves to extend their natural lives."

"That's how he's lived so long," said Caina. "His necromancy."

"Yes," said Halfdan. "But even during the height of the Fourth Empire, the master magi of that time could rarely live for longer than two hundred, two hundred and fifty years. Yet Maglarion is still here." Halfdan took another sip of wine. "Well, you know what happened during the War of the Fourth Empire. The Magisterium broke into factions, and slaughtered each other, and the Ghosts helped the Emperors regain control of the Empire and subdue the magi."

"No slavery, no necromancy," said Caina.

Halfdan nodded.

"Why wasn't Maglarion killed with the rest of the necromancers?" said Caina.

"Because he was smart enough to leave the capital before the Fourth Empire fell and the Fifth Empire was established," said Halfdan. "We think he traveled the nations outside the Empire, studying the necromantic traditions and lore he found there. Maat, most probably, studying the ruins of the Kingdom of the Rising Sun."

"The Maatish scroll my father took from the smugglers," said Caina. "That was why he came to Aretia."

"He returned to the Empire about a hundred and fifty years ago," said Halfdan. "He started gathering students, taking them from among the ranks of the magi, and making allies among the nobility. The Magisterium, of course, claims to oppose the use of necromancy - but the magi want power, and Maglarion has power beyond anything any living magus can wield today. He's always been friendly with the Kindred and the Istarish slavers' brotherhood. He uses the assassins to get rid of his enemies - as happened in Kaunauth - and the slavers will deliver...raw material for his necromantic experiments."

"He's been doing this for a century and a half?" said Caina. "Why doesn't anyone stop him?"

"The Ghosts have stopped him," said Halfdan. "Time and time again. The slavers draw our attention, or his students overstep and kill too many people with their necromantic sciences. The Ghosts track them to their lair and kill the students and the slavers alike. And then Maglarion disappears for a few years and starts all over again in another part of the Empire."

"But why haven't the Ghosts killed Maglarion?" said Caina.

"We've tried," said Halfdan. "Five times. Five times the Ghosts sent their best nightfighters to ambush Maglarion. And every last time, Maglarion killed them. Every single one of them."

"All of them?" said Caina.

Halfdan nodded.

"But what does he want?" said Caina. "All this death...a man doesn't kill that many people, if he doesn't want anything. What does he want?"

"We don't know," said Halfdan.

Caina blinked. "We don't?"

Halfdan shook his head. "It's not as if he will tell us, after all. He influences the nobility, but he doesn't seem to want to rule the Empire. He takes students from the Magisterium, but he doesn't seem to care whether the magi rule the Empire or not. I think he regards the nobility and the magi as tools to use and discard as he pleases." Halfdan shrugged. "Does he want more arcane science, more sorcerous power? Maybe he simply enjoys the bloodshed and carnage, and lives for nothing more than that? Or perhaps he wants to live forever, become immortal? I don't know."

"Until we know," said Caina, "we won't be able to stop him."

"No," said Halfdan. "But we can remain on guard against him. Especially now that he has allied himself with Lord Haeron." Halfdan shook his head. "Haeron probably thinks that Maglarion is serving him, the fool. Well, Haeron Icaraeus was already an enemy of the Emperor and of the Ghosts. If he's allied himself with Maglarion, then we have all the more reason to oppose him."

They sat in silence for a moment. Caina remembered Maglarion, remembered his calm, cold voice, the ghostly green light flashing beneath the patch covering his left eye.

The way he had butchered her father and his servants.

Why had he done all those things? What did he want?

"You should get to bed," said Halfdan. "We shall have a long day tomorrow."

"We're leaving?" said Caina.

"You'll see," said Halfdan.

The next morning they left Mors Insidion.

"We're going to Malarae?" said Caina.

"The Imperial capital itself," said Halfdan. "We need to put some things in motion against Lord Haeron. And you need to begin the next step of your training. We've taught you to fight, and now it's time you learned to be subtle."

"What does that mean?" said Caina.

Halfdan smiled. "You'll find out."

CHAPTER 15
THE IMPERIAL CAPITAL

They left Vytaagia, followed the Imperial Highway through the Disali hills, and returned to the rolling plains around the Bay of Empire. Soon they reached Croton, where only four years past, Caina had arrived, traveling by fishing boat with Riogan and Komnene and Halfdan.

It seemed a lifetime ago.

But instead of turning east for Disalia, this time they turned northwest, taking the Imperial Highway as it followed the coastline. Travelers filled the road, endless streams of merchant wagons piled high with goods, liveried couriers riding back and forth, detachments of Malarae's Civic Militia patrolling the roads, proud in their chainmail, red cloaks, and plumed helmets.

On the third day out from Croton, they reached the Megaros River, broad and placid, its surface filled with endless lines of cargo-laden barges and rafts.

And on the western bank of the Megaros stood Malarae, capital of the Empire of Nighmar.

Caina gaped at it.

She had never seen anything so vast.

Halfdan told her that over a million people occupied Malarae, and Caina could believe it. The city stretched as far as she could see, even rising up the slopes of the mountains beyond the river. Countless warehouses lined the harbor and crowded the river's banks, and ships beyond count filled the quays and docks. Beyond the docks she saw the vast mansions and soaring towers of the Imperial nobility. The Magisterium aided in their construction, using their sorcery to help lift and shape the stone, and some of the towers rose hundreds of feet over the surrounding city. Amidst the mansions she saw the vast halls of the merchant collegia, or the soaring domes crowning the temples to the Empire's gods.

And beyond, sitting upon an outthrust spur of the mountain, stood the massive towers and buttressed walls of the Imperial Citadel, seat of the Emperors of Nighmar, a fortress-city in its own right. Five different Empires had risen from Malarae, spanning thousands of years of history, yet the Citadel had never fallen. The purple banners of the Emperors had flown from the Citadel's battlements for centuries.

Halfdan chuckled at her expression. "What do you think?"

"It's...big," said Caina.

Riogan snorted. "Eloquent."

No bridges crossed the Megaros River, Halfdan explained, partly as an ancient defense against barbarian tribes from the east, and partly to keep the river clear for merchant traffic. So they took a massive ferry across the Megaros, a broad raft laden with travelers and merchants, tended by hard-faced rivermen who handled the craft with skill. They docked, and went ashore into a bustling market square. Caina saw dozens of varieties of fish for sale, along with squids and crabs and octopi and stranger things.

"Fishmongers' Square," said Halfdan.

"Where are we going?" said Caina.

"To teach you to be subtle," said Halfdan.

"What does that mean?" said Caina.

To her surprise, he answered. "Haeron Icaraeus is active in Malarae. We need spies here. Our friends in the Vineyard have taught you to fight. Well and good. Now we shall teach you to be subtle. We will teach you how to be a spy. How to remain unseen, even in a crowd. How to blend in and remain unnoticed." He smiled. "And I have just the right teacher in mind for you."

They crossed Fishmongers' Square, making for the broad street that led into the city's heart. Caina's eyes darted back and forth, taking in the crowds. That man was a carpenter, obviously, to judge from his callused hands and heavy hammer. That woman, a seamstress. That man, a bricklayer. And that boy in the ragged shirt and...

Caina jumped forward, seized his wrist, bent it back. The boy squealed in alarm and tried to break away, but she held him fast.

"Give it back," she said.

"I don't know what you're talking about!" he gasped.

She twisted him around to face Riogan.

"Give it back," she said, "or that fellow will cut your throat."

The boy dropped Halfdan's belt pouch into her hand, and she released him. He sprinted away and vanished into the crowds.

"Very good," said Halfdan as she handed the pouch to him.

"Was that a test?" she said.

"Not at all," said Halfdan. "The fellow did pick my pocket. But you handled it very well."

"Theodosia," said Riogan, "is going to love her."

"Well," said Halfdan, "let's introduce them, shall we?"

They walked further into Malarae, along a broad avenue crowded with people. Massive statues stood on marble plinths, stone images of armored men on horseback, or warriors lifting their swords in defiance of unseen enemies. The Via Triumphalis, Halfdan called the street, and the statues depicted long dead Emperors and Lord Commanders who had defeated the Empire's enemies, earning the right to a statue.

Soon they left the docks and the working neighborhoods behind, and came to the city's wealthier districts. Caina stared at gleaming mansions and soaring towers, their facades adorned with statues and reliefs, at lush gardens and bubbling fountains. They passed through plazas lined with shops selling countless luxuries and rarities, silks and spices and gems from Anshan and Istarinmul.

Finally, they stopped before a building with a columned facade and a high dome that rose two hundred feet over the plaza.

"What is this?" said Caina. "A temple?"

Halfdan laughed. "Hardly. Welcome to the Grand Imperial Opera."

"The opera?" said Caina, her lip crinkling. Her mother had loved the opera, had often complained how she missed the Imperial opera companies in Malarae and Artifel.

"Of course," said Halfdan. "Actors and singers generally come from the dregs of the Empire. The nobility and the wealthy merchants hold them in disdain...but come to their shows anyway. And since the nobles hold them in disdain, they don't bother to hold their tongues in front of actors."

"And so the Ghosts have many friends among the actors and musicians," said Caina.

"Quite right," said Halfdan.

He led them around the flank of the massive building, away from the grand entrance, to a narrow wooden door in the back. Halfdan knocked, waited. An iron plate in the door slid aside, and Caina saw the gleam of eyes.

"Sign?" growled a voice in High Nighmarian.

"Let tyrants beware," said Halfdan in the same language, "let the wicked fear, and let the sorcerers tremble, for in the shadows wait the Ghosts."

The voice grunted. "Good enough. It's been a while, Basil."

"So it has," said Halfdan. "Is she here?"

"Aye. Primping, as usual," said the voice. "She'll want to see you."

The door swung open, and they walked into a narrow stone corridor, lit only by glowing glass globes hanging from the ceiling. Caina remembered those spheres from Maglarion's lair and shivered.

"They use enspelled globes for light?" said Caina.

"Everyone in Malarae does," said Halfdan. "The capital's Magisterium chapterhouse manufactures them by the thousands, sells them cheaply but at great profit. It's how the Magisterium finances itself, mostly."

The corridor ended in an enormous workshop with a wooden ceiling supported by massive wooden beams. Workmen hurried back and forth, swarming over some sort of wooden construction, hammers and paintbrushes in hand. They were building sets for the opera, Caina realized. She saw vast trapdoors in the ceiling, with pulleys and ropes ready to raise the sets as needed.

Halfdan steered them through the chaos until they came to a row of doors on the far wall. One of the doors stood open, light spilling into the gloomy workshop. Inside Caina saw a woman sitting upon a stool, admiring herself in an large mirror. The woman was in her late thirties, perhaps her early forties, with long blond hair and pale gray eyes. She was a bit plump, but tall enough to bear the extra weight with grace.

She turned at their approach, and her face lit up with a brilliant smile.

"If it isn't Halfdan!" said the woman in High Nighmarian, her voice rich and rolling. "You rascal!"

"Theodosia, my dear," said Halfdan. "You're looking well."

"Flatterer," said Theodosia, planting a kiss upon Halfdan's cheek. "I look old and used up, a withered crone, and cannot get even the most desperate of men to look at me."

"You are many things," said Halfdan, "but used up is not one of them." He sighed. "A pity we are not alone. I could prove you wrong most effectively."

Caina blinked. This was a side of Halfdan she had not seen before.

"Easily accomplished," purred Theodosia. She leveled a finger at Riogan. "You. Wait outside. Try not to kill anyone." She paused for a moment. "Unless it's really necessary, of course."

Riogan gave a sardonic little bow, something almost like a smile flickering over his lips. "Your discretion fills me with pride, great lady."

"Bah. I am not a lady, and you know it," said Theodosia, but she smiled as she said it.

Caina turned to follow Riogan.

"No," said Theodosia. "You stay."

Caina stopped, and Riogan shut the door behind him.

"So," said Theodosia, turning to the mirror once more. The table before the mirror held a truly astonishing array of cosmetics and wigs.

"How bad is it?"

"Bad enough," said Halfdan. "You remember what I told you about Maglarion, I trust?"

Theodosia's eyes flicked to Caina, just for a moment. "Aye, I do."

"He's apparently started working with Haeron Icaraeus," said Halfdan. Theodosia swore, several times.

"Undoubtedly Lord Haeron thinks that Maglarion is working for him," said Halfdan, "but I suspect Maglarion has his own ideas."

"No doubt," said Theodosia. "What does he want?" She scoffed. "Lord Haeron, he is a rich fool, and like all rich fools, he wants to be Emperor. But what does Maglarion want?"

"That is one of the things I would like you to discover," said Halfdan.

Theodosia sighed. "I shall try. My eyes and ears watch Lord Haeron night and day. But, oh, a fat fool he may be, but he is as clever as a snake. Very cautious, very careful. He has left no evidence we can use against him."

"Then perhaps we should simply kill him," said Halfdan.

"Easier said than done," said Theodosia. "He guards himself most carefully, and is clever enough to hire competent guards."

"Well," said Halfdan, "we'll just have to be cleverer, won't we?"

Caina blinked. "You're the circlemaster of Malarae."

Both Halfdan and Theodosia looked at her.

"I told you she was clever," said Halfdan.

"Indeed you did," said Theodosia. She smiled and tapped one finger against her lips. "Halfdan also said you were most observant. Tell me what you see about me."

Caina shrugged, looked at Theodosia for a moment, and then at the room.

"Well?" said Theodosia.

"You're a widow," said Caina, "and you have at least two children, both sons. They probably went into the Legion or the Civic Militia."

"The scar from the ring," said Theodosia, tapping her finger, "and the candles?"

"Yes," said Caina. It was common for mothers with children in the Legions or the militias to light votive candles to Markoin, god of soldiers.

"What else?" said Theodosia.

"You're carrying at least three knives," said Caina, "two in your boots, one in your belt, and I would wager that you have more that I haven't been able to find. You've had a bad cold, and only just got over it. And you dye your hair."

Halfdan burst out laughing.

"I most certainly do not!" said Theodosia, touching her hair.

Caina shrugged. "But you have all those bottles of dye on the table, and I can see the stains where your hair brushed the walls while still wet."

Theodosia sniffed. "How did you know about the cold?"

"The spots on the mirror, from sneezes," said Caina. "You haven't cleaned them off."

"So I see," said Theodosia, tapping her finger against her lips again. "Well, Halfdan said you were clever, and I see he was right. No doubt he had Riogan teach you to kill, hmm? There is more to being a Ghost than killing and fighting. You must know how to disguise yourself. How to blend in, whether you are dancing at a noble ball or strolling the slums. You must know how to mask yourself so well that your best friend and dearest lover could not recognize you."

"How?" said Caina.

"Why, I shall teach you," said Theodosia, spreading her arms. "For I am Theodosia of Malarae! I first strode upon the stage of the Imperial Opera as a girl of fourteen, and I have played every part and sung every aria from the 'Queen of Anshan' to the 'Slave of Istarinmul'. First, let us see what you can already do. Can you sing?"

"Sing?" said Caina, nonplussed.

"Yes. Can you sing? It is a simple question," said Theodosia.

"I don't know," said Caina. "I've never really tried."

"Well, then, sing this," said Theodosia, and she sang a phrase in her rich, rolling voice.

Caina hesitated, took a deep breath, and sang the phrase. Or tried to, anyway.

Theodosia winced. "Ah, so you cannot sing. Well, I simply won't use you on the stage, that is all. Halfdan tells me you can speak many languages, yes?"

Caina nodded.

"Though I sing best," said Theodosia, switching to Caerish, "in High Nighmarian, since all the greatest arias are written in High Nighmarian."

Caina answered in Caerish. "I'm afraid I wouldn't know. I have never been to Malarae, before today."

"Is that so?" said Theodosia, switching to Kyracian. "It must have been an impressive sight, coming into the city for the first time. I was born here, and Malarae is the queen of cities."

"There are very many beautiful buildings," said Caina in the same language, "and all those statues. It must have been dreadfully expensive."

Theodosia laughed, and started speaking in Anshani. "There have been Emperors for thousands of years, and each one wants to be remembered as a great ruler. So every Emperor throws up a new theater, or a new tower, and names it after himself, in hopes that he will be remembered as a great Emperor. The construction makes a dreadful lot of noise, but we do get many fine buildings out of it."

"And this theater?" said Caina in Anshani. "It's called the Grand Imperial Opera. Why isn't it named for an Emperor?"

"Actually," said Theodosia, switching to Cyrican, "it is technically named the Theater of Iconias, for the Emperor who ordered it built during the early years of the Third Empire. But it is the most prestigious theater in the Empire, and 'The Theater of Iconias' is quite a mouthful, so it is mostly called the Grand Imperial Opera."

"A nickname, then," said Caina in Cyrican. "So I see."

Theodosia clapped her hands. "Delightful!" she said in High Nighmarian once more, speaking to Halfdan. "How many other languages can she speak?"

"I don't know," said Halfdan. "Caina, how many languages do you know?"

"High Nighmarian," said Caina, "Caerish, Saddaic, Disali, Kagarish, Cyrican, and Anshani. Oh, I learned Kyracian at the Vineyard, and I think I picked up a few of the curse words in Vytaagi."

"How did you learn all those tongues?" said Theodosia.

"My father," said Caina, blinking as she remembered. "He taught me. When...he still could."

"Ah," said Theodosia. "Now, then. Can you do accents?"

Caina frowned. "Accents?"

"You speak fluently," said Theodosia, "in whatever language. The trouble is, you sound like a proper young noblewoman, no matter what tongue you use. It will do no good if I teach you to disguise yourself as a lowborn girl, or as a mercenary soldier, and you sound like a Nighmarian noblewoman."

A mercenary? Caina wondered how she could possibly disguise herself as a man. "So...you mean I should speak with an accent? Like Saddaic or Anshani was my first language, and I learned High Nighmarian later?"

"Exactly," said Theodosia. "Try High Nighmarian with a Caerish accent, first. Everyone speaks Caerish, so that should be easiest."

Caina thought for a moment. Halfdan spoke with a Caerish accent. Most of the time.

"Aye?" she said at last, trying to speak as Halfdan did. "How's this, then? Talking this way makes my teeth hurt."

Theodosia and Halfdan shared a look.

"Passable," said Halfdan.

"But not good enough," said Theodosia. "We shall practice. Yes, you may not be able to sing, but you definitely have potential. When I am finished with you, you shall be able to disguise yourself as anything from a starving beggar to a highborn lady, and no one shall look twice."

"You're going to stay with Theodosia for a time," said Halfdan. "You'll masquerade as her assistant, just as Theodosia masquerades as an opera singer."

"Masquerade?" said Theodosia. "Masquerade? I am the finest soprano to sing the Imperial capital for a hundred years! I masquerade as nothing."

Halfdan smirked, and made a little bow. "My apologies, madam. You are indeed the finest soprano in the city, and nobles and merchants come from across the Empire to bask in the wonder of your voice. The fact that you deign to act as circlemaster of Malarae in your spare time is a wondrous blessing for the Ghosts, and we regularly fall to our knees and thank the gods for sending you to us."

"That's better," said Theodosia.

"I want you to keep an eye on Haeron Icaraeus," said Halfdan. "Find out what he intends. If you can find a way to bring him down, good, but do not put yourself or your people at unnecessary risk. He is too careful and too dangerous to confront directly, for now."

"What about Maglarion?" said Theodosia.

"If you can find out what he wants, or what he hopes to gain by working with Lord Haeron, then do so," said Halfdan. "But do not confront him directly." He looked at Caina, and then back at Theodosia. "Haeron Icaraeus is dangerous, but next to Maglarion, he's little more than a petulant child. Maglarion has exterminated entire Ghost circles before, and if he thinks you are a threat to him, he will take action."

"We shall be as shadows," said Theodosia. "He will never even know that we are here." Her smile returned. "I do hope you shall stay for dinner. I have found the most delightful Anshani chef."

"Alas," said Halfdan, "I need to be on ship for Cyrica by the evening tide." He took Theodosia's hands. "Take care of yourself, and look after Caina. She's very clever, and will be a great help to you." He looked at Caina, put his hard hand on her shoulder. "And do as Theodosia bids you. She knows what she's about."

Caina nodded, biting her lip. Halfdan had looked after her for almost four years now.

On impulse, she slipped out of his grasp and hugged him, hard.

"You be careful, too," she said.

Halfdan smiled.

"My dear child," he said. "I'm always careful."

He bowed once more and left.

Caina stood in silence for a moment.

"Well," said Theodosia. "Halfdan is a marvelous fellow, but he always gives me a great deal of work to do. Shall we get to it?"

CHAPTER 16
THE PRICE OF IMMORTALITY

Maglarion stood in the darkness below Malarae, gazing upon his bloodcrystal.

It had grown.

A few years ago, it had been the size of his fist. But Lord Haeron had kept him well-supplied with slaves, and Maglarion killed them all, feeding their life forces into the bloodcrystal. Bloated with the stored energy from hundreds of deaths, it had swelled to the size of a small child. Its power had increased, as well. When he had created it, it could absorb the energy from any death within thirty or forty yards.

Now it could absorb the power from any death within a half mile.

Which meant that it grew constantly, even without Maglarion's attention. A million men, women, and children lived in Malarae, and some of them died every day. A few days ago, a woman had been raped and knifed within a few blocks of the Grey Fish Inn. The bloodcrystal captured the energy of her death, storing the power within itself. An inattentive child had been crushed beneath the wheels of a wagon. His life force, too, drained into the bloodcrystal.

Every death made the bloodcrystal a little larger, a little stronger. Soon it would have the power to capture the energy from any death within the entire city.

And then Maglarion's real work could begin.

He smiled, running a hand over the bloodcrystal's rough side. It shone constantly now, pale green flames flickering in its depths. Sometimes faces formed in the flames, images of those deaths captured by the bloodcrystal. That pleased Maglarion. The lives of his victims, after all, had no purpose – save to be harvested by him.

Now, to begin.

A wooden podium stood before the bloodcrystal, holding the dagger and the Maatish scroll he had taken from Sebastian Amalas's library. Maglarion raised the dagger and slashed his palm. Blood welled from the cut, and he extended his hand over the bloodcrystal.

The blood sizzled and hissed when it struck the dark surface.

Maglarion began to chant, reading the ancient spell from the scroll, gesturing with the bloodied dagger. Power built in the air, his fingertips crackling with emerald flame. The bloodcrystal pulsed and throbbed in answer.

Maglarion waved his bleeding hand, spraying more droplets over the bloodcrystal, and released the power.

The crystal blazed with green light, and Maglarion felt the stored power in the crystal pressing against his mind and soul, joined by the Maatish spell's link.

And then the power erupted through him.

Maglarion shuddered and fell to his knees, breathing hard, eyes wide. The power raged through him like a molten river. The Maatish spell had joined him to the bloodcrystal, linking its stolen life force to his own, and now that vast reservoir of power enhanced his strength.

He lifted his hands, watching the cut upon his palm vanish, the skin repairing itself. And still stolen strength and vitality surged through him. The liver spots vanished from his hands, the skin tightening.

Amazed, he climbed to his feet without the use of his cane. Years ago, one of the Ghosts' interminable attempts on his life had almost succeeded, leaving him with a bad limp that even his necromantic prowess could not quite heal. Yet now the limp was gone, and his left leg worked without the slightest hitch.

His left eye, of course, did not heal.

But he had plucked it out himself, after all.

He strode across the cellar to the mirror upon his worktable and gazed at his reflection. For centuries, now, he had looked like a white-haired man in his late sixties, face lined and worn. Now he looked like a man in the vigor of his early forties, his hair more black than gray.

His laughter rang over the cellar.

He would transcend the flesh, in the end. He would leave his body behind, and live as pure power, immortal and invincible for all time. This renewed vitality, this rejuvenation, was just the first step.

He had indeed put the harvested lives of his victims to good use.

And even as the thought crossed his mind, he felt someone die within reach the bloodcrystal.

For the briefest moment he had contact with the flickering life force. An old man, dying of sickness, alone in his room. And then the energy released by the death drained into the bloodcrystal. The crystal shivered as it grew slightly larger, and Maglarion closed his eyes with the pleasure of it. The old man had been weak, his life force little more than a flickering ember, and yet its consumption had filled Maglarion with ecstasy.

What would it be like, he wondered, when he devoured all of Malarae?

An image of the old man's face flickered in the bloodcrystal, and then vanished in green flame.

He turned, saw Ikhana descending the cellar stairs.

"Master," she said, stopping before him. "Lord Icaraeus has gathered the Restorationist nobles. They would…"

She stopped, staring at him, and he had the distinct pleasure of seeing shock cross her cold face, for the first time in over a century.

"My dear Ikhana," said Maglarion, spreading his hands. "You seem surprised."

"You are…younger," said Ikhana, her face returning to its usual empty expression.

"Do you remember what I told you?" said Maglarion, stepping closer to her. "That first day, when you tried to kill me?"

There were, he realized, other advantages to a rejuvenated body. Ikhana's face was cold, and her eyes empty, but she was really very beautiful.

A hint of fear showed in those cold eyes.

"You said you were the master of death," said Ikhana, "that life and death themselves were yours to command."

"Yes," said Maglarion, shoving her to the floor, "and I still am."

He took her, then and there, upon the cellar floor, the first time he had lain with a woman in centuries. She did not resist. She did not even try. And why should she? The black dagger had enslaved her to him, body and soul, and he owned her more thoroughly than a fool like Haeron Icaraeus could ever own his slaves.

But her eyes glittered by the time he was done, shining with the same icy lust he saw when he gave prisoners to her and the dagger.

Ikhana only respected power…and Maglarion had power.

"Come," he said, rising to his feet. "Let us see what our good friend Lord Haeron has found for us."

Like most nobles, Lord Haeron maintained a townhouse in Malarae, to use when the business of the court called him to the Imperial capital. Of course, Lord Haeron of House Icaraeus was one of the most powerful men in the Empire, and his townhouse was a sprawling ten-story pile of marble, ringed with gardens and fountains, with a massive tower rising four hundred feet above the mansion. Lord Haeron's guards, hard-faced, cold-eyed men, prowled the grounds, laden with arms and armor. Lord Haeron had many enemies, the Ghosts among them, and did not neglect his personal security.

Some of the guards escorted Maglarion and Ikhana into the mansion. He enjoyed their caution in his presence, the way they checked their weapons and never let their eyes leave him for long.

Little good it would do them.

The nobles awaited him in one of the mansion's smaller ballrooms, sipping from flutes of wine. Haeron had had the wit, at least, to banish the servants from the ballroom, posting guards at the doors. Servants were often friendly with the Ghosts.

Slaves were better than free servants. Easier to kill, when necessary.

Maglarion looked over the nobles, Ikhana trailing behind him. Most of the prominent Restorationist nobility in the Empire had come. There was Lord Haeron, the center of attention, a dozen lesser nobles nodding at his every word. There was Lord Macrinius, handsome and dashing. There was Lady Aureon, vain and primped, flirting with sour-faced old Lord Corthios. Even some Militarist nobility had come, to his surprise, but he knew them all.

He had known their ancestors.

In some cases, he had killed their ancestors.

Haeron Icaraeus crossed the room, the lesser nobles trailing after him. "Ah, Master Maglarion. So good of you to..."

He stopped, frowning, and looked hard at Maglarion's face.

"So good of you to come," he said, as if he had not noticed anything amiss. He lifted his voice, addressing the nobles. "My friends! You might have wondered why I invited you here tonight with such secrecy. Well, you are men and women of vision, every one. You wish to see our Empire returned to economic and social order, to see slavery reestablished in every province and in Malarae itself. You wish to see the arcane sciences used for the benefit of the Empire and the nobility. And you wish to see that upstart fool of an Emperor brought to heel. Tonight, I wish to introduce you to a worthy ally of our noble mission - Maglarion, once a Master of the Magisterium of the Fourth Empire."

A surprised murmur went through the assembled nobles.

Maglarion's reputation proceeded him.

"My lords and ladies," said Maglarion. "How would you like to live forever?"

Silence answered this pronouncement. Haeron frowned, and Lord Macrinius looked skeptical, as did a few of the other lords.

"You know that during the Fourth Empire," said Maglarion, "the necromantic sciences had not yet been banned. That the magi used these sciences to extend their lifespan for centuries. I am the heir to their secrets, and I can pass them on to you, if you support my work. Think of the possibilities - a society of immortal nobles, ruling forever over a powerful and vigorous Empire, an Empire where the lower classes know their place."

One of the nobles laughed. "Do you seriously expect us to believe that?" A young man, with close-cropped blond hair and bright blue eyes, his arms heavy with muscle. Lord Alastair Corus, Maglarion recognized, Militarist lord and tribune in the Eighteenth Legion. "Immortal nobles, indeed. Lord Haeron, thank you for the hospitality, but I'm afraid I've wasted quite enough time with a one-eyed charlatan today."

He bowed in Haeron's direction and left.

"I assure you," said Maglarion, "that every word I am speaking is the truth."

That was a lie, of course, but they didn't need to know that.

"Doubtful," said Lord Macrinius, brushing some dust from the sleeve of his coat. "Lord Haeron has a fondness for collecting rogue sorcerers, and I'm sure you can perform an impressive trick or two. But we are hardly ignorant peasants to be impressed by a conjurer's showmanship. We know our history, 'Master' Maglarion. Even the most powerful necromancers of the Fourth Empire could not extend their lives beyond two and a half centuries, and they could only bestow a few additional decades upon their followers."

"And I have surpassed them," said Maglarion. "I have lived for almost four centuries."

Some of the nobles laughed at that.

"Indeed?" said Macrinius. "Do you truly expect us to believe that without proof? Undoubtedly you will say that you can brew an elixir of immortality, provided you have just enough of our gold. And then you'll disappear to make the same pitch to the satraps of Anshan, or perhaps the emirs of Istarinmul. Haeron, you ought to hang this scoundrel from his heels as a warning to others who would cheat the Lords of the Nighmarian Empire."

"Proof, you want?" said Maglarion, his voice soft. "Then proof you shall have."

He walked to a table, shoved aside silver plates of delicacies, and climbed upon it.

"What are you doing?" said Haeron, scowling. Even Ikhana appeared surprised.

"Do you want proof, my lords and ladies?" said Maglarion. "Then behold! I have mastered death, and the power of life itself is my plaything." He undid his black coat and ripped open his white shirt, exposing his chest.

"What is the meaning of this?" said Haeron, his face darkening. Undoubtedly he did not like to look the fool in front of his sycophants.

"Watch," said Maglarion.

He drew the dagger from his belt and slammed it home in his chest, between his ribs.

That...rather hurt.

The nobles stared at him, shocked. One woman screamed. Blood gushed over Maglarion's hands, and he twisted the dagger, driving it deeper into his heart. Then he ripped it free, the blade glistening.

His heart stopped beating. His vision darkened, and Maglarion toppled off the table.

He felt himself hit the marble floor, and everything went black.

Then power surged through him, burning and potent, drawing him back from the darkness. His eye of flesh swam back into focus, staring up at the ballroom's ceiling. A furious argument filled his ears. Some of the nobles stood over him, gesturing and shouting. Ikhana waited nearby, a hungry expression on her face. No doubt she thought herself rid of him, and wanted to kill everyone in the room.

"What sort of foolishness was this, Haeron?" said Lord Macrinius. He sounded affronted. "Did you invite us here to watch some madman kill himself?"

"How was I to have known?" said Haeron. "The man had skill with the necromantic sciences, I saw that with my own eyes." He snorted. "Undoubtedly it deranged his mind, gave him delusions of grandeur. Well, better to learn that a tool is flawed sooner rather than later, no?"

"And how much trust did you place in this man?" said Lord Macrinius. "We cannot afford any missteps, not with the Ghosts snapping at our heels."

"Ghosts!" said Lady Aureon. "There are no such thing as the Ghosts."

Haeron's voice hardened. "Do not think to..."

Maglarion drew in a deep breath and started to laugh.

The effect on the nobles was...gratifying.

Haeron flinched, all the color draining out of his thick face. Macrinius fell silent, shocked. Aureon shrieked, perfumed hands flying to her painted face. Some of the others swore, while others just stared in shock. Every man and woman among them knew what death looked like, and Maglarion had just killed himself in front of them.

And then returned.

He climbed to his feet, the bloodcrystal's power surging through him. He spread his arms, letting them see his blood-soaked shirt, the wound on his chest closing itself. Ikhana stared at him, her mouth working. Twice in one day, now, he had managed to shock her.

"I believe, my lord Macrinius," said Maglarion, smiling, "that you wished to see proof?"

"How?" said Macrinius at last.

"The necromancers of old lived for two centuries," said Maglarion. "But I have surpassed them, I have delved deeper into the necromantic sciences than they ever did. And I have mastered death itself - as you can see with your own eyes."

The wound on his chest finished closing.

"My dear Lord Macrinius," rumbled Haeron, "did you really think that I would associate myself with a charlatan?"

"Aid me, my lords and ladies," said Maglarion. "Give me the materials I need to continue my research. The gods may promise life eternal to their followers - but only I can give it to you. Aid me, and I shall give you the Empire. Aid me, and you shall rule over the Empire forever - forever young, forever strong, and forever immortal."

Maglarion watched their faces. They were convinced. They were his.

He would make good use of these men and women.

Before he killed them all, of course.

CHAPTER 17
MASQUERADES

Caina soon settled into a routine at the Grand Imperial Opera.

The singers and the musicians and the stagehands tended to sleep late, so she awoke before dawn. While they slept, she went to the deserted workshop and practiced her unarmed forms for an hour, until her breathing came hard and fast. After that, she bathed, and ate a breakfast of bread and cheese, sometimes an egg or two.

And then she helped Theodosia.

The Imperial Opera, Caina soon learned, was the most prestigious opera company in the Empire. Every major city had one, and Malarae had a dozen - but the Emperor himself patronized the Grand Imperial Opera, and only the finest singers performed upon its stage. Theodosia usually sang to rapturous applause three or four nights a week.

"Makeup, my dear, is an art," said Theodosia one night, as Caina helped her prepare. "Too little is ineffective. Too much, and you look like a painted whore." She paused. "Unless, of course, you want to look like a painted whore. In which case too much is exactly the right amount. But the right amount can make you look twenty years older, or ten years younger - looking younger is always harder for women. It can even make you look like a different woman entirely, or even a man. Watch."

Caina applied the makeup to Theodosia's face, following the woman's precise directions. It was difficult, but not that different from disarming Halfdan's practice traps. At least no needles erupted from Theodosia's face.

"Do you see?" said Theodosia, gesturing at the mirror. She did, indeed, look ten years younger.

"Yes," said Caina. She was beginning to see how a nightfighter might find makeup useful.

"For the rest of the night," said Theodosia, adjusting her hair one last time, "you'll run errands for the Seneschal. Also, you'll speak only Caerish. Use a...Saddaic accent, I think. You see, makeup is only part of it. If you want to fool people into thinking that you are a servant, you must act the part. Your stance, your gestures, your expression, your accent...all of them must say 'I am a servant' or 'I am a washerwoman' or whatever disguise you choose to take. Do you understand?"

Caina thought it over. "No."

"Good," said Theodosia. "For understanding comes only with practice." She got to her feet. "And now my audience awaits."

For the rest of the night, Caina obeyed the theater's Seneschal, a nervous, sweating man who nonetheless ruled the Grand Imperial Opera with an iron fist. The various nobles and merchants attending the opera wanted wine, or refreshments, or messages delivered, and Caina did their errands. She did her best to act like a servant, keeping her eyes downcast, her accent Saddaic, and her stance and posture diffident and respectful.

Quickly she realized why Theodosia wanted her to do this.

The nobles paid no attention to servants. None whatsoever. They regarded the servants as something like furniture, or perhaps horses - something used when needed, but otherwise ignored. They spoke freely in front of her, too freely. She soon learned that one lord slept with the wife of another. That another nobleman contracted with smugglers to bring Cyrican spices into the city, avoiding the Emperor's tariffs.

From time to time she had a moment to stop, to listen to the opera.

Theodosia could indeed sing. Her voice filled the theater, one moment softer than silk, the like the blast of a proud trumpet.

The nobles even stopped plotting to listen to her.

Caina delivered a tray of breaded shrimp to the private box of Lord Haeron Icaraeus, and she took her first look at the man who had allied himself with Maglarion. Lord Haeron was stout and bearded, his expression and posture accustomed to command. Five hard-eyed men lounged about Lord Haeron, hands resting near their sword hilts, and another man first tasted everything Haeron ate and drank.

For a single terrified moment, Caina wondered if she would see Maglarion himself among Haeron's entourage, but there was no sign of him.

She supposed the sort of man who lurked in abandoned ruins, draining blood from virgin girls, was not the sort of man to come hear Theodosia sing.

Then Theodosia finished her aria, and the entire theater rose in thunderous applause.

Even Lord Haeron clapped a few times.

###

After the opera finished, Caina returned to the chaos of the workshop. The stagehands hauled the sets back into the place, and the singers and the chorus departed to get drunk. She fetched tools and wine, running back and forth at the Seneschal's bidding.

One of the singers stopped in her path. A man named Lucien, about twenty or so, handsome with dark hair and bright eyes. He was a bass, and had sung alongside Theodosia in the opera's final duet.

"Ah," said Lucien in Caerish, "you have some wine for me, yes?"

"Of course," said Caina, lifting the tray.

He took a long drink. "Singing, it is such thirsty work. I have seen you - you are Theodosia's new assistant, no? But I do not know your name."

"My name is Marina," said Caina, using the alias she had chosen.

"Marina," said Lucien, rolling the name around his tongue. "I am very pleased to meet you." He touched her arm, briefly. "My name is Lucien. You may have seen me on stage."

"I did," said Caina. "You sing very well."

His smile widened, and he touched her hand for just a moment. "You do me too much honor. Too much honor, indeed. I wish you could have been on stage with us. You would have looked very fine."

"Thank you," said Caina, wondering what he wanted. She looked around for Theodosia, or the Seneschal, hoping for an excuse to get away.

And as she looked away, Lucien glanced at her breasts, just for a moment.

Oh. Right.

He was very handsome, she had to admit, and she did like his eyes, and the way his smile flashed across his face. And he could indeed sing well, almost as well as Theodosia. For a moment Caina wondered what it would feel like if he kissed her.

To her great annoyance, she felt her cheeks grow warm.

But he had soft hands. What did he know of pain, of suffering, of hardship? A man like Riogan could break Lucien in the space of three heartbeats.

Caina saw Theodosia crossing the workshop, still in the elaborate jeweled gown and diadem worn by the "Queen of Anshan."

"Ah," she said. "Theodosia needs me. Excuse me."

She hurried away before Lucien could respond.

Theodosia stood before her mirror, examining herself.

"Well?" she said. "What did you think?"

Caina thought for a moment. "You sounded good."

"Good?" said Theodosia. She took a glass of wine and drained it in one gulp. "Good? I sounded good? Is that all you have to say?"

"I don't know very much about music," said Caina. "But I still think you sounded good." She frowned. "Even Lord Haeron clapped a few times."

Theodosia gave an indelicate snort. "Ah! Now there is high praise." A glint came into her eye. "So you see why I had you run the Seneschal's errands?"

Caina nodded. "The nobles, they're...they're so," she searched for a word, "stupid." Theodosia laughed. "They talk about illegal things in front of the servants. They don't even see servants. It's like..."

"Furniture," said Theodosia. "They think of servants as furniture."

Caina nodded. "I hope I wasn't like that with my father's servants."

"Oh, you probably were," said Theodosia. "Of course, you were just a child, so you didn't know any better. But now you do. Be warned, however, not all the nobles are fools. Some of them are halfway clever. Lord Haeron, for instance, probably assumed that all the servants were spying on him. He didn't say anything incriminating, did he?"

Caina shook her head.

"Exactly," said Theodosia. "You can learn a great deal about a man by talking to his servants. They say the best measure of a man is how he treats those in his power, after all, and servants see everything. And if they hate their master, they will be more than happy to share all his secrets with you." She smiled. "The next show, I think we shall have you mingle among the lords' servants. You can tell them what a cruel mistress I am, how I beat you and insult you at every turn. Then they will share their masters' secrets with you."

"You don't mind me spreading lies about you?" said Caina.

"Well. One does have a certain reputation to maintain," said Theodosia, "and opera singers are supposed to be ever so difficult. I never saw the point, myself. Too much work. Now help me out of this costume."

Caina obeyed, helping Theodosia to wash the intricate makeup from her face.

"You know," said Theodosia, "Lucien seems rather taken with you."

Caina laughed. "He's too old for me."

"He's only twenty. And you're...what, sixteen?"

Caina nodded.

"Many girls are married by the time they're fifteen," said Theodosia. "I was married at seventeen myself."

"Are you trying to find me a husband?" said Caina, undoing the elaborate laces on the back of Theodosia's costume.

"Oh, certainly not," said Theodosia. "It would be unwise of you to take a husband, I think. Not unless you no longer wished to be a Ghost nightfighter. Still, Lucien is very handsome, is he not? Not terribly bright, I'm afraid, but no one man can possess every virtue...and he is very handsome."

"He is," said Caina, helping Theodosia out of her coat.

"You are quite capable of taking care of yourself, I'm sure," said Theodosia. "Halfdan would have seen to that. Still, if you want to...ah, enjoy yourself with Lucien, or anyone else, for that matter, feel free to do so. Halfdan told me a bit about you. Most girls your age have to worry about getting pregnant if they enjoy themselves, but you wouldn't."

"No," said Caina, blinking. "No...I suppose I wouldn't, at that."

Her voice caught a little on the last word.

Theodosia looked at her, and her face fell.

"Oh," she said. "Oh, Caina. I'm sorry. I've rather made a fool of myself, haven't I? I forgot how painful this must be for you." She reached out, took Caina's hand. "You wanted children very badly, didn't you?"

"Yes," said Caina.

Theodosia smiled. "I didn't. I didn't even think about it, but it sort of...happened. Ah, my sons have been a trial to me...but, still, I would not trade them for anything. Forgive me for being so thoughtless."

"It's all right," said Caina. She shrugged. "It's been almost five years since Maglarion killed my father and left me barren. I should be used to it by now."

"Some scars never really heal," said Theodosia.

Caina sniffed, rubbed at her eyes. "That sounds like the sort of thing Halfdan would say."

"Well, he did tell it to me," said Theodosia, and Caina laughed. "He also likes to say that the best cure for sorrow is work. So, let's keep you busy, shall we?"

And true to her word, Caina kept busy. Theodosia knew countless tricks of makeup and disguise, and as the months went by she taught every last one to Caina. Soon Caina knew how to disguise herself as anything from a starving commoner to a highborn lady. From time to time Theodosia had her don a disguise, and walk unseen and unnoticed among the crowds of Malarae.

It was a strange feeling, but one that Caina enjoyed.

She spent time among the nobles' servants, regaling them with tales of Theodosia's erratic moods and irrational demands. Soon they shared lurid tales of their own. Many of the Restorationist nobles abused their servants, who in turn had little compunction about spying upon their masters.

And many of the nobles had secrets, though most were harmless. One lord carried on affair with three different merchants' wives, another schemed to steal control of a copper mine from a rival, and still a third planned to embarrass the Lord Governor of the Pale at a ball.

But sometimes the lords had darker secrets; correspondence with slave traders, or shelter for renegade sorcerers, or secret messages sent to the Empire's enemies.

Caina suspected Theodosia sent Riogan, or someone like him, to pay those lords a visit.

Theodosia kept Caina practicing different accents. Sometimes Caina spent the entire day speaking High Nighmarian with a Caerish accent, or Cyrican with a Saddaic accent, or Anshani with a Kyracian accent. She taught Caina to alter the pitch and tone of her voice, when to slur her words and when to speak faster, and soon Caina could disguise her voice with ease, picking from a dozen different voices and accents.

Lucien's attentions to her did not flag, either. Caina would have been more impressed had she not known that he had slept with a dozen different women at the Grand Imperial Opera.

One day he cornered her in a narrow hallway.

"It grieves me," Lucien said, "to see you working so hard. Theodosia does not appreciate you, Marina."

Caina shrugged. "She keeps me from starving, no? And she even let me go on stage once or twice."

Lucien scoffed. "As an extra! Little more than scenery! You deserve more. You should be on stage with me, in jewels and in silks." He touched her shoulder for a moment. "I can arrange that."

"I can't sing," said Caina.

"You wouldn't have to," said Lucien. "Your beauty alone would fill the theater with song."

Caina laughed. "That's a terrible line."

But he did indeed look handsome. And he always smelled nice, too. Malarae stank of salt and fish and tar and worse things, as one might expect in a city of a million people, but somehow Lucien always managed to smell nice.

"But," she said, "you are almost charming enough to pull it off."

"Almost?" he said. "You wound me terribly. I think you are very bold, Marina."

Caina shrugged. "Boldness has its uses."

"Really?" said Lucien. "Then perhaps I shall be bold."

And before she could react, he leaned closed and kissed her.

That...felt nice. It felt very nice. He was good at it; undoubtedly he had had a lot of practice. A warm flush spread through Caina, her heart beating faster. Why shouldn't she enjoy herself? She wanted children, a family of her own, but that would never happen. Why shouldn't she indulge?

Then Lucien's right hand came to rest on her left breast, his left digging into the waistband of her skirt, and the warm feeling went away.

The reflexes Akragas had drilled into her took over, and both her hands clamped about Lucien's right wrist. Before he had a chance to shout, she twisted his right arm behind him, put her foot in the small of his back, and slammed him into the stone wall. Lucien toppled to the floor, eyes wide, blood pouring from his nose.

And he started to cry.

Caina stared at him, attraction dissolving into incredulous contempt. She hadn't even hit him that hard, certainly not hard enough to break his nose or loosen his teeth. And he was crying over it? She had been hit much harder than that.

She had been hurt much worse than that.

"You hit me!" said Lucien, gazing up at her in bewilderment. "Why?"

"It's nice to be asked first, you know," said Caina, and left without looking back.

Lucien left her alone after that.

"Tonight, we shall disguise ourselves as men," announced Theodosia.

Caina blinked. "We shall?"

Theodosia opened the closet next to her mirror, dragged out a heavy brass-bound chest. "You've been keeping an eye on Lord Macrinius for me."

"I have," said Caina. Lord Macrinius was a powerful Restorationist noble and a friend of the Magisterium, second only to Haeron Icaraeus in prominence. He also enjoyed the Grand Imperial Opera, attending almost every performance. Caina had been keeping very close watch over him. Macrinius invariably met with several Istarish merchants during the operas, and usually left with them.

"Haeron Icaraeus," said Theodosia, opening the chest, "has been smuggling slaves into Malarae. We don't know what he's doing with them, or why."

"He's working with Maglarion," said Caina, shivering at the memory. "I can guess what he's doing with them."

"Whatever he's doing with them," said Theodosia, "we're going to stop him. Lord Macrinius has many friends in Istarinmul, and contacts among the slavers' brotherhood. He's buying slaves in the Istarish markets, and smuggling them into Malarae."

"Can't the Harbormaster stop him?" said Caina.

Theodosia rummaged through the chest. "Macrinius is smart enough not to bring his slaves into the city's harbor. He brings them ashore at one of those little towns along the Bay of Empire that turn a blind eye to smugglers. Then he has them transported via wagon to the city."

"How do we stop him?" said Caina.

"Simple," said Theodosia. "We find proof, irrefutable proof, that he purchased slaves and brought them into the Empire. We then make sure that proof just happens to find its way before the magistrates. Lord Macrinius then flees the Empire, if he's lucky...or loses his head, if he's unlucky. And if we're very lucky, we find the proof we need to bring down Lord Haeron, as well."

"And that, I assume," said Caina, "is why we have to dress like men."

"Exactly," said Theodosia, pulling clothing out of the chest. "I have a contact in Lord Macrinius's household. One of his clerks. The man's a spineless worm, but he hates Macrinius. For the right amount of gold, he can give us the proof we need. We're going to meet him at midnight in one of the dockside taverns."

"This is like the plot of the 'Queen of Anshan'," said Caina.

Theodosia grinned. "Precisely. Though I doubt I should sing an aria in the tavern. That might draw attention."

They dressed as caravan guards. Hundreds of merchant caravans came to Malarae, and caravan guards were a common sight. Caina rubbed sweat into her black hair, let it fall in greasy curtains over her face. Then she applied makeup to her jaw and chin, giving her face a coating of rough stubble. She dressed in a ragged tunic, dirt-stained trousers, and heavy, worn boots. Over her clothes she put on a coat of leather armor with steel studs, a threadbare green cloak, and a belt with short sword and dagger around her waist.

She barely recognized herself in the mirror. She looked like a man. A smallish man, but a man nonetheless. And Theodosia's transformation was even more dramatic. She looked like a grizzled veteran of a hundred battles, hard-eyed and capable.

"How do I look?" said Theodosia, her soprano voice a shocking contrast to her appearance.

"Terrible," said Caina.

"Splendid!" said Theodosia. Her voice changed to hissing rasp. It sounded as if she had been stabbed in the throat. "Let us visit the tavern."

Caina concentrated, and answered in a new voice of her own, a snarling growl. "Aye."

###

A short time later they came to the Hanging Pirate.

The dockside taverns all had colorful names; the Hanging Pirate, the Captain's Wife, the Grey Fish Inn, the Grief Reef. No doubt each one had an amusing legend behind the name. But they all had the same crowds of drunken sailors and caravan guards and laborers, the air heavy with the smells of sweat and beer and ringing with laughter, argument, and off-key song. The only women were serving maids, or prostitutes.

And yet Caina strolled unnoticed through all of them.

Part of her mind wondered at that. But most of her mind focused on maintaining the disguise. On walking like a man, with a confident swagger. On glaring at anyone who looked at her wrong. And it worked. She looked like any other caravan guard looking to get drunk.

No one looked at her twice.

"You there!" said one of the prostitutes, stepping into Caina's path. The woman was haggard, her eyes shining with a feverish light. "You looking for a good time? You seem like a handsome lad."

Caina was so surprised that she almost forgot herself, but practice kept her expression indifferent, her stance amused. "Aye? What're you charging, then? I won't pay more than a clipped copper."

The prostitute took offense. "A clipped copper! Scoundrel! I'll..."

"Enough of that," snarled Theodosia. "We've business. You can tumble the local ladies later."

She led Caina through the tavern crowd.

"I'm offended," murmured Theodosia into Caina's ear, speaking in her normal voice. "No whores propositioned me."

"Perhaps I look nicer," said Caina.

"That must be it," said Theodosia. "Do you see our friend?"

Caina scanned the Hanging Pirate's common room and nodded. "That has to be him."

A nervous-looking man sat at a table in the corner, huddled over a clay mug of wine. Unlike the rest of the men, he did not look as if he had ever raised his fist in anger. His clothes were clean and neat, and ink stained his narrow fingers.

He would probably get robbed on his way home.

"Aye, that's him," said Theodosia, returning to her disguised voice. "I wonder why the fool wanted to meet in the Hanging Pirate, of all places."

"Let's find out," said Caina.

They crossed the room. Theodosia dropped into the chair opposite the man, slouched and confident. Caina stood over them, keeping an eye on the crowd.

"I'm waiting for someone," said the man, fidgeting.

"Well, we're someone," said Theodosia. "See, I heard a funny rumor.

They say there's a clerk who works for Lord Macrinius, a man named Otton. That he's tired of his lord treating him like a slave, wants to see his lord pay. But Lord Macrinius is powerful and rich. So the clerk looks around for someone who can bring Macrinius to ruin."

Otton licked his lips, stared at them for a moment. He looked around. At last he leaned forward.

"You're...you're Ghosts?" he whispered.

"The Ghosts are a fool's tale," said Theodosia. "But we're no friends of Macrinius, I tell you true. So if you have something we can use against him...aye, we will use it."

"I can't do it," said Otton, shaking.

For a moment Caina thought Otton would leave, but he kept talking.

"I can't do it any more!" said Otton, burying his face in his hands. He shuddered for a moment, then looked up. "Lord Macrinius...Lord Macrinius is buying slaves. At first I didn't care, thought it nothing more than another cargo. But then I saw one of the...the 'shipments'...the children crying...gods!"

He buried his face in his hands again.

"Here, man," said Theodosia, picking up the clay mug. "Drink. It'll clear your head."

Otton nodded and drank. "I...I can't do it any more. I can't sleep. I hear the children crying all the time, even in my dreams. I can't live like this. I have to do something. Here." He reached into his coat, drew out a book, and shoved it at Theodosia.

"What's this?" said Theodosia.

"A copy of a ledger," said Otton. "My master is a very frugal man, and keeps track of every copper coin. This is the record of his slave dealings. The ships they came on, the number of slaves, the amount he paid for them, where he stored them. All of it."

"You've put yourself at great risk, doing this," said Theodosia, paging through the ledger. "This could ruin Lord Macrinius. If he finds out about this, he will have you killed."

"I know that," said Otton, rubbing his face. "And if he kills me...well, he kills me. At least I'll face the gods with a clean conscience." He shoved away from the table and stood. "Do what you will with it. I'm done."

He left.

Theodosia sat in silence for a moment. And then she said, "That man near the door, do you see him?"

Caina nodded, taking care not to stare. The man leaned against the wall, watching the crowd with a cool eye. Lean and clean-shaven, he looked as if he knew how to handle a weapon.

He was obviously not a sailor or a mercenary guard.

"He's been watching Otton," said Theodosia. "Macrinius probably hired him to keep an eye out for disloyal servants."

Caina took a deep breath. "I think he's a Kindred assassin."

Theodosia cursed. "You're sure?"

Caina watched as the assassin touched the dagger in his belt. "Pretty sure."

The assassin stretched, finished his mug of wine, and left.

"Let's go," said Theodosia. "Or else Otton's going to meet the gods even sooner than he thought."

They hurried across the Hanging Pirate's common room.

"The two of us can't take a Kindred assassin in a straight fight," murmured Caina.

"Of course not," said Theodosia. "Which is why it's not going to be a straight fight."

Caina nodded. She approved.

They stepped into the narrow dockside street, the cobblestones slick, the air heavy with the scents of gull dung and dead fish. Otton walked with his hands in his pockets, his head down. The Kindred assassin followed, making no effort to conceal his movements. And why bother? Caina doubted a man like Otton would notice a herd of rampaging elephants in his path.

"Otton," called the assassin.

Otton stopped, turned.

Caina started running.

The assassin drew his dagger, and Otton's eyes bulged. "Lord Macrinius knows well to how to repay disloyalty."

Caina snatched a throwing knife from her sleeve and flung it.

The blade buried itself in the assassin's bicep. The man spun with a bellow, and sent his dagger hurtling at Caina's face. She twisted to the side, boots skidding on the damp cobblestones, and the blade clattered against the ground. The assassin yanked another dagger from his belt and lunged at her, ignoring his wounded arm. Caina jumped back, the dagger blurring past her head. The Kindred assassin kept coming, slashing and hacking.

So he didn't see it when Theodosia stepped behind him and buried a dagger in his back.

The assassin shuddered, back arching in agony. Theodosia ripped her blade free and slashed it across his throat. The assassin toppled, landing facedown in a pool of his own blood.

She handled a dagger well, for an opera singer.

"Just as well we're near the harbor," muttered Theodosia, cleaning the dagger on the dead assassin's pants. "Easiest way to dispose of corpses."

"You...you killed him!" said Otton.

"Aye," said Theodosia. "There are some loose bricks against that wall. We'll need them to weigh down the body."

Caina nodded and started collecting bricks. Fortunately, the street remained deserted, save for Theodosia, Otton, and the dead assassin.

"That man was a Kindred assassin," said Theodosia, speaking in her normal voice.

Otton looked ill.

"Macrinius probably hired him to hunt down anyone who might betray him," said Theodosia.

"Then Lord Macrinius knows," said Otton. "I'm finished."

"No," said Caina, dropping the bricks on the corpse. Like Theodosia, she spoke in her own voice. "You'll disappear with us, and we'll dispose of the corpse. Lord Macrinius while realize that something is amiss, but he won't realize how serious. Until it's too late."

Theodosia gave her an approving nod. Then she stripped off her cloak and wrapped the corpse in it, pausing for Caina to add the bricks.

"You'll go into hiding with us," said Theodosia. "Safer that way. Less chance Macrinius will track you down."

"If...if you say so," said Otton. He blinked. "Wait...you're both women?"

Theodosia grinned. "Welcome to the Ghosts."

"But you're women!"

"Then I'm glad we have a strong man like you along," said Theodosia, "to help carry the corpse to the harbor. Now grab his damned feet and lift."

Otton sighed, but helped lift the dead assassin.

CHAPTER 18
DOWNFALL

"I have no head for figures," said Theodosia after they returned to the safety of the Grant Imperial Opera. "Go through this ledger. Tell me if it has anything useful."

So Caina did. She spent the entire next day reading the ledger, with Otton explaining the more obscure parts of it to her. The poor man was frightened of her, but he kept orderly records.

Then Caina looked over the final page. Her eyes widened, and she ran to Theodosia's room.

"This is it," said Caina, pointing at the ledger.

Theodosia looked up from her mirror. "This is what?"

"How we're going to get Lord Macrinius, and maybe even Lord Haeron, too," said Caina. "See this entry, this one here?"

Theodosia squinted at the page. "Macrinius paid ten thousand denarii to the Istarish slavers' brotherhood for three dozen slaves."

"But that's not the important part," said Caina. "He's already paid for the slaves...but they're not going to arrive for another three days."

Theodosia blinked, several times...and then a pleased smiled spread over her face.

"That's...that's good?" said Otton, hovering in the doorway. Caina might have frightened him, but he seemed downright terrified of Theodosia.

"My dear fellow," said Theodosia, "that's very good. Everyone knows that Lord Macrinius dabbles in slave trading, but there's never been any proof. But if we find a score of slaves chained in his cellar, then there's no hiding it. No amount of bribery or political influence will save him then. He'll be finished, and if he's lucky he'll flee the Empire before the Emperor has him beheaded for slave trading and treason."

"So...you're going to catch him in the act?" said Otton.

"Precisely," said Theodosia.

"How?" said Caina.

"We're going to give him some bait that he cannot resist," said Theodosia. Her smile widened. "Me."

###

Riogan arrived the next morning.

Caina saw him as she practiced her unarmed forms alone in the deserted workshop. She finished an unarmed throw, and she turned, she saw Riogan leaning against a pillar, watching her. He looked much as she remembered; the same close-cropped blond hair, the same cold eyes, the same dark clothing and weapons ready at hand.

For a moment they stared at each other.

Then Riogan stepped forward, his hand blurring. His arm shot forward and sent a throwing knife hurtling for her face. But Caina saw the movement coming, and she sidestepped, the knife whirring past her. Her hand dipped into her sleeve, drawing a throwing knife of her own.

But Riogan did not move, save to laugh.

"You've gotten better, girl," he said, his eyes bright with mockery. "A few years ago, that knife would have torn your throat open."

"I've been practicing," said Caina, watching him for any threatening movements. "What are you doing here?"

"Killing people who need killing," said Riogan. "And carrying messages for Halfdan. Though I came at the right time. You could use my help."

Caina nodded. Riogan did not like her, but that was unimportant. He was very good at what he did. And if Theodosia's plan was going to work, they would need all the help they could get.

"Probably," she said at last.

"A shot at Lord Macrinius," said Riogan. "An idea to warm the heart, it is."

"I suppose you have a grudge against him?" said Caina.

Riogan laughed. "Hardly. But he's one of Haeron Icaraeus's strongest lieutenants. And anything that discomforts Haeron Icaraeus is a fine thing."

###

Three nights later, Theodosia sang upon the Grand Imperial Opera's stage, singing the lead of "The Hunter's Marriage", a romantic story full of bawdy songs and innuendos, and it seemed to Caina that Theodosia sang her arias of passion and lust right into Lord Macrinius's box.

Macrinius watched her, enraptured. For once he did not plot and scheme. Instead he simply sat and watched Theodosia sing. He accepted the trays of delicacies that Caina brought him, and the glasses of wine, but he never took his eyes from Theodosia.

And he kept drinking the wine. Specifically, the wine laced with a powder Komnene had taught Caina to prepare, a powder that inflamed the passions of anyone who consumed it. It had a bitter taste, but the wine masked it, and Macrinius was so enraptured by Theodosia's performance that Caina supposed she could have given him a glass of vinegar and he would not have noticed.

The opera concluded, and Macrinius surged to his feet, applauding.

"You," he said after a moment, pointing at Caina. "Girl. Come here, now."

Caina did a curtsy and approached, head bowed. "Yes, my lord?" she said, speaking with a thick Caerish accent. "Do you wish something?"

"Theodosia of Malarae," he said, sweat standing out on his forehead. "Do you know her?" He began scribbling onto a piece of paper.

"Why, of course, my lord," said Caina. "She's the finest singer in all of Malarae, all the Empire, and the jewel of the Opera, so she is."

"Yes, yes, of course," said Macrinius, folding the paper and shoving it into Caina's hand. "Give her that note. If you bring back a message from her, you'll get a denarius. Go!"

Caina did another curtsy and ran.

She returned with Theodosia herself, still clad in her stage costume.

Macrinius gave Caina a denarius and promptly forgot about her.

"My lord Macrinius," said Theodosia.

Macrinius rose to his feet, smiling. "You came yourself?"

"Of course," said Theodosia. "How could I ignore a message from so noble a lord? And your letter was so...fervent."

"How could it not be?" said Macrinius. "Your performance was magnificent. Splendid beyond words. I simply cannot describe it."

Theodosia laughed and did a polite little curtsy, one that gave Macrinius a look down the front of her costume.

Macrinius started to sweat some more.

"My lord is too kind," said Theodosia.

"I hope you will not think me too forward," said Macrinius, "but would you care to accompany me to my townhouse for some...refreshment? That performance, that magnificent performance, must have been most draining."

"Oh, it was, my lord, it was," said Theodosia. "I shall be most happy to tell you about it, in private."

Macrinius took her hand. "My coach awaits us, my dear." His voice was almost a purr.

"Oh, but let me change first," said Theodosia. "And let me take two of my servants. The girl," she fluttered a hand at Caina, "and my footman."

Macrinius frowned.

Theodosia laughed. "I may not be a lady, my lord, but surely you cannot expect a woman to travel without her servants?"

Macrinius blinked. "Well...that seems reasonable. Do not take too long, my dear."

"I shouldn't dream of it," said Theodosia, beckoning to Caina. "Come along, Marina. I want to change clothes, and quickly."

"Yes, madam," said Caina, following Theodosia from Lord Macrinius's box.

Riogan leaned against the wall outside the box, clad in the livery of a footman.

"It's time?" said Riogan, falling in step alongside Caina.

She nodded.

A cold smile spread over Riogan's face.

So Caina and Riogan hung on the outside of Macrinius's elaborate coach as it rattled through Malarae's streets. The coach rolled through Macrinius's gates, past well-armed and vigilant guards, and stopped at the foot of Macrinius's ornate mansion, its walls studded with reliefs and statuary.

Theodosia let Macrinius guide her from the coach and into the mansion's opulent entrance hall, Caina and Riogan trailing after them, along with Macrinius's own servants and bodyguards.

"Such a large house you have, my lord," said Theodosia, looking around with wide eyes.

"Why, this modest little hovel?" said Macrinius with a disparaging gesture. Caina took Theodosia's cloak, folded it over her arm. "It is nothing. Merely a place to sleep when I have business in the Imperial capital. You should see my villa in Cyrica. In summer, when the crops are ripe, and the fields are like seas of gold. Ah, now that is a magnificent sight." He smiled, took her hand, and kissed it. "Though not so much as you, my dear."

Theodosia gave a little laugh. "You flatter me, my lord."

"Why, it hardly counts as flattery if it's the truth," said Macrinius.

Theodosia kept smiling as Macrinius led them through the mansion, pointing out statues and armor and various historical relics from House

Macrinius's history. Soon Lord Macrinius had one arm around Theodosia's shoulder, and she leaned against him, laughing at his jokes.

Finally they reached Macrinius's bedroom.

"Leave us," said Macrinius, looking at his bodyguards. "All of you. Now."

The bodyguards bowed and escorted Caina and Macrinius down the stairs, to a small room near the kitchens. The room had some cots, and a small fireplace, but was otherwise bare.

"You two will stay here tonight," said one of the bodyguards. "His lordship will probably be finished with your mistress by tomorrow morning. One of us will come for you then. Don't leave, and don't wander about the mansion. We catch you outside this room, you'll get a beating. If you're lucky."

"Yes, sir," mumbled Riogan, not meeting the man's eyes. "You won't have any trouble from us, sir."

"See that we don't," said the bodyguard.

He left, locking the door behind him.

Caina's lip twitched in amusement.

"Now?" she said.

"Not yet," said Riogan. "They'll check on us at least once. Count to a thousand."

Caina nodded and started counting in her head.

She had gotten to six hundred and ninety-four when she heard the rasp of a footstep outside the door. "Do you think his lordship will marry our mistress?" said Caina in her thick Caerish accent. "That would be ever so grand, aye? Our mistress would become a lady, and wear silks and jewels and furs, and we would get to live in this fine house..."

"Shut your yap, girl," said Riogan in the same accent, "and let me get some sleep, or you'll feel the back of my hand."

The footsteps faded away.

"I have to say," murmured Riogan in his usual cold voice, "you are the most annoying serving girl I have ever met."

"Thank you," said Caina. "Shall we get on with it?"

Riogan nodded.

Caina climbed to her feet and stripped off her serving maid's dress. Beneath she wore loose-fitting black pants, a long sleeved black shirt, and black boots. A belt around her waist held throwing knives, a coil of rope, a collapsible grapnel, and a few other useful tools. From her belt she drew out a black mask, tugged it over her face, and a pair of black leather gloves. Riogan tossed aside his servant's livery, revealing similar clothing.

"This way," said Riogan, crossing to the window. He raised a dagger, lifted the latch on the shutters, and pushed them open. He had prowled around Macrinius's mansion last night, scouting out the grounds and the buildings, and knew where the slaves were held.

Or so he claimed.

Riogan jumped out the window, and Caina followed. It was a short drop to the ground, only seven or eight feet, and Caina landed besides him, her legs buckling to absorb the force of the fall. Riogan led her around the mansion's bulk, their boots making no sound against the earth. From time to time a patrolling guard came into sight, and they ducked into concealment until the guard passed.

Then they came to the cellar doors.

Gardens ringed Macrinius's mansion, dotted with bushes and trees and statues and small bubbling fountains. In the middle of a garden lay a pair of doors, no doubt leading down to a cellar. Nobles often built such cellars on their grounds to keep wine and cheese and meat cool in the heat of summer.

But to judge from the two guards keeping watch over the doors, Lord Macrinius stored something other than cheese in his cellar.

Slaves, most likely.

Caina crouched behind a bush, Riogan waiting besides her. The guards stood talking with each other, making no effort to keep watch on their surroundings. Obviously, they did not expect trouble.

Riogan watched them for a moment longer. Then he gestured, pointing at the man on the left, and made a slashing motion with his other hand.

Caina understood.

Riogan circled around the cellar doors, moving like a shadow. Caina did the same, keeping herself behind the guards. She remembered training with Halfdan at the Vineyard, remembered creeping up to touch the other Ghosts on the shoulder before they noticed her presence. It was just like that.

Except Macrinius's guards noticed her, they would kill her.

Best not to think about that.

Caina stopped behind the guard, drawing a dagger from her boot.

In one smooth motion she straightened up, clamped one hand over the guard's mouth, and ripped the dagger across his throat. Blood spurted across her gloved fingers. He screamed into her hand, but she sawed the blade back and forth, and soon he choked on his own blood. Caina eased him to the ground, so his fall would not make any undue noise.

She shivered. She had killed before. The thugs at the tavern in Kaunauth. The Kindred assassin in the street. Her mother. But never before had she killed in cold blood.

She didn't like the feeling, not at all.

But she could worry about it later.

She heard a faint thump as Riogan levered his own guard to the ground. He rummaged through the dead man's belt for a moment, then pulled free a long iron key. A moment later he undid the lock on the cellar doors. The door swung upward to reveal a dark staircase descending into the earth.

Torchlight glimmered in the depths.

"Pull the corpses onto the stairs," murmured Riogan into her ear. "Less chance someone will stumble across them."

Caina nodded, dragged her dead guard onto the stairs as Riogan did the same. Then Riogan closed the cellar doors behind them, and they descended, boots making no sound against the cold stone. The stairs ended in a gloomy, vaulted cellar, similar to the place where Maglarion had held Caina captive years ago. Half the chamber had been cordoned off with iron bars, and behind those bars huddled fifty or sixty naked women and children.

The slaves. Kidnapped from their homes, no doubt.

Suddenly Caina did not feel so bad about killing the guard.

Five of Macrinius's men kept watch. Three sat at a wooden table, laughing and playing cards by the light of a lantern. A fourth man leaned against a pillar, watching the game, and a fifth walked back and forth before the iron bars.

The three men playing cards drank from a barrel of wine sitting against one pillar, from time to time filling their clay cups with it.

Riogan caught Caina's eye, gestured at the barrel. She nodded and crept towards it, taking care to remain silent. The thick pillars holding up the roof provided plenty of cover, along with the tangled black shadows thrown by the lanterns. Step by step she drew closer to the barrel.

At last she reached it, and her hand dipped into her belt, drawing out a small pouch. It held another of the powders that Komnene had taught her to make. Caina opened the pouch and number the entire contents into the barrel.

Then she settled against a pillar to wait.

The men kept playing cards, laughing and drinking, and soon refilled their cups. Yawns replaced laughter, and their speech grew slurred and slow. Then one man fell face-first onto the table, wine spilling across the floor.

The man pacing before the iron bars turned. "What's this? Bad enough you're drinking on watch. Now you're sleeping?"

"Marl," said one of the seated guards, his eyes heavy. "I think...I think there's something wrong with the wine..."

Then he, too, passed out.

Marl scowled, and the man leaning against the pillar straightened up. "Bah! They drank themselves senseless. Lord Macrinius will have our..."

Then Riogan exploded out of the darkness, a dagger in either hand,

and killed the man against the pillar in a single smooth motion. But Marl leapt forward and drew his sword, his blade flying for Riogan's head. Riogan backed away, dodging and blocking with his daggers, but Marl kept at him, face grim and focused.

Until Caina's throwing knife landed in Marl's thigh. He staggered a step, and that was all the opening Riogan needed. One blade plunged into Marl's throat, another into his chest, and he went down.

The slaves began to shout, some of the children crying.

"Good throw," said Riogan.

"Thanks," said Caina, wrenching her knife free from Marl's calf.

"Calm the slaves down," he said, crossing to the table. "I'll find the keys."

Caina crossed to the iron bars, and the slaves drew back in fear. She couldn't blame them. They looked half-starved.

Not surprising, given what Maglarion probably had planned for them.

"We are here to rescue you!" she said, speaking Caerish in her disguised voice. "The Emperor will not let his people suffer, and Lord Macrinius shall answer for his crimes. Those of you who have children, make certain they are ready to travel. Help those too weak to stand!"

"But..." began one of the women, clutching a boy of seven or eight.

"Do as I command!" roared Caina, and the slaves complied.

She turned just in time to see Riogan finish cutting the unconscious guards' throats.

"Why did you kill them?" she murmured, keeping her voice low. "There was no reason for it."

The mask concealed his face, but she imagined his lip curling in contempt. "Because there was no reason not to. You don't leave live enemies behind you, girl. You've learned to kill, but you're still too soft for this." He gestured at the slaves. "Besides, are you going to argue that they didn't deserve to die?"

Caina had no answer for that.

Riogan helped himself to Marl's sword and handed her a ring of iron keys. "This is going to be the hardest part. Get the slaves moving."

Caina unlocked the iron door and stepped into the cage. The slaves had been chained to metal rings set in the wall, and she moved down the line, unlocking them as quickly as she could.

"Get on your feet and start moving," she told the slaves. "And keep quiet! Your lives depend on it."

They obeyed, for the most part, though the children kept whimpering.

Riogan pushed open the doors, and they hurried across Macrinius's gardens, making a straight line for the gate. Four men still stood guard at the gate. There had been no clever way to neutralize the gate guards, no way to sneak past them or avoid them.

They were going to have to fight their way out.

Like Riogan had said, the hardest part.

"Stay together," said Caina. "Anyone who runs off on their own is going to die."

The guards turned, eyes widening as they noticed the mob of escaping slaves, and reached for their weapons.

Riogan moved first.

He sprang forward with a bloodcurdling yell, sword in both hands, and struck. The blade crunched into an astonished guard's neck, blood welling over the gleaming steel. But by then the other men had their swords out, and they came at Riogan in a rush.

Caina was ready for them.

Her throwing knife lashed out, struck a guard's armored chest, bounced away. But the blow distracted the man long enough for Caina to jump onto his back and rip her dagger across his throat. But then another guard was on her. She managed to kick free of the dying man in time to avoid the first sword blow, but the pommel caught her on the temple, and she fell hard to the ground. The guard's sword plunged down, and she managed to roll aside. Behind them, she saw Riogan locked in a furious duel with the final guard. He couldn't help her.

And Caina had to face her guard in a fair fight.

Not good.

So she would make the fight a little less fair.

Her hand dipped into one of the pouches at her belt, drawing out a handful of black powder, and she flung it into the guard's face. Luck was with her, and some of the powder connected with the guard's eyes, and the man screamed in sudden agony.

She darted close, her dagger ending to his pain.

Another scream, and Riogan finished his guard.

"Move!" he growled, gesturing at the slaves with the bloody sword. "Move, damn you, move!"

He pushed open the gates, and the slaves streamed through them.

###

A short walk took them to a watchtower of the Civic Militia. The Militia, Malarae's police and garrison force, had fortified watchtowers scattered throughout the city. And Theodosia had said that Ghosts took care to keep friends among the Militia's officers.

Riogan banged on the tower's door until it swung open. A man in the red surcoat and chain mail of the Civic Militia stepped out, a plumed helmet on his head and a baton of office in his hand. A centurion, then.

And unless Caina missed her guess, the centurion was Tomard,

Theodosia's eldest son.

She hid a smile behind her mask.

Theodosia did enjoy pulling strings. Certainly, Tomard did not seem surprised, or even fazed, by fifty naked slaves turning up at his doorstep.

"Aye, then?" Tomard said in Caerish. "What's all this?"

"These slaves escaped at great peril of their lives from the cellars of Lord Macrinius," said Riogan, handing over the ledger that Otton had given them. "I suggest you move at once to seize any evidence before Lord Macrinius destroys it."

Tomard took the ledger, paged through it.

"Mother, Mother," he muttered to himself, "you do have a flair for the dramatic, don't you?" He looked at Riogan. "If you're who I think you are, you'd better disappear, now." He turned and bellowed into the watchtower. "Men! You, you, you! Get blankets and food for these fellows! The rest of you, with me! We get to arrest a lord tonight!"

Riogan and Caina vanished into the night.

The Civic Militia arrested Lord Macrinius, despite the furious protests of Lord Haeron Icaraeus and a half-dozen other Restorationist lords, but the evidence was overwhelming. Nearly fifty eyewitnesses, describing their illegal imprisonment in Macrinius's cellar. The ledger the Civic Militia had found with the slaves. And a host of other documents taken from his mansion, proving beyond a doubt that he had been engaged with Istarish slavers, kidnapping Imperial citizens and selling them as slaves.

Lord Haeron and the others withdrew their protests, leaving Macrinius to his fate.

The Emperor himself pronounced Macrinius's sentence, and a few weeks later, Caina stood in the crowd and watched the executioner behead Macrinius in the Grand Market below the Imperial Citadel.

"I am disappointed," said Theodosia a few days later, examining herself in the mirror. The rumors that she had been involved in the Lord Macrinius's ignoble downfall had only enhanced her reputation. The Grand Imperial Opera had been full to bursting the past few nights

"Why?" said Caina.

"We got Macrinius," said Theodosia, "but no evidence on Lord Haeron. The man is too clever."

"At least we did get Macrinius," said Caina.

Theodosia glanced at Caina. "And yet that troubles you. What is it?"

Caina hesitated. "You slept with him."

"I did," said Theodosia. She smiled. "And I must say, for a scoundrel and a murderer he was quite a skillful lover. Pity he was involved in slave-trading." She adjusted her hair. "That troubles you, I take it?"

Caina nodded.

"My dear," said Theodosia, "we have spent the last several months arranging Lord Macrinius's death. If I had sent you into the night with a dagger and a vial of poison to see him dead, you would have done it, no?"

"I would have killed him," said Caina. "He deserved it. It's just...seducing him seemed wrong."

Theodosia smiled, took Caina's shoulder, guided her to stand in front of the mirror.

"Caina," said Theodosia, "you've learned to fight with your hands and with your knives and with your mind. And you are a very lovely young woman, even if you don't see that yourself. If you chose, you could destroy a man without raising a finger against him."

"That seems wrong," said Caina.

Theodosia shrugged. "As compared to killing him?"

Caina had no answer for that.

"We are Ghosts," said Theodosia, "and we do what we must, to guard the Empire from tyrannical lords and slavers and corrupt sorcerers. And if we should happen to enjoy it along the way," she smiled, "well...why not?"

"I don't know," said Caina. As a child, she had wanted a family of her own, vowing that she would be a better mother than Laeria Amalas. But that would never happen. She would never have children. And if she could use her body as a weapon against men, why should she not?

Maybe she should have let Lucien seduce her.

"I don't know," said Caina again.

"Well, think on it," said Theodosia. "Meanwhile, help me with my makeup. I have an aria to sing."

After the performance, a man waited in Theodosia's room.

Caina stopped, hand dipping into her sleeve for a throwing knife. The man had graying black hair and arms heavy with muscle. He wore the robe and cap of a prosperous merchant, a trimmed beard framing his lips, and...

Caina grinned. "Halfdan!"

"You've grown," said Halfdan, smiling back.

"Well, it's been a year," said Caina.

"Theodosia told me you did well, very well, with Macrinius."

Theodosia walked into the room, and stopped. "You rogue! You return at last!"

"So," said Halfdan, "I heard you sent Macrinius to heaven before you sent him to hell."

Theodosia actually blushed.

"Well done, both of you," said Halfdan. "Macrinius was one of Haeron Icaraeus's most powerful supporters. Lord Haeron will find his loss a heavy blow."

Theodosia snorted. "Better if we had found evidence to rid ourselves of Lord Haeron, as well."

"He was too careful for that," said Halfdan. "But we will have him, sooner or later." He looked at Caina. "And it's time for you to have another teacher."

Caina bit her lip and nodded.

"Ah, you will take her from me?" said Theodosia. "I do not know what I will do without her."

"You can apply your own makeup," said Caina.

"Yes, but I do not want to," said Theodosia. She laughed, and hugged Caina. "Be careful, child. You have great things ahead of you, I think. And you are welcome to attend my performances at any time. Just so long as you don't try to sing."

Caina hugged Theodosia back, and left with Halfdan.

CHAPTER 19
COUNTESS MARIANNA NEREIDE

Halfdan was disguised as a jewel merchant, Basil Callenius of Marsis, and so he took her to an expensive inn. He had his own coach and footman, and a pair of servants to look after his clothes and goods.

"This is a nicer disguise than Marcus Antali," Caina murmured.

"A jewel merchant is a superb disguise for spying upon the nobility," said Halfdan. "Nobles love jewels, after all."

The next morning they took the coach from the inn. Halfdan had given Caina a new gown to wear, blue with black trim, and she was startled to find herself admiring her reflection in the coach's window.

Theodosia must have worn off on her.

"Who is to be my next teacher?" said Caina.

Halfdan looked up from the coach's window. "Your last teacher. You're almost ready."

"Who, then?" said Caina.

"The circlemaster of Malarae," said Halfdan.

Caina frowned. "Theodosia is the circlemaster of Malarae."

"One of Malarae's circlemasters," said Halfdan. "As I'm sure you've observed, Malarae is a rather large place. Over a million people live here, and tens of thousands of visitors at any one time. Keeping track of everything that the Ghosts need to know about is...difficult. So Malarae has multiple circles, covering different parts of the city. Theodosia is circlemaster of one, but there are others."

Caina nodded. "What will this circlemaster teach me?"

"How to be a noblewoman," said Halfdan.

Caina laughed. "My father was Lord of House Amalas and Harbormaster of Aretia. Technically, I am a noblewoman."

"Yes, but you don't know how to act like a noblewoman," said Halfdan.

Caina shrugged. "Theodosia taught me to masquerade as one."

"I'm sure she did," said Halfdan. "But masquerading is one thing. The Emperor and the Ghosts have many enemies among the nobility, and we need more eyes and ears among them. You might know how to masquerade a Nighmarian noblewoman of high birth, but do you know how to act like one? You've spent a third of your life around spies, assassins, and opera singers, and I rather doubt your mother took the time to instruct you in social graces."

"She didn't," said Caina.

"So if you are to spy for us among the nobles," said Halfdan, "you need to learn these things. How to dress, how to speak, how to walk. The forms of etiquette and courtesy the nobility require. How to command servants. How to dance."

"Theodosia taught me to dance," said Caina. "She even had me on stage a few times."

Halfdan laughed. "Aye? Well, believe me, the sort of dancing you can do on stage at the opera is rather different than the sort of dancing that is acceptable at a noble ball."

A short time later the coach stopped before townhouse, smaller than Macrinius's sprawling pile of a mansion, but much less ostentatious. A small garden, full of flowering bushes, ringed the townhouse, threaded with paths of white stone. Caina followed Halfdan from the coach, and a footman in livery greeted them at the door.

"Basil Callenius, master merchant of the Collegium of Jewelers, and his daughter Anna to see Lady Julia Morenna," said Halfdan.

"Of course, sir," said the footman. "I shall announce you at once."

The footman led them up a flight of stairs and into a sitting room with high windows overlooking the garden. A woman sat in a chair, looking out the windows, a distant look on her face. She was a little older than Theodosia, and much smaller, with black hair well on its way to gray. A maid stood besides her, holding a silver tray with a teapot upon it.

"Lady Julia," said Halfdan. "I am honored to see you once again."

The maid busied herself pouring out three cups of tea.

"Of course you are, Basil," said Julia, extending a thin hand. Halfdan bowed over it and kissed the heavy gold ring on one finger. "Whenever you appear, I always wind up spending entirely too much upon jewelry. It's positively scandalous." She spoke High Nighmarian with cool precision. "This is the daughter I've heard so much about?"

"Aye," said Halfdan. The maid handed a teacup to Caina, the fine porcelain warm against her fingers.

Julia nodded. "Leave us," she commanded, and the footman and the maid bowed and withdrew.

Something in that imperious voice irritated Caina.

"So," said Lady Julia, after the servants withdrew. "I heard you've been busy."

"Well," said Halfdan, "I do like to keep occupied."

Julia smiled. "Lord Macrinius had such a...dramatic fall, didn't he? Who would have thought that he would be foolish enough to smuggle slaves into the Imperial capital? Or that the slaves would be bold enough to break free, escape their chains, and report his crimes to the Civic Militia? One wonders if the slaves had some help."

"I wouldn't know about that," said Halfdan.

Again that little smile crossed Julia's face. "Of course not. Though I do wonder. Why did Macrinius do something so stupid?" She sighed and took a sip of the tea. "Though he was, if you will forgive the phrase, never the sharpest sword in the armory."

"A common trait among Restorationist nobles," said Halfdan.

"Sadly true," said Julia. "Yet why risk bringing slaves into the city? For the principle of the thing? Macrinius did not seem the sort of man to lay his life down over principle. For money, perhaps? But surely he could not earn enough money trading slaves to justify the risk."

"Almost certainly Macrinius bought those slaves because Haeron Icaraeus ordered him to do so," said Halfdan, "and Haeron wants to give those slaves to Maglarion."

Julia blinked, once. Evidently Halfdan hadn't told her about that part yet.

"Maglarion is here?" said Julia.

"He's allied himself with Haeron Icaraeus," said Halfdan. "I don't yet know the details of their pact. I suppose Maglarion promised to kill Haeron's foes or to put him upon the throne; he's made such deals before. And in exchange, Haeron provides Maglarion with slaves."

"Why?" said Julia.

"Raw material," said Caina, her voice quiet as she remembered. "Maglarion's a necromancer. He uses the blood of living victims to fuel his spells. Evidently he finds it easier to get slaves from someone like Lord Icaraeus than to go out and kidnap them himself."

"But why do this in the Imperial capital?" said Julia. "Necromancy is practiced openly in Anub-Kha, or in Anshan. Slavery is legal in Istarinmul and the Cyrican provinces. Maglarion could carry out his...experiments in peace there, without fear of the Ghosts. Why do such things here?"

"I don't know," said Halfdan, "and that's what you're going to find out. I know that Haeron Icaraeus is gaining allies among the nobility, and that his followers invariably wind up dabbling in the slave trade. None of the other Ghost circles are in a position to infiltrate Haeron's meetings. You are, however. Find what Maglarion wants. Whatever he promised Haeron is bad enough. Whatever Maglarion wants for himself is probably much worse. Caina will help you."

Julia's gray eyes shifted to Caina.

"Train her to act as a proper young Nighmarian noblewoman," said Halfdan. "She'll help you. And she has variety of skills you will find most useful."

"As you wish," said Julia.

"Caina, do as Julia bids you, just as you did for your previous circlemaster," said Halfdan.

"I shall," said Caina.

Halfdan bowed, kissed Julia's ring once, and left.

Caina and Julia stared at each other for a moment.

"You don't like me very much," said Julia, "do you?"

Caina blinked. "I...just met you. That seems premature."

"But," said Julia, lifting a finger, "you don't like me. Do you."

"No," said Caina.

"Why not, if I might ask?" said Julia.

"You...remind me of my mother," said Caina.

Julia reminded Caina of Laeria Amalas a great deal. Julia's appearance, her perfectly arranged hair and gown, her jewelry, everything reminded Caina of her mother, of how Laeria used to obsess over every last detail of her appearance.

"Ah," said Julia. "You and your mother are not on speaking terms, I take it?"

"She's dead," said Caina. "I killed her."

Julia's face went still. "May I ask why?"

"She was a novice of the Magisterium," said Caina, "but they put her out because she was too weak. So she sold me to Maglarion, in hopes that he would teach her the arcane science that the Magisterium never would."

"I see," said Julia. "Your mother...she was Lady Laeria, was she not? Laeria, who married Sebastian Amalas?"

Caina blinked. "How did you know that? Did you know them?"

"I did, years ago," said Julia. "I used to live in Artifel, before my husband and son died. I knew your mother, when she was a novice in the Magisterium motherhouse. She was smart and ambitious, but eaten up with pride. Your father once served a term as Lord Governor of Outer Ulkaaria. Did you know that?"

Caina shook her head.

"That was when your mother met your father," said Julia. "I had hoped that he would be good for her, that he would temper her arrogance." She sighed. "Instead, she saw your father as a means to advancement. But he was not interested in further Imperial magistracies, and wanted to return home to Aretia."

"He did," said Caina. "My mother...used to berate him for not seeking an Imperial magistracy."

"I had heard that slavers killed Sebastian and Laeria six or seven years ago," said Julia. "I had no idea that they had a daughter. You look just like Laeria, you know."

"I do not!" said Caina, her hands curling into fists. At once she berated herself for the outburst. Halfdan and Theodosia had taught her better than that, and she forced herself back to calm.

"You do," said Julia. "It was not an insult. Laeria was quite a lovely young woman, even if her heart was rotten."

"What...what was my father like, when you knew him?" said Caina.

"Diligent," said Julia. "But distracted. I suspect he became Lord Governor of Outer Ulkaaria because it was expected of him, but he wanted nothing more than to return to Aretia and live in peace and quiet with his books. A wise young man, really. Our Empire would be better for it if more men desired to live in peace and quiet, rather than seeking honor and power."

"Perhaps he was not so wise," said Caina, "if he was fooled by my mother."

Julia almost smiled. "Your mother could be very charming, when she put her mind to it." She rose, setting aside the cup of tea. "And so can you. Maglarion and your mother hurt you, and you desire revenge."

Caina said nothing.

"But you are only one girl," said Julia, "and you cannot defeat your enemies with knives and fists. No. You must use a softer way. A subtler way. If you can charm them, convince them that you are in fact their friend...then they will never see the knife coming, will they? Not until it is too late. The nobility of the Empire is a nest of serpents behind smiling masks, child. And I can teach you to move among them."

Caina remembered how her mother had become so charming whenever someone of sufficient rank or wealth visited Aretia.

An ability that Caina might find useful herself.

"All right," she said at last.

###

So Lady Julia Morenna taught her the arts of a noblewoman.

There was more to it than Caina expected.

Some of it she had learned from Theodosia already. All the little tricks of cosmetics to make herself look more beautiful. How to make her eyes look larger, her cheekbones sharper, her lips redder. How to pick gowns that flattered her form without revealing too much...unless the time was right to reveal more, of course.

Quite a bit of it Caina did not know.

When to wear silk, or linen, or velvet, or damask, depending upon the weather and the formality of the occasion. What sort of jewelry to wear. Theodosia had worn very little jewelry. Most of it had been costume jewelry, glass gems set in cheap metal, and she had worn it only while on stage. But Julia had a vast store of jewelry, and she explained its uses to Caina.

"Men, by and large," she said, "do not care about jewels. They will see that you are wearing them, which means you are a woman of station, and that is enough. Women, however, wear jewelry the way that peacocks wear feathers. Especially noblewomen, and wealthier commoners. The wife or daughters of a prosperous merchant will very often wear silver, with amethysts and sapphires. Nobles wear gold, with rubies and diamonds and emeralds. Unless, of course, you are simply wearing jewelry to enhance your appearance." She held up a silver chain adorned with sapphires. "This would work marvelously for you, I think. The silver, a contrast with your black hair. And the sapphires, to match those lovely blue eyes of yours."

They spent a great deal of time going over etiquette. Caina already knew the history behind some of it. The Empire was old, and some of the noble Houses traced their lineage back for thousands of years. Older Houses had more prestige than younger ones, and the oldest Houses of all, the eight First Houses that traced their descent back to the founding of the Empire - only members of their blood could sit upon the Imperial throne.

"House Amalas was founded in the Third Empire," said Julia, "by a valiant Legionary the Emperor raised to the nobility. But we cannot have you going about under your real name, can we? You shall be...Marianna, of House Nereide, I think. Yes. House Nereide went extinct during the War of the Fourth Empire, so that should be a suitable identity for you."

She taught Caina the elaborate rules of etiquette surrounding the balls and feasts of the nobility. The rules of precedence, how the older Houses always went first...unless the lord of a younger House had been made a Count or held an Imperial magistracy. How to address a lord, a lady, a master magus, a high priest, a merchant. How to command servants with suitable dignity - firm enough that they did not think you weak, yet not harshly enough to make them spit in the wine.

One of Julia's servants, an old man with a prissy demeanor, spent several days teaching her to dance as the nobles did, slowly and with stately dignity. Caina found she rather enjoyed it. It was not all that different, really, from the unarmed forms she practiced every morning until her heart raced.

###

Three weeks later, Julia declared that Caina was ready for her first ball.

She spent the better part of the day getting ready, with the assistance of no fewer than three maids. She bathed, perfumed, shaved, coiffed, and finally got dressed in a flowing gown of blue silk with black slashes on the hanging sleeves, and intricate black embroidery across the bodice. It dipped lower in front than Caina would have expected, but that left room for a delicate silver necklace, a sapphire hanging from the chain. Silver earrings with sapphires went in her ears, and Julia had found a ring with the sigil of House Nereide, which Caina put on the third finger of her right hand.

Her father's ring she kept with her, tied to a leather cord around her left wrist, hidden beneath her sleeve.

After they finished, Caina gazed at herself in the mirror. The blue gown fit well, and the sapphires sparked in their silver settings. Her black hair had been piled in an elaborate braided crown, the current fashion among Malarae's nobility, and makeup made her eyes look larger.

Julia had been right. Caina looked almost exactly like her mother.

She shivered in disgust, and resisted an urge to smash the mirror.

But if gowns and jewels and cosmetics were weapons she could use against the magi, against Maglarion...then she would use them, and use them well.

That night they took Julia's coach to the mansion of Lord Corthios, a Restorationist noble and one of Lord Haeron's supporters.

"So what are we looking for here?" said Caina, smoothing the blue silk of her skirt.

She did rather like the way it looked on her.

"Anything interesting, of course," said Lady Julia, peering out the coach's windows at the dark streets of Malarae. "The nobles socialize at these balls. So naturally there's a great deal of scheming and plotting that the Ghosts want to overhear. Lord Corthion is one of Haeron Icaraeus's chief supporters among the Restorationists, so Lord Haeron himself will probably put in a brief appearance. Especially after poor Macrinius's unfortunate tragedy, alas." She smiled, briefly. "Though not all nobles come to scheme. Some attend to get drunk and eat too much food, or to seek out new companions in the bedchamber. And some simply enjoy dancing."

"Are you a Restorationist?" said Caina.

Julia laughed. "Of course not, child. I am a Ghost circlemaster. My sympathies lie with the Loyalists. But Lady Julia Morenna pays no attention to politics. Lady Julia Morenna is a meddling busybody of a widow who delights in playing matchmaker."

Which was part of Caina's disguise. "Countess Marianna Nereide" was a rural noblewoman who had come to the Imperial capital seeking a wealthy husband. And naturally, Countess Marianna had sought the aid of Lady Julia Morenna, well-known for her ability to play matchmaker.

"I think," said Caina, "that your public face is as much a disguise on you as this gown is on me."

Julia lifted her eyebrows. "Of course it is. Ah, here we are."

The coach came to a stop and the footman opened the door. Lord Corthios's mansion was smaller than Macrinius's, but not by much. Every window shone the enspelled glass spheres the novices of the Magisterium churned out and sold by the thousands. Liveried servants hastened back and forth, bearing trays of delicacies. Nobles stood in small groups in the gardens, chatting.

Lord Corthios greeted his guests at the door, one by one. Caina had seen him several times at the Grand Imperial Opera in Lord Haeron's box, and she knew what he looked like. An old man, balding, thin and hard as an old root.

She stopped to do a curtsy before him, and only long practice kept the surprise from her face.

Lord Corthios looked younger.

Not very much younger. But there was more muscle on his frame than Caina remembered, she could swear it. His hairline had moved closer to his forehead. and his white hair had turned iron gray. He must have dyed it.

But why would he have dyed it gray?

Julia's voice cut into her thoughts. "My lord, it pleases me to introduce Marianna, a Countess of House Nereide."

"An honor," said Corthios, bowing over her hand and planting a dry kiss upon her fingers. He stared down the front of Caina's gown as he straightened up, and his smile widened. "I do hope we shall have some time together later in the evening. The duties of a host can be so burdensome."

Caina smiled at him. "I hope so as well, my lord."

She followed Julia into the ballroom.

"Boor," muttered Julia.

"Does he look younger to you?" said Caina.

"Younger?" said Julia. "Now that you mention it, yes. I thought that he had dyed his hair. But he almost looks…almost looks as if he put on some muscle, as well. Perhaps he's started training. Almost certainly that is it."

But it still bothered Caina.

###

She spent the rest of the night circulating with Julia. A score of different noblemen asked Caina to dance, and to her very great surprise, she found that she enjoyed dancing with them.

And she learned things, too. The noblemen wanted to impress her, the pretty young Countess from the rural provinces, and so told her things. About their wealth, their power, their connections. About the high offices and honors they held. About the powerful lords – like Haeron Icaraeus – they counted as friends.

She saw Haeron Icaraeus himself later that night, standing with his usual cluster of bodyguards and followers.

With the notable exception of Lord Macrinius, of course.

But Haeron himself looked younger. His hair and beard were thicker, and he looked as if he had lost weight.

Perhaps Julia was right, and he had been taking better care of himself.

But she remembered listening to Maglarion lecture as she lay chained upon that metal table, telling his students that necromancy could bring renewed youth and everlasting life...

Then a hand closed about hers, and Caina found herself face to face with a lord. A man in his late twenties or early thirties, she thought, with close-cropped blond hair and blue eyes. The hand that gripped hers was hard and strong, and he looked as if he knew how to use the ornate sword that hung at his belt.

"Let's dance," he said, and pulled her along. Caina had no choice but to follow, unless she wanted to fall on her face.

"It is customary, my lord," she said, voice icy, "to ask first."

He smiled and lifted his eyebrows. "Well, you obviously wanted to dance. So it was only polite to dispense with the pleasantries and get right to the point. Besides, you were looking at fat old Haeron with such a baleful expression. It is the duty of a lord to rescue a lady from such dark thoughts."

"I most certainly was not!" said Caina. "I would never be so rude as to stare." At least she hoped not. Haeron Icaraeus was paranoid, and if he realized that she had been looking at him...he might start to draw conclusions.

The lord laughed. "Or he'll think that you want him, the randy old goat."

Caina blinked, and realized that he was teasing her. Which was a relief. She hadn't been staring at Haeron after all.

Though this lout was still teasing her.

She opened her mouth to reply, and he spun her around, arm coiling about her waist.

A lout who happened to dance very well.

He spun her into the first steps of the "Tiger and the Gazelle", a complicated, intricate dance, and Caina answered in kind. She expected him to stumble, to miss a step, but he never did, and his confident smile never wavered. Caina wished that her skirt did not hinder her movements, but the unarmed forms had made her legs strong, and she kept pace with him.

When they finished, they bowed to each other, as the dance required. Caina was surprised to hear a smattering of applause from the surrounding nobles. Apparently they had made something of a spectacle.

"You dance very well, my lady," said the lord. "You must be new to the capital. I am sure so skillful a dancer could not have escaped my notice for long."

"Tell me your name," said Caina, "and perhaps I will tell you mine, my lord."

A lie. She would not tell him her real name, after all.

He smirked, bowed over her hand, and planted a kiss on her signet ring. "Alastair, Lord of House Corus, at your service, my lady."

"Marianna, Countess of House Nereide," said Caina.

"Perhaps we'll have the opportunity to dance again," said Alastair.

He bowed once more, and left.

"You two made quite the stir," said Julia.

Caina felt her face redden, much to her annoyance. "Tell me about him."

"He's married, for one," said Julia.

Caina was surprised to find herself disappointed.

"Beyond that, he's a tribune in the Eighteenth Legion," said Julia. "He spends half his time in the field with the Legion, and the rest of it here in the capital. He's a notorious womanizer. And a Militarist lord; he probably owns a few slaves in the Imperial Pale, off the records. He's friendly with Haeron Icaraeus, but not closely allied with him."

"Oh," said Caina, even more disappointed. A good dancer he might have been, but if he was a friend of Haeron Icaraeus, and a slaveholder, she wanted nothing to do with him. "What does he do for Lord Haeron?"

"Carry messages, mostly," said Julia. "Haeron has friends among the officers of the Legions. Lord Alastair brings them messages when he travels north to the Pale and his Legion. And sometimes the Legions take slaves from the barbarian tribes outside the Pale. Alastair arranges to have them smuggled back to Malarae. Exotic barbarian slaves often fetch high prices."

"I see," said Caina.

"If you want to be his mistress," said Julia, "that's your decision, of course, but I wouldn't recommend it. Granted, he is quite charming. But he doesn't know anything useful enough to justify the bother of seducing him.

What else did you learn?"

"Lord Basilikos," said Caina, "has made an agreement with Lord Haeron..."

She launched in a concise description of everything she had learned that night of the nobility's endless jockeying for status and power.

"Good," said Julia. "You see? These balls are not such a waste of time after all."

"No," said Caina. "They're not. And the dancing is really rather enjoyable."

Her eyes strayed back to Alastair Corus as she spoke, and she made herself look away.

###

So Caina attended balls under Julia Morenna's watchful eye, sometimes as many as three or four a week. She danced with lords, and spoke with ladies, and made friends with powerful and wealthy merchants.

Very often she danced with Alastair Corus, even if he was a slave trader. And married. It was not as if his wife ever came to the balls.

And she soon noticed something disturbing.

"All of them," she murmured to Julia one night, standing in the corner of a noble's ballroom. "All the Restorationist lords who follow Haeron. They all look younger."

Julia said nothing.

"It's Maglarion's necromancy," said Caina. "He said he could make people younger. That's why Haeron and the others are working with Maglarion. He's promised to make them immortal. And that's why Haeron is buying so many slaves. Maglarion's killing them, using their blood to make his followers younger."

"And what does Maglarion get out of it?" said Julia.

"I don't know," said Caina.

But they had to find out. Before it was too late.

CHAPTER 20
MORTAL WOUNDS

Months passed, and Caina attended more balls with Julia. On other nights she went to the Grand Imperial Opera, heard Theodosia sing, and flirted and chatted and gossiped with the nobles. Sometimes she attended chariot races at the Imperial Hippodrome, placing wagers on the charioteers and listening to the nobles discuss business.

She grew adept at charming lords and merchants and magi, gleaning secrets that they did not wish her to know. From time to time she donned a plain wool dress and masqueraded as Julia's serving maid. As her experiences with Theodosia had taught her, nobles never noticed servants, after all.

And sometimes Julia had her break into a mansion in the dead of night, clad all in black, to plant a letter or to steal one, or to dose a noble's wine with an aphrodisiac or a sleeping draught. Caina came to think of Julia as a spider sitting in a vast web of intrigue.

And Caina helped her spin that web.

One day a liveried messenger, solemn in a silver-trimmed black coat, arrived at Julia's townhouse bearing a scroll sealed with Lord Haeron Icaraeus's personal sigil.

It was an invitation. Lord Haeron would celebrate his fiftieth birthday with a grand ball, and he requested the honor of Lady Julia's and Countess Marianna's presences.

"Interesting," murmured Julia, as she and Caina sat over tea. "Interesting, indeed. I have been trying for years to get an informant into

Icaraeus's mansion. The man is simply too paranoid, and his security too rigid. If Lord Haeron knows that someone has betrayed him, or if he even suspects betrayal, he unleashes the Kindred."

"Do you think he knows that we are Ghosts?" said Caina. "That you are a circlemaster?"

Julia took a moment to sip her tea. "Possibly. But I doubt it. Lady Julia Morenna, as you know, is a meddling old busybody with no interest in politics. Besides, I am not wealthy enough or powerful enough for Lord Haeron to take an interest in me."

"Then why send you an invitation?" said Caina.

"To show his power, of course, and his wealth," said Julia. "It would not surprise me if he sent an invitation to every noble, every magus, and every sufficiently wealthy merchant in the city."

"What about me?" said Caina.

"I doubt he's thought about you at all. 'House Nereide' has even less power and influence than House Morenna," Julia smiled for a moment, "and Countess Marianna Nereide, my dear, has established a reputation as an empty-headed flirt."

"Thank you," said Caina. She had worked hard at that, after all.

"If he does think about you," said Julia, "it's no doubt as a potential sexual conquest. But I doubt he's even aware of you."

"Charming. So," said Caina, "what shall we do about this invitation?"

"Why, we shall accept," said Julia. "It would be terribly rude to ignore it, would it not?" She smiled. "Besides, I've wanted to look around the Icaraeus mansion for quite some time. Wasn't it thoughtful of Haeron to give me the chance?"

She rang a bell, summoning her servants to fetch pen and paper so she could write a response.

A week later, Julia's coach rattled to a stop outside the sprawling grounds of Haeron Icaraeus's mansion.

Caina descended from the coach, her blue skirts gathered in one hand. The mansion was enormous, ten stories of gleaming marble fronted with ornate columns, intricate bas-reliefs, and hundreds of statues in heroic poses. A colossal tower rose four hundred feet from its core, no doubt built with the aid of the magi. The gardens ringing the mansion almost seemed like a forest in themselves. Hundreds of coaches surrounded the mansion, and Caina saw throngs of people, clad in their most ornate finery, making their way across the gardens.

"I think Haeron invited half the city," murmured Julia.

Caina looked down the streets. "He even has tents set up, to give free food and wine to the commoners."

"Of course," said Julia. "Haeron would like the commoners to toast his health...so long as they do not get too close to him."

They walked through the crowds of nobles, towards the mansion's grand doors. Caina saw armed men strolling through the crowds, wearing the livery of House Icaraeus, swords and daggers in their belts and crossbows cradled in their arms.

"Kindred assassins," she murmured to Julia.

"You're certain?"

She watched one of the assassins adjust a dagger. "Yes."

There were another group of armed men. They wore black, segmented armor, like Legion armor but far more ornate. Each man wore a purple cloak, and bore a black shield embossed with the eagle of the Empire.

"The Imperial Guard," said Julia. "The Emperor himself will make an appearance tonight."

"Why?" said Caina. "I thought Emperor Alexius and Lord Haeron hated each other."

"They do," said Julia, "but Lord Haeron is still one of the most powerful lords of the Empire. Courtesy requires that the Emperor put in an appearance. So they will exchange polite compliments while smiling, even though they detest each other."

"Which is what you've been teaching me to do," said Caina.

Julia laughed. "Quite right. Come. Let's exchange polite compliments of our own with Lord Haeron."

As they drew closer to the crowd at the mansion doors, Caina's skin began to crawl, and she felt...something in the air, a faint electric tingle that made her stomach twist.

Sorcery.

"There's...a lot of sorcerous power here," said Caina.

Julia glanced around the crowd. "Someone's casting a spell? There are at least a score of master magi here."

"I don't think that's it," said Caina. "It feels like...someone's cast a lot of very powerful spells here, and recently."

"Maglarion?" said Julia.

"It could be," said Caina. "I don't know."

"Keep your eyes open," murmured Julia.

And then they stood before Haeron Icaraeus.

"My lord Haeron," said Julia, performing a deep curtsy, and Caina followed suit. "Honor to you on this felicitous day."

"Thank you, my lady," said Haeron, his voice a deep rumble as he sketched a shallow bow in return and kissed Julia's ring.

"I must say," said Julia, "you are looking quite well."

He did. The ball was in celebration of his fiftieth birthday, but Haeron

Icaraeus could have passed for thirty-five. He was slimmer than Caina remembered, more vigorous, more energetic.

"Clean living," said Haeron, smiling. His dark eyes flicked to Caina. "And this is…"

Caina did another curtsy.

"Countess Marianna, of House Nereide," said Julia.

"A pleasure, my dear," said Haeron, kissing Caina's ring again. "Perhaps I shall have the opportunity to speak with you later."

But he turned away, dismissing her presence. No doubt he had already forgotten her.

Good.

She followed Julia into the mansion's ballroom. It was an vast space, large enough to hold Julia's entire townhouse, four stories high with elaborate marble-railed balconies ringing the walls. Crystal chandeliers dangled from the ceiling, holding hundreds of the Magisterium's glowing glass spheres. It must have cost an unspeakable amount of money.

"What now?" said Caina.

"We mingle," said Julia. "And look around. We've never had a chance to get into Icaraeus's mansion before. See if you can find anything interesting."

Caina nodded and began wandering across the ballroom floor. Nobles, merchants, and magi stood in small knots, talking and drinking wine. Musicians played soft music from the corners, and servants hurried back and forth. The tingling sensation against her skin got worse, and the scars on her belly tightened.

That hadn't happened for a long time.

Was Maglarion himself here?

She shivered at the thought.

"Your expression, my lady, is positively baleful."

Alastair Corus stopped before her, stark in his black coat and boots, sword hanging at his belt. He passed her a silver flute of wine, and Caina took it.

"It is rather colder in here than I expected," said Caina, sipping at the wine. "That's all."

"Ah," said Alastair. "Is that it? I've been in many battles, my lady, and I've seen the faces of the men as they charge the enemy. I daresay you could put a fright into them."

Caina raised an eyebrow. "You are saying, sir, that I look like a charging Legionary? How terribly flattering."

Alastair laughed. "I made a botch of that, didn't I?" He hooked his elbow through her arm. "Come, let us walk together. That will help keep you warm."

Caina pulled free from him. "Perhaps you should walk with your wife, instead."

A grimace flickered over his face. "I would be delighted to walk with my wife, if she did not hate me so much."

Caina blinked. "Your wife hates you?"

He had never mentioned that before.

"The soldiers under my command," said Alastair, "they are not supposed to marry. But many of them have women in the camps and the garrison towns. They have something to look forward to, when they return from the field." His mouth twisted. "But not me. My wife has always hated me. Our fathers forced us to marry, and she has never forgiven me. She thinks that I'm beneath her, you see."

"My...mother," said Caina. "My mother treated my father in much the same way. I'm sorry."

Alastair shrugged. "Well, what's done is done. So you can hardly blame me if I decide to attend balls and walk with lovely women instead of going home to listen to my wife complain that I will not give her more money for shoes."

Caina thought for a moment, and then smiled.

"You know," she said, "I think a walk would warm me up."

And it would give her an excuse to look around the mansion.

Alastair laughed. "Perhaps I cannot fit you into my schedule."

"So you'd rather go home to your wife?" said Caina.

Alastair sighed. "You make an excellent point."

He extended his arm, and Caina grinned and put hers through it.

"Well," she said, "where shall we walk? Lord Haeron's mansion is so grand. I should really like to see more of it."

Alastair snorted. "Grand? Gaudy and tasteless is more like it. A giant marble monument to the tiresome old blowhard's vanity. But if you want to see more of it, see more of it you shall. I could never refuse a pretty woman anything."

Caina laughed and turned her head.

Maglarion was staring at her

She froze in sudden terror.

He stood on the highest balcony, arms clasped behind his back, gazing down at the ball. And like Haeron Icaraeus and Lord Corthios, he looked younger. Much younger, in fact. His hair was black and thick, his arms and chest heavy with muscle beneath his coat. Yet she recognized his face, his expression, the black patch covering his left eye.

She would recognize him anywhere.

He stared at her, and Caina was a child again, chained to that cold metal table as Maglarion raised his glittering dagger to her father's throat...

"Countess?" said Alastair. "Marianna? Are you all right?"

And then Caina realized that Maglarion was not staring at her. He was simply looking over the ballroom. Even if he had noticed her, no doubt he only saw yet another noblewoman in a silk gown. If he remembered her at all, he would remember a terrified girl in ragged, bloodstained clothing.

Alastair frowned at her. Caina chastised herself for losing control.

"That man," she said, recovering her poise, "that fellow on the balcony, the one with the patch over his eye. Who is that?"

"That charlatan?" said Alastair with a laugh. "He's one of Lord Haeron's pets. An outlaw magus, or a renegade sorcerer. The man claims to have all sorts of mystical powers to roll back death and aging. His hair was white at first, but now he's dyed it black." He laughed. "The more foolish noblewomen take that as proof that he has power over death."

"A charlatan," murmured Caina. "Of course."

Charming Alastair might have been, but he was not very observant.

Then Caina saw Julia walking along the balcony, speaking to another noblewoman. Maglarion's head turned, and he stared at them for a moment. A smile spread over his face, and he started after Julia.

He walked without a limp and a cane now, Caina noticed.

Dread rose in her throat. Julia had never seen Maglarion, had only heard him described as an old man with a cane. She would never recognize him, not until it was too late, and if Maglarion decided to harm her…

"Excuse me for a moment," said Caina. "I will return quickly."

Alastair frowned. "Does my company displease you so, Countess?"

"Not at all," said Caina.

"Don't tell me you're going to go talk to that old charlatan," said Alastair. "He'll fill your head with nonsense."

"Of course not," said Caina. "But my dear friend Lady Julia is very vain, and she is susceptible to such charlatans. If I leave her alone with him, he'll have her spending a fortune on potions and other nonsense."

Alastair titled his head. "You…have more grit to you than I expected, my lady."

"Perhaps you'll see more of my grit yet, my lord," said Caina, and she slipped his grasp.

She hurried up the stairs to the fourth-story balcony. The gallery beyond was deserted, save for a lone Kindred assassin, keeping watch on the guests below. Caina looked back and forth, her heart racing. Perhaps Maglarion had moved on. But she still had to warn Julia against him…

A voice came to her ears, kindly and wise, and she shivered in recognition.

It was Maglarion.

"You are more prominent than you think, Lady Julia of House Morenna," he said. "Your web of social influence extends throughout the capital and beyond."

"You are too kind, sir," said Julia, her voice smooth as glass. "I am only a poor widow who enjoys the company of a few friends. Nothing more."

Caina ducked behind a pillar and peered around it.

She saw Julia standing near the ornate marble railing, Maglarion a few paces away. Julia wore her polite smile, the one she used when dealing with lords she found offensive. Maglarion's expression was predatory. He looked like a wolf cornering a sheep.

Looking at him made Caina's skin crawl. She felt the arcane power rolling off him, like waves of heat rising from an inferno. He seemed stronger, so much stronger, than he had seven years ago. Had he always been this powerful, and she had never realized it? Or had he indeed gotten stronger?

"A poor widow," said Maglarion, touching her wrist. "It need not be so."

Julia's smile thinned. "You are too forward, sir. Too forward by far."

"Not at all," said Maglarion. "I propose not a crude liaison, but something better." His voice dropped. "You can be young again, Lady Julia."

Julia gave a mocking little laugh. "You can roll back age, then? Time itself?"

"I can," said Maglarion. "I have mastered the arcane sciences to a degree not seen since the Fourth Empire. The magi of the modern Magisterium are as children next to my power. And I can make you a young woman once again."

Julia said nothing.

"You've seen what I've done for Lord Haeron, Lord Corthios, Lady Aureon, and the others," said Maglarion. "Do they not look younger, the years wiped from their faces? Join us. I can do the same for you. I will make you young again. You are a widow, you say? You can find a new husband, one worthy of you, can bear sons and daughters again. All this I will give you if you follow me."

Julia shivered. "I...I..."

Caina had never seen her so flustered.

"Do your scruples stop you?" said Maglarion. "Cast them aside. They are only chains that hold you back. I can give you immortality. Surely that is worth any price."

"Immortality?" said Julia. "The nature of man is mortal. His fate is to die. At what price comes your immortality? I have heard that Haeron Icaraeus buys vast quantities of slaves...slaves that always seem to disappear. What use do you find for them, I wonder?"

"It is the natural order of things," said Maglarion, his smile hardening. "The weak prey upon the strong. And with the aid of arcane science, the strong can use the weak to live forever. So, Lady Julia Morenna? Are you weak or strong?"

"Your definition of strength is flawed," said Julia, lifting her chin. "To accept one's fate with courage…that is strength. Slaughtering innocents to stave off inevitable death, that is weakness. And cowardice."

"Or blind folly," said Maglarion. "I have conquered death itself. What matter the price?"

"No," said Julia, her voice and face cold. "Thank you, sir, for your most generous offer. But I am afraid that I must decline."

She turned to go.

"I think not," said Maglarion.

He gestured, and Caina felt a surge of arcane power.

And Julia froze in place.

"I'm afraid you know too much now, my lady," said Maglarion. "More than is…healthy, shall we say? You claim to have no political interests, but I suspect you are friendly with the Loyalists. Which means you'll run and tell your little tale to the Ghosts. And the Ghosts are an annoyance that I can do without."

Caina's heart pounded with terror. Maglarion was going to kill Julia.

Or do worse things to her.

"So I'm going to have to silence you, I'm afraid," said Maglarion, stroking her cheek. Julia trembled, but did not move, caught in the power of his spell.

Caina had to act.

She ripped the left sleeve from her gown and wound it around her head, forming a makeshift mask. Then she kicked off her heeled boots, the marble floor cold against her bare feet.

Then she glided forward without a sound.

She didn't dare get too close to Maglarion. She suspected his powers would make it difficult, if not impossible, to catch him unawares. And her only chance was to catch him by surprise. Her terror remained, but her mind became cold, focused, clear. Akragas and Sandros and Halfdan and Riogan had trained her well.

The Kindred assassin still walked through the pillars of the gallery, looking left and right. Caina crept behind him, slipping a throwing knife into her hand. Then she leapt, her arm wrapping about his throat, her feet tangling in his ankles.

The assassin was good. He twisted, pushing her away, but Caina hammered the handle of the throwing knife into his skull, behind his ear. He went rigid, and Caina slammed the handle down twice more. The assassin went limp, and she lowered him the floor.

She yanked his crossbow free from his harness. In his belt she found a small vial of poison, as she expected. She jammed a quarrel into the bow, drawing back the bolt, and poured the poison over the quarrel's razor-edged head.

Then she crept across the balcony, the crossbow ready in her hands.

One shot. She had one chance at this.

Maglarion still stood before a paralyzed Julia, touching her face. He hadn't killed her yet. He liked to talk, Caina remembered, and enjoyed listening to himself.

"I could just wipe your memory," said Maglarion. "But you had the temerity to mock me. Not that your opinion matters at all, of course. But it showed that you are weak, unworthy to attain immortality as I have."

Caina crept closer, raising the crossbow. Sandros had shown her how to use them, but she'd never been very good. Closer. She had to get closer. The heavy quarrel could explode Maglarion's head like a rotten melon. If she hit him wrong, the quarrel would go right through him and into Julia.

"So I will kill you," said Maglarion. "But simply cutting your throat...ah, that would be wasteful, would it not? Especially when I can harvest your death. Death is like...fire, you know. Just as fire produces warmth and heat, so does death produce power. Power that a skilled necromancer can use and store." His smile widened, and he patted her cheek. "I think I'll feed your life force to Lord Haeron. A birthday present for him, eh?"

Caina leveled the bow. A little closer, a little closer...

"Come with me," said Maglarion, and Caina felt another surge of power. Julia took a step forward, face slack, eyes glassy. "Follow me, and you shall see wonders and horrors. Before you die..."

He turned, and his good eye widened as he saw Caina.

She squeezed the trigger. The crossbow heaved, and the heavy quarrel plunged into Maglarion's chest. Blood splashed across his white shirt, and he staggered back.

She threw aside the bow and ran at him, a throwing knife falling into her hand. She flung the blade, and then another, both knives burying themselves in Maglarion's mutilated chest, the blows knocking him back against the marble railing. Then she drew her last throwing knife and leapt upon him, burying the blade in his throat. He toppled, and she shoved.

Maglarion overbalanced and tumbled over the railing.

She heard his bones shatter as he struck the ballroom's hard marble floor.

Julia flinched and shook her head, the glassy look vanishing from her eyes. Shocked screams rose from the ballroom. Caina ducked behind the railing, relieved that she had thought to mask herself, and peered through the ornate balustrade.

Maglarion lay motionless in a pool of his own blood.

She could not believe it had been that easy. That man had terrorized the innocent for centuries, and she had killed him in the space of a few heartbeats.

Then Maglarion started to move.

He pushed himself to his feet, and Caina heard the crackling as his broken bones moved back into position.

A horrified silence fell over the ballroom.

Maglarion reached up, ripped the quarrel and the throwing knives from his chest. Blood gushed over his hands, further soaking his shirt, but the wounds closed as Caina watched. He sighed, and massaged his torn throat as the wound closed.

"That," he announced, his voice rusty, "hurt."

He looked up, and Caina flinched.

The fall had torn away his eye patch. A green bloodcrystal filled his left eye socket, shining with the emerald fire that Caina associated with necromantic spells. It had been there all along, she realized, enhancing his sorcery, and no doubt giving him other abilities.

A poisoned bolt, three throwing knives, and a forty-foot fall hadn't killed him.

They hadn't even hurt him very much.

Maglarion's good eye narrowed as he stared at her, and she felt the surge of power.

"Stop him!" Caina screamed. "He's planning to assassinate the Emperor!"

The Imperial Guards took one look at the bloody man with the growing green eye and rushed him.

"Run!" Caina yelled, grabbing Julia's arm.

Maglarion gestured, and the Imperial Guards flew backwards, seized by invisible force. He lifted his hand, pointing at the balcony, and Caina felt the sudden sharp spike of arcane power, like tiny needles digging into her skin.

She ran faster, half-dragging Julia along.

Maglarion thrust out his palm, and the balcony...

...exploded.

The roar filled Caina's ears, and the shock knocked her to the ground. Shards of shattered marble rained in all directions. Caina scrambled to her feet, pulling Lady Julia along with her.

She risked a glance over her shoulder, saw the Imperial Guards running at Maglarion. But Maglarion made a hooking motion, and the falling debris from the shattered balcony changed direction and rained upon the charging Guards in a storm of stone. Chunks of marble smashed black helmets and crushed black cuirasses, and the Guards fell dead to the floor. Caina heard screams as the terrified nobles fled the ballroom.

She saw Maglarion turn towards the damaged balcony, felt his sorcerous strength gather for another strike.

"Go!" said Caina, pulling on Julia's arm. "Run. Run!"

They sprinted across the damaged gallery, towards the stairs.

Then the entire mansion shook like a dying animal, and the roar of collapsing masonry filled her ears. Maglarion had simply ripped apart the balconies, she realized, letting them fall in an avalanche to the ballroom floor. Her heart raced with terror, and she half-ran, half-stumbled down the trembling steps, Julia behind her. She had been terrified of Maglarion, and his voice had filled her nightmares for years.

But she had never dreamed that he possessed that kind of raw power. Little wonder he had lived for centuries.

Little wonder the Ghosts had not been able to kill him.

Caina led Julia through the mansion's back corridors, past crowds of terrified servants, and into the gardens. Their coachman had fled in the chaos, so they made their way back to Julia's townhouse on foot.

Maglarion did not pursue them.

The attack threw the Imperial capital into an uproar.

Rumors filled Malarae about the renegade sorcerer who had attacked Lord Haeron's birthday celebration, a dozen different contradictory accounts repeated in the taverns and inns. Some said that the sorcerer had arrived to kill Lord Haeron, and Lord Haeron's allies among the Magisterium had fought him off. Others said that Haeron had hired the sorcerer to kill the Emperor, and the Ghosts had ambushed the sorcerer, killing him before the Emperor could arrive.

In a few days, both Lord Haeron and the Magisterium announced a reward of a hundred thousand denarii for the man's head.

Caina laughed aloud when she heard that.

Four days after the attack, she went to join Lady Julia for tea.

Halfdan stood next to Julia's chair, again disguised as the wealthy merchant Basil Callenius.

"My dear," he said, putting down his cup of tea, "you really made quite a stir."

Caina shrugged. "I didn't know what else to do. Maglarion would have killed Julia, otherwise."

"Or worse," said Julia, taking a sip of tea. "Caina saved my life, and possibly my soul, as well."

"I should have done more," said Caina.

Halfdan snorted. "You put a poisoned crossbow bolt into him, two throwing knives into his chest, cut his throat open, and threw him off a balcony. I fail to see what else you could have done. It's going to take more than sharp steel and a vial of poison to kill Maglarion."

"Do you really think Lord Haeron has turned on Maglarion?" said Caina, thinking of the bounty.

"Do you?"

"Of course not," said Caina. "Lord Haeron looks fifteen years younger. I think he's been buying slaves and turning them over to Maglarion, who then kills them and feeds their life force into Haeron. I doubt a man like Haeron Icaraeus would give up eternal youth over a shattered ballroom and a few dead Imperial Guards."

"That was my thought as well," said Halfdan. "The bounty is just a bluff to convince the Emperor that Lord Haeron is taking this 'rogue sorcerer' seriously. And the Emperor is not convinced. Julia, I've just returned from a meeting with the Emperor."

Julia blinked. "What did His Imperial Majesty say?"

"Emperor Alexius is certain that Haeron Icaraeus and his Restorationist followers have been working with a necromancer, using the lives of slaves to make themselves younger," said Halfdan. "The Emperor believes that Lord Haeron plans to seize the throne for himself, using Maglarion's powers for support. And the Emperor doesn't know what Maglarion wants, but whatever it is, it is not in the best interest of the Empire or its people."

"His Imperial Majesty has a gift for understatement," said Caina.

"He does," said Halfdan, "but he can take drastic action, when he feels it necessary. The Emperor wishes the Ghosts to take direct action against Lord Haeron and Maglarion."

"Direct action?" said Caina.

"Whatever is necessary to secure their downfall," said Halfdan.

"I don't know how much use I will be to you," said Julia. "Undoubtedly Maglarion will find it most suspicious that a masked Ghost arrived to save me from Maglarion. At the very least, Lord Haeron will suspect that I am...more friendly with the Ghosts then I let on. He may even try to have me killed."

"We'll arrange additional guards for you," said Halfdan. "And you still have many friends among Malarae's nobility. See what you can learn from them."

"Will I assist Julia?" said Caina.

"No," said Halfdan. "You'll be coming with me, to the Vineyard."

"A new teacher?" said Caina, hiding her disappointment. She wanted to stay here, continue the fight against Lord Haeron and Maglarion.

"No," said Halfdan. "No more teachers. You went up against Maglarion and you survived."

Caina scowled. "He survived."

"I doubt you could have done anything to kill him," said Halfdan. "And you are the first Ghost in centuries to face him and survive. No, you are ready. You will take the final oaths of a Ghost nightfighter, and then you will return here, to join our effort against Lord Haeron."

Julia smiled. "Thank you for my life, child."

"And thank you for your lessons," said Caina.

Julia laughed. "I merely polished what was already there. She's ready, Halfdan. You have made her into a deadly weapon for the Ghosts."

"I hope so," said Halfdan, "for we shall need every weapon we have to defeat Maglarion."

He left the townhouse, and Caina followed him.

CHAPTER 21
NIGHTFIGHTER

It had been years since Caina had last set foot in the Vineyard, but it had changed little in that time. It still stood tall and strong among the Disali hills, the river rushing along the base of its crag. The guards walked the walls, and the workers bustled about the terraces.

Caina frowned.

"Something amiss?" said Halfdan.

"It seems smaller than I remember it," said Caina, shaking her head.

"Not really," said Halfdan. "You've just grown."

The gates swung open at their approach, and Halfdan and Caina led their pack mules inside.

###

Komnene awaited them.

"By Minaerys," she murmured, catching Caina in a hug. "Look at you. You were a little girl when last I saw you." She held Caina out at arm's length, looking at the fine gown and the expensive cloak. "You could cause quite a stir at a ball in the Imperial capital, I think."

Caina grinned. "I already did. Though I was wearing a mask at the time."

Komnene blinked. "That was...sensible of you."

"Come," said Halfdan. "Let's get some food."

###

They had a fine dinner in the villa's hall, with wine from the Vineyard.

Caina did not like wine, even after her time with Julia and Theodosia, but even she had to admit that this wine almost tasted good.

"Is this a special occasion?" she asked Halfdan.

He nodded. "After dinner, go to your old room in the wall. Change into the clothes you find there. Then go to the watchtower. There's a path in the cliff behind the tower, heading to the crest of the hill. Follow the path. I will meet you there."

Caina nodded and kept eating.

It was past sunset by the time they finished dinner.

Caina walked to her old room in the wall. It was just as she had left it - the same narrow bed, the same battered dresser, the same stone walls and floor. Though like everything else in the Vineyard, it seemed smaller than she remembered.

Black clothes lay across the bed.

Caina stripped out of her gown and changed into the loose-fitting black trousers and long-sleeved black shirt. Leather boots went on her feet, and each of the boots held a dagger in a hidden sheath. A belt went around her waist, holding knives, lockpicks, a coiled rope with a collapsible grapnel, and other useful tools. Leather gloves went over her hands, and leather bracers over her forearms. Each bracer held another hidden throwing knife.

She kept her father's signet ring beneath her shirt, hanging from a slender chain around her neck.

Then she left the room and climbed to the Vineyard's highest terrace, circling around the watchtower. As Halfdan had said, she saw a path zigzagging its way up the face of the cliff.

Caina took a deep breath and started to climb, taking care to keep her balance in the moonlight.

A fire blazed atop the hill's rocky crown.

Halfdan waited before the fire. Komnene stood besides him, hands folded. Next to her waited Riogan, leaning on his spear, his expression its usual mask of cold indifference. Akragas and Sandros waited there, along with a dozen other Ghosts that Caina did not know.

"It was here," said Halfdan, speaking in Disali, "at this very spot, that the Ghosts began. The Disali farmers and herders met here, terrified from the tyranny of Ashbringers, and vowed to fight back from the shadows. And it was here, on this hill, that they met with Emperor Cormarus, and swore to serve him in exchange for his aid against the Ashbringers. And thus it has been, ever since. The Emperor defends the commoners from the tyranny of the nobility and the magi, and we aid him."

A wind blew along the hilltop, making the flames dance.

"And now," said Halfdan, "you are one of us. If you want."

"What do you mean?" said Caina.

"This is your last chance to walk away," said Halfdan. "If you wish, we can find a place for you. A priestess of Minaerys. A noblewoman in the capital. An independent merchant. Say the word, and you can have whatever life you choose."

Caina shook her head. "And walk away from what Maglarion has done? No."

"I warn you," said Halfdan. "Once you join the Ghosts, once you become one of us...you will remain a Ghost for the rest of your life. You will serve us as a nightfighter, one of the Emperor's elite spies and assassins. Our enemies will probably kill you in the course of your duties. Yet if you are injured, and cannot serve as a nightfighter, you will remain a Ghost, whether as a nightkeeper, or a circlemaster, or as one of the eyes and ears. Even if you live for a hundred years, we will find a way for you to serve. Do you understand? Even if you marry, even if you rise to wealth and power...you will remain a Ghost. For the only way to leave the Ghosts is through death."

"I understand," said Caina. "And I am not turning back. Not now."

Komnene looked saddened by that.

"So be it," said Halfdan. "Then are you ready to take the oath, to join the Ghosts as a nightfighter?"

"I am," said Caina.

Halfdan nodded, and switched to High Nighmarian. "Do you swear, then, to serve the Ghosts, to follow the commands of the circlemasters, upon pain of death?"

"I so swear," said Caina in the same language.

"Do you swear to keep the secrets of the Ghosts, and to never reveal a Ghost to our enemies, upon pain of death?"

"I so swear," said Caina.

"And do you swear to forever stand against the enemies of the commoners, the magi, the nobility, the slavers, and all those who would prey on the people of the Empire, upon pain of death?" said Halfdan.

"I so swear," said Caina.

Halfdan stepped forward, gripped her forearms, and kissed her once on each cheek. One by one each of the other Ghosts came forward and did the same.

"Then you are one of us," said Halfdan. "Riogan."

Riogan smirked raised his arm.

Something black flowed and rippled in his grasp, seeming to merge and blend with the shadows thrown by the fire.

"Take it," said Riogan.

Caina hesitated, then took the flowing black thing.

It was a cloak, she saw, lighter than any fabric she had ever seen. Amazed, she held it up, and even as she lifted it, it kept blending and merging with the shadows.

"What is it?" she said.

"A secret known only to the Ghosts," said Halfdan. "Only we know the process of making shadowcloth, of weaving the shadows themselves with common silk. It is the cloak of a Ghost nightfighter. Wear it, and you can hide within the shadows themselves. And it offers additional protection, as well. While you wear it, your mind cannot be harmed by sorcery."

"Though there's nothing stopping a magus from crushing your skull with a spell," said Riogan.

"Put it on," said Halfdan.

Caina donned the cloak and pulled up the cowl. It felt almost weightless, yet she saw how it blurred into the shadows, making it seem as if she were part of the darkness.

It felt...

It felt right.

"Welcome home, nightfighter," said Halfdan.

"Your first task," said Halfdan, as they ate breakfast. "Julia told me you made the acquaintance of Lord Alastair Corus."

Caina paused, a cup of tea halfway to her lips. "I did. Do you want me to kill him?" She would regret that. Alastair might have been a slaver and a friend of Lord Haeron, but she had enjoyed dancing with him.

"Not necessarily," said Halfdan. "I want him stopped. He's not closely allied with Lord Haeron and the Restorationists, but he does errands for them, shuttling slaves and money from the Imperial Pale to the capital. You're going to deal with him. First, make certain that he is no longer useful to Lord Haeron. That is your main task. Second, try to find any evidence implicating Lord Haeron. Third, if at all possible, try to use Lord Alastair to hamper Lord Haeron's slaving operations. If you do..."

"If I do," said Caina, "then we can flush Maglarion into the open."

Halfdan nodded. "And then we can deal with him."

Caina blinked. "How? I put a poisoned crossbow bolt through his lungs. If that doesn't kill him, what will?"

"Let me worry about that," said Halfdan. "For now, find a way to ruin Lord Alastair. Some sort of public scandal would be best." He paused. "Try not to kill him unless absolutely necessary."

Caina nodded.

###

She left the Vineyard later that morning, once again in the guise of Countess Marianna Nereide, attended by servants Halfdan had chosen.

The cloak, along with her weapons and tools, waited in her saddlebags.

CHAPTER 22
STOLEN LIVES

Maglarion stood alone in the Grey Fish Inn's cellar.

The ghostly green light from his bloodcrystal threw back the darkness.

The thing had grown immense. A few years ago it had been the size of a small child. Now it was a monolith of black crystal, nine feet tall and three across, green flames writhing like tortured things in its depths. Sometimes the flames formed faces, images of those whose life forces it had captured.

It had grown vast with stolen power.

So much power, in fact, that it had healed the wounds the masked woman had inflicted in a matter of seconds.

Infuriating, that. It had been a very long time since anyone had gotten close enough to hurt him so badly. A Ghost, most likely, probably assigned to infiltrate Lord Haeron's birthday ball. And an exceptionally cunning one, as well, to recognize the presence of mind-controlling sorcery. Most men would have assumed that Maglarion was speaking quietly to Lady Julia, not invading her mind with a spell.

But not that masked Ghost.

It didn't matter. Undoubtedly the woman lay dead in the wreckage of Haeron Icaraeus's ballroom.

A lot of people had died that night.

He smiled and ran a hand along the bloodcrystal.

A lot of people had died...and his bloodcrystal had captured the power released from their deaths.

The bloodcrystal could trap the energy released from any death within seven miles of the Grey Fish Inn, now. That covered most of Malarae, even a few of the nearby villages. Every day, people died in Malarae. Every day, fresh life energy flowed in the bloodcrystal, into Maglarion. Every day he grew stronger, his sorcery more powerful.

Killing slaves was almost unnecessary at this point. Save for the tedious necessity of placating his noble followers, of course.

Very soon now, he would be ready to cast the final spell in the ancient Maatish scroll.

For once he had enough life energy stored in the bloodcrystal, the power would reach...a critical mass. It would transform. Ascend. Just as wood burst into flame when exposed to enough heat, so too would the bloodcrystal's power erupt.

And that power would belong to Maglarion.

He only needed one thing, just one thing more...

Something prickled against his senses.

He turned, saw Ikhana enter the cellar, her pale face ghostly in the bloodcrystal's light.

"Master," she said. "Lord Haeron would speak..."

Boots thumped against the stairs, and Haeron Icaraeus stalked past Ikhana, fists clenched, face tight with fury.

"My lord Haeron," murmured Maglarion, still smiling.

"I thought I would find you skulking in this pit," said Haeron. "What in the hell were you thinking?"

"One of the Ghosts tried to kill me," said Maglarion. "I admit my response might have...lacked a certain subtlety."

"A certain subtlety?" roared Haeron. "A certain subtlety? You made me look a fool before half the lords of the Empire! What good is Lord Haeron's word, if he cannot protect his guests under his own roof from a rogue sorcerer?"

"Perhaps you should have kept the Ghosts from penetrating your mansion," said Maglarion. "You boasted of your security often enough."

"Now the Ghosts know for certain that I plan to move against the Emperor!" said Haeron, his shout ringing off the walls. "And I must engage in this mummer's farce of the 'hunt for the rogue sorcerer', all while the Ghosts sniff about my affairs."

Maglarion laughed.

Haeron's face darkened. "Do you find this funny? Do you?"

Maglarion did. Listening to Haeron Icaraeus was like listening to a child. Or a donkey that had somehow learned to imitate human speech. Maglarion was beyond him, beyond his petty schemes and his petty little games of power. Haeron Icaraeus still thought that political power was true power. He was wrong.

Sorcery was the only true power. And through it, Maglarion would live for millennia after Haeron's bones had crumbled into dust.

Especially since Maglarion would kill Haeron Icaraeus himself.

"Funny?" said Maglarion at last. "No, not in the least." He spread his hands. "I suppose, my lord, that I should simply surrender to you. You can turn me over to the Magisterium for the bounty. A hundred thousand denarii."

Haeron blinked in surprise.

"A hundred thousand denarii will buy quite a lot of things," said Maglarion. He began to walk in a circle around Haeron. "Weapons. Women. Power. So many things. Perhaps you can go to the Great Market and buy...say, another ten years of life?"

Haeron began to sweat.

A smile flickered across Ikhana's face, and she touched the black dagger at her belt. She had learned the hard way, long ago.

Stolen life force was...addictive.

It was time Haeron Icaraeus learned the same thing.

"So, my lord," said Maglarion. "I have wronged you, most horribly. Undoubtedly it will cost a vast fortune to repair your ballroom. I can give you immortality, of course...but what is that, weighed against money? Surrender me the Magisterium, my lord!" He held out his wrists, smiling. "Let me know the just punishment for my horrid crimes."

He bit back his laughter as Haeron Icaraeus struggled. No doubt Haeron realized that he ought to send Maglarion away while he still had control over his own mind. But it was far too late for that.

Even if Haeron himself did not yet know it.

"Well...I suppose circumstances sometimes spin out of control," said Haeron. "So long as you take greater care in the future...I can overlook this indiscretion."

Maglarion gave a mocking little bow. "Very gracious of you, my lord. Very gracious indeed."

Again Ikhana's lips twitched in something almost like a smile, her eyes predatory as she stared at Haeron.

"Perhaps you will permit me to use a bloodcrystal on you?" said Maglarion. "If you are to rule the Empire for eternity, after all, then you need to keep up your strength."

Haeron nodded, his eyes glittering in eagerness. "I will permit it."

Maglarion crossed to the far wall. A dying slave hung in chains, covered in half-healed cuts and slashes. Maglarion drew his dagger and ripped it across the slave's throat, hot blood welling over his fingers.

He felt the man's life force drain into the great bloodcrystal, and shivered in pleasure.

But there was still enough lingering power for him to take the slave's blood and shape it into a lesser bloodcrystal, one no bigger than his thumb. He crossed the cellar once more, laid his free hand on Haeron's forehead, and drained the lesser bloodcrystal, releasing its stolen life force to into Haeron.

Haeron shuddered, his eyes going wide. He looked a few years younger when Maglarion finished, his face smoother, his hair thicker than it had been.

"I think," said Maglarion, "that it is time I moved."

"Oh?" said Haeron, his voice slurred. "Where?"

"The great tower in your mansion," said Maglarion. "The chamber at the top." He gestured at the massive bloodcrystal. "I wish my primary bloodcrystal moved there at once."

Lord Haeron, still drunk on the infusion of fresh life force, did not argue.

"If you are not going to kill him," said Ikhana, "then you should let me kill him."

Maglarion and Ikhana stood in the round chamber atop the great tower of Lord Haeron's mansion, five hundred feet above the ground. The high, narrow windows had a magnificent view of Malarae, even of the Imperial Citadel on its mountain spur.

But the view was unimportant. House Icaraeus's ancestral mansion lay close to Malarae's heart. From here, the bloodcrystal's life-draining aura covered the entire city. Even now he felt fresh death feeding into it, increasing its power.

Making him stronger.

"Patience, my dear," said Maglarion. "Fear not. Haeron Icaraeus shall die at his appointed time."

Followed by a great many other people.

Including Ikhana, now that he happened to think about it.

His bloodcrystal stood in the center of the chamber, concealed by heavy tarps, lest some sharp-eyed Ghost glimpse its glow through the windows. A wooden podium waited before the bloodcrystal, a dagger and the Maatish scroll lying upon its surface.

Maglarion crossed to the podium, read the scroll for a moment. Then he lifted the dagger and whispered a spell. Something like rancid oil spread over the dagger's surface, and then it began to gleam with green flames.

He lifted the tarp and scratched the dagger's tip across the bloodcrystal's side.

And black blood oozed from the scratch. It dripped the floor, sizzling and boiling like fat in a hot kettle.

Maglarion needed only one more thing to achieve true immortality, to transcend the flesh forevermore.

He needed a great deal of death.

And in the black blood sizzling on the floor, he had found the instrument to bring about those deaths.

CHAPTER 23
SEDUCTION

Caina decided upon a simple plan.

She would stay with Julia and attend the nobility's endless balls and feasts. Sooner or later she would run into Alastair Corus again, and this time she would respond to his advances. When he invited her to his townhouse for dinner, she would go.

And after she had taken a look around, she could return at night, break in, and carry off whatever evidence she found. His correspondence, most likely. Lords often maintained a voluminous correspondence, and if Alastair was smuggling slaves for Lord Haeron, he might mention it in his letters. Or perhaps Alastair kept a ledger to record his earnings. Lord Macrinius had, after all.

Either way, the letters or the ledger would ruin him, perhaps send him to the executioner's block.

###

A few days later Caina waited in the ballroom of Lady Aureon, another of Lord Haeron's allies. Nobles and wealthy merchants stood in small groups, talking and drinking. Caina accepted a glass of wine from a servant and pretended to drink. She wore a green gown with black trim, tighter across the chest than she preferred. In fact, it left her shoulders and a good part of her bodice exposed.

But that was all right. It was part of the plan.

Lady Julia had told her that Alastair would almost certainly be in attendance, and Caina did not have to wait long. He strode into the ballroom, clad in his usual close-fitting black coat and trousers, sword and dagger at his belt.

She stared at him until he noticed her, then she looked down and smiled, as both Theodosia and Julia had taught her to do.

As she expected, he walked over.

"Countess Marianna," he said, catching her hand and kissing her signet ring, "so good to see you again."

"And you, my lord," said Caina. "I..."

He kept his grip on her hand and spun her into a dance.

Caina laughed, despite herself. "I thought I told you that it was customary to ask first!"

"To ask what?" said Alastair. "How much work it took to get into that gown? At least three hours, I'll wager."

"It is customary to ask a lady before you dance with her, my lord Alastair," said Caina.

"Why, I already did ask," said Alastair.

"I think not," said Caina. He spun her again, his free hand cradling her back. He did it flawlessly. When she had regained her balance, she said, "I would remember it if you did."

"I did," said Alastair. "At that festive little gathering of Lord Haeron's, as you might recall. You wandered off, and the next thing I knew the ballroom was exploding. Most distressing."

"Exploding buildings are like that," said Caina.

"What?" said Alastair. "Don't be absurd. I am a tribune of the Eighteenth Legion of the Empire of Nighmar. Exploding buildings are simply part of my duties. I was simply distressed that we never got to finish our dance."

"Well, that was your fault," said Caina. "You said that Haeron's pet sorcerer was a charlatan, and instead he ripped apart half of Haeron's mansion with his spells!"

Alastair frowned. "It's just as well you got Julia away from him. She is rather entertaining, for a meddlesome old woman, and I wouldn't want her in the clutches of some deranged foreign sorcerer." He snorted. "Sorcery. Magi are too much trouble, mark me well."

Caina raised an eyebrow. "Then why are you on such friendly terms with Lord Haeron? All the rumors say the Restorationist lords are friendly with magi and foreign sorcerers."

Alastair sighed. "Rumor and calumny." He dropped his voice. "And just between you and me, Haeron Icaraeus is a tedious bore. They say he's hard and loveless. Not true. He is in fact deeply in love."

Caina frowned. "So what does he love?"

"The sound of his own voice," said Alastair.

She burst out laughing at that.

"So then," she said, once she had recovered herself, "if he is such a tedious bore, why do you associate with him?"

Alastair sighed. "Money, my dear lady, money. House Corus, alas, was never wealthy, and my father drank away what little wealth we had." His eyes tightened, and Caina realized that she had never seen him drink or eat to excess, the way other nobles did. "And while serving as a tribune in the Eighteenth Legion bestows honor and glory, it brings in very little money. And so I must turn to commerce to support myself."

"So," said Caina, frowning, "you're not a Restorationist? Or a Militarist?"

Now it was Alastair's turn to burst out laughing. "You shock me. A Restorationist? You think I want the magi to rule the Empire? The magi are incapable of governing themselves, let alone the Empire. Or that the Lord Commanders of the Legions should choose the Emperor? My lady, I've met most of the Lord Commanders, and I wouldn't trust them as far as I could throw them. And some of them are quite fat."

"Then you don't really care about politics?" said Caina.

"Not particularly," said Alastair. "I just want to get paid." He sighed. "Someday, I'll have enough money. Then I can buy a pleasant villa along the Bay of Empire, settle down with a wife and some children."

That was something Caina would never know. Ghost nightfighter she might be, but she still felt a pang at that.

"Then I can leave all the nonsense of Imperial politics behind me, once and for all," said Alastair. He stared at her for a moment, and then smiled. "I didn't expect you could get me to talk about that. You know, you're rather cleverer than I thought."

Again Caina's eyebrow came up. "So you thought me a fool, my lord?"

"Not particularly," said Alastair. "But one doesn't expect to find intelligence in a lovely woman, and you, my dear Countess, are most lovely. And a surprisingly adept conversationalist. We should continue this talk tomorrow, I think, at my townhouse. My cook can prepare an excellent roast lamb."

Caina smiled. "I would like that."

And to her surprise, she meant it. And not just because she wanted to reconnoiter his townhouse.

The next evening she arrived at Alastair's home.

To her surprise, it was smaller than Julia's. Considering Alastair made at least some money smuggling slaves for Haeron Icaraeus, she would have expected a larger house. Perhaps he spent it all on fine clothes.

A liveried servant met her at the door, led her inside. The townhouse's hall looked much as she expected. Trophies of war hung on the wall, armor and swords from the barbarian lands beyond the Imperial Pale. A small shrine to Markoin, the god of soldiers, occupied one table, and a banner of the Eighteen Legion hung from the ceiling.

"Lord Alastair will be with you shortly," said the footman. "He apologizes for his absence, but urgent business delayed him."

"Very well," said Caina, putting bored impatience into her voice. "I hope his lordship will not keep me waiting too long."

The footman bowed and departed.

Caina wandered over to the wall, picked up one of the barbarian swords. The blasted thing was heavy! How did the barbarians wield them in battle? Still, she supposed it had to be heavy, to punch through the Legionaries' heavy armor...

A woman's shout cut into her musings, and Caina spun, eyes looking back and forth.

She was alone. But she heard angry voices coming from the stairs.

"You are useless, Alastair, useless!" A woman's voice, shrill and angry. "Utterly worthless! I cannot believe my father forced me to wed you! The next time you go north, perhaps you should do us all a favor and get yourself spitted upon a barbarian sword. Death in battle is the only accomplishment you will ever have."

"What more do you want from me, Nerina?" Alastair's voice lacked its usual casual insouciance. "I've already given you all the money I have, and then some. You spent it all. There's no more, not until I finish some more...business with Lord Haeron."

"Then I suggest you find some more, fool," said Nerina. "I expect to be supported in the manner that I deserve."

"That you deserve?" said Alastair, his voice incredulous. "You have a wardrobe full of gowns and boxes full of jewels. You have a dozen maids waiting on your every whim...at least, you did, until you dismissed them all without cause. You can eat the finest foods whenever you wish. All of this, I might add, I paid for. How have I failed to support you in the manner you deserve?"

"If you were a man," said Nerina, "a strong man, then you would have the money. You find a way to get the money, to get what I deserve." She scoffed. "Enough! I cannot bear to look at you for another second! I am going to visit my sister."

"Nerina," began Alastair.

Caina heard heavy footsteps. A few moments later she saw a coach with the sigil of House Corus drive past the house, the shape of a woman visible through the windows.

She turned, and saw Alastair standing on the stairs, looking at her.

"You look," he said with a smile, "as if you're going to use that sword on me."

Caina blinked, looked at the heavy sword, and felt her face redden. "It...well, I heard shouting."

"Alas," said Alastair. He took the sword and returned it to the hooks on the wall. "One of the maids neglected to polish my boots. I don't care, of course, but I have a reputation for fearsome cruelty to maintain, so I had to shout at her. Merely a formality, you understand."

"It sounded like you were fighting with your wife," said Caina.

Alastair sighed, and the smile drained from his face. "Nerina is...difficult. My father arranged the marriage. It hasn't gone very well, I'm afraid."

"My mother used to talk like her," said Caina, voice quiet.

Alastair scowled. "And you approve, do you?"

"I hated my mother."

His scowl turned to a surprised smile. "Really? Well. I knew there was a reason I liked you," he looked her up and down, "asides from the obvious, of course. But it's terrible gauche to point out the obvious."

"Terribly," said Caina.

He took her hand and kissed it. "Shall we eat?"

Dinner was indeed excellent. Caina even liked the wine.

And bit by bit, she worked her way past Alastair's glib charm.

All he had ever wanted, he told her, was to be a soldier, a Lord Commander of a Legion. To serve and defend the Empire has his fathers had done before him. He wanted, Caina realized, to be like one of the noble lords of old, to go out on campaign to defend the Empire, and then return home to his wife and sons and daughters.

Caina blinked in surprise. "So you wish children, then?"

"Of course!" said Alastair. "What man could say otherwise?"

"Sometimes we want things we cannot have," said Caina.

Alastair sighed. "True enough. Still, better to strive for them than to sit forever yearning and moping, no?"

"Spoken like a true soldier of the Empire," said Caina.

"And now you flatter me, my lady," said Alastair.

After dinner they walked on the townhouse's flat roof. It was a small townhouse, by the standards of Malarae's nobility, but it still stood five stories high, and had a large roof. There was ample room to walk, to look at the towers and domes of Malarae, to gaze up at the stars.

Alastair took Caina's hand in his as they walked, and to her surprise she did not pull away.

"So what do you want, my lady?" said Alastair.

"Oh, merely the world, I suppose," said Caina, "and everything in it."

Alastair winced. "Now you sound like Nerina."

"Which means you think I sound like my mother," said Caina. "A cruel thing to say, my lord."

He tugged her hand, spun her around to face him.

"Then what," he said, "do you want?"

Caina blinked, caught off guard, and for a moment her poise wavered.

"Children," she said at last, voice quiet. "I...want children."

"That's rather easy to arrange," said Alastair.

"Not for me, it isn't," said Caina. She cursed herself for a fool, but told him anyway. "I had a...a carriage accident, when I was a girl. I was stabbed through the belly by a...a broken axle. I can't have children. Not now, not ever."

"Oh," said Alastair. "I'm sorry."

She had miscalculated. A barren woman was an object of pity and scorn. Her goal had been to get closer to him, to find his letters and his ledgers...

He touched her cheek, and she looked up at him. "What a pair we must make. You want children, but cannot bear them. I want children, but my wife refuses to have anything to do with me."

Caina tried to smile. "It's like an opera."

"A bad opera," said Alastair. "Sometimes I think that life is a cruel farce, a joke played upon us by malevolent or indifferent gods. Perhaps they take pleasure in watching us suffer."

"There is so much suffering in the world," said Caina, "but I will fight against it."

"How?" said Alastair.

She hesitated, realizing that she had said too much, been too honest. "There...are ways. I...will feed the poor, I will find them shoes and clothing, and..."

"You surprise me," said Alastair. "I...never would have expected such things from you."

"And you are repulsed?" said Caina.

"Not at all," said Alastair. "Perhaps...someday, when I have more money, I can assist you. I...have been forced to do many things that I am not proud of. To hear you talk this way, it gives me comfort."

"It is a cruel world," said Caina. "I suppose we must take what comfort we can."

"You're right," said Alastair, leaning forward.

He was going to kiss her, she realized.

A dozen thoughts flashed through her mind. He was married. His wife

JONATHAN MOELLER

seemed like a pettier version of Laeria Amalas. This was only a delusion, a fantasy. He wanted children, and she could never have them. And undoubtedly there had been other mistresses before her, and he would certainly take more after she left Malarae.

But he was different than what Caina had expected. Maybe Theodosia had been right. Maybe she should take what comfort she could. And she could do this without consequence, could she not? She could not become pregnant, could not bear a bastard child.

And there was one other thought.

A virgin's blood, Maglarion had said, as he cut into her belly. A virgin's blood could fuel all manner of useful necromancy. She still had nightmares about lying on that metal table.

And perhaps if she were no longer a virgin...perhaps that would never happen to her again...

So when he kissed her, she kissed him back.

A short time later they ended up in Alastair's bedroom, still kissing. Caina started pulling off her gown, her hands trembling with excitement and a little fear.

She stopped.

Alastair was staring her exposed stomach.

At her scars.

Heat flooded into her face.

"Don't," she said, half-turning away, "don't...don't stare at me like that, I..."

"Shh," said Alastair, putting his fingers over her lips. "Do you think they make you ugly? They do not."

He took her face in both hands and kissed her again.

Eventually, she got out of the gown, and he carried her to the bed.

Later Caina lay entwined with Alastair as he slept, her head pillowed on his chest. He had scars, as well, old wounds across his arms and shoulders and ribs. She had seen enough violence in her life to recognize the scars from a sword. Whatever his wife thought of him, Alastair was a brave man, brave enough to lead his Legionaries from the front.

His wife.

Caina's mouth twisted. Nerina was unworthy of him. And yet she was still his wife, which made Caina an adulteress. Her mother, she was sure, had seduced married men, more than once. Was Caina any better than her?

She did not like the thought.

And Alastair was a slave trader, little better than the Istarish slavers who worked for Maglarion.

She liked that thought even less.

But she did like the way Alastair felt, lying against her, liked it very much indeed. Little wonder Theodosia had encouraged her to do this. And she had his trust now. It would be easy to find his letters and his ledger.

And perhaps she could encourage him to stop trading slaves, even to join forces with the Ghosts.

That hopeful thought filled her mind as she drifted off to sleep.

###

The next few days settled into a pleasant routine. She and Alastair had dinner together, or they danced at one of the balls. Once they simply went for a long coach ride north of the city, along the river, taking in the view of the mountains and the Imperial Citadel.

And at night, they returned to his bedroom.

Four nights later, Caina saw her chance.

She woke up, blinking, and found herself alone in Alastair's bed. She rolled over and saw Alastair writing at a desk against the far wall, a stack of letters spread across its surface. An annoyed frown covered his face, but he kept writing.

His correspondence.

"What is it?" murmured Caina as she sat up, holding the blanket to herself.

He looked up at her, smiled, and returned his attention to his papers. "Nothing of importance. Just...some business matters, that's all."

She thought she glimpsed Lord Haeron Icaraeus's seal on one of the papers.

"Why don't you come back to bed?" she said.

"In a moment," he said, still writing.

Caina sat up straighter.

"Alastair," she said, letting the blanket fall away. "Come back to bed."

He stared at her for a moment, his smile widening. Then he swept the papers into a single stack, shoved them into a drawer of the desk, and locked it.

"I suppose business can wait," said Alastair.

Caina grinned and let him draw her down to the bed.

After they finished, she rested her head on his chest, staring at the locked drawer.

CHAPTER 24
CONSEQUENCES

Tomorrow night, Caina decided as she listened to Alastair breathe.

She would drug Alastair's wine at dinner. After he slipped into unconsciousness, she would break into his desk, make off with his correspondence, and leave Malarae. Halfdan awaited her at Trinus, a fishing village on the eastern bank of the Megaros River. After this, Caina would have to abandon her "Countess Marianna Nereide" disguise, of course, but that was no great concern. She could create a new disguise easily enough.

She drifted off to sleep in Alastair's arms, thinking over the plan. She hated to deceive and betray him like this.

But he had brought it on himself. He should not have traded in slaves.

###

Caina awoke to angry shouting.

She reached for the dagger she always kept under her pillow, and found nothing. Caina always kept a weapon close at hand, even while sleeping, but Marianna Nereide did not.

Alastair was gone, the blankets thrown aside, as if he had risen in haste.

Then the door burst open, and Alastair backed into the room.

His wife Nerina stalked after him.

She was short, even shorter than Caina, with the stout build of a sedentary woman and the bloodshot, dark-circled eyes of a heavy drinker. And a tremor in her hands that spoke of an addiction to more exotic drugs.

Her bloodshot eyes focused on Caina, full of hatred and contempt.

"So this is your little whore, Alastair?" said Nerina. She wore a rich gown of Anshani silk, and the jewels glittering on her fingers could have paid for Alastair's townhouse a dozen times over. "Or the newest one, at any rate, hmm? A stupid little slip of a girl." She laughed. "Did you buy her from one of your slaver friends? Or did she agree to share your bed for some coins? I cannot imagine why any woman would share your bed otherwise."

"You said you would be visiting your sister for another three days," said Alastair, voice tight with anger.

"I changed my mind," said Nerina. "I thought I'd come back and catch you with one of your whores. I wonder what my father would think of it. Maybe I can get him to challenge you to a duel."

Alastair's hands curled into fists, but he said nothing. Caina wondered why he didn't stand up to her, why he didn't fight back.

"Nerina," he began.

"Imbecile," said Nerina. "I deserve better than this. I deserve better than to come home and find my useless husband in bed with some empty-headed whore. I deserve better than you."

His face turned crimson, but he said nothing.

It was easier for him to say nothing, Caina realized. Easier for him to say nothing, and keep his head down, and ignore his wife's rages until she left. Much as Sebastian Amalas had done with Laeria.

Alastair was weaker than she had thought.

"And what about you, whore?" said Nerina, shoving her way past Alastair. "Do you have anything to say for yourself?"

"What is there to say?" said Caina. "You're right. I slept with your husband. It was...it was not the right thing to do, but I did it anyway."

"Marianna," said Alastair, "don't antagonize her..."

"Shut up," said Nerina. "Well? Was it worth it? I hope whatever he paid you was enough to endure sleeping with him."

She slapped Caina.

"Well?" said Nerina.

"Don't touch me," said Caina.

"I'll do whatever I want to you," said Nerina. "Well? Was it worth it?"

She drew back her hand for another slap.

Caina's reflexes took over.

She caught Nerina's wrist on its descent and twisted. Nerina's watery eyes widened in shock and pain, and Caina surged to her feet, heedless of her nudity, Nerina's wrist still caught in her grip. She sidestepped, twisting Nerina's arm behind her back. Nerina shrieked, her free hand clawing for Caina's face. She was half again Caina's weight, and probably stronger, but Caina knew what she was doing, and had better leverage.

She drove her knee into Nerina's back. Nerina overbalanced and landed on her face, Caina on top.

Alastair gaped.

"I told you," said Caina, "not to touch me."

"Get off me!" screamed Nerina, starting to sob, "get off me, get off me, get off me!" Her words blurred together in one long wail of pain and fear.

"Marianna," said Alastair, "please, just...let her go."

Caina released Nerina's arm and climbed back to her feet, bracing herself in case Nerina came at her again. But she needn't have worried. Nerina fled from the bedroom, wailing, and did not look back.

They stood in silence. After a moment, Caina picked up the blanket and wrapped it around herself.

"Why," said Alastair, blinking, "why did you do that?"

"I told her not to touch me," said Caina. Overpowering Nerina like that might not have been the best idea. If Alastair realized she was a Ghost...

"But...but she's a daughter of a noble House!" said Alastair, shaking his head. "Her father is Lord Sardon!" Caina knew the name; he was one of Haeron Icaraeus's supporters, a Restorationist lord of middling influence. "I can't just...gods, when her father hears about this..."

"Damn it, Alastair," said Caina.

He fell silent, blinking at her.

"Maybe you brought this on yourself," said Caina. "I doubt I'm the first woman she's found in your bed. But...you shouldn't let her treat you like that."

"I can't..."

"Divorce her," said Caina.

Alastair flinched. "Are you...you cannot be serious. My father forced me to marry her. If I divorced her, Lord Sardon would ruin me for it. I'd be penniless."

"So what?" said Caina.

"So what?" said Alastair, incredulous.

"Yes," said Caina. "You're miserable, and you'll keep jumping from mistress to mistress until you drink yourself to death or your wife hires a Kindred assassin to pour poison into your wine. If you divorce her, yes, Lord Sardon will probably ruin you. And what would you lose? You waste all your money on her whims anyway! So you can either be poor and miserable...or you can be poor and free." She took a deep breath. "You want to be an officer in the Legion? You'll be free to do that, without the necessity of your...side business to pay for Nerina's luxuries. And you'll be free to take a different wife."

Alastair blinked. "You mean...you?"

"No." It hurt more than Caina had expected to say that. "A wife who can give you sons and daughters."

Alastair opened his mouth, closed it again. He stood like that for a long time, and then his face hardened.

"You're right," he said at last. "I've been a fool. I know what I have to do; I've known what I've had to do for a long time." He took a deep breath. "Thank you."

Caina nodded.

And someone screamed as Alastair reached for the bedroom door. He threw open the door, racing to the stairs, and Caina followed him, holding the blanket around herself.

He stopped so suddenly that Caina almost walked into his back.

"Oh, gods," he groaned.

Nerina Corus hung from the railing, a curtain knotted around her neck. Her eyes bulged from her purple face, tongue swelling over her lips.

And Caina had thought that she could sleep with Alastair without consequence.

Alastair dashed forward, tore the curtain from the railing, and Nerina collapsed in a boneless heap to the floor. He raced down the stairs and rushed to her side, but he was too late. Caina knew death when she saw it, and Nerina was dead.

She stared at the corpse, numb. Her fault. If she had thought of a better way to handle Alastair, if she had thought of a better way to get those letters...

The letters.

The part of her mind that Halfdan and the others had trained, the cold part, realized that she had a perfect opportunity to seize his correspondence.

Caina slipped into the bedroom as Alastair and the servants gathered around Nerina's corpse. None of them noticed as she closed the door. She hurried across the room, rooted through her discarded gown, and drew out a slender wire hidden in the belt.

Then she set to work on the locked drawer.

It was a good lock, but Halfdan had trained her on far more intricate mechanisms. It took her only a moment to release it and yank the drawer from the desk. She the stack of letters and a small ledger, wrapping them in a pillowcase. Then she pulled on her gown as quickly as she could manage.

She hesitated. If she left now, Alastair would realize that she had taken his papers, once the shock and grief cleared his mind. And he might realize that she was a Ghost.

There was an easy solution to that.

Alastair, like most nobles, used the Magisterium's glowing glass globes for illumination at night. But the servants still used candles, and a candle sat atop the nightstand, along with some flint and tinder.

Caina set the blankets on fire and tugged them upon the floor. The flames spread to the thick carpet, and she snatched up the bundle of documents and hurried to the window. Alastair's bedroom was on the top floor, but a copper drainpipe ran down the wall, and Caina could use that to escape easily enough.

She looked at the bedroom, at the flames chewing into the walls and floor.

"I'm sorry, Alastair," Caina whispered, and went out the window.

She stayed long enough to watch the fire engulf the townhouse, to watch Alastair take charge of the Civic Militia to fight the flames.

And then she slipped away into the night.

CHAPTER 25
CHOICES

The next day Caina took a ferry across the Megaros River.

She was dressed again as a mercenary, the same disguise she and Theodosia had used while working to bring down Lord Macrinius. No one paid any attention to a caravan guard wearing a ragged cloak and dusty leather armor, or to the wrapped bundle of oddments slung over one shoulder.

The ferry arrived at the Imperial Highway's docks, and she walked the few miles north to Trinus.

The village was nothing more than a few houses and docks clustered by the river. The villagers made their living harvesting clams from the mud flats and selling them in Malarae's markets. And according to Halfdan, the villagers supplemented their incomes by hiding smugglers and criminals from the Civic Militia.

The perfect place for the Ghosts to hide.

The village had one ramshackle tavern overlooking the river. Caina pushed open the door, her boots thumping against the floorboards. Only a little light penetrated the grimy windows, and perhaps a dozen men, fishermen and mercenaries, sat nursing clay mugs of wine. One gray-haired caravan guard sat in a corner, eyes glinting behind a curtain of greasy hair.

Halfdan.

Caina crossed the room, sat down across from him, and set the bundle on the table.

Halfdan looked at her, his face expressionless.

"I made a botch of it," said Caina in Caerish. To anyone watching, they would look like two men conversing over cups of wine.

"Did you?" said Halfdan in the same language. "That's not what I

205

heard."

"What did you hear?" said Caina.

"Lord Alastair's mansion burned down," said Halfdan. "Apparently, his wife found him in bed with another woman, and she hung herself in retaliation. The scandal has quite ruined his reputation. He'll have no choice but to leave the capital and rejoin the Eighteenth Legion on the frontier."

"I was the one," said Caina.

"To do what?"

Caina sighed. "I was the one she found in bed with Alastair."

"I see," said Halfdan. He reached for the bundle. "What's this?"

"Alastair's correspondence," said Caina. "It's mostly letters from Haeron Icaraeus. He talks about how he wants 'merchandise' brought from the Pale, but it's plain he's writing about slaves. The ledger records how much Haeron paid Alastair for the slaves. He made a lot of money, and he spent it all buying things for Nerina."

Halfdan shuffled through the papers. "How did you get these?"

"After Nerina hung herself," said Caina, "Alastair was...distracted. I broke into his desk and stole the papers, and I set the house on fire to cover my escape. He probably thinks I got frightened and fled the city...the way he thinks I fled after Maglarion went berserk at Haeron Icaraeus's mansion."

Halfdan nodded, turning over one of the letters. "That makes sense."

Caina took a deep breath. "I made a mess of it and I'm sorry."

Halfdan snorted. "You think so, do you? Everything went rather well."

Caina blinked. "You...approve of what I did?"

Halfdan shrugged. "You did what I asked, did you not? I told you to make certain Lord Alastair would no longer be useful to Lord Haeron, and you did. Alastair Corus's reputation is ruined. Once he leaves Malarae, the only way he will return is as Lord Commander of his own Legion. Which is quite possible, given his ability as a soldier, but that will take years. I also asked you to find incriminating evidence against Lord Haeron." He hefted the bundle of papers. "This isn't incriminating - Icaraeus is too clever for that - but it's still useful. It will help us plan our next move against him. You did reasonably well, all told." He frowned. "Your identity as 'Marianna Nereide' is probably compromised...but that would happen sooner or later, in any case."

"But...Nerina Corus...she killed herself," said Caina.

"So?" said Halfdan. "It's not as if you killed her. She chose to hang herself. Not you."

"But...I..."

"Ah," said Halfdan. "You blame yourself for it."

Caina nodded.

Halfdan shrugged. "You needn't. Nerina Corus was...unbalanced. Even before she married Alastair. And you weren't Alastair's first mistress, and you won't be his last. If you hadn't set Nerina off, something else would have. Sooner or later she would have killed herself to spite Alastair."

"But I led her to it," said Caina. "I provoked her."

"Maybe you did," said Halfdan. "And if it troubles you, you'll have to live with it. I sent you to Malarae disguised as a noble...but I left the rest in your hands. I told you to disgrace Alastair and get his letters, but how you did it was up to you. You chose to seduce him and steal the letters from beneath his nose. I do not disapprove. It worked, did it not? Yet you needn't have done so. You might have disguised yourself as a maid, and worked your way into the household until you could seize the letters and escape. Or you could simply have broken in at night and stolen them. You're certainly skilled enough to pull it off." He snorted. "In fact, I almost stabbed you when you sat down. I didn't recognize you at first."

"Theodosia," said Caina, "said I should use my appearance as a weapon. That it was easier to cloud a man's mind than to fight him."

Halfdan nodded. "That does sound like Theodosia. But you're not Theodosia, are you?"

"No," said Caina. "No, I'm not."

She sat in silence for a moment.

"I shouldn't have done it," she said, "the way I did. I got Nerina Corus killed. She was a vicious wretch...but I pushed her to kill herself." She shook her head. "Theodosia can do as she wishes...but I will use my mind as my weapon. Not my appearance."

"Then you're at peace with this?" said Halfdan.

"Not really," said Caina. "But I've made my mistakes. I won't make them again."

"Good," said Halfdan. "The only ones who do not learn from their mistakes are the dead. And we have work to do before we die yet." He shoved the letters back into the bundle. "Do you know what the Grand Kyracian Games are?"

Caina frowned. "They're held in Malarae every ten years, to celebrate the Third Empire's victory over Old Kyrace." The nobles held chariot races and gladiatorial games. During the Fourth Empire, when the magi ruled, the enslaved gladiators fought to the death. Now volunteers only fought to first blood, while the Emperor gave free bread and wine to the city's population. Nobles from across the Empire gathered in Malarae for the Games, along with tens of thousands of commoners.

"They begin in a month," said Halfdan. "And if Haeron Icaraeus is going to move against Emperor Alexius, he will do so then. And if he does, he'll probably have the aid of Maglarion's sorcery."

Caina nodded.

"In the meantime," said Halfdan, tapping the bundle, "Lord Haeron is bringing a huge shipment of slaves into Malarae, at least a hundred of them. The letters you've found confirm it."

"What are we going to do?" said Caina.

Halfdan smiled. "We're going to free the slaves, bring down Lord Haeron, and kill Maglarion. Come along."

He left the tavern, and Caina followed him.

CHAPTER 26
PLAGUEBLOOD

The great bloodcrystal pulsed, sickly green light spilling out from the edges of the concealing trap.

Every pulse resonated in Maglarion's blood and bones.

And every pulse made him stronger.

He walked to the tower chamber's rain-beaded windows, gazing at the city of Malarae spread out beneath him. Night had fallen, yet still he saw light; the glow surrounding the nobility's mansions, the fiery light of foundries and bakeries, the light from the taverns and the inns. The Grand Kyracian Games would soon begin, and thousands more people had flooded into the city, filling the inns.

More death.

Maglarion shivered as he felt the energy from another death drain into the bloodcrystal. A mugging, he thought. Some fool killed for the few coins in his pocket. The fresh power flowing into the bloodcrystal pleased him, but it was insignificant.

Very soon now, he would pour more power into the bloodcrystal.

So much more.

He gazed at the darkened sky, watching the rain fall into the city.

"Tell me," he said at last, "have you ever thought about the rain?"

Ikhana crossed to his side, her face expressionless. Save for the ugly glitter in her eyes, of course.

"Master?"

"The rain," he said, gesturing at the window.

Ikhana shrugged. "It falls. It makes it easier to move unseen at night. What of it?"

"Have you ever considered," said Maglarion, "how it touches everyone in the city?"

She stared at him in puzzlement.

"Rich and poor, young and old, the rain falls upon them all," said Maglarion. "Is that not what the poets say? One rainfall can cover an entire city, even one the size of Malarae."

Ikhana remained indifferent.

"Tell me something else, then," said Maglarion. "If you wanted to kill everyone in Malarae, how would you do it?"

Ikhana blinked. "There are a million people in Malarae, Master. Perhaps a million and a quarter, once the Grand Kyracian Games begin."

Maglarion sighed, whispered a spell, and clenched his fist.

Invisible force seized Ikhana, flung her to the floor. For a moment his sorcery held her in its crushing grip, and she trembled like a dying rabbit. Then he gestured again, releasing her from the spell.

"That is not what I asked," said Maglarion, as Ikhana climbed to her knees. "How would you kill everyone in the city?"

Ikhana licked her lips. "My dagger." She touched the black blade at her belt. "I would go into the street, kill the first man, woman, or child I saw. And I would kill, and kill, and kill, until they were all dead, until their life energies filled me."

"Eloquent as ever," said Maglarion. "But what if you wanted to kill them all at once? Every last man, woman, and child in the city, all dying in the same moment. How would you do it?"

For a moment confusion touched her empty face. "It...is not possible, Master."

"Is it?" said Maglarion. "What if one were to, let us say, poison the rain itself? The rain that falls upon rich and poor and young alike? What would happen then?"

"Such a thing is impossible." said Ikhana. "Not without the aid of great sorcery..."

Her voice trailed off, her dark eyes glancing at the bloodcrystal beneath its tarp.

Then a smile, like a corpse's rictus, covered her face.

"You're going to kill them all," she breathed.

"Bring me a goblet," said Maglarion.

Ikhana hastened to do his bidding.

She did not know, of course, that she would die with the rest of them. Maglarion hoped to see her expression once she realized it. She had been an excellent servant, after he had broken her will. But once he finished, once he cast the final spell upon the Maatish scroll and left the flesh behind...he would have no further need of servants.

Ikhana returned with a pewter goblet. Maglarion took it, crossed to the great bloodcrystal, and threw back the tarp. Green flames writhed in the crystal's depths, and he saw faces, countless faces, swimming in the darkness. The faces of all those whose life energies had drained into the bloodcrystal.

He drew a dagger, scraped it across the bloodcrystal's side, and held out the goblet.

Black blood oozed and bubbled from the gash, and spilled into the goblet. The gash soon closed, repaired by the bloodcrystal's vast reservoir of power, but not before the black blood filled the goblet. It lay in the cup like liquid darkness, darker than the night, darker than the bloodcrystal.

The pewter corroded at its touch.

"What is it, Master?" said Ikhana.

"Death," said Maglarion. He smiled and lifted the goblet towards her. "Pestilence. Would you to care to drink?"

She shied away from it, hand twitching towards her dagger. As well she should. The black blood could not harm Maglarion. His link with the great bloodcrystal protected him. But if Ikhana drank it, if even the smallest drop touched her skin, she would die. Neither the dagger nor stolen life energy could save her from the substance in the goblet.

"You're certain, my dear?" said Maglarion, stirring the black blood with a finger. She had acquired a sensitivity to arcane energies decades ago, and no doubt she felt the dark power within the goblet. "You don't wish to drink? Truly?"

"No," whispered Ikhana, and the hint of fear he saw upon her face pleased him.

"Wise of you," murmured Maglarion, setting the goblet upon a table.

Ikhana glanced at the doorway. "Lord Haeron is coming."

"I know," said Maglarion.

She looked at him, nostrils flaring. "You will kill him?"

He would. And soon.

"Not quite yet," said Maglarion.

The door opened, and Haeron Icaraeus strode into the tower chamber, proud and confident in his finery...and his newfound vigor and youth.

How Maglarion looked forward to watching the pompous fool die.

"My lord Haeron," said Maglarion, sweeping into a grand bow. "I was hoping to speak with you soon."

"Oh?" said Haeron. "Why is that?"

"Because," said Maglarion, "I have devised the means by which I shall kill the Emperor for you."

That was true, at least. The Emperor would die.

Along with many other people.

"How?" said Haeron, rubbing his hands together.

"The Emperor is guarded, as you know, night and day by the Imperial

Guard," said Maglarion. "And his regalia of office was created by the magus-emperors of the Fourth Empire, and protects him from almost all forms of sorcery." He gestured at the goblet. "But it will not protect him from this."

Maglarion knew that one of the Emperor's rings protected him from sorcery, and another from most poisons.

But his rings could not stop a plague.

"What is it?" said Haeron, reaching for the goblet.

Ikhana grinned.

That alone made Haeron freeze in place.

"I would not touch that, my lord," said Maglarion, "if I were you."

"Is it...poison?" said Haeron, peering at the blackness in the goblet. "The Emperor's regalia shields him from poison."

"But not from this," said Maglarion. "It is not a poison. Think of it as a...plague, my lord, for lack of a better word. Anyone who drinks a single drop of this...plagueblood, or has a single drop touch his skin, will die. And there is no defense, no cure, no medicine that will stop it."

Haeron scowled. "But will it not be obvious that someone poisoned the Emperor?"

"Not at all," said Maglarion. "The Emperor is in his sixties. An old man." Maglarion, who had lived for four centuries, smiled at the thought. "It will look as if some pestilence claimed him."

A pestilence unlike any ever seen before.

"Yes," murmured Haeron, stroking his beard. "It could be done. It could indeed be done. He does not even have to drink it, you say? It need only come in contact with his skin? That would simple to arrange. One of the Kindred could do it, certainly."

"And then Emperor Alexius would die," said Maglarion, watching the lust burn in Haeron's eyes. "The lords of the Empire would gather to elect his successor. And your path to the Imperial throne would be clear."

"We should wait until the Grand Kyracian Games," said Haeron. "Most of the nobles will have gathered in the city for the Games anyway. I can take the throne in short order, then."

"My thought exactly," said Maglarion, keeping his smile hidden.

"Good," said Haeron. "Think of the great works I shall perform as Emperor! The magi shall return to a position of respect. Slavery will once again bring prosperity and order. And an immortal Emperor and a council of immortal nobles shall rule over the Empire forever. With your help, of course. When I sit upon the Imperial throne, you shall have whatever reward you wish."

Maglarion bowed again. "The gratitude of the Emperor, and the opportunity to practice the arcane sciences, is all the reward I require."

Even that was true, as well.

"Though I should like to test it, first," said Haeron, "before we risk it upon the Emperor himself."

"As you wish, my lord," said Maglarion. He had no objection. Death only made him stronger, after all. "One of the slaves in the next shipment."

"No," said Haeron, smiling. "I have better idea. Someone has failed me, and I wish to make an example of him."

Maglarion listened, intrigued, and laughed aloud when Haeron finished.

Haeron was a fool...but even a fool sometimes spoke wisdom.

A few hours later Lord Alastair Corus walked into Haeron's study.

His eyes were bloodshot, his face unshaven, his clothes rumpled. He looked, Maglarion thought, like a defeated man.

"Ah," said Haeron, turning from the rain-streaked windows. "Alastair. Do come in, my friend."

Haeron's study was larger than the houses of many commoners, with a massive oak desk, a thick carpet, and polished shelves filled with books. Maglarion doubted that Haeron had read a single one of them. Flames danced in an enormous marble fireplace, and two overstuffed chairs sat before the fire, a gleaming end table between them.

A pitcher of wine sat on the table.

"My lord Haeron," said Alastair, his voice tired. "You wished to see me."

Maglarion watched from the corner, his presence masked by a simple spell.

"I did, I did," said Haeron, putting a hand on Alastair's shoulder and guiding the taller man to the chairs. "I understand that you've suffered some...reversals, Alastair. I should like to hear about them."

Alastair sat down, rubbing his face, and Haeron sat across from him. "You do, do you? Well, here it is. I met a woman."

"Who?" asked Haeron.

"Countess Marianna Nereide," said Alastair. "A minor House, from the Saddaic provinces."

Maglarion had a dim recollection of the name. There had been a House Nereide during the Fourth Empire, though he assumed they had all been killed. No doubt some cousin or another had survived in the provinces to carry on the family name.

"She was...unlike anyone I had ever met," said Alastair. "I fell for her." He rubbed his face again. "And then Nerina found us...and Marianna stood up to her. I thought...I thought for a moment I could do the same. And then Nerina hung herself. Marianna...Marianna must have been so frightened that she fled. Someone knocked over a candle and my townhouse burned."

He lapsed into silence.

"The...papers describing our business dealings?" said Haeron.

"Gone," said Alastair. His mouth twisted in a bitter grin. "You needn't fear exposure. They were in my desk, and there's nothing left of my desk but ashes."

"Good," said Haeron. "If those papers had been lost, I would have been forced to see to your ruin, my friend, just as I did for poor Macrinius."

Alastair nodded, indifferent.

"But this is still a very grave scandal," said Haeron. "Nerina's father is furious, and demanded that I bring you to ruin. Let me be blunt, Alastair. It is in your own best interest that you leave the capital, and return to the field with the Eighteenth Legion. I'm afraid you will be unable to return to Malarae for some time."

"I know," said Alastair.

"But who knows what the future may hold?" said Haeron. "Any man may rise high in the Legions. Perhaps one day you shall return as Lord Commander of the Eighteenth, fresh from a victory over the northern barbarians."

It was all Maglarion could do not to laugh.

"Perhaps," said Alastair.

"I suggest you leave tomorrow," said Haeron. "And a with a drink, of course, to see you off."

Maglarion released his spell and stepped forward, holding a goblet. He filled the goblet from the pitcher, the red wine sparkling in the fire's light.

Strange, considering the drop of plagueblood he had mixed with the wine.

"Very well," said Alastair, taking the goblet. "I wish...I just wish I knew where Marianna had gone. That I could explain things to her." He took a long drink of the tainted wine.

"Of course," said Haeron, leaning forward.

"Could you find her?" said Alastair. "I could write her a letter, and..."

His eyes fell on Maglarion, and his voice trailed off.

"You," he whispered. "You're that sorcerer..."

All at once his hands began to shake. The goblet fell from his hands, the wine spilling into the thick carpet. Sweat beaded on his forehead, his skin turning splotchy.

Alastair began to scream, and Maglarion laughed.

CHAPTER 27
THE BAIT

The warehouse had weathered brick walls and a roof of red clay tiles, like thousands of others crowding the docks of Malarae.

But most warehouses did not have a pair of Istarish guards pacing back and forth before the locked doors, hands resting on the hilts of their swords, their eyes scanning the night.

Caina crouched in the shadows across the street, watching the guards from behind a stack of empty barrels.

She wore the black clothes she had received at the Vineyard, a black mask covering her face, and her shadow-woven cloak around her shoulders, the cowl up. Knives rested in her belt, and her daggers in their boot sheaths.

Her father's ring hung from its cord around her neck, hidden beneath her shirt. Riogan had laughed at that, but she did not care.

She remained motionless, watching the guards. They looked very much like the Istarish slavers who had held her captive seven years past; the same sort of leather armor, the same style of swords, the same merciless eyes. Perhaps they had even come from the same group of slave traders. Hard men, she knew, men who knew how to use their weapons.

But clearly they did not expect any trouble. They barely walked twenty paces from the warehouse's entrance, and did not bother to circle the building. Sometimes they stopped and talked for few moments in quiet voices.

Caina waited.

One of the guards strolled towards the pile of barrels, gazing down the street at the harbor, and Caina saw her chance. She glided forward, dagger low in her hand, boots making no noise against the ground. Four quick

215

steps, and she was behind the guard, the shadow-cloak flowing around her like living darkness.

She slapped a gloved hand over his mouth and cut his throat.

Blood splashed over his leather armor, and Caina's hand absorbed his scream. He tried to fight back, but Caina kicked out, tangling her leg in his, and the guard lost his balance.

He did not get up again.

Caina straightened up just in time to see Riogan finish the second guard. Like Caina, he wore all black. He also wore a shadow-cloak, and it blurred the edges of his form, making him merge and vanish into the darkness. Sometimes she had a hard time even seeing him.

"Hide the bodies," said Riogan, his voice a quiet rasp.

Caina nodded, dragged her dead guard to one of the empty barrels, and stuffed him inside. Riogan paused long enough to pluck a ring of keys from his dead guard's belt, and then hid the corpse in the alley alongside the warehouse.

Then he beckoned, and she followed.

They did not go through the warehouse's front doors, circling instead to the back. Riogan produced a rope and grapnel and flung it. The grapnel caught on the roof tiles, and Riogan scrambled up the rope, Caina following. Four square holes stretched in a line down the center of the roof. Light wells, no doubt, to spare the warehouse's owners the expense of illumination.

They crept to the edge of the nearest well and looked down.

Right away the stink hit Caina's nostrils.

The interior of the warehouse looked like a cattle pen, but instead of cows and mules, the wooden stalls held people. Each stall contained five or six naked men and women, chained together by collars around their necks. Utter despair crushed their features, and some wept quietly. A dozen Istarish slavers stood guard. Some wandered back and forth in the aisles between the stalls, while seven of them sat at a table, drinking and playing cards.

Just as they had done in the cellar below Macrinius's mansion.

Neither the guards nor the slaves saw them. They didn't look up. No one ever looked up.

Riogan pointed, and Caina followed him.

They stopped at the light well by the warehouse's far wall. There were more stalls below, Caina saw, but this end of the warehouse was otherwise deserted. She unhooked her own rope and grapnel from her belt, drove the grapnel's claws into the clay tiles, and let the rope fall.

Still no one noticed.

She slithered down the rope, dropped into a crouch behind some empty crates, and waited. No sounds of alarm came from the guards. Caina counted to a hundred, and then beckoned to Riogan. He came down the rope in a controlled fall, his boots making no sound when they struck the floor, and crouched besides her.

"They're drinking from a barrel next to the lantern," hissed Riogan into her ear. "Poison it."

"And the others?" whispered Caina.

"Take them one by one. Hide the bodies in the empty stalls."

That would be difficult. But half the slavers were already drunk, and the other half looked careless. No doubt they thought that Lord Haeron Icaraeus's influence would shield them from interference.

They would learn otherwise in short order.

The only light came from a pair of lanterns, one on the card table, the other on the floor next to the barrel of wine. And the lanterns threw plenty of dark and tangled shadows over the stalls, which meant that Caina found it easy to glide from shadow to shadow, remaining unseen and unheard. She passed within three paces of some of the collared slaves, and they did not notice her.

The barrel stood open, two-thirds full of blood-colored wine. Caina reached into her belt, drew out a small pouch of powder Komnene had taught her to prepare, and dumped it into the barrel. The wine bubbled for a bit, and then went still. Caina slid into the shadows as one of the Istarish slavers pushed from the table, walked to the barrel, and filled his cup. Nerina's death had wracked her with guilt, but she had no qualms about killing these men, these slave traders who sold their victims to Maglarion's dark sciences.

Of course, the powder wouldn't kill them, but merely knock them out.

Halfdan wanted information.

She saw one of the guards walk down an aisle of stalls, hand on his sword hilt, and she glided after him, reaching into her belt. She did not draw a dagger or a knife. That would make too much noise, and the smell of blood might give her away. Instead she lifted a heavy cloth pad, soaked with another concoction that Komnene had taught her to mix.

The guard paused at the end of the aisle, stretched, and started to turn.

Caina jumped up behind him, wrapping her left arm around his neck, her right hand slamming the cloth pad over his mouth and nose. He flailed, drew breath to scream...and Caina felt him relax as the pad's fumes filled his lungs. She sidestepped, and let him fall into the dirty straw of an empty stall.

She looked around. Still no one had noticed.

She drugged two more of the guards before the elixir mixed into the cloth pad lost its potency. Circling to the next aisle of stalls, she saw more unconscious guards lying on the floor. Riogan had been busy.

She settled in the shadows to wait.

The drug she had mixed into the wine would not take effect right away. But one by one the Istarish slavers sitting at the table began to nod off. One fell backwards and toppled to the floor.

The final slaver rocketed to his feet, eyes wide.

"Casim?" he said, staring at the fallen man. "Casim?"

Caina stepped from the shadows, a dagger in hand.

The slaver flinched and reached for his sword.

"Casim isn't getting up," she said, using the rasping voice that Theodosia had taught her. "Neither are the others."

Riogan stepped out of the darkness, masked face hidden beneath his shadow-cloak's cowl, daggers gleaming in either hand. The slaver backed away, sweat pouring down his face.

"I suggest," said Caina, "that you throw down your sword, give us your keys, and surrender. Otherwise you can join your friends on the floor."

Gulping, the slaver threw down his sword and raised his hands.

"Smart man," said Riogan.

In short order, Caina and Riogan had the slavers tied up and the prisoners freed.

Tomard's company of Civic Militia arrived to take terrified slaves in hand. As militiamen swarmed over the warehouse, Tomard stepped into the darkened corner where Caina and Riogan waited, wrapped in their shadow-cloaks.

"Mother told me that I'd find something interesting here," he murmured, taking off his crested helmet and running a hand through his sweaty hair. "Though she didn't tell me how interesting. A hundred slaves and nine slavers!"

"We'll want to speak with the slavers before you hang them," said Caina.

"Aye, that can be arranged," said Tomard, putting his helmet back on. "Bah! This stinks of politics. A wise militiaman keeps his nose away from the games of the lords and the magi. You Ghosts bring me too much trouble."

"There are no Ghosts," said Caina, "only…"

"Yes, yes, I know," said Tomard. "The Ghosts are a rumor concocted by fools to explain their failures." He snorted. "Though isn't the first time I've seen a rumor bring down slavers."

###

The next morning Caina disguised herself as a common serving woman and walked to the Grand Imperial Opera.

The workshop below the great stage looked much as she remembered it. The same wooden sets, the same tools, the same stage hands sleeping off last night's wine on cots and blankets. The door to Theodosia's room stood open, and Caina saw Theodosia herself sitting before the mirror, adjusting her makeup.

Theodosia turned and smiled.

"There you are," she said. "Halfdan said you would be along shortly. Hand me that brush, will you?" Caina crossed to the table, picked up the brush, and handed it over. "I've had just devil of a time replacing you, you know. The girls I have now don't know the difference between rouge and face powder! My life is an unceasing parade of tribulations."

"That must be dreadful," said Caina, trying not to laugh. "How you ever find the strength to bear up under such trials, I'll never understand."

"Insolent girl," said Theodosia, and then she laughed and caught Caina in a hug. "It is good to see you again. Halfdan tells me you've been making all sorts of trouble for Lord Haeron."

"I made Maglarion blow up Lord Haeron's ballroom," said Caina.

Theodosia smile widened. "I saw Haeron at the opera the following week. I've never seen a man scowl so fiercely for so long." The smile faded. "I...also heard what happened with Lord Alastair. I'm sorry it turned out that way."

"So am I," said Caina.

"Nerina Corus was a dreadful harpy," said Theodosia. She sniffed. "Why, the woman once talked entirely through 'The Queen of Anshan!' And while I was singing the lead, no less! Lord Alastair should have divorced her years ago and never looked back."

Caina looked away. "He doesn't have to worry about that now, does he?"

Theodosia studied her for a moment. "Are you in love with him?"

"No," said Caina.

"You're sure?" said Theodosia.

"I...liked him," said Caina. "A lot. He was charming and witty and...he was..."

"A good lover?" said Theodosia.

Caina felt herself flush, but nodded. "He was. But...I couldn't respect him. He was weak. Too weak to stand up to his wife, too weak to do anything but take the path of least resistance." Her expression hardened. "And he was a slave trader. That stinking warehouse full of slaves? He did things like that because it was easier than confronting Nerina. I didn't respect him…and I respect myself less, for seducing him."

Theodosia nodded. "I think you may have been seduced yourself, my dear."

"You did tell me I should find a lover," said Caina.

"True," said Theodosia, picking up a small jar of makeup. "But I didn't tell you to seduce a married man and terrorize his wife to suicide, did I?"

Caina sighed, closed her eyes. "No. That was my mistake."

Theodosia nodded. "Just so long as you know it. Mistakes are unpleasant, of course…but they become so much worse when you refuse to learn from them."

"I don't want to do it that way again," said Caina. "Learn a man's secrets by seducing him."

"Perhaps that's just as well," said Theodosia. "You're a lovely young lady, my dear…but you're smarter than I am, and vastly more dangerous in a fight. Halfdan sharpened that mind of yours into a knife; you might as well use it to stab somebody. Hand me that bottle, will you?"

"Why are you putting on makeup now?" said Caina, handing over the bottle. "It's barely past dawn. Are you doing performances during the day now?"

"Of course not," said Theodosia, dabbing around her eyes with a brush. "But Halfdan and Lady Julia will be arriving shortly so we can decide what to do about Lord Haeron and his pet necromancer. And I am not going to look slovenly in front of Lady Julia. That woman already thinks far too much of herself as it is. Now help me pick a dress."

Caina laughed, and did as she was told.

Halfdan arrived a short time later, dressed in the furred robe and cap of Basil Callenius, master merchant of the Imperial Collegium of Jewelers. Lady Julia walked on his arm, elegant in a gray gown with black trim upon the sleeves and hem. Riogan followed, wearing the chain mail and livery of a bodyguard, sword and dagger ready at his belt.

Something strange rested in his left hand.

It was a staff, about seven feet high, but wrapped in tight strips of leather. The staff's top bulged beneath the leather wrappings, and Caina wondered if it was a spear of some kind.

Rekan followed them, wearing the black robe and red sash of a magus. Caina's lips thinned as she saw him, and she remembered their practice sessions in the Vineyard, his repeated failures to break into her mind.

He scowled. Evidently, he remembered her too.

Halfdan and Julia walked to join Theodosia, but Riogan stopped before Caina, his cold eyes on her face.

"You did well, last night," said Riogan, "killing that guard."

Caina shrugged. "Just like slaughtering goats."

Riogan blinked, and then laughed. "Yes. I remember. I thought to scare you. But it seems you are made of sterner steel than I thought. Or perhaps Halfdan and the others made you harder."

"The guard was a slave trader," said Caina. "He kept children locked naked in a filthy pen for money. I don't have any regrets about killing him."

"Come here, you two," Halfdan said. "We have plans to make."

Caina walked to Halfdan's side.

"I'll put this simply," said Halfdan. "If Haeron Icaraeus is going to move against the Emperor, he'll do it during the Grand Kyracian Games. Most the Empire's nobility will attend, and if Emperor Alexius dies...or is murdered...the nobles will convene the Imperial Council and elect his successor. All the Restorationist and most of the Militarist nobility is on Haeron's side already. He can bribe or bully the undecided lords, push aside the Loyalists, and get himself elected the next Emperor. And once Emperor, he would lift the bans on necromancy and slavery."

"We know all this, Halfdan," said Julia. "What are we going to do about it?"

"It's very simple," said Halfdan. "We're going to stop him."

"How?" said Theodosia. "Has the Emperor ordered us to assassinate him?"

"If necessary," said Halfdan.

Caina was surprised. The Emperor, Halfdan had told her, preferred to have the Ghosts work quietly, subtly. Only rarely did he order direct assassinations.

"That won't be easy," said Caina.

They all looked at her.

"I've seen his bodyguards," said Caina, "when he came to the opera. He doesn't go anywhere without at least a dozen Kindred assassins around him. And I've seen the inside of his mansion. There were even more Kindred assassins there."

"You took that assassin on the balcony," said Julia, "and I suspect Riogan could handle more."

"A dozen at once?" said Riogan. "Even I might find that challenging."

"Our tasks," said Halfdan, "are threefold. First, we will kill Haeron Icaraeus if at all possible. Second, we will attempt to disgrace him, or find irrefutable and incontrovertible evidence of his crimes. If we can find that, the Emperor can order Haeron arrested, or even force him into exile."

"And the third task?" said Riogan.

"We will kill Maglarion," said Halfdan.

Silence answered that.

"How?" said Caina at last.

"Perhaps it is not even necessary?" said Rekan. The very thought of striking at Maglarion seemed to unnerve him. "The man's arcane power is immense. Surely, if we deal with Lord Haeron, Maglarion will disappear back into the shadows."

"If Haeron is going to strike at the Emperor," said Halfdan, "he will almost certainly use Maglarion to do it. And he has terrorized the people of the Empire for centuries. It is past time Maglarion was brought to account for his crimes."

"Obviously," said Caina, "but how are we going to do it? I put a poisoned crossbow bolt through his lungs, cut his throat, stabbed him, and kicked him off a fourth-story balcony. He was on his feet against in a matter of seconds."

"He must have a reserve of necromantic energy, of stolen life force, that he can draw upon," said Rekan. "One strong enough to heal any injury he takes, even mortal wounds."

"Probably one of the bloodcrystals you saw him make," said Halfdan to Caina. "If we can do enough damage to him, enough physical damage, we can overwhelm the bloodcrystal's reservoir and kill him."

Theodosia snorted. "How shall we do more injury than that? Will we have to chop him up, burn the pieces, and scatter the ashes?"

"Perhaps not," said Halfdan. "Riogan?"

Riogan nodded and pulled the wrappings from his staff.

It was, in fact, a spear. The shaft was lusterless black wood, dark and grim, topped with a two-foot silver blade. Caina stared at it, fascinated. The silver seemed...odd. Wrong, somehow. Just looking at it seemed to make her eyes hurt.

Rekan took a half-step back in alarm.

"What is that?" said Caina. "It...is that enspelled?"

"No," said Halfdan. Riogan chortled.

"Is that..." said Julia.

"Yes," said Halfdan. "Ghostsliver."

Rekan muttered a curse.

"What is ghostsilver?" said Caina.

"A rare form of silver, found only in the mountains of the Imperial Pale," said Halfdan. "Only the Ghosts know about it - hence the name, obviously."

Caina held her hand over the blade. She didn't feel a tingle, as she did in the presence of sorcery, but something...else. It was almost like a vibration, something that made the bones of her hand tremble.

"You feel something?" said Halfdan. "I thought you might. People who have an sensitivity to sorcery can often feel the presence of ghostsilver."

"But what does it do?" said Caina.

"Ghostsilver is highly resistant to sorcery, almost immune to it," said Halfdan. "Which means that a ghostsilver blade can pierce a magus's defensive wards, can destroy even the most potent enspelled objects."

"And that means," said Caina, "that means if we can get close enough...we can use this spear to kill Maglarion!"

Her hand curled into a fist next to the blade. All the blood on Maglarion's hands, all his victims over the centuries. They could be avenged at last.

Her father could be avenged at last.

"That assumes we can get close enough to Maglarion to use the spear," said Julia.

"We can," said Halfdan. "We have bait."

"Bait?" said Caina. "What bait?"

Halfdan smiled. "You."

"Me?"

"Or, rather, Countess Marianna Nereide," said Halfdan. "The one who brought Lord Alastair Corus low. Countess Marianna is rather notorious."

Caina looked away.

"That means you'll have drawn Lord Haeron's attention," said Julia. "Lord Alastair was one of his men, after all, and he must suspect the Ghosts."

"And more importantly," said Halfdan, "you will draw Maglarion's attention. He hasn't survived this long by ignoring threats. If he decides to come for you...we'll be ready for him. Or, more specifically, Riogan and that ghostsilver spear will be ready for him."

"Lord Haeron is throwing a number of balls before the Grand Kyracian Games begin," said Julia. "Naturally, I have been invited to them." Theodosia sniffed. "You'll come as well, as my guest. Halfdan will be your seneschal, Riogan will be your bodyguard...we'll say you were so frightened by what happened at Lord Haeron's ballroom that you hired him for your protection. Sooner or later, you'll draw Maglarion's notice."

"And then we'll have him," said Halfdan.

"So Marianna is your name," murmured Rekan.

Caina shook her head. "It's an alias, of course."

"That plan puts her in great danger," said Theodosia.

"Of course it does," said Caina. "I'm a Ghost nightfighter. Great danger is what I do. And if I can spend my life to stop Maglarion... it would be worth the cost."

Theodosia frowned, but said nothing.

"And since we are speaking of Maglarion," said Rekan. "I believe I have uncovered part of his plan."

"Oh?" said Caina. "You know what he wants?" She had wondered that for seven years. Why all the games with the slaves and the nobles and the bloodcrystals? What did Maglarion want?

"As you know, several of the Magisterium's master magi are...somewhat sympathetic towards him," said Rekan. "I have heard rumors. Apparently, Maglarion is going to teach them some of his arcane sciences."

"In exchange for what?" said Halfdan. "He would do nothing for free."

"In exchange for a storm," said Rekan.

"A storm?" said Caina. "A thunderstorm?"

"Exactly," said Rekan. "The master magi of the capital's chapterhouse know something of the old Kyracian science of stormsinging. Maglarion has asked them to conjure a storm over Malarae."

"A hurricane?" said Halfdan. "Something to destroy the city?"

"No," said Rekan. "The master magi lack the power for such thing. No, Maglarion merely wants a...rainstorm, nothing more. A heavy, soaking rainstorm, large enough to cover the entire city. The sort farmers would like."

Caina thought it over.

"Why?" she said at last.

Rekan smirked. "I know not. You are the Ghosts, so skilled at ferreting out secrets. Perhaps you can find out."

"Do you know when?" said Halfdan.

"Within the month," said Rekan. "Perhaps within a few days. I could not learn any more."

"Whatever Maglarion intends with this storm," said Theodosia, "it can't be good."

"Then we'd better stop him first," said Caina.

###

Later Caina practiced her unarmed forms in a deserted corner of the workshop. Throws, punches, kicks, and leg sweeps until her heart pounded and sweat dripped down her forehead.

"You've kept up with it, I see," said Halfdan.

Caina stopped, saw him approaching. "It's kept me alive more than once."

"Good," said Halfdan, and took a deep breath.

"What is it?" said Caina.

"Alastair Corus is dead."

She remembered the final expression on Alastair's face, the twisting grief and pain as he cut down Nerina's corpse. She remembered him laughing, remembered him taking her in his arms...

"He's dead?" whispered Caina.

Halfdan nodded.

"How?" she said at last. "He...didn't kill himself, did he? He couldn't have. He wouldn't have."

"I don't believe so," said Halfdan. "I think he was poisoned."

"Poisoned? Who did this?" said Caina.

"Tomard sent the report," said Halfdan. "One of the Civic Militiamen found Alastair's body in the street. Tomard thinks Alastair was poisoned, but he's not sure. And Tomard was...disturbed enough that he wants one of us to come look at the body as soon as possible."

Caina frowned. A man could not rise to a centurion's rank in the Civic Militia without a level head, and Tomard was one of the steadiest men she had ever met.

"Wait," she said, her mind working through the shock. "Tomard thinks Alastair was poisoned? Surely he's seen men killed by poison before. Which means...which means he's not sure how Alastair was killed, and if it was enough to disturb him..."

"You want to come?" said Halfdan.

"Yes," said Caina.

They disguised themselves as mercenaries and left the Grand Imperial Opera.

CHAPTER 28
BLACK SORCERY

Night had fallen by the time they reached the Civic Militia's fortified watchtower.

It was the same watchtower where Caina and Riogan had taken the slaves after freeing them from Lord Macrinius's cellar. Nor was it far from Haeron Icaraeus's mansion. In fact, she could see the massive shape of the Icaraeus mansion, its proud tower soaring into the night.

Her hand curled into a fist. If Haeron had killed Alastair, he was going to pay for it. And if Maglarion had killed him...it was one more death to lay at his feet.

Halfdan pounded on the door until a grim-faced militiaman opened it.

"Aye?" he said in Caerish. "We're not hiring recruits. Be off with you."

"We don't wish to join," said Halfdan. "Your centurion is Tomard, aye?"

"What of it?"

"We've a message for him," said Halfdan. "Tell him the shadows are waiting."

The militiaman scowled, but a silver coin from Halfdan improved his disposition, and he vanished into the tower. A short time later Tomard appeared, a suspicious look on his face. He seemed steady ever, but...

Caina realized he was afraid.

"Aye?" Tomard said.

"Let the tyrants beware," said Halfdan in High Nighmarian, "let them fear the shadows..."

Tomard grunted. "For in the shadows wait the Ghosts." He switched back to Caerish. "Mother sent you?"

"She did," said Halfdan.

"Follow me, then," said Tomard, leading them into the watchtower. They walked through the central room, past militiamen eating and drinking at trestle tables. Tomard unlocked an iron-banded door, revealing the stairs to the tower's cellar. "You two eaten yet?"

"We're not hungry," said Halfdan.

"That wasn't an offer," said Tomard, picking up a lantern. "It's a warning. Once you see what...happened to Lord Alastair, you'll have a hard time keeping your dinner down."

Caina shivered.

Tomard led them down the curving stairs to the cellar, a massive vaulted room with barrels and crates stacked against one wall. A table rested in the center of the room, covered by a stained cloak.

A misshapen form lay beneath the cloak.

Caina blinked. She felt the faint tingle of sorcery, and the cold, queasy feeling she had come to associate with necromancy. It was coming from the thing lying beneath the cloak.

"That's him?" said Halfdan.

"Aye," said Tomard, setting the lantern on the floor. "Brace yourselves. This...isn't pretty."

He pulled the cloak away.

And it took every ounce of self-control Caina had not to scream.

Alastair Corus, or what was left of him, lay on the table. Caina recognized him, but only just. A huge black cyst covered the left side of his face, so large that it had burst his eye from the socket and distorted his mouth, the mouth that had kissed her, into a distorted grin. More of the huge cysts covered his arms, his legs, and his torso, and a few of them had burst open, yellowish-black slime leaking to stain the wood of the table.

"You idiot!" said Halfdan. "This isn't poison! He died of some pestilence. What were you thinking, bringing him here? You should have burned the corpse at once! As it is, you've probably infected half..."

"It's not a pestilence," said Tomard.

"He's right," said Caina.

Halfdan fell silent and looked her.

"Those cysts," said Caina. "What kind of pestilence could do that? And he was lying in the street. Anyone who passed by would have caught the plague. Every militiaman in this tower would have caught it."

"Then if it's not a plague," said Halfdan, "it must be some kind of poison."

He didn't know, Caina realized. For the first time in the seven years, she had seen Halfdan taken aback.

"Look at those cysts," she said, stepping closer to Alastair's body. The queasy tingling against her skin grew stronger, sharper. "I don't think a natural poison or disease could have done this."

"Sorcery, then?" said Halfdan.

Caina lifted a hand, held it a few inches from Alastair's face. It felt like tiny needles pierced her skin.

"Necromancy," she said

Tomard muttered an oath and raked a hand through his hair.

"You're sure?" said Halfdan.

"I can feel it," said Caina. "Maglarion did this, I'm certain."

But why? If Maglarion had wanted Alastair dead, surely there were simpler ways to do it. One of Haeron's Kindred assassins, or some poison in a glass of wine. Why this hideous death?

Perhaps it was for some necromantic purpose.

She remembered the day Maglarion killed her father. It felt like it had happened hours ago, not years, as she looked at Alastair's corpse. Maglarion said that death released necromantic power, power that could be trapped in a bloodcrystal and used by a skilled practitioner of the necromantic sciences...

Was that why he had killed Alastair in such a hideous fashion? To harvest his death for power?

The storm. Why did Maglarion want the magi to conjure a storm over Malarae?

The answer seemed just out of reach.

"He's planning something," whispered Caina.

"Planning what?" said Halfdan.

"I don't know," said Caina. "But this...I think this is just the beginning. He's been working to something, for all these years. The Maatish scroll. All those slaves. The bloodcrystals. And now poor Alastair, and that storm...he's going to do something even worse than this." She looked at Halfdan. "We've got to stop him."

"We shall," said Halfdan, looking at Tomard. "We've seen enough. Burn this, and quickly. Whatever killed Lord Alastair might not be catching, but best not to take any chances."

They turned to go. Caina hesitated over the body, and reached for an intact patch of skin on Alastair's left hand.

"Oh, Alastair," she whispered. Something inside her seemed to break, and she felt tears in her eyes. "I'm sorry. I'm so sorry."

And as she touched his hand, a blast of icy power erupted from him and surged up her arm.

Caina stumbled with a startled gasp. Ghostly green flames crackled up and down Alastair's twisted limbs. Brighter flames shone in his eyes, and the crawling tingle of necromantic sorcery grew stronger, sharper.

And Alastair's corpse started to move.

Caina jumped back in alarm as Halfdan and Tomard shouted. The corpse sat up, jerkily, like a puppet controlled by an unsteady hand. Its head twisted back and forth, and Caina heard bones grinding in its neck.

And then the corpse lunged for her, fingers hooked into claws.

Caina sidestepped, yanked the dagger from her belt, and slashed. But she realized the futility of it even as her dagger ripped across Alastair's arm. He was already dead. How could she use a dagger to kill a man already dead? The blow staggered the corpse, but it soon recovered its balance and turned to face her.

Tomard bulled past her, shield on his arm, broadsword ready. He smashed the corpse in the face with the heavy shield, and lashed out with the broadsword, severing Alastair's right arm at the elbow. The corpse staggered, but punched at Tomard with its remaining arm. Tomard managed to get his shield up, but the force of the blow shattered the thick wood, knocking him back.

The severed arm began crawling of its own accord towards Tomard, pulling itself along by its fingers.

Caina looked around, mind racing. Their weapons were useless. She needed something else, she needed...

One of the barrels along the wall caught her eye.

Lamp oil.

She dashed forward, plunged her dagger into the corpse's back. The thing stiffened as she ripped the blade free, and it came after her in a shuffling run. Caina leapt up and smashed the dagger's handle into the barrel's spigot. Lamp oil gushed free, spraying the corpse.

She dashed past the table, seized the lantern, and flung it at Alastair's body with all her strength.

Harsh light filled the cellar as the corpse erupted in raging yellow flames. The puddle of lamp oil went up around the corpse as well, the fire spreading across the barrels and boxes stacked against the wall.

And the other barrels of oil.

"We should probably run!" said Caina, hurrying towards Halfdan.

Alastair's corpse thrashed once more and collapsed motionless into the spreading flames. The fire seemed to cancel whatever necromantic spell had violated his body.

Caina raced up the stairs after Halfdan and Tomard.

A short time later they stood outside and watched the tower burn. The walls were stone, but the floors and stairs were wood, and the flames devoured them in short order. Tomard organized the militiamen into a bucket line, pulling water from the nearby Naerian Aqueduct.

"I don't know how I'm going to explain this to the Lord Commander," said Tomard.

"Tell him the truth," said Halfdan.

Tomard snorted. "Oh, yes, that will certainly go over very well. 'Sorry, Lord Commander, but I had to burn down the tower to stop a devil-infested corpse.' Yes, he'll certainly believe that." He glanced at Caina. "Did you really have to burn down the tower?"

Caina shrugged. "Would you rather be in there with the devil-infested corpse?"

"Ah...no," said Tomard. "The two of you had better go. Else there will be awkward questions later."

Halfdan nodded, and Caina followed him into the night.

"What do you think?" said Caina.

"First Alastair's townhouse, and now a watchtower. You have a remarkable knack for burning down buildings."

Caina sighed.

"It was probably a trap," said Halfdan, "set to go off in case a magus or someone with sorcerous ability touched at the corpse."

"I don't have sorcerous ability," said Caina.

"But you can sense the presence of sorcery," said Halfdan. "That might have been enough to trigger the trap."

"But why would Maglarion go to the trouble?" said Caina.

The slaves. The bloodcrystals. The storm. And now this.

What did he want?

"I don't know," said Halfdan. "Perhaps we can kill him before he reaches his goal, whatever it is."

They returned to the Grand Imperial Opera in silence.

CHAPTER 29
THE PACT OF THE MAGI

Caina dressed for Lord Haeron's ball in grim silence.

She chose a blue gown with black scrollwork on the sleeves. The bodice was uncomfortably tight, but the hanging sleeves left plenty of room to conceal throwing knives. She piled her hair in an elaborate crown, donning a silver choker chain with a thumb-sized sapphire in the center. Her father's signet ring she hid on a cord around her left wrist.

If she had to confront Maglarion, she wanted that ring with her.

At last she took a deep breath and examined herself in the mirror. She looked like a pretty young noblewoman without a thought in her head. Her mother must have looked like this, twenty years ago.

She did not look like a woman planning to kill a centuries-old necromancer.

That was the point.

She went to join the others.

###

A short time later the coach stopped before the ostentatious marble pile and massive tower of Lord Haeron's mansion. Riogan and Halfdan opened the coach's door, and Caina and Julia descended. Dozens of coaches waited around the mansion, and Caina saw hundreds of nobles wandering through the gardens.

"How are you going to sneak the spear into there?" said Caina. Already she saw the Kindred assassins prowling among the guests, silent in their dark livery.

Riogan smirked and touched his belt. A broad-bladed short sword hung there, and Caina realized that it was the spear. Or, at least, its blade, attached to a sword hilt.

"I prefer the spear," said Riogan, "but it's tricky to sneak into a party. Even for me."

He wore leather and chain mail, and addition to the spear blade, carried a pair of daggers and a sword strapped to his back. Halfdan wore a seneschal's robes, but he, too, carried a dagger and a sword at his belt. Julia had chosen a sleek green gown, jewels glittering at her throat and fingers, but Caina was sure she had a dagger hidden someplace.

"Let's go," murmured Halfdan. "Stay cautious."

He led them though the crowds of chattering nobles. Caina caught snatches of conversation as she passed. Most of the nobles discussed the upcoming Grand Kyracian Games. More than a few nobles praised Haeron's seeming youth and vigor, and speculated on what he would do as Emperor.

Caina did her very best not to grind her teeth, to keep her expression cool.

The scaffolding covering the half-rebuilt ballroom improved her mood somewhat. Instead of the damaged ballroom, Halfdan led them to the Grand Hall instead, only a little smaller than the ballroom, a huge chamber lined with granite pillars, the vaulted ceiling carved with reliefs celebrating House Icaraeus's long history.

Haeron Icaraeus waited by the tall double doors to greet his guests.

"Julia, my dear," he rumbled, catching Julia's hand and kissing it. He looked even younger than Caina remembered, stronger and healthier. The life force of more murdered slaves, no doubt. "So good of you to come. Especially after the...unpleasantness at my previous ball."

"I would not miss it, my lord Haeron," said Julia, her voice smooth as glass. "It is the duty of all loyal daughters of the Empire to celebrate our triumph over Kyrace."

"Indeed," said Haeron. "And I see you have brought a guest?"

His dark eyes turned towards Caina. The last time, he had barely noticed her. This time, she had his full attention.

She made herself look nervous and did a curtsy. "My lord Haeron. An honor."

"A pleasure," he said, taking Caina's hand and kissing it. "I've heard quite a bit about you, my dear."

"Have you, my lord?" said Caina. "All lies and calumnies, I am sure."

"It was a tragedy, about Lord Alastair Corus, was it not?" said Haeron. "Such a dreadful pestilence."

"Yes," said Caina, keeping her voice smooth. Anger curled inside her. Alastair had been a fool, but he did not deserve to have a monster like Haeron Icaraeus gloating over his grave. "It was most tragic."

"You were very close to him, were you not?" said Haeron.

"He enjoyed the honor of my company," said Caina.

"Oh, he did, he did," said Haeron. "Did you know he came to me before he died? He wanted counsel. You had ruined his life, after all, and he didn't know what to do. Was he the first man you ever took into your bed?"

"That," said Caina, "is hardly an appropriate question."

Haeron smirked. "I was merely curious. Usually, a young woman falls for the first man she takes into her bed, but you were only the latest of Alastair's mistresses. Yet his wife killed herself over you, and Alastair was so heartbroken that he died of a plague." He laughed. "And here you are, utterly untroubled. You bear close watching, Countess. A woman as cold-hearted as you would make a potent ally or a dangerous enemy."

"Lord Haeron," said Julia, her voice frosty, "it is hardly dignified to discuss such matters in public, is it? Certainly it is beneath the dignity of a man who might be the next Emperor of Nighmar."

Haeron's eyes narrowed. "As you say, my lady. A pleasure speaking with you both."

He turned his attention to the next group of nobles, and Caina and the others walked into the Great Hall.

"He suspects something," murmured Caina.

"Of course he does," said Halfdan. "He knows that someone arrived to save Julia from Maglarion. And he knows that you were involved with Lord Alastair. Seeing you with Julia made him suspicious. And with any luck, it will make Maglarion suspicious, and he will show himself."

"Fat bastard," muttered Riogan, glancing back at Haeron, who was hardly fat any longer. "I should have cut his throat then and there."

"Yes, that would be subtlety, indeed," said Halfdan. "Keep watch."

Caina nodded. If Lord Haeron decided that she and Julia were a threat, if he decided to have them killed...he could do it easily. Caina saw a dozen Kindred assassins prowling throughout the hall, ignored by the noble lords and ladies. It wouldn't even take a blade or a crossbow quarrel. An "accidental" fall from a balcony, a drop of poison in the wine...

"Are you well?" said Julia. "You look...ill."

"I'm fine," said Caina. "I..."

She frowned.

She did feel ill.

And as she concentrated, she felt the presence of necromancy all around her. Faint, tenuous, like smoke rising from a distant fire, or the smell from a half-buried corpse.

But it was there nonetheless.

"Sorcery," said Caina, frowning. "There's...a great deal of necromantic power here, I think." If she closed her eyes, she could almost feel it beating upon her face like the sun. "Whatever Maglarion's doing...it's here. In this mansion."

"Do you think Maglarion would be bold enough to show himself openly?" murmured Julia. "Half the guests at Haeron's birthday saw his face. And the Magisterium still has that 'bounty' on his head."

"I don't know," said Halfdan. "Let see if we can draw him out, shall we?"

Caina and Julia moved from group to group of nobles, Halfdan and Riogan trailing after. They accepted glasses of wine from servants, and made polite small talk with the nobles. Caina pretended to listen to their talk of balls and weather and Imperial politics, but her eyes scanned the room whenever she had a chance. Maglarion was here, she was sure of it.

Then she saw him.

He stood on the high balcony running along the length of the Great Hall, watching the crowd with amused interest. A patch hid the glowing green crystal embedded in his left eye socket, and he wore a cloak with the hood pulled up, no doubt to keep anyone from identifying him.

But Caina could never forget him, no matter how much she wanted to.

"Excuse me, sirs," said Caina, moving away from a group of nobles. Riogan looked up as she approached, and she whispered into his ear.

"There," she said. "On the balcony, behind me. In the cloak."

"That's him?" said Riogan. "Fellow with the patch over his eye?"

Caina nodded.

Riogan grunted. "Shorter than I expected. He's talking to someone."

Caina turned, looking up just long enough to see Maglarion talking to a stout lord in an expensive blue coat.

"We're taking him," said Riogan. "Now."

"Just like that?" said Caina.

Riogan nodded. "He's isolated on that balcony. Best chance we'll have. You distract him, and I'll creep up from behind and ventilate his guts with the ghostsilver blade. Now make up an excuse."

Caina stepped to Julia. "I feel the need to stretch my legs. I think I will take a walk. Up to that balcony, perhaps. There's a fascinating man I've wanted to talk to for some time."

Both Julia and Halfdan looked at her, eyes hard, and then nodded.

"Do be careful, my dear," said Julia.

"Not to worry," said Caina. "Raccard here," she glanced at Riogan, "will deal with anyone who threatens me, I'm sure."

"Good luck," said Halfdan, "my lady."

Caina nodded and followed Riogan across the Great Hall. A narrow flight of stairs led up to the balcony. Caina wished that she was wearing her shadow-cloak. It would have ruined her disguise, of course, but so long as she had it on, Maglarion could not break into her mind.

Not that it would stop his spells from shattering every bone in her body, of course.

She reached the balcony, Riogan a half-step ahead of her.

Maglarion was gone.

She looked around, saw him vanishing into a hallway, the stout lord in the blue coat walking before him. Riogan jerked his head in that direction, and Caina nodded, her heart racing. Would Maglarion recognize her face? She doubted it - she had been only one among his hundreds, even thousands, of victims. If he realized who she was, he might kill her on the spot. Or perhaps he would try to find out how she had escaped from his lair all those years ago.

But if he remembered her from Lord Haeron's birthday, he would kill her on sight.

Either way, she had to distract him long enough for Riogan to strike.

The hallway was long and high, statues and busts standing in niches along the walls. Caina saw Maglarion vanish into a door of polished wood. She took a deep breath and followed. She would go in, get his attention, and give Riogan the chance to...

"Where are you going?"

The voice was toneless. Caina turned, as did Riogan.

A tall, pale woman crossed the hallway towards them, dressed all in black. A black dagger hung in a sheath at her belt, her hand curled around the hilt. Her face was emotionless. Almost lifeless. Caina had seen corpses with more expression. The woman's pale eyes were cold, almost like looking into a frozen pond. Caina had seen eyes like that before, had...

Recognition shot through her.

Ikhana. Maglarion's lieutenant.

She felt a nauseated tingle as Ikhana stepped forward. The dagger, Caina remembered. Ikhana had claimed that it could drain life energies from its victim and into its wielder. At the time, Caina had been too terrified to care. But now she felt the aura of dark power surrounding the weapon.

"Where are you going?" said Ikhana, her voice still dead, but her knuckles tightened around the dagger's hilt.

Caina drew up her chin. "It is not any of your concern, servant. I am a Countess of the Nighmarian Empire and may go where I wish. Now be off, or else I'll tell Lord Haeron of your insolence, and he'll have you beaten black and blue."

"I know you," said Ikhana.

"I've never seen you before," said Caina.

Riogan stepped forward, hand on his sword hilt. "You offer my mistress impertinent words, wench. Get out of our way or you'll feel the back of my hand."

The sight of Riogan with hand on sword would have frightened most people. But Ikhana did not move, did not blink her icy eyes.

"Where have I seen you before?" she murmured. "Have I seen you before? No...I think not. But you are familiar. Yes. That is it. You remind me of someone. Someone the Master knew."

Caina felt a drop of icy sweat trickle down her spine. The woman's monotone, her motionless eyes, made her seem like a dead thing. Ikhana remembered her. Or she remembered Laeria Amalas, and Caina looked like her mother.

She had to distract Ikhana.

The answer came to her.

"Raccard," she said, putting a whine into her voice, and curling her arms around Riogan's neck. She had the brief satisfaction of seeing astonishment shoot into his cold eyes. "Raccard, you said we could sneak off together. And if Lady Julia ever found out about this, oh, I'd never heard the end of it. Raccard, make her go away."

She planted a kiss on his cheek and rested her head against his shoulder.

"Woman," said Rekan, his voice gruff. "My mistress, ah...she is feeling ill, and needs to lie down. Find her a bed she can use, now."

Ikhana's eyes narrowed in contempt, and she walked away without another word.

Caina disentangled herself from Riogan as soon as Ikhana was out of sight.

"What is the matter?" said Riogan, smirking. "My lady is too good for a romp with her bodyguard?"

"We have work to do," said Caina.

Riogan's smirk vanished. No doubt he was more interested in killing Maglarion than kissing her. Or anyone. "Did you see where he went?"

"That door," said Caina.

Riogan nodded. "Then let's finish this. You distract him, I'll gut him."

Caina reached for the door a crack, stopped.

"What is it?" said Riogan.

Her skin tingled. "He's casting a spell."

"At us?"

"No," said Caina. "And it's not...it's not powerful." She took a deep breath and opened the door.

Beyond she saw a cavernous, darkened sitting room, with overstuffed couches and chairs resting on at thick carpet. Double doors opened onto a broad balcony, Maglarion standing near the marble railing.

Six men in the black robes and purple sashes of master magi stood with him.

"Stop," hissed Caina.

"What?" murmured Riogan.

"There are master magi with Maglarion," said Caina. "Six of them. Not even you can sneak up on all of them."

"Go," said Riogan. "We'll try again later."

Caina started to step back, then stopped. One of the magi wore a red sash instead of a purple one, and she recognized his face.

Rekan.

"Rekan's here," said Caina.

Riogan cursed. "He's supposed to be at the Magisterium's chapterhouse."

She dropped into a crouch and crept forward, skirts gathered in one hand. Riogan scowled at her for a moment, but followed. Caina huddled behind one of the massive couches and peered around the edge, listening. She didn't dare come any closer. She knew that Maglarion could reach into the minds of others, and he might sense her presence, or Riogan's. Or one of the master magi might have similar powers.

"We respect you, of course, Maglarion," said one of the master magi, a balding man with a crooked nose. "You were one of the great magi of the Fourth Empire, and none of us can match your skill. Furthermore, your ability to survive for such a span of time is indeed remarkable. But you ask a great deal of us. The Magisterium is under constant pressure from the Ghosts and their allies among the nobles, and Emperor Alexius detests us. Flashy displays of power draw...unwelcome attention. As Lord Macrinius learned, you might recall. The storm you wish us to conjure will draw a great deal of unwelcome attention."

"True, Caprinius, I ask a great deal of you," said Maglarion, smiling as he always smiled, "but I offer much in return. Observe."

He gestured.

The fat lord in the blue coat floated into Caina's field of vision, suspended in the power of Maglarion's spell.

"Who is that?" said Caprinius.

"Some lord or another," said Maglarion. "He recognized me, and threatened to turn me over to the Magisterium unless I used my sorcery to enspell a wife for him."

The magi laughed.

"You fear the Ghosts and their noble allies? You fear the Emperor?" said Maglarion. "With this, you need not fear them ever again."

He reached into his coat pocket and drew out a glass vial. Black fluid filled the vial, thick and viscous, and looking at it made the tingling sensation against Caina's skin worse.

And yet...she felt drawn towards the vial. Pulled towards it, like iron towards a lodestone. She blinked in confusion. She had never felt anything similar in the presence of sorcery before.

"What is that?" said Caprinius. "Some manner of poison?"

"Not at all," said Maglarion. "Poisons have antidotes. This does not. Think of it as...oh, a pestilence, let us say. An illness in a bottle. Lord Haeron likes to call it 'plagueblood'. Rather melodramatic, but it does capture the essence of the thing." He pulled the cork from the vial. "You may want to stand back. Plagueblood is rather virulent."

Caprinius, Rekan, and the other magi took several prudent steps back.

"One drop," said Maglarion, standing before the floating noble, "would be sufficient to kill at least ten thousand men, should it be mixed into their drinking water."

"You'll make him drink it, then?" said Caprinius.

"Of course not," said Maglarion. "If I let him open his mouth, he'll start to scream. And that might disturb Lord Haeron's ball. One must keep one's priorities in order."

The magi shared a laugh, and Maglarion let a single drop of black plagueblood fall upon the skin of the lord's throat.

Their laughter soon stopped.

The lord thrashed and struggled against the grip of Maglarion's spell. As Caina watched, black cysts bloomed across his face and hands. The arms of his coat and the legs of his pants bulged as cysts swelled beneath the fabric. The cysts burst in rapid succession, tearing the poor man's face to shreds, thick yellow pus and black blood oozing down his neck and shoulders.

Just as Alastair Corus had suffered, no doubt.

Caina curled her shaking hand into a fist, willing it to stillness. She wanted to save the nobleman, wanted to bury her throwing knives in Maglarion's neck. But that would do no good. She had no weapon that could hurt Maglarion. Riogan had the ghostsilver blade, but even he could not move fast enough to kill Maglarion before he killed them both.

So she did nothing and watched the nobleman die.

Maglarion flicked a finger, and the corpse tumbled into the sitting room, blood and slime soaking into the thick carpet.

"Remarkable," said Caprinius, though he sounded a bit ill. "Forgive the question, but...ah, are we in any danger of infection?"

"None," said Maglarion. "That is the beauty of it. Plagueblood is only contagious if its maker wishes it to be so."

"Remarkable," repeated Caprinius.

"Do you see the possibilities?" said Maglarion, returning the cork to the vial. "Plagueblood is a weapon against which there can be no defense. You can destroy the Ghosts and their allies among the lords with ease. The Emperor himself can die, if you wish. Once I teach you the secrets of creating plagueblood, no one can stand against you. No one."

The magi said nothing, but Caina saw the greed shining in their eyes.

"Yes," said Caprinius. "You...speak wisdom, Maglarion."

"In exchange for all that," said Maglarion, spreading his hands, "conjuring a rainstorm over the city seems like a small price to pay."

"So it does," said Caprinius. He bowed to Maglarion, low and formal. "You shall have the storm you desire. Tomorrow night."

"Thank you, master magus," said Maglarion. "I look forward to our collaboration."

The master magi and Rekan bowed, and started towards the door. Caina slid backwards along the couch, Riogan moving besides her, avoiding the eyes of the magi.

"Rekan," said Maglarion, voice quiet.

Rekan stopped, turned. "What do you wish of me, Master?" Despite the dead man on the floor, despite the fact that Rekan was almost certainly a traitor, Caina was amused. Rekan had always been so arrogant. Now he hung on Maglarion's words like a dog crouching before its master.

"I have...an extra task for you," said Maglarion.

Rekan returned to Maglarion's side.

"Do you know Graywater Square?" said Maglarion.

"I do," said Rekan.

"You're familiar, then, with the fountain there?" said Maglarion.

Rekan nodded. "A remarkably fine fountain for such an impoverished district of the city. I believe it feeds off the Naerian Aqueduct."

"Indeed," said Maglarion. He held out the plagueblood vial, and Rekan took it. "Take this and poison the fountain."

"Master?" said Rekan.

Maglarion smiled. "I wish one final test of the plagueblood. I am curious to see how long its effects will last. Graywater Square is quite crowded. I suspect...oh, two or three thousand people draw their drinking water from that fountain. I want to see how many of them shall die."

"Quite a few of them, I should think," said Rekan, tucking the vial into his robes. "And you will send others into the city with the same mission, yes? To spread chaos before Lord Haeron takes the throne?"

"Do not trouble yourself with that," said Maglarion. "Others shall deal with the Naerian Aqueduct itself tomorrow. Merely do as I bid. Fulfill my commands, Rekan, and you shall have the reward I have promised. You shall have it to the full."

Something ugly kindled in Rekan's eyes. "Yes. Master."

"Good," said Maglarion, walking around the nobleman's body. "Oh, have some of Haeron's servants tend to the corpse." He smiled. "They're rather used to it, by now."

CHAPTER 30
MY NAME IS CAINA

Caina tensed, preparing to tackle Rekan from behind.

But he stayed too close to Maglarion, and both sorcerers left the sitting room.

She took a deep breath, ignoring the smell of blood and decay from the dead nobleman, and hurried across the sitting room. Then she opened the door and slid into the hallway, hand tight around the handle of a throwing knife.

Both Maglarion and Ikhana were gone. But she saw Rekan striding onto the balcony, black robes billowing around him. No doubt he was in a hurry to carry out Maglarion's instructions.

To kill all those people in Graywater Square.

Unless Caina stopped him.

She started after Rekan.

Riogan's hand closed about her shoulder. "Where do you think you're going?"

Caina gave him an incredulous look. "To stop him."

"Foolishness," said Riogan. "He might have allies. Better to tell Halfdan. That way we can feed Rekan false information, and dispose of him later."

"And what about all those people in Graywater Square?" said Caina.

Riogan shrugged. "Not our problem."

Anger blazed up in Caina, and she almost struck him.

"You tell Halfdan," said Caina. "I'm going after Rekan."

Riogan did not let her go.

"I'm going after Rekan," said Caina, "unless you stop me."

"Foolish girl," said Riogan, but he released her shoulder.

"Just tell Halfdan what happened," said Caina, and she hurried after Rekan.

She did not have a hard time following him through the crowds. Rekan's black magus robe made sure that even nobles gave him a wide berth. Caina followed as closely as she dared, murmuring apologies as she slipped past frowning nobles and scowling merchants. Then Rekan walked onto the grounds, and Caina hesitated.

No one in their right mind troubled a brother of the Imperial Magisterium, and Rekan could walk wherever he wanted. But a noblewoman in silk and jewels had no such luxury, especially in a rough neighborhood like Graywater Square. Almost certainly Caina would draw unwelcome attention, perhaps even robbers.

And if she was delayed, if Rekan got too far ahead of her...thousands of people in Graywater Square would die.

But Caina knew Malarae, and she knew the fastest way to Graywater Square. If she moved quickly, she could intercept Rekan.

She sprinted to Halfdan's coach.

Shutting the door behind her, she knelt before the seat. A moment's work had the secret compartment open, and she pulled out a bundle of clothing.

The darkness of the shadow-cloak fell over her hands.

In a moment she stripped out of the blue gown and donned the black nightfighter clothes, the mask hiding her face, the cowl pulled up. She still smelled of perfume, but there was no time to wash. At least the shadow-cloak shielded her mind from any spells Rekan might throw at her.

She left the coach and hurried into the night, keeping to the shadows. Caina moved as fast as she dared, leaving the nobles' mansions behind, entering the districts of the merchants and craftsmen. Yet she saw no sign of Rekan. If he had gotten past her, if he had taken a horse instead of walking...

Then she saw him in the dark street, stark and tall in his black robes. Caina hurried after him, flowing from shadow to shadow, her cloak blurring with the night. Plans flitted through her mind. Should she confront him? Perhaps he would tell something useful about Maglarion. Should she try to capture him? Almost certainly he knew something about Maglarion's plans.

Or should she simply kill him? Almost certainly she could not take him in a straight fight. If he brought his sorcery to bear against her, he would kill her quickly.

And if Caina died, Rekan would murder everyone in Graywater Square.

A dagger in the back, then. Before he had a chance to use his spells. Quick and easy, if not necessarily clean.

She slipped a dagger from the sheath in her right boot. Step by step she closed upon Rekan, her feet making no sound against the street. From time to time Rekan stopped, glancing over his shoulder, but Caina melted into the shadows, and waited until he started walking again.

The neighborhood changed from the sturdy houses of prosperous merchants to the tall, blocky squares of the apartment towers that housed Malarae's poor. The air stank of smoke and soot, rising from the foundries and charcoal burners dotted among the apartments.

And Rekan walked into Graywater Square. A half-dozen apartment towers encircled the broad plaza, their lower levels occupied with shops and taverns. Merchant stalls and peddlers' booths, closed for the night, stood in rows. A massive fountain of carved stone adorned the plaza's center, decorated with statues, water falling from their arms to splash in shallow pool. In the distance, Caina saw the tall stone arches of the Naerian Aqueduct.

Rekan stopped, and Caina hesitated. Maybe she had been wrong about him. Perhaps he had only been playing along with Maglarion. Had Halfdan had ordered him to uncover Maglarion's secrets?

Then Rekan smirked, drew the plagueblood vial from his robe, and walked towards the fountain.

Caina made up her mind.

She broke into a run. Rekan froze, turning as he heard her footsteps, but he was too late. Caina sprang upon his back, arm wrapping about his throat, dagger angled to slide between his ribs and into his heart.

She stabbed, all her strength and momentum behind the blow.

But the blade rebounded as if it had struck a stone wall.

Caina blinked in astonishment, felt the tingle against her arm.

Sorcery. Evidently Rekan had had the foresight to ward himself against steel weapons.

He bellowed, and Caina felt another surge of power as his will lashed out. Invisible force struck her, ripped her from his back, sent her flying. He didn't hit nearly as hard as Maglarion, but hard enough. Caina struck the ground, rolling to absorb the momentum, and scrambled back to her feet, dagger ready.

Rekan stared at her, eyes wary. Her skin crawled as he gathered arcane power for another spell.

"So," said Rekan. "Halfdan finally figured out that I played him false, did he? Is that you, Riogan?"

Caina said nothing.

"Turn around and run," said Rekan, "and I might let you live."

Still Caina said nothing.

"You can't stop Maglarion," said Rekan. "You can't even kill him. I heard how the Ghosts tried to assassinate him. A crossbow bolt through the chest and a fall from the balcony, and he survived." He smirked. "Run along, or I'll hand you over to Maglarion...and you wouldn't like that at all."

"You betrayed the Ghosts," said Caina, speaking in her rasping, disguised voice. She stepped to the side. Steel couldn't touch him, but flesh could; she had gotten an arm around his neck, after all. If she could get close enough, find something else to use as a weapon... "Why?"

Rekan laughed. "You actually ask why?" Caina took another step to the side. "The Ghosts paid me in mere gold. Maglarion will pay me with immortality. Can you match that price, Ghost?" He flexed his fingers, and Caina felt the tingle sharpen against her skin. "One last chance, Ghost. Leave, and I'll let you live."

"No," said Caina, taking one more step to the side. Empty clay pots and jars stood on the counter of a nearby booth.

Rekan blinked in surprise. "No? You dare to challenge my power..."

"If you were going to kill me," said Caina, "you would have done it already. You wouldn't have wasted time with that idiotic speech about immortality."

Rekan's eyes narrowed. "Let us see about that."

He thrust out his hand.

But Caina was already in motion. She seized one of the jars and flung it. The jar struck Rekan in the face and shattered, and he stumbled back with a scream, blood flying from his mouth. Invisible force lashed at Caina, but his aim was off, and she spun past the spell.

She grabbed another pair of jars and ran at him. Rekan staggered, leaning against the fountain as he recovered his balance, and she flung another jar at him. He tried to dodge, but Caina anticipated it, and the jar bounced off his chin. Rekan stumbled and Caina crashed into him, smashing the final jar across his face. The magus slumped back against the edge of the fountain, stunned, and Caina grabbed his collar, intending to shove his head under the water until he stopped breathing.

Even a master magus would have trouble casting spells then.

Rekan screamed and flung out a hand. Invisible force erupted in all directions, making the fountain's water erupt. The blast knocked Caina backwards, sent her sprawling to the ground, her mask knocked askew, her cowl falling back. She scrambled to her feet, but Rekan lifted his hand and pointed.

His will hammered into her mind like a thunderbolt.

Caina fell to one knee before him, grimacing. She felt his mind rummaging through her thoughts like a groping hand, and without her cowl, she was not protected from his mental attacks.

"Lie down," growled Rekan, blood dripping from his lips. "I order you to lie down."

Caina fought back, as she'd fought against her mother, as she'd fought against Rekan himself in the Vineyard. She rallied her rage, pushing Rekan's will further and further back. Rekan's eyes bulged with strain, sweat dripping down his face to mingle with the blood.

Caina shuddered, and her mask slipped all the way off.

Rekan's eyes widened in astonishment.

"Marianna!"

His will wavered.

Caina leapt forward, all her anger pushing aside Rekan's mental attack, and seized one of the pottery shards from the ground. She crashed into Rekan, burying the broken shard in his throat. Rekan fell besides the fountain, choking on his own blood, and Caina stared into his terrified eyes.

"My name," she hissed, "is Caina."

She pushed the pottery shard into his throat until he stopped thrashing.

Then Caina climbed off Rekan and looked around, tugging her mask and cowl back into place. No one had noticed their fight. Or if anyone had, they knew better than to interfere in a fight between a magus and a shadow-cloaked figure.

She dug through Rekan's sash. If the vial of plagueblood had shattered during their fight...

Her fingers closed about something icy cold.

It hadn't.

Caina lifted the vial, staring at it. She felt its necromantic power, the concentrated death gathered within the glass. It should have repulsed her.

And yet...and yet it did not.

She felt drawn to the plagueblood. As if it were a missing part of her that she had only now rediscovered. For a moment she felt an overwhelming urge to remove the cork and drink.

Remembering what had happened to Alastair and the fat noble made the urge easy to resist.

She tucked the vial into her belt. Leaving Rekan's corpse in the open would warn Maglarion that something had gone amiss, so she looked around for a wagon to steal.

###

Later that night she sat in one of the rooms below the Grand Imperial Opera. Halfdan, Riogan, Theodosia, and Julia stood nearby, while Rekan's corpse lay sprawled upon a table. The great theater had been rebuilt and renovated a dozen times over its history, creating a maze of forgotten rooms and corridors below the workshops.

Theodosia knew them all, of course. Including the best place to hide the body of a slain magus

"That was," said Halfdan, when Caina had finished telling her story, "a very foolish risk you took."

Caina nodded. "I know." She leaned against the wall. Rekan's spells had given her more bruises than she had thought, and the cool stone felt good against her back. "But I did it anyway."

"And well you did," said Julia, while Riogan scoffed. "He would have murdered all those people, otherwise." She shivered. "All those children."

"You could very easily have been killed," said Halfdan.

"I know," said Caina, again. "But I wasn't. And if I could have stopped him at the cost of my life...for three thousand people, that would have been a fair bargain, I think."

"The Ghosts defend the Empire's commoners," said Halfdan, face grave. Then he smiled. "You did well, Caina. A risk...but it paid off."

Riogan grunted, but said nothing.

"I lived in Graywater Square when I was a child," said Theodosia, voice quiet. "I drank from that fountain every day." She shivered. "That Maglarion wanted to poison that water and kill so many people...gods, but I should not be surprised at the depth of his evil, not any longer."

"But why?" said Julia. "What could he possibly gain from it?"

Riogan shrugged. "He's a magus, a necromancer. Why not?"

"No," murmured Caina, staring at Rekan's corpse. "That's not it."

"What, then?" said Riogan. "Have you figured it out?"

Caina took a deep breath, thoughts tumbling through her mind.

"Power," she said. "It's about power. Power is the only thing Maglarion cares about. I remember...I remember him talking about bloodcrystals."

"What exactly is a bloodcrystal?" said Julia.

"A product of necromantic science," said Halfdan. "A necromancer can use blood to create a kind of crystal, when then can store stolen life energy. Sort of like a...reservoir of power the necromancer can tap at will."

"Or a drain," murmured Caina. "A sponge."

All those people drinking from the fountain. So much death, all at once...

"A drain?" said Halfdan. "What do you mean?"

"Maglarion made bloodcrystals that absorbed the power from any death within a certain radius," said Caina. "I watched him demonstrate." She remembered her father, sagging in the slavers' grip as Maglarion buried the dagger in his chest. "He killed my...he killed a man ten paces from a bloodcrystal, but the power released from his death drained into the crystal. Made it larger, made it start to glow. It astonished his students. They had never seen anything like it." Thoughts clicked together in her head. "He must have learned how to do it from my father's Maatish scroll, from the necromancers of the Kingdom of the Rising Sun. And he must have spent the last seven years learning how to make plagueblood. And...and..."

And just like that, the answer came to her.

It was so simple.

So simple, and so horrifying.

"I know what Maglarion wants," she said.

They stared at her.

"Power," said Caina. "He's going to use the plagueblood to poison Malarae's aqueducts, to kill thousands of people at once. He'll use his bloodcrystals to trap the sorcerous power released by their deaths, to make himself stronger. That's why he allied himself with Haeron Icaraeus. He doesn't care about Lord Haeron, he doesn't care about the Empire, and he doesn't care about anything except arcane power. But allying with Lord Haeron gave him access to all the slaves he needed for his experiments."

Halfdan swore. "And it put him in the largest city in the Empire. Where he could poison thousands of people at once, absorb the most power. You said that Maglarion claimed he could make the plagueblood contagious?" Caina nodded. "The vial he gave to Rekan was probably contagious. Gods, if that had gotten into the fountain, if the victims had spread the plague...he could have killed tens of thousands."

"That storm," said Riogan. "That's why he ordered the magi to conjure that storm tomorrow night. He's going to use it as a distraction while he poisons the aqueducts."

"The Naerian Aqueduct," said Halfdan. "You said he mentioned that to Rekan. The Naerian Aqueduct feeds the most populous districts of Malarae. If he pours the plagueblood into the aqueduct...he could kill half of the population."

"No," said Caina, shaking her head. It made perfect sense, but...she was sure they were missing something.

Only she couldn't see what.

"Tomorrow, then," said Halfdan. "We'll take Tomard's company of Civic Militia, set a trap for Maglarion where the Naerian Aqueduct enters the city. If we ambush him, Riogan can kill him with the ghostsilver spear before he poisons the aqueduct or bring his powers to bear against us."

Theodosia nodded. "I will let Tomard know. You'll put in a good word for him with the Lord Commander of the Civic Militia, won't you? He's still in trouble over that watchtower Caina burned down."

"It was necessary," said Caina, still staring at Rekan's corpse.

What was she missing?

"I shall," said Halfdan. "Get some sleep. Tomorrow night's going to be busy."

Caina nodded and got to her feet.

Everything they said made perfect sense. The bloodcrystals fed on the power of death, and the quickest way for Maglarion to kill a great number of people was to upend a vial of plagueblood into the Naerian Aqueduct.

Yet why did she feel as if she had overlooked something of grave importance?

She did not sleep well that night.

CHAPTER 31
THE STORM COMES

The Naerian Aqueduct surged down the foothills.

It was an astonishing feat of engineering. One of Emperor Alexius Naerius's distant ancestors had redirected one of the mountain streams, the Legion's engineers carving a fresh channel down the foothills. A great stone conduit had been built to carry the water into Malarae, rising ever higher on stone arches as the hills descended. At its highest point, the aqueduct rose a hundred and fifty feet on its arches.

The Ghosts waited in the foothills, overlooking the conduit.

"Why here?" Caina had asked Halfdan.

"The Naerian Aqueduct feeds a lot of fountains," said Halfdan. "If Maglarion dumps the plagueblood into the water here, it will reach every last one of them."

Caina hoped Halfdan was right. If he was not, a lot of people were going to die.

Fifty militiamen from Tomard's company waited on the rocky hillside, concealed behind boulders. They would deal with any slavers Maglarion brought as bodyguards.

And hopefully they would distract Maglarion long enough for Riogan to use the ghostsilver spear. He waited besides Caina, motionless as death itself, the spear ready in his hand. Caina stood besides him, wrapped in her shadow-cloak, flexing the muscles in her arms and legs to keep them from stiffening.

A boot scraped against stone. Caina turned, reaching for a throwing knife, and saw Tomard crouching behind Halfdan.

"The lookouts say someone's coming," said Tomard. "About thirty men. Istarish slavers, by the look of them. And a tall fellow in a hooded cloak."

Caina's gloved hands curled into fists.

Maglarion.

Riogan shifted his grip on the ghostsilver spear.

"Surround the slavers," said Halfdan, voice low. "Give them once chance to surrender, and if they don't, kill them all. And the man in the cloak...our nightfighters will deal with him." He gestured at Caina and Riogan. "Don't fight him unless absolutely necessary. He's a necromancer, and extremely dangerous."

"First demon-infested corpses, and now necromancers," muttered Tomard. "I should have listened to Mother and become a carpenter."

He hurried off to join his men.

A short time later the slavers arrived. Thirty of them, as Tomard had said, armored in steel-studded leather, swords and daggers in their belts. A tall, cloaked figure led them, one hand resting on the hilt of a sheathed dagger. Caina frowned. That didn't look at all like Maglarion. In fact, it looked like...

The figure pulled back the hood, revealing long white hair and pale, lifeless eyes.

Ikhana.

Tomard's men surged to their feet, weapons in hand. The slavers yelled in alarm and drew their swords. Ikhana looked back and forth, her empty expression never changing.

"We've got you surrounded!" Tomard's voice rang out. "Throw down your weapons and surrender! You'll only get one chance!"

Ikhana shivered, her eyes going wide, a strange look coming over her face.

Lust.

"Kill them!" she screamed, ripping the black dagger from its sheath at her belt. "Kill them, kill them all in the name of the Master!"

The slavers yelled and charged the militiamen, brandishing their weapons. Tomard bellowed a command, and the militiamen stood their ground, lifting their shields to form a solid wall of oak. The slavers crashed into them, swords clanging against armor and shields, and militiamen and slavers alike fell to the rocky ground. But the shield wall held, and more slavers died than militiamen.

And then Ikhana joined the battle.

She leapt forward with terrifying speed, moving with a grace and power that made Riogan look clumsy by comparison. The black dagger blurred in her hand, its edges burning with green fire. She struck left and right with the weapon, the glowing edges only scratching two of the militiamen.

Yet both men fell, screaming, and shriveled before Caina's eyes. One moment they were vigorous men in their thirties. A heartbeat later they were fifty, and then twice that. And then only bones and dust remained in their armor.

Ikhana's dagger did, indeed, steal life.

Ikhana screamed in ecstasy, her eyes alight with wild glee, the dagger blazing with ghostly fire. She wheeled and killed another militiaman with a slash, laughing, and sprang at Halfdan. Halfdan backed away, sword held in guard, and Caina raced towards them, dagger ready.

But he would be too slow, Caina saw. Halfdan was a competent fighter, but Ikhana moved like lightning.

And she could kill with a single scratch from that dagger.

Ikhana danced past Halfdan's guard, dagger raised for the kill...

Then Riogan was there, the ghostsilver spear stabbing and thrusting. Burning dagger met ghostsilver blade a dozen times in half as many heartbeats. Riogan whirled the spear, the butt swinging for Ikhana's head, but she glided backwards, and stabbed for Riogan's belly. He dodged backwards, completing the spear's spin in time for the blade to deflect the black dagger.

Ikhana glided back, her face alight with glee, laughing all the while.

It gave Caina all the opening she needed to throw a knife.

Ikhana staggered as the blade buried itself in her shoulder. Caina flung another, and another, knives striking Ikhana's chest and throat. Ikhana staggered, pale eyes blazing with fury, and went to one knee.

Then a slaver stumbled past her, sword raised to block a militiaman's blows, and Ikhana buried her dagger in his hip.

The man screamed, but not for long, as green fire flashed through his veins and crumbled his flesh and bone to dust. The knives fell from Ikhana's flesh as the ghostly flame flashed through her, healing her wounds. Riogan raced at her, spear gripped in both hands for a deadly thrust, but Ikhana leapt to her feet and stabbed for his face. Riogan twisted aside, the blade missing his jaw by inches.

"Come, come, little Ghosts," crooned Ikhana, beckoning with the dagger. "Do you know how many of your kind I have slain over the centuries? Come and die!"

"You talk too much," said Caina, letting the shadow-cloak billow loose over her shoulders.

She risked a glance at Riogan, saw him nod.

"Very well," said Ikhana, and she leapt at Caina.

Caina dodged the flame-wreathed dagger. Ikhana was fast, faster than Riogan, faster than Akragas. Caina blocked one stab, deflected another, dodged a third. Still Ikhana came, dagger moving faster than a serpent's tongue. Caina twisted to the side, cross-stepped...

...and let her billowing cloak slam into Ikhana's face.

Ikhana hissed, clawing the cloak aside. It only delayed her for a second, but it was enough. Riogan lunged forward, the ghostsilver spear plunging into Ikhana's belly. Ikhana howled in fury, falling upon her back as the spear pinned her to the ground. Caina kicked the black dagger from Ikhana's grasp, and its green flames winked out.

She looked around for more enemies, but the battle was over. Tomard and the militiamen had killed most of the slavers, and the few survivors had surrendered.

"Gods," muttered Riogan, still gripping the spear's shaft. "If I'd known she could fight like that, I would have had Halfdan make this damn thing into a crossbow bolt."

"But what if you missed?" said Caina.

Riogan grunted and started to pull out the spear.

"No!" said Caina. "Don't finish her. Not yet." She looked at Ikhana as Halfdan joined them. "Where is Maglarion?"

Ikhana laughed. Despite the spear buried in her belly, she showed no pain. "Not here, fool. As you can see."

"But he is beaten nonetheless," said Halfdan. He stooped over Ikhana and pulled something from her belt. A metal flask, and from the sudden crawling chill Caina felt, no doubt filled with plagueblood. "He will not poison the aqueduct, and he will not grow strong on the lives of the innocent."

"Is that what you think?" said Ikhana, and she laughed again. "That this was about the aqueduct? Fool, fool. Ever and always, you Ghosts are fools."

A flash of light came from the south, followed a few seconds later by the rumble of thunder. The storm, Caina realized. The storm the master magi had conjured for Maglarion.

She stared at the aqueduct, the water pouring through it.

Water...

"Perhaps you should be more forthcoming," said Riogan, giving the spear a push.

Ikhana laughed again. "Kill me, if you wish. The Master will only raise me up to serve him once more. He has more power than you know. And soon he will have more power than you can imagine. He shall be a god, and I shall be his right hand, to slay forevermore in his name."

"I doubt that," said Halfdan. "Maglarion treats his servants as tools, to be cast aside when they fail. And you failed, didn't you?" He lifted the flask of plagueblood. "He will not trouble himself over you, unless he kills you to cover his tracks. So I suggest you make this easier on yourself."

Ikhana sneered and said nothing.

Caina listened with only half an ear. Instead she stared south, to the storm clouds rolling in from the Bay of Empire. Lightning flashed and crackled, illuminating the clouds. A massive storm, one that would unleash torrents of rain upon Malarae, over the entire city...

The realization felt like a knife plunging into her skull.

"Oh, gods," she whispered.

Halfdan frowned at her, as did Riogan.

"The storm," said Caina. "He's going to poison the storm itself. That's why he had the magi conjure it. He's going to mix the plagueblood into the rain. He'll kill everyone in Malarae."

Her mind reeled. There were a million people in Malarae. Maybe a million and a quarter, with the crowds for the Grand Kyracian Games. How many slaves had Maglarion fed into his bloodcrystal over the last seven years? A few hundred? A few thousand? That much stolen life had given him the ability to heal mortal wounds in a matter of seconds.

And if a few thousand innocent lives had given him that ability, what kind of powers would he draw from the energies of a million stolen lives?

It made sense. Horrible, horrible sense.

"Yes," hissed Ikhana, eyes glittering. "The Master will transform the storm into a rain of plagueblood. He will kill everyone in Malarae. A million lives, snuffed out at once. The necromantic power released shall be vast beyond reckoning...and the Master shall draw it into his great bloodcrystal. The power will transform him. He will leave mortal flesh behind, to live as pure spirit, as pure power, forevermore." She laughed, high and wild. "He shall be as a god."

"We'd best get away from Malarae, now," said Riogan.

"No!" said Halfdan. "We must stop him."

"And how shall we do that?" said Riogan. "Maglarion could be anywhere in the city. We'll never find him in time to stop the spell. Best to get away with our own lives, now, while we still can. Why should we die with everyone else in Malarae?"

Everyone.

Caina thought of Theodosia, of Julia, of the stagehands at the Grand Imperial Opera, of Julia's maids and servants, of the nobles and merchants, of the teeming crowds she had seen every day in Malarae, of the uncounted thousands who lived in the city, filling it with noise and stink and life.

Dead. All of them.

"No," she said. "I know where Maglarion is."

They looked at her.

"Lord Haeron's mansion," said Caina. "I felt something there, some concentration of necromantic power. It must be the bloodcrystal he'll use to trap all those lives. It's there, in Lord Haeron's mansion. If we go now we might still make it in time."

"Madness," said Riogan.

"Come or not, I don't care," said Caina. "But I will not let Maglarion kill everyone in Malarae." She held out her hand. "If you're not going to come, then at least give me the spear."

Riogan stared at her for a moment, then growled a curse. "Fine! I'll help you. Haeron Icaraeus's life is mine. I can't kill him if Maglarion does."

"Go," said Halfdan. "I can't keep up with you two. I will send word to the Ghosts in the Imperial Guard, bid them send every available man to Haeron's mansion."

Caina nodded and ran as fast as she dared down the rocky hillside

CHAPTER 32
THE FINAL SPELL

The Magisterium's messenger bowed low before Maglarion.

"The master magi send word, sir," he said. "They have conjured the storm, as you wished. It should reach the city at any moment now."

Maglarion smiled.

"Good," he said. "Please extend my gratitude to the master magi. And tell them that they shall receive their reward in full, this very night."

Oh, they would.

The messenger bowed once more and left, leaving Maglarion alone in the tower chamber. After a moment he started to laugh.

The "master" magi, indeed. During the height of the Fourth Empire, they would have been little better than half-trained novices. Still, Maglarion had put the fools to good use.

His smiled widened.

He had put quite a few fools to good use.

And he was at last ready. True immortality would be his. He would ascend in might, to live forevermore as power and strength.

There was just one thing left to do.

He walked to the great bloodcrystal and tore aside the tarps, filling the chamber with ghostly green light.

A year ago, the bloodcrystal had been half again Maglarion's height. Now it stood twenty feet tall and ten wide, its jagged top brushing the domed ceiling. Green flames blazed and writhed in its black depths. The faces of his victims appeared and disappeared in the green glow. Maglarion laid a hand on its rough surface, and felt the power pulsing within...the power that his, thanks to his link with the bloodcrystal. Power beyond the reach of weaklings like the master magi, power beyond the ability of a fool like Haeron Icaraeus to comprehend.

He looked out the south windows, saw lightning over the bay.

Power that would soon increase beyond reckoning.

The long and difficult spell to imbue the clouds with plagueblood would drain a substantial part of the great bloodcrystal's reserves. But once plagueblood fell from the skies, once Malarae started to die, Maglarion would receive that power back a thousand times over. A million times over. The necromantic power released from all those deaths would surge into the bloodcrystal...and through the link, into Maglarion himself.

Maglarion would devour it all.

True immortality at last.

He supposed that he was about to destroy the Empire of Nighmar. The Emperor would die, along with most of the nobles. The provinces of the Empire would fracture into civil war and chaos...and pestilence, too, if travelers happened to carry Maglarion's plague from the desolate capital. But the death of the Empire did not matter in the slightest. The Empire was peopled with mortal men and women, men and women whose lives had no meaning and no purpose.

The only purpose to their existence was to be consumed as Maglarion saw fit.

Raindrops splattered against the tall windows.

Almost time now.

And no one could stop him.

The Ghosts could try, of course, but he had misled them. Sending Rekan to the fountain in Graywater Square, and Ikhana to the Naerian Aqueduct had been nothing more than diversions. If they succeeded, well and good – his bloodcrystal would absorb the resultant deaths. Of course, he was reasonably sure that the Ghosts had killed Rekan, and that they would kill Ikhana.

No great loss. Especially since their deaths would keep the Ghosts away during the final spell.

He crossed to the wooden podium before the bloodcrystal. A dagger rested on it, along with the ancient Maatish scroll that he had taken from Sebastian Amalas's library seven years ago. He looked over the hieroglyphs, refreshing the ancient spell upon his mind one final time.

Footsteps sounded against the tower stairs.

Maglarion shivered in anticipation.

He turned as Lord Haeron Icaraeus entered the chamber.

"You wished to see me?" said Haeron, his voice holding a threatening edge. After all, one did not summon Lord Haeron.

"Yes, my lord," said Maglarion. "I have good news for you."

He fell silent.

"Well?" said Haeron. "What is it?"

"I have devised a means for using plagueblood to kill the Emperor," said Maglarion.

That part was true.

Haeron blinked, and then smiled. "You have? Excellent! And I will not be suspected?"

"I can assure you, my lord," said Maglarion, "that no one will suspect you in the slightest."

Which was also true.

"When can you do it?" said Haeron.

"Why, I have already begun" said Maglarion. "The Emperor will probably die by sunrise. Certainly before night comes again."

Haeron frowned. "So soon, you say? But…I've barely had time to prepare. My support is strong among the Restorationist nobles, but I need additional allies among the Militarists before I can crush the Loyalists."

"My lord," said Maglarion. "You are a man of destiny, fated to bring great change to the Empire. And power comes to those bold enough to seize it."

Haeron gave a sharp nod. "Yes. Yes. It is as you say. Very well. How precisely will you kill the Emperor?"

Maglarion lowered his voice. "Are you sure you want to know?"

He was going to enjoy this.

Haeron scowled. "Tell me, sorcerer. Now."

"Very well," said Maglarion, beckoning Haeron to the podium. "Do you know what this is?"

"A Maatish scroll," said Haeron, voice impatient. "You've explained this to me already."

"Plagueblood was an…innovation of the Maatish necromancer-priests," said Maglarion. "With it, they terrorized their enemies and their subject peoples, and kept the Maatish empire under an iron fist for centuries. They had a spell, you see," he gestured at the windows, "to charge the rain itself with plagueblood. If a city rebelled, they conjured a storm over it, infused their rain with plagueblood, and sat back to watch the city die."

He watched the thought worm its way through Haeron's mind.

Haeron's reaction was most entertaining.

"Are you insane?" thundered Haeron. "Our agreement was for you to kill the Emperor, not everyone in Malarae! I want to rule over the Empire, not a graveyard! I forbid this!"

"As you wish, my lord," said Maglarion. "It's just as well, since I cannot proceed. I'm missing a final catalyst for the spell."

"What catalyst?" spat Haeron.

"Royal blood," said Maglarion. "The spell to infuse storm clouds with plagueblood requires an offering of royal blood. Which is why the Maatish necromancers used the spell rarely, of course. The pharaohs, and their families, were loathe to give up their blood."

Haeron snorted. "Just as well, then, that you will find neither kings nor pharaohs in Malarae, sorcerer. The Emperor and the nobles rule the Empire, not a king. Trouble me no more with this nonsense."

He turned to go.

"My lord?" said Maglarion. "One more question."

"What?" said Haeron, glaring over his shoulder.

"Did you not tell me that in ancient times, the House of Icaraeus ruled over Cyrica as kings?"

"Yes, that's true," said Haeron, turning around, "why…"

He saw understanding come over Haeron, saw him turn to run.

Too late.

Maglarion flicked a finger, wrapping Lord Haeron in bands of arcane power. Haeron froze in mid-step, trapped in the grip of Maglarion's sorcery. Maglarion gestured, and Haeron floated towards him.

He retrieved the dagger from the podium and a goblet from the worktable, and strode towards Haeron. On impulse, he released the portion of the spell that bound Haeron's mouth. He wanted to hear what Haeron had to say.

Maglarion did want to enjoy this.

"Release me!" bellowed Haeron. "I demand that you release me at once. You'll regret this, sorcerer. I'll watch you die for days!"

First would come bluster.

Maglarion ripped open Haeron's sleeves.

"I tell you, release me!" said Haeron. "I can make it worth your while, once I am Emperor. Power, riches, lands, whatever you desire, it is yours!"

And then bargaining.

Maglarion walked towards the bloodcrystal, Haeron floating after him, still struggling against the invisible bonds.

"Let me go!" shrieked Haeron, eyes wide as he stared at the dagger. "Let me go, let me go, let me go!"

And then begging.

Maglarion turned, green flame crackling around his fingers, and cut Haeron's left wrist, catching the blood in the goblet.

And last came the screaming, the terrified, frantic wails of a trapped man with no escape.

"Why do you scream so?" murmured Maglarion, watching the goblet fill. "You told me so yourself. The strong do as they like, and the weak suffer." He smiled. "It is only the natural order of things."

Haeron shrieked and sobbed and begged all the more. Maglarion ignored it, painting sigils in blood upon the floor, encircling the bloodcrystal's dark mass. At some point Haeron fell silent. No doubt he had died from blood loss. His usefulness to Maglarion had ended.

He released the spell, and Haeron's corpse crumpled to the floor. A flick of his fingers, and the body slid across the floor to the wall, conveniently out of the way.

One more sigil painted around the bloodcrystal's base.

And then it was finished.

He was ready. At long last, he was ready.

True immortality would be his.

Trembling, Maglarion crossed to the podium, tossing aside the bloody dagger and goblet. He cleared his mind and focused, drawing the words of the final spell to the forefront of his thoughts. Then he began to chant, drawing arcane power into himself, more and more, until he thought he would burst from it.

The bloodcrystal pulsed with green flame, matching his heartbeat. The massive thing shivered, sweating drops of black plagueblood. The plagueblood floated into the air, whirling around the bloodcrystal, faster and faster, wreathing it in a halo of liquid darkness.

Maglarion shouted and clapped his hands.

Power screamed out.

And the bloodcrystal erupted in answer.

A pillar of emerald flame exploded from the bloodcrystal. Maglarion's spells protected him, but the force tore away the domed ceiling, blasted out the windows, and ripped away most of the walls. For a moment shattered debris tumbled in every direction, and then the tower chamber stood open to the air, the storm raging around Maglarion.

The column of emerald flame stabbed into the sky, piercing the storm clouds themselves. The lightning arcing from cloud to cloud took a greenish tinge, the air crackling with necromantic power. More plagueblood swirled around the bloodcrystal's mass.

Maglarion's shoulders shook with exertion, his head ringing, but he laughed. When he finished the spell, the spinning cloud of plagueblood would ascend the pillar of flame, mingling with the storm. Plague-tainted rain would fall upon Malarae, killing those it struck, filling the aqueducts and the cisterns with death.

Within a day Malarae would die.

And their deaths would lift Maglarion to true immortality at last.

Exultant, he flung out his hands and began screaming the spell's final words.

CHAPTER 33
BLOOD AND VENGEANCE

Haeron Icaraeus's mansion loomed in the darkness, visible even in the pouring rain. Liveried guards stood at the gates, while Caina saw Kindred assassins prowling the grounds.

Her skin tingled and crawled, reacting to the sorcery-fueled storm raging overhead. And she felt something else, a nexus of dark power swirling within the mansion, stronger than anything she had ever sensed before. It was like looking at the sun...if the sun gave out black light, light that froze instead of warmed.

"So it's in the mansion, but you don't know where," growled Riogan.

"We'll sneak past the guards," said Caina, thinking fast. "Once we're in the mansion, we find Maglarion and kill him before he casts his spell."

It sounded simple enough.

"Yes," said Riogan. "We'll sneak past a dozen Kindred assassins. That should certainly..."

The tingling against Caina's skin doubled, and redoubled, until it was almost physical pain.

Then green light flared overhead, and Caina looked up just in time to see the top of the mansion's tower explode. The thunderclap was enormous, even louder than the storm overhead, and for an instant a cloud of broken stone wreathed the tower's shattered crown. And then a pillar of emerald flame burst from the tower, stabbing into the clouds. Green lightning leapt from cloud to cloud, and Caina felt wave after wave of necromantic power pulsing from the tower.

"I think I know where Maglarion is," she said.

Riogan swore. "He's finished the spell!"

"No," said Caina, drawing a dagger in either hand. "Not yet. We'll have to fight our way in. Run!"

Caina sprinted for the gates, Riogan following. They were probably going to die, she realized. She was capable in a fight, and Riogan was better, but they couldn't defeat Haeron Icaraeus's guards and assassins by themselves.

But the guards took one look at the pillar of fire and ran, terror on their faces. She saw servants fleeing the mansion, and even the Kindred assassins were running. Caina had spent so much time around sorcery that she had grown numb to it.

Though looking at the pillar of flame, she could understand their reactions.

"That's our chance!" she hissed to Riogan. "Go!"

They raced through the gates, dodged the fleeing guards and servants, and entered the mansion. Caina knew her way through the maze of corridors from her previous visits. The mansion trembled and shuddered, dust falling from the ceiling, and she wondered if the force of Maglarion's sorcery would bring the entire place down before she could reach him.

Then they sprinted up the tower stairs, Caina's breath coming fast and hard, running through round chamber after round chamber. The pulsing throb of necromantic sorcery against her skin grew sharper and colder. Then she saw green light from above, and realized they were almost there...

Blue light flashed, and a jolt of pain went down her arms.

"Stop!" she hissed. Riogan came to a halt behind her, leaning on the ghostsilver spear to catch his breath.

"What?" he said, and then fell silent as he saw the faint wall of blue light shimmering across the stairwell.

"A ward," said Caina. She waved her gloved hand in front of it, and felt a wave of stabbing pain. "A powerful one, too. I...I don't know what will happen if we touch it." They had to get past it. Halfdan had said that ghostsilver spear could pierce spells. Could it break the ward?

"We go up," said Riogan, crossing to the chamber's tall, narrow windows. "Climb the walls. If Maglarion sees us, he'll kill us the minute we come up the stairs. But I doubt the old devil warded the windows. If we take him unawares, I can have the spear through his heart before he realizes anything is wrong."

Caina nodded as Riogan lifted the butt of the spear and smashed a window.

"I'll go up this side," said Riogan. "You take the other. We'll play this the way we planned at Haeron's party. You distract Maglarion, and I'll kill him from behind."

Caina nodded again. "Riogan?"

"What?"

"Good luck."

He gave sharp nod. "You as well."

Caina shattered a window with the handles of her daggers and stepped onto the sill. Rain and wind lashed at her, threatening to send her tumbling to the mansion's roof hundreds of feet below. But she kept her balance as she pulled the rope from her belt and flung it. The grapnel caught on the tower's shattered crown. Caina gave it several tugs, took a deep breath, and started to climb.

A few moments later she reach the tower's top.

The first thing she was Haeron Icaraeus. Or his corpse, rather. He lay crumpled against the jagged ruins of the wall, face frozen with fear and horror.

His alliance with Maglarion had not ended well.

Maglarion himself stood perhaps thirty feet away, his coat billowing in the wind. The bloodcrystal in his left eye socket blazed with light, and he stood with his arms raised to the heavens, face uplifted as he screamed the words to a spell. Caina felt the arcane power swirling around him, vast and strong as an ocean tide.

But the great bloodcrystal captured the whole of her attention.

Caina had never seen anything like it.

The thing stood twenty feet high and ten wide, a jagged monolith of gleaming black crystal, wreathed in a swirling cloud of plagueblood. Ghostly green fire danced in its depths, the flames forming faces. So many faces. For a horrified moment Caina saw her father's face in the flames, and the servants of House Amalas that Maglarion had butchered so long ago, and then Alastair and Nerina.

But even that was only peripheral.

Because she could feel the great bloodcrystal.

It felt...the hideous thing felt like it was a part of her, almost like a limb. She felt every flash and pulse of the flames in its depth, felt it shuddering and trembling with stored power. She felt the draining aura radiating from the thing, vast enough to cover all of Malarae, the aura that would drink the deaths from every man, woman, and child in the city when the rain of plagueblood fell.

It was pulsing in time with her heartbeat.

How? How was that even possible?

She saw a dark flicker behind Maglarion. Riogan rolled over the ruined wall and landed on his feet, the ghostsilver spear in hand. Step by step he crept closer to Maglarion.

Any moment Maglarion would notice him.

Caina scrambled to her feet, making no effort to conceal herself.

"Maglarion!" she yelled.

He spun, the spell faltering, astonishment on his face. Then his good eye narrowed, his hand came up, and Caina felt the crawling tingle as his power closed around her.

The ghostsilver blade erupted from his chest.

Maglarion staggered, hands raking at the air. Riogan ripped the spear free, the blade dimmed beneath a thick coating of blood, and buried it in Maglarion's back again. Maglarion dropped to one knee, right eye wide with shock, his shoulders slumped. Caina felt the vast spell shudder and come to a halt.

They had done it.

The bloodcrystal blazed with emerald light.

Maglarion snarled and flung out a hand, invisible force seizing Caina. For a panicked instant she thought the spell would blast her off the tower, send her tumbling to her death. But instead she floated into the air, immobilized by Maglarion's will. She saw Riogan caught in the same way, shuddering as he tried to break free from the spell.

Maglarion gripped the spear below the blade and pulled it free from his chest, foot by bloody foot. After he got it loose, he spent a few moments coughing and shuddering. But wave after wave of power washed out from the bloodcrystal, the hideous wounds on Maglarion's chest and back shrinking with every pulse.

Had he become so strong that nothing could kill him? Not even a ghostsilver blade?

He was linked to the bloodcrystal, Caina realized. It poured so much power into him that he could heal any wound, recover from any injury.

He was invincible.

A little later Maglarion levered himself to his feet, leaning on the spear like a staff.

"Ghostsilver," he said, his voice rusty. "Very clever. It would have worked, a year or so ago. But I've moved beyond that. I've moved far beyond that."

The wounds on his chest vanished, and he tossed the spear aside. It clattered across the floor and came to rest against Haeron Icaraeus's corpse. The great spell still raged against Caina's skin, waiting for Maglarion to continue.

"Ghost nightfighters," he said, looking from Riogan to Caina. "You Ghosts are so damnably persistent. Like cockroaches, really. Again and again I smash you, and again and again you come to die." He smiled. "At least you had the wit to wear those shadow-woven cloaks. That's why I didn't sense your approach. But let's see who you are, hmm?"

He threw back Riogan's cowl and mask. Riogan scowled at him, and Maglarion laughed.

"I know you!" he said. " Haeron told me about you. The Kindred assassin who refused to murder the child. Haeron put an enormous bounty on your head for that."

"Guess you didn't care for the fat bastard either," said Riogan, glancing at Haeron's corpse.

"No," said Maglarion. "I did not. Tell me. You had a life of wealth and power as a Kindred assassin, and you cast it aside to save the life of one worthless child. Was it worth it?"

Riogan sneered. "If it meant I could defy a miserable craven like Haeron, and a bloody-handed devil like you, then yes."

"Haeron indeed was a miserable craven," said Maglarion. "But he had his uses, so I kept him alive. You, however, are of no use to me. Your death shall be far worse than his."

He gestured, and some of the plagueblood whirling around the bloodcrystal struck Riogan in the face.

Riogan snarled. Then he started to scream. The veins in his face turned black, and cysts swelled beneath his jaw, his nose, his eyes, his armor bulging as the cysts spread. His screams redoubled, raw and horrible and worse than any sound Caina had thought Riogan could ever make.

Then one of the cysts swelled in his throat, cutting off his air, and the screams stopped.

Maglarion let Riogan's deformed corpse fall to the floor. The bloodcrystal pulsed, and Caina felt it drink in the power released from Riogan's death.

Maglarion turned to face her, smiling.

Caina trembled, trying not to scream. She was eleven years old again, chained to that cold metal table, watching as Maglarion approached with the dagger in hand.

Only this time Halfdan was not coming to save her.

And once Maglarion killed her, he would kill everyone in Malarae.

She had failed.

"And who might you be?" said Maglarion. "Let us find out, before you join your comrade."

He reached up, pulled back Caina's cowl, and tossed aside her mask.

His good eye widened in astonishment.

"Laeria Amalas?" he said.

Caina glared at him, forced herself not to show fear.

"No," murmured Maglarion, taking her chin in his hand. "No...too young, though you are her very image. Her...daughter? Yes. That fierce little girl Laeria sold to me? Still alive? Amazing."

"You killed my father," said Caina.

Maglarion ignored that. "And you survived for seven years? I thought I had killed you." He shook his head and rubbed the ragged hole in his coat. "That was an oversight. When the Ghosts poisoned those fool magi...they must have saved you. Taken you in, trained you to become a weapon." He laughed. "Little good it has done you."

"Better to fight than to let you do whatever you please," spat Caina.

Maglarion laughed. "You fought back, and I still did whatever I wished. What a fine joke this is!" His hand tightened on her chin. "I created you. By accident, true, but I made you what you are. The Ghosts forged you into a weapon, and I assume you spent the last seven years dreaming of the day you would finally strike me down and avenge your useless father. And now that day has come!" He leaned closer, good eye bright with mirth. "Tell me...is it everything you dreamed it would be?"

Caina said nothing, every muscle straining against the invisible force that held her fast.

Useless. She might as well have tried to move a mountain of iron.

"Of course," said Maglarion, releasing her and stepping back, "you failed to kill me, which means you've wasted your entire life." He spread his arms, gesturing at the vista of Malarae around them. "If you're here, you've figured out what I will do. I should keep you alive to watch your precious Empire die. But I made the mistake of keeping you alive once before. You see, your life, your father's life...their only purpose was to be used as I pleased. Think on that as you die, dear child."

He gestured, and a spray of plagueblood kept from the cloud and struck Caina in the face.

It was cold, so terribly cold, and Caina gasped, the plagueblood filling her nostrils and mouth. She felt it trickle down her throat, the terrible cold spreading through her chest and stomach. She waited for the agony to begin, for the cysts to erupt from her flesh.

Instead, for a brief moment, she felt...better. As if something long-lost had been returned to her at last.

Then the cold sensation faded.

Nothing else happened. No cysts, no pain.

Nothing.

The plagueblood hadn't killed her. It hadn't even hurt her. Her eyes darted back and forth, glimpsing plagueblood leaking from cracks in the great bloodcrystal...

The bloodcrystal.

Realization struck Caina.

It was the same bloodcrystal. The one Maglarion had made from her blood in that cellar. The one he had used when he killed her father. No wonder she had felt such a terrible attraction to it, to the vials of plagueblood taken from Rekan and Ikhana. Even now, swollen with the stolen lives of thousands, it was still the same bloodcrystal, made from Caina's blood.

Which meant the plagueblood was made from her blood. It was part of her. A stolen part, but part of her nonetheless.

She was immune.

Maglarion stared at her, the beginnings of surprise on his face.

If he realized that she was immune, he would crush her skull. Or simply throw her from the top of the tower.

Caina opened her mouth and started to scream at the top of her lungs, throwing her head back and forth. Her arms and legs trembled, and she sobbed, her groans of pain mixing with shrieks of agony.

Theodosia would have been proud.

Maglarion's concern melted into a sneer. "The same as all the others," he murmured. "A little stronger, perhaps, but the same as all the others."

As Halfdan had told her long ago, people saw what they expected to see.

He watched her wail for a moment. Then he turned his back to her, walked to the podium, and lifted his arms. Again he declaimed the ancient Maatish spell in a thunderous voice, and Caina felt the power swirl in the air, the great spell moving forward once more.

He was almost finished. A little more power, and the plagueblood would infest the clouds themselves.

But his invisible grip on Caina faded as more and more of his strength poured into the great spell. Then it released her, and she let herself collapse in a limp heap. Maglarion glanced back at her, once, and Caina did not move, did not even let herself breathe.

He looked back at the bloodcrystal, his arms and voice trembling with exertion.

Caina rolled to a crouch, making no sound.

Her hand curled about the ghostsilver spear's haft, the blade's strange vibrations traveling up her arm, and she lifted the weapon. She had a clear shot at Maglarion's back. Three running steps, and she would bury the spear in his torso.

Just as Riogan had done.

Maglarion would heal the wound in a moment, and this time he would make sure to kill her. Even if she impaled him with the spear and threw him from the tower, the bloodcrystal's power would restore him...

The bloodcrystal.

Caina's gaze fixed on it. It was the heart of Maglarion's power. It held the stored life energies of his victims, the stolen lives that made him strong. It was the bloodcrystal that made him invincible and immortal.

And Halfdan had said that a ghostsilver blade could destroy even the most potent enspelled objects.

Maglarion's voice rose to a triumphant shout, his spell reaching a climax.

Caina made up her mind.

She leapt forward and stabbed the spear with all her strength and rage behind it.

The bloodcrystal looked like obsidian, shiny and hard, yet the ghostsilver spear plunged into it like soft butter. A spray of plagueblood erupted from the impact, along with hundreds of tiny specks of green light. A web of cracks spread over the crystal's surface, and Caina felt the ghostsilver blade straining against the bloodcrystal, arcane power flowing up her arm.

Maglarion screamed, screamed as he had not when Caina had shot him, when Riogan had stabbed him. He staggered back, hand clenched to his side, good eye wide with shock and pain.

"Stop!" he said, raising his hand.

Caina ripped the spear free and stabbed again. The bloodcrystal shuddered, trembling like a dying thing, and the pillar of emerald flame flickered and sputtered. More plagueblood sprayed from the side, more of those tiny spheres of green light. Maglarion howled and fell to one knee, clutching his side as if the spear had been buried in his flesh. She saw flecks of gray appear in his black hair, saw thin lines spread over his face.

The tiny spheres of green light spun around the tower's top, moving faster and faster.

Maglarion snarled, beginning a spell, and Caina ripped the spear free and drove it even deeper into the great bloodcrystal. A storm of green light erupted from the crystal, spinning around the tower, and plagueblood sprayed everywhere. Maglarion shrieked, aging before Caina's eyes. He looked as she remembered from that terrible day in her father's library, an old man with wild white hair, face lined and seamed.

"You were right!" screamed Caina, twisting the spear. "You turned my mother into a monster! You killed my father!" She stabbed again and again and again. "You turned me into a Ghost!"

Maglarion struggled to stand, teeth bared in a snarl.

The whirling spheres of green light grew larger, swelling into faces. Images. Shades of the dead, of Maglarion's many victims.

Caina wrenched the spear loose.

"You shouldn't have done that," she said, and threw herself at the bloodcrystal, all her weight behind the ghostsilver spear.

The blade sank into the black depths.

And with a hideous scream the bloodcrystal shattered, splitting in two like a lightning-struck tree.

Maglarion fought to stand.

One spell, one spell to tear that impudent child to bloody shreds. Yet every stab of that damned spear into the bloodcrystal sent waves of hideous pain through him, worse than anything he had ever known.

And then the bloodcrystal shattered.

Agony filled his veins like molten lead. His link to the bloodcrystal disintegrated, withering like a dry leaf in flame, and the backlash only redoubled his pain.

He heard someone screaming, realized it was him.

Green light exploded out, throwing him back, and he slumped against the ruined wall.

The spinning lights swelled, growing larger and larger, taking on human shapes.

They weren't spinning around the tower, he realized.

They were spinning around him.

The shades of all those he had killed, all those he had fed to the bloodcrystal. Sebastian Amalas and his servants. The slaves he tortured to death in the cellar of the Grey Fish Inn, the slaves he slew to give Haeron and his followers renewed youth. Rekan and Ikhana and Haeron Icaraeus and countless others.

All of them.

Staring at him.

For the first time in centuries, Maglarion felt a frisson of fear.

No. No. It wasn't possible. It was not possible!

Fear became terror.

The shades came at him in a rush. He raised his hands to ward them off and lost his balance, tumbling over the tower's side.

He fell, screaming.

And when he met the ground there was no bloodcrystal to heal him.

CHAPTER 34
A CHILD OF THE GHOSTS

The pillar of green flame vanished. The lightning lost its greenish tinge as the storm abated, the rain slackening.

After a long moment, Caina staggered back to her feet.

The great bloodcrystal lay in shattered chunks across the floor, surrounded by pools of plagueblood. Even as Caina watched, the crystal shards crumbled into black ash, the plagueblood drying into dust. Caina ran her fingers through the dust, and felt no trace of power from it, not the slightest hint of sorcery.

The bloodcrystal's power had been broken.

She picked up the ghostsilver spear, its blade charred, and took a deep breath. She had seen Maglarion fall, carried by the shades of his victims. Had the dead truly taken their vengeance on Maglarion? Or had the stolen life energy, released from the bloodcrystal, overwhelmed Maglarion?

Caina didn't know.

But she would not believe Maglarion was dead until she saw the body.

To her surprise, the Maatish scroll still rested upon the podium. It had survived the rain and the bloodcrystal's destruction. No doubt the Maglarion had laid protective spells upon the scroll. The scroll that he had killed her father to claim. The scroll that held the secrets of making bloodcrystals and plagueblood.

Caina pierced the scroll with the spear's blade. The protective spell crackled and faded in a flash of blue light, and the scroll crumbled to dust.

After that, she closed Riogan's eyes, and then descended the tower, spear in hand.

She found Maglarion's body sprawled across the grounds.

He had claimed to be four hundred years old, and now his corpse truly looked the part. Little more than a skeleton draped in withered skin remained, a few wisps of pale hair encircling a liver-spotted skull. His right eye stared at the sky, frozen in terror, while the green bloodcrystal flickered in his left socket.

To judge from his expression, whatever he had seen in the final instants of his life had not been pleasant.

It was over.

Maglarion was dead.

Caina lifted her father's ring and kissed it. Then she jabbed the ghostsilver spear into the green bloodcrystal, watched it crumble into ash. For so long, she had hated Maglarion. For seven years he had filled her nightmares. She dreamed about killing him again and again. To keep him from hurting others, of course, but also to repay her father's death.

And now it was over.

The sound of boots caught her attention. Tomard's militiamen swarmed through the gates, swords and shields at the ready, looking up at the broken tower. Caina supposed that the explosion must have been visible throughout the city.

Halfdan approached, looking at Maglarion's corpse with amazement.

"You killed him?" said Halfdan.

"Riogan's dead," said Caina, voice quiet. "He stabbed Maglarion with the spear, but it didn't work, and Maglarion hit him with plagueblood. Riogan...didn't die well."

Halfdan blinked. "How are you still alive?"

"Maglarion did the same to me," said Caina. "But...it was my bloodcrystal, the one he had made from my blood. The same one, after all these years. I think it made me immune to the plagueblood." She shrugged. "So I took the spear and stabbed the bloodcrystal. That seemed to work."

Halfdan shook his head. "Amazing. I...never considered that. I knew he must have been using a bloodcrystal to store all those stolen lives, but...the same one?" He gave a quiet, tired laugh. "The fool doomed himself."

"I think those stolen lives destroyed him," said Caina. "It was like the shades of the dead came out of the bloodcrystal and threw him from the tower."

"Perhaps they did," said Halfdan. "We should go. That explosion will draw every militiaman and magus in the city."

Caina nodded and followed Halfdan and Tomard out the gates. "What do you think people will say happened here?"

"Why, whatever I tell them to say," said Halfdan. "I plan to start a few rumors."

###

Lord Haeron's death and the fall of House Icaraeus shook the Empire.

Later Caina heard dozens of conflicting stories describing what had happened that night. Some claimed Haeron had been plotting with an army of renegade sorcerers to overthrow the Emperor. Others said that Haeron had been murdered by an outlaw magus. Still others swore that Haeron had planned to use the outlaw sorcerer to overthrow the Emperor, only to die when the sorcerer betrayed him.

That, Caina thought, was closer to the truth than most would ever know.

The Imperial Guard swarmed through Haeron's mansion, and discovered proof of his complicity in slave trading and necromancy. The Emperor stripped House Icaraeus of its titles and honors, and Haeron's surviving relatives fled the Empire.

The Restorationist nobles collapsed into chaos. Haeron had been the foremost of their number, and the exposure of his crimes discredited the Restorationist cause. Many lords switched their support to the Loyalists, distancing themselves from the Magisterium. Even those who fervently wished to restore slavery found it expedient to keep their views to themselves.

A few rumors, a very few rumors, claimed that the Ghosts, the Emperor's spies and assassins, had orchestrated Lord Haeron's downfall.

But no one took those rumors seriously. Every sensible man knew that the Ghosts did not exist.

A week later Caina said goodbye to Theodosia and Julia, and left with Halfdan, a half-dozen guards, and a train of pack mules. Halfdan disguised himself as Marcus Antali, merchant of middling prosperity, and Caina as his daughter.

"I want to take the ghostsilver spear back to the Vineyard," said Halfdan. "We may have need of it in the future, if we encounter another sorcerer of Maglarion's power."

Caina nodded.

Now she rode a mule as their pack train followed the winding Imperial Highway into the rocky Disali hills.

What would become of her now, she wondered? Half her life had been spent in training, preparing to become a Ghost nightfighter.

Preparing to face Maglarion, she realized.

But now he was dead, her father and the other victims avenged, and Malarae saved.

What would Caina do now?

###

A week later Caina stood on the Vineyard's highest terrace, working through her unarmed forms. She practiced the forms for two hours every day, and another two with throwing knives and daggers, and spent more time in the Vineyard's library, reading.

It distracted her.

Sometimes she thought about seducing one of the guards. Perhaps Theodosia had been right. Perhaps she could find comfort in a lover's arms.

But Caina could not have children, could never have a family, no matter how much she wanted one. Seducing a guard would be as hollow as what she had shared with Alastair.

###

Later she sat in Komnene's infirmary, drinking tea.

"You were right to warn me," said Caina.

"About what?" said Komnene. She looked older than Caina remembered, had taken to walking with a cane.

"About becoming a weapon," said Caina.

Komnene set down her tea and waited.

"I thought...I thought I wanted to do this to save others, to keep Maglarion from hurting others the way he killed my father, the way he hurt me," said Caina.

"And you did," said Komnene. "You and Riogan both, and Halfdan and the others. You stopped him from killing a million people in Malarae. And thousands more afterward. Millions, even, if that vile plague of Maglarion's spread. You and Riogan saved all those lives, Caina."

"I know. But in my heart," said Caina, "I did it for revenge." She closed a fist. "And now that is over. What...what shall I do now?"

Komnene gave a gentle smile. "You will know."

Caina laughed. "Perhaps you were right, and I should have been a priestess of Minaerys."

"No," said Komnene. "For if you had listened to me, no one would have stopped Maglarion, and millions would have died. I think joining the Temple would be a poor fit for you. When you are confronted with evil, you do not contemplate, or pray - you take action." She smiled. "My dear child. You've grown strong, and your pain has made you wise. You will know what to do."

Caina hoped she was right.

###

That night Caina had another nightmare.

A different one, though. This time she watched Maglarion finish his great spell, plagueblood exploding into the sky. And poisoned rain fell from the clouds, and Malarae died around her.

All because she had failed to stop him.

Caina awoke, certainty filling her like iron.

She was Caina Amalas. Sebastian's daughter. Maglarion's victim. Halfdan's student.

But she was also a Ghost nightfighter. And there were other men and women like Haeron Icaraeus in the Empire, lords who would restore slavery, who would terrorize the defenseless and the poor. There were corrupt magi like Rekan, dabbling in necromancy and blood sorcery. And maybe there were even sorcerers who shared Maglarion's power and the depth of his evil.

Who would stop them?

She would stop them.

Caina rose, went to seek out Halfdan.

It was past time that she got back to work.

THE END

Thank you for reading CHILD OF THE GHOSTS. Turn the page for a sample chapter from GHOST IN THE FLAMES, the next book in THE GHOSTS series. To receive immediate notification of new releases, sign up for my newsletter at this web address:

http://www.jonathanmoeller.com/newsletter.html

GHOST IN THE FLAMES BONUS CHAPTER
CHAPTER 1 PYRES IN THE NIGHT

Caina thought she might have to do some killing, so she dressed for business.

In many tales, the Emperor's Ghosts were always women of perilous beauty, clad in skin-tight black leather. Caina thought that ridiculous. Black leather made too much noise, and reflected too much light. Instead she wore loose black clothes, black gloves, and a black mask that concealed her face. Around her waist went a leather belt of throwing knives and other useful tools, and she secured a heavy dagger in each of her boots.

Next came the cloak.

Light as air and blacker than night, it was a wondrous thing. Halfdan had told her that only the Ghosts knew the making of these cloaks, fused together of spider silk and captured shadows. It mingled and blurred with the shadows around her, and when she pulled up the cowl, it made her face all but invisible.

Last, the ring.

It was a man's signet ring, heavy and thick; she wore it on the first finger of her left hand, beneath the glove. It was old and nicked, the sigil worn smooth with use. Unlike everything else Caina carried, it could not be used as a weapon, nor did it have a practical use.

But she wore it anyway.

Night lay over the city of Mors Crisius, and Caina glided from shadow to shadow.

Long ago, she had been told, the city had been prosperous, built around the tomb and mortuary cult of some long-dead Emperor. But the city's harbor had worn away, bit by bit, and the merchant ships went instead to Rasadda. Mors Crisius had become a sleepy town of fishermen, farmers, and mortuary priests, and now only pirates and smugglers made use of its decaying harbor.

Along with worse people.

Caina stopped and stared at Vanio's townhouse.

It looked like the townhouse of a thousand other prosperous merchants. White walls, a roof of fired red tiles, a paved courtyard ringed within a low wall. It did not look at all like a home of a man who would kidnap fellow Imperial citizens and sell them as slaves.

But, then, appearances lied. Caina knew that well. She took a deep breath and went to it.

She sprang up, caught one of the ornamental metal spikes crowning the wall, pulled herself up, and waited. The courtyard lay quiet, its flagstones worn and smooth, a fountain bubbling by the gate. One of Vanio's watchmen strolled towards the house. He wore a studded leather jerkin, his belt heavy with sword and dagger. The watchman opened the main door and vanished into the house. No other guards emerged.

Beneath the cowl and the mask, Caina's lip curled. Vanio's security was barely adequate to keep out common thieves, let alone one of the Emperor's Ghosts. No doubt Vanio thought himself safe from the retribution his crimes had earned.

Well, that might change, tonight.

She counted to three hundred, but no other watchmen appeared, and she saw no signs of life from the house. Caina dropped into the courtyard, the black cloak pooling around her. A single light gleamed in one of the windows, no doubt where Vanio's guards sat earning their keep. She crossed the courtyard and tried the front door. It was locked, of course, and the lock was a fine one, but Caina had seen worse. She knelt, pulled some tools from her belt, and set to work.

Her skill made short work of the lock. Caina pushed the door open as slowly as she could. Within she saw a darkened atrium, the floor covered in an expensive mosaic, but heard nothing.

The smell hit her at once.

Caina slipped into the atrium, pulling the door closed behind her. The smell was stronger in here, thicker and heavier. For a moment Caina thought that the house had caught fire, but she saw no smoke, no signs of panic. She had never smelled anything quite like it. It was a burnt, greasy odor, almost like fat dripping upon a fire. Or like burnt pork.

Burnt pork? Were the watchmen trying to cook something?

Caina shook her head and crept into the townhouse, her boots making no sound against the floor. She glanced around, and noted that Vanio had done quite well for himself. Like so many of these provincial merchants, he had done his utmost to copy the High Nighmarian style. The mosaic beneath her feet showed the Emperor Crisius triumphing over Corazain the Ashbringer. Freestanding marble statues littered the halls, along with busts resting in niches, all copies of famous artworks in the capital. The statuary alone must cost twice what every fisherman in Mors Crisius earned in a year, and the rare woods in the doors had come from the forests of Varia Province on the other side of the Empire of Nighmar.

Someone like Vanio could not make that kind of money doing something honest.

Caina crept through a dining room, the gleaming table set with polished silver, and found the stairs. She had reached the landing when she heard the voices, saw the gleam of light. Caina sank into a corner, her cloak blending with the shadows, and waited. The voices came louder, and Caina realized that two men stood at the top of the stairs, one of them holding a lantern. The watchmen, most likely.

They were speaking in Saddaic. Fortunately, she knew the tongue.

"What in hell's name is that stink?"

"Damned if I know," said a second man. "You did the last walk. Are they cooking anything?"

"It's past midnight! All of Vanio's servants are lazy dogs. You'll not see any of them out of bed before dawn."

"Something must be burning."

"I told you," said the first man, irritated, "I already walked around the house. I didn't see any smoke. The house is not on fire."

"Then why is the smell getting worse?"

The first man spat. "Must be coming from one of the inns. Cooking a pig for tomorrow's stew or something. What of it? It's no concern of ours."

"The nearest inn's a half-mile away! Something's burning, I tell you. Maybe we should wake old Vanio."

"Are you mad? You know how that greedy bastard loves his sleep. Wake him now and we'll be out of work before dawn. Do you want to go back to work on a fishing boat? Or into the Legions? No, we'll do nothing, and that's that."

"I still think something's burning," said the second man. "What if something is on fire? Do you think Vanio'll keep us on if we let his house burn down?"

"Damn you, nothing's on fire," said the first man. "You worry worse than an old woman. But if it'll shut you up, we'll go look." Boots clicked against the stairs.

Caina flung herself backwards, rolled over the landing's railing, and ducked under the massive table. She slipped a throwing knife from her belt, the blade tucked against her gloved hand to hide its gleam. Two of them.

275

Not good. She adjusted her grip on the blade and braced herself.

The watchmen came down the stairs, and Caina saw that there were in fact three of them. The third man, older than the other two, hadn't opened his mouth. The first watchman carried a lantern, and all three wore studded leather jerkins and carried swords and daggers on their belts.

For a moment Caina thought they would see her. The watchman lifted his lantern, throwing shadows across the dining hall, and Caina remained motionless. They walked past her, and their eyes glanced over the table without alarm. Caina blinked in surprised relief. She heard them open the front door and walk into the courtyard. Apparently they hadn't noticed the opened lock.

Caina hurried up the stairs, cloak flowing behind her. The stairs opened into a narrow upstairs hallway, with two doors on the left and one on the right. She had spied out Vanio's townhouse yesterday, and knew that the left doors opened into the study and the solar, while the right door lead to Vanio's bedchamber.

The burnt smell was very strong up here, almost overpowering. The air almost tasted of it, even through her mask. No wonder the watchmen had complained. Caina crossed the hall, listened at the study door for a moment, and swung it open.

The study shared the townhouse's ostentatious opulence. The shelves held the sort of works an educated man was expected to own; histories of the Nighmarian Empire, lives of the Emperors, treatises on oratory and virtue. A thin layer of dust covered most of the books, except for a trio of weighty histories in the corner. She pushed aside the books, and saw the gleam of a safe built into the wall.

Caina grinned, produced her tools, and got to work. The safe, like the lock on the front door, was excellent work, but Caina had seen better. After a short time, she tugged and the door swung open. Only one thing lay in the safe, a battered merchant's ledger, worn with much use. Caina took the ledger, carried it to the window, and flipped through the pages.

Her mouth tightened into a hard line. The ledger detailed Vanio's inventory of slaves. It seemed that he specialized in buying children at cut-rate prices from impoverished peasant farmers, and selling them at an enormous profit to the Carthian and Alqaarin merchants who dealt in such things. He also turned a substantial profit dealing in artworks, old Saddai and Kyracian artifacts and the like, but the bulk of his money came from selling children. Caina closed the ledger, her hand twitching towards the knives in her belt. A short detour on her way out, a quick slash of her knife, and the villainous scum would die choking in his own blood...

No. Not yet. Halfdan had only wanted evidence, not blood. And the Emperor had declared slaving a crime against the Empire, and the penalty for a crime against the Empire was worse than anything Caina had time to inflict upon Vanio now. She closed the safe, replaced the books, tucked the ledger under her arm, and made for the door.

She stepped into the hallway just in time to see the watchmen come up the stairs.

Caina froze in the doorway. For a moment she thought the watchmen wouldn't see her. They were arguing about the smell again, and none of them even glanced towards the study door.

"I'm telling you," said the man in the lead, "that damned smell is worse! Where the hell is that coming from?" He looked around, glancing at the study door.

His eyes got wide.

"Gods!" he said, fumbling for his sword, "what the hell is..."

Caina stepped forward and flung a knife, her foot forward, her arm thrown back, her back arched. Her entire body snapped like a bowstring. The knife hurtled forward and buried itself in the man's throat. He fell to his knees, gagging. The other two watchmen leapt past the fallen man, yanking their swords from their scabbards. Caina threw the heavy ledger. It caught the older man in the face, and he stumbled back with a curse, bouncing off the door to Vanio's bedchamber.

The last man ran at her, his sword a silvery blur.

Caina stepped back and yanked the daggers from her boots. She did not want to take the man in a fair fight. She had trained with short blades for years, along with the open-handed fighting style favored by the Ghosts. She was quick and agile, but she was not a large woman, and she simply did not have the raw strength to fight toe-to-toe with most men.

No matter. She had learned long ago that to fight fair was to lose.

The sword came towards her head, and Caina caught it in a cross-parry between her daggers, her arms straining with the effort. Her left foot lashed out and slammed hard into the man's knee. He gasped with pain, leaning forward, and Caina disengaged and whirled to the side. The watchman stumbled forward, and as he did Caina slashed with her right hand. The blade opened the artery in his neck, and the watchman toppled, blood spurting between his fingers as he vainly tried to stem the flow.

Caina turned just in time to meet the older, silent watchman's attack. He came at her with both sword and dagger, and he knew how to use his weapons. Caina retreated before his advance, her blades working to beat aside his attacks. She sent a knife spinning for his face, but a flick of his sword sent the blade clattering to the floor. Sooner or later he would pin her against a wall, and that would be that.

In a fair fight.

Caina reached up and undid the black silver brooch that pinned her cloak. It came loose and dangled from her right hand, a drape of shadow billowing from her arm. The watchman stopped, frowning at her, and Caina flung the cloak at his face. He sneered and slashed his dagger to knock the cloak aside.

But mundane steel passed through the shadow-spun cloak without touching it, and the black cloth fell over him. He snarled in fury and clawed at his face, his sword sweeping back and forth before him. Caina ducked below the waving sword and drove her dagger into his gut. The watchman screamed and fell to his knees, the cloak slipping from his face, and Caina dragged her blade across his throat.

He joined the others on the floor a few seconds later, his blood pooling across the tiles.

Caina retrieved her cloak and stood, breathing hard. She stared down at the bodies, and the blood staining the floor and walls. They would have killed her, and not thought twice about it. Yet her stomach still twisted with nausea. Suddenly she was eleven years old again, and she saw the men lying sprawled on the floor of her father's library, their glassy eyes staring at the ceiling...

Later. The noise might have woken the servants. And there was no way Vanio could have slept through the racket. She had to get out of here now. Caina retrieved her knives, picked up the dropped ledger, and started for their stairs.

And stopped.

The burnt smell was stronger. Much stronger. Almost overpowering. Caina turned, puzzled. She saw that the door to Vanio's bedchamber stood partway open. For a moment she thought Vanio himself had opened it, but the door must have been knocked ajar during the fight.

The burnt smell poured out through the open door.

Caina hesitated for a heartbeat. She ought to get out of the townhouse, now, before someone discovered the bodies. Yet that smell. Had Vanio taken to burning pork in his bedchamber? It made no sense, and Caina did not like things that made no sense.

She pushed the door open the rest of the way and glided into the bedchamber.

If the townhouse was opulent, the bedchamber was palatial. Her boots sank into a rich, thick carpet. Tapestries hung from the walls, and the wooden furniture gleamed. A massive double bed stood in the center of the room, draped in curtains. The smell was very bad in here, almost overpowering.

It was coming from the bed.

Again another memory from that awful day came to her, as she crossed her father's study, her heart pounding with terror, towards the chair at his desk...

Caina shook aside the memory. She crossed the room, flung open the curtains, and found the source of the awful stench.

Vanio himself lay sprawled across the silken sheets.

Or, rather, what was left of Vanio.

His corpulent body had been reduced to a twisted mass of black char, his fingers curled into shriveled claws, his mouth yawning in an eternal scream, his eyes and nose blackened pits. His teeth seemed shockingly white in the black ruin of his face. The smell rolled off his charred flesh in nauseating waves. Grease seeped from red cracks in his torso, staining into the silken sheets.

Impossible.

Caina stepped back, staring at the gruesome corpse. Vanio looked as if he had been roasted atop a pyre, or burned at the stake. Yet she saw no fire damage to the bed or the room, no smoke stains on the walls. Had he been burned elsewhere and carried here? That made no sense either. Caina had been able to sneak into the townhouse, but she doubted a pair of men carrying a charred corpse could have managed the same feat.

Her mouth tightened. That left only...

"Murder!" shrieked a woman's voice from the hallway. One of the maids, no doubt. "Murder! Murder! Master Vanio!"

Time to go.

Caina tore the curtain from the bed, wrapped her fist in it, and smashed the window. Leaded glass fell in a rain to the courtyard below. She threw the ledger out the window, and then went through herself, finding easy footholds in the townhouse's stonework. More lights came on in the windows, and Caina heard more shouts, followed by a shrill scream from the broken windows.

No doubt the poor maid had found Vanio's corpse.

Caina dropped into the courtyard, retrieved the ledger, and scrambled over the wall. More screams and panicked shouts came from the house, but it didn't sound as if anyone had spotted her. Caina had only wanted to get in and out with Vanio's ledger, and she hadn't wanted to kill anyone. How had things gone so wrong?

Well. She hadn't planned on finding a charred corpse, for one thing.

Caina broke into a full run, the cloak billowing out behind her like a living shadow.

To continue reading GHOST IN THE FLAMES, *visit this link:*
http://www.jonathanmoeller.com/ghostintheflames.html

ABOUT THE AUTHOR

Standing over six feet tall, Jonathan Moeller has the piercing blue eyes of a Conan of Cimmeria, the bronze-colored hair a Visigothic warrior-king, and the stern visage of a captain of men, none of which are useful in his career as a computer repairman, alas.He has written the DEMONSOULED series of sword-and-sorcery novels, the TOWER OF ENDLESS WORLDS urban fantasy series, THE GHOSTS series about assassin and spy Caina Amalas, the COMPUTER BEGINNER'S GUIDE sequence of computer books, and numerous other works. Visit his website at:
http://www.jonathanmoeller.com

CPSIA information can be obtained at www.ICGtesting.com
Printed in the USA
BVOW03s2232020614

355224BV00008B/154/P